Darkchild

Bluesong

And still to come . . .

Starsilk

in a magnificent Berkley trade edition

Berkley Books by Sydney J. Van Scyoc

BLUESONG
CLOUDCRY
DARKCHILD
SUNWAIFS

BLUESONG

SYDNEY J. VAN SCYOC

BERKLEY BOOKS, NEW YORK

BLUESONG

A Berkley Book / published by arrangement with
the author

PRINTING HISTORY
Berkley trade paperback edition / May 1983
Berkley edition / July 1984

ISBN: 0-425-07130-8

For Ruth and Van

BLUESONG

ONE
KEVA

It was morning and mist rose from the slow-running stream, cloaking the streambank where Keva walked. In the distance she heard the hiss of geysers. Nearer, topweeds eddied gently upon the water's surface, yellow throats closed against the heaviness of dawn.

Keva shivered, not from the cold but from the dreams she had left behind in Oki's hut. Fire—she had dreamed fire again, a diffuse brightness rimmed on all sides by jagged mountain peaks. As she watched, it overflowed the basin of mountains and lapped against the sky, rising higher and higher until its smouldering heat pervaded all her dreams. She had wakened with her lungs burning and her cheeks flushed. Wakened with the feeling she was about to see something she did not want to see, something so frightening, so confusing . . . Shaking, she had pulled on her clothes and stumbled from the hut, leaving Oki and Lekki still asleep.

The sense of a burning sky was so real it was upon her still, despite the mist and the running water. Keva pulled her padded jacket close, hot and cold at once. Why did she dream of fire in the mountains when Oki said she had never seen the mountains that lay to the north? Par sat on the streambank sometimes with children at his feet and told tales of women who lived in the mountains and drew the sun's fire as easily as Oki drew water from the warmstream. He called them barohnas, and he had many stories of the barohnas and the people they ruled because at one time the warmstream people had lived in the mountains too.

Although Keva was too old now to sit at Par's feet, his stories had been much in her mind these past days. She had accepted them with no question when she was young, but recently some sense of incompleteness had begun to disturb her, as if Par had drawn his tales short of the truth. Was that why she dreamed of fire so often? Because she was worrying at the details of Par's tales? Or did she dream of fire because she *had* seen the mountains—when she rode behind the bearded man? Because she did know something of fire? Something she had put aside? Something she did not want to examine?

Keva glanced around, almost expecting Oki to appear in her nightcloak with denials. Oki said she had never seen fire in the mountains or heard the strange, grinding rumble that sometimes woke her sobbing from her sleep. Oki said she had never ridden a white steed with blowing mane and heard a bluesong that had no words. Oki said there had been no bearded man. Oki said Keva had always lived beside the warmstream, daughter of weeders lost one day when the bottomweeds, their stems unfurled to take the sun, had snarled shut at the approach of storm and dragged their vessel to the bottom.

Keva frowned, walking deeper into the mist. What Oki told her was more plausible than the notion that she had come from the mountains. Yet there was something inconsistent in Oki's manner. Why, if she were only telling Keva's story as it had happened, did her heavy features become so rigid when Keva questioned her? And however hard she tried, Keva could not summon memory of her parents. She could not remember their touch, the smell of their clothes, or the sound of their voices, not even here, where the mist eroded the boundary between past and present.

Yet she remembered the bearded man clearly, the dark of his eyes, the restless way he looked and moved. He was a roaming man, a searching man, and for a while she had searched with him.

Or she had dreamed she searched with him.

Keva tugged at the sleeves of her jacket, trying to warm her fingers. No, she didn't believe she had dreamed the bearded man, no matter what Oki said. Moving softly, Keva crept to the water's edge and peered at her reflection. She was tall and slender. Even haloed by obscuring mist, her hair was the color of night, hanging straight and smooth to her shoulders. Her eyes were at once bright and dark, her brows finely arched. Her lips and nose were cleanly made, and her hands were narrow, with nails that showed pink against her bronze skin.

All this told her the bearded man was no dream. None of the fisher-people looked as she did. Their brows were thicker, their bodies heavier, their hair rougher. And none were so dark, like a shadow upon the water. The only person like herself was the bearded man.

If he were a fantasy why had she created him in her own image, down to the finest detail?

And the bluesong—she could call back scraps of it sometimes, when the sun was bright. It came to her as clearly as if it sang in the trees, a high, wordless yearning. Yet actually the song had come from a blue silk sash the man wore at his waist when he rode.

A silk that sang? That was more fanciful than any tale Par had ever told. Yet she remembered its voice. Puzzled, Keva walked upstream to the rocky place where the geysers played. She watched them, lost in thought, until the sun rose and the bottomweeds sent their thick stems slashing through the water's surface. Turbulence lashed at the streambank and the topweeds opened reluctant throats.

Sighing, Keva turned back toward the fisher village, leaving the streambank to walk among the trees. Their trunks were broad and mossed. Morning shadow pooled dark and cold at their bases. Even her footsteps were lost in their silence.

Preoccupied, she did not realize she had disturbed Oki at her cache until she heard Oki's surprised grunt and looked up to see her back hastily from the base of a hollow tree. Keva halted, startled by her foster-mother's damp consternation.

Oki scrubbed her stained hands on her loose trousers, her heavy shoulders hunched defensively. "Tip leaves from the newest fire-growth," she said quickly. "There's nothing here but tip leaves for medicine."

Keva's brows rose. Did Oki think she would disturb her cache? When the smallest fisher-child knew she must never disturb a private cache without permission? "I didn't see anything," she said.

Oki's heavy head bobbed involuntarily. "Fire-growth," she repeated, stepping away from the hollow tree. For a moment she stared at Keva with damp anxiety, as if she expected to be questioned. Then she scrubbed perspiration from her face and said sharply, "You left without laying the fire under the boiling pot this morning. Have you gathered wood?"

Keva hesitated. Laying the fire was her foster-sister's chore, but Lekki had probably gone hunting bark-beetles with her friends and forgotten. And Keva was anxious to escape Oki's challenging gaze. "I'll gather the wood now," she said quickly, turning back through the trees.

She had already laid the fire and filled the pot when Oki returned to the firepit, still scrubbing her hands against her trousers. Grunting, Oki sorted briskly through the fibers piled nearby. Silently they set to work boiling and pounding fibers to be woven into cloth. Keva fell to the rhythm of the work, briefly forgetting the things that puzzled her.

At midday the bottomweeds stretched erect, straining toward the sun, and the weedfishers launched their vessels into the stream. Soon they were calling across the water, diving after the edible roots and bulbs that grew in the mud at the bottom of the stream. Teal, tallest of the young weedfishers, splashed and called more loudly than the others, his bragging smile inviting Keva to admire his prowess.

She did not respond. She was of an age now to pull moss from the trees and sew a mattress to share with Teal. Others her age had already sewn their first mattresses, but the warm days of spring roused no desire in Keva to do so.

I don't have moss thoughts because moss burns when there is fire.

Moss burns. Keva shivered as the image of fire smouldered in her mind. *Fire.* "Oki—" she said impulsively.

Oki turned from the pounding stone, warily.

"Oki—I dreamed about the burning in the mountains again last night."

Oki's face stiffened, the heavy plane of cheek and jaw turning rigid. "You dream too much," she said shortly.

Keva shook her head, refusing the rebuff. Instinctively she knew everything was related: her dreams, the bearded man, the bluesong. And Oki could tell her about them if she would. Keva was sure of it. "Oki—tell me about the women in the mountains. The barohnas."

Stiffly Oki stood, her face grim. "There is nothing for you to know about those women."

If there were nothing, why did Oki always respond to questioning with such prickly anger? "I have to know," Keva insisted. "What they look like, how they live—Oki, tell me." The stories Par told the children had the taste of fantasy, of tales passed through so many generations of storytellers they had lost all but the barest flavor of truth. But there were other stories—stories passed among the adults, and Oki knew them. Keva was certain of it. Otherwise why did perspiration stand on Oki's stiff face, just as it had when Keva surprised her at her cache? *"Tell me."*

Oki's jaw clenched, a stubborn resistance. "What they look like?" she demanded roughly. "They look nothing like you or me. They look more like the women who come from the plain with the herds in summer. Dark and tall—Par has told you that. How they live? They live in mountain ways, and if you were meant to know those ways, you wouldn't be a daughter of warmstream weedfishers. We live here where the barohnas never come because we want to know nothing about them and their mountain ways."

"But you know something," Keva argued. "The weedfishers came from the mountain valleys once. Par told me they used to live there with the mountain people, in stone halls." Surely that much of what Par said was true. The rest, the stories of barohnas lifting heavy boulders and making them dance in the air, the stories of stone eyes that saw long distances—tales, surely; only tales.

Oki's hands bunched on her trousers, kneading the coarse fabric. Her mouth twisted bitterly. "The weedfishers lived in the mountains—yes—before they were weedfishers. And they left because they would not live there any longer. There were things happening in the mountains that should never happen when people live together."

"Things—are they still happening?"

"Now?" Oki's face darkened. "What does it matter if they're happening now? Our people left the mountain valleys so many generations ago we don't count them. We were pale white-haired people when we left, like the serfs who slave for the barohnas. We *were* serfs then, and now we're free people—with no look of the stonewarrens upon us. We've changed that much.

"But the barohnas haven't changed. No matter what the plains women tell us when they come with their herds, they haven't. Perhaps they don't use their fire to burn their serfs now. Perhaps they don't make war from valley to valley. But today is only one moment in time. So long as the barohnas can draw fire from the sun, they will burn again—and we will stay here where they never come."

Keva's eyes narrowed. Challenged, Oki was suddenly willing to talk. "But Par never—"

"Par never tells the children the ugly things," Oki said bitterly. "He's like a child himself—lost in pretty tales. So you grow up ignorant. You've never heard about serfs turned to ash in their fields and children blinded because the barohnas decided to make war on one another. No storyteller will tell you those things when he can weave a pretty story of palaces and orchards and children with hair the color of mist."

Reluctantly Keva nodded. Par's tales had been that: pretty. And if he had not told the children about the burnings—her mind raced quickly ahead—what other things had he expunged from his tales? What bitter things? Because if there were no bitter things, why did she always wake in pounding terror when she dreamed of fire in the mountains? And the bearded man—were there ugly things to be told about him too? About the people he came from?

What people could he have come from? Keva pressed her temples and her thoughts took an instinctive leap. "He's one of them," she realized aloud. "Par told us the barohnas are dark and tall, and the man I rode with was dark and tall. He was their kin." And since he *was* dark, not fair, he was not serf but master—an ugly thing in itself, if what Oki said were true. If the barohnas used their fire not just to warm the valleys and thaw the ground for planting but as a weapon.

And if she had been riding with him, traveling in his care, under his guardianship—

Oki's heavy face contracted. "There was no bearded man. Your father was a weedfisher. Your mother built her hut upstream of mine when I lived in the southern village and I was there to tie the cord when you were born. They went on the water one day—"

"No." Keva rejected the familiar litany. The story of her birth and her parents' death meant no more now than it ever had. She could not remember her parents and she could not remember the southern village where Oki said she was born.

But if she closed her eyes, she could feel the bearded man's surging white steed between her legs, could see him bent over the animal's neck, dark hair knotted over one ear—could smell the leathers he wore.

The weedfisher who had been her father? For all the memory she had of him, he might never have existed.

Had he existed? Catching her breath, Keva peered up at Oki. If Par told stories that were less than the truth, what about Oki? Had Oki told her the truth—any of it? Or had she told her a story full of measured lies?

The sharpness of her gaze cut Oki like a blade, taking her breath. Oki's stained hands dropped and her face sagged, losing all its dogged certainty. A grey stain spread under the surface of her skin.

Before she could regain her composure, before Keva could follow her own thoughts to their logical conclusion, there was a cry from the farthest trees. Keva turned as other cries followed, conveying the alarm. Oki scrubbed her stained hands on her trousers, the grey of her face deepening. She hesitated for only a moment, mouth twisting, then turned and ran heavily toward the shouting voices.

Keva hesitated, then ran after her. She gathered what had happened as she ran, from the voices that relayed the alarm through the trees. The beetle hunters had been scratching at the loose bark of an ancient grey alder when a spinner had darted from its nest to sink poisoned claws into one of the hunters. The name that was called back through the trees was Lekki's.

Lekki! Keva's breath came hard and her blood beat a protective fury. Lekki, her foster-sister, Lekki with her teasing grin and unruly hair.

The bloating had already begun when Keva and Oki reached the grey alders. Lekki thrashed blindly against every hand, her hair matted with perspiration, her clawed leg grossly swollen. Her eyes were half-open, but there was no teasing light in them now, no awareness at all. Keva caught her breath in a painful sob. She had seen spinner poisoning before, had seen how quickly it worked. Too soon the venom would make Lekki's fingers thick, would swell her eyelids and close her throat, choking her.

Oki had seen spinner poisoning too. She threw herself down, pressing her daughter's thrashing body to the ground. "Be still! You'll make the poison spread."

Reason came briefly to Lekki's glazed eyes. "Mah—?" The half-uttered word was thick.

"Be still." Oki peered around at the gathering fisher-people, agonized. Keva read her thought from her eyes. There was no remedy effective against spinner poisoning except firetips—the shiny tip leaves from the quick-withering vines that grew in soil scorched by a recent lightening strike. Oki had found fresh firetips that morning and hidden them in her cache. But no one could calm Lekki as she could. No one could hold her quiet and keep the poison from rushing through her bloodstream. If she left her to go to her cache—

"I'll go," Keva said, half choking. "I'll bring the leaves. Oki—I'll go."

Keva expected a quick nod, a hurried command. Instead Oki hesitated, holding Lekki's thrashing body to the ground.

"*I'll go*," Keva insisted, poised to run.

"Yes," Oki said at last, a harsh whisper. "Go."

Keva wasted no time wondering at Oki's reluctance. She pushed through the gathered people and ran, her breath burning in her throat. *Lekki*—her early memories were distorted, disordered, many of them not accessible at all, but she remembered how lost she had been before Lekki was born, before she had had Lekki to bathe and feed and look after. Only as she watched Lekki grow had she begun to feel she was one of the fisher-people, as Oki insisted she was.

But she was not. Crisis made her mind work quickly and revelation came with rushing certainty as she ran through the trees. The bearded man—*could only be her father.* Otherwise why did Oki refuse to talk about him? Why did she insist upon a drowned weedfisher father whenever Keva mentioned him? Otherwise why was she so like him, with black hair and bronze limbs and arched brows?

She stumbled against a heavily mossed tree and gripped its rough trunk, not wanting to follow her thoughts to their logical conclusion. If the bearded man were her father and if he were kin of the barohnas—

But if she were kin of the barohnas, why had she been left here with the weedfishers? Why had Oki raised her as her own, feeling as she did about the barohnas? Oki had always treated her with a bristling, hovering possessiveness. Could Oki behave so to someone who was kin of the barohnas?

Had Oki even told her the truth about the barohnas, or had she spoken from spite?

There were no answers. Keva's blood ran as swiftly as her thoughts. Reaching the hollow tree, she knelt and tore out plugs of moss. She reached into the dark cavity and pulled out several wrapped bundles of herbs and medicinals. It was easy to tell which were firetips, even without unwrapping the bundles. The feel of the fresh leaves was springy and there was a sharp, distinctive odor.

Catching her breath, Keva jumped up and ran back through the trees. By now someone would have fetched water and pounding tools and someone else would have opened the wound to make it bleed. If the tip leaves were potent enough, if Lekki could stand the bleeding—

Lekki was struggling for breath when Keva returned. The fisher-women worked over her silently, one making a poultice and pressing it to the wound, another occasionally lifting off the poultice to squeeze fresh blood from the gash, Oki stroking Lekki's hair to keep her still. Keva watched, shivering, her throat closed so tightly she could hardly swallow.

When half the afternoon was gone, the swelling eased and Lekki began to breathe freely again. The women carried her to Oki's hut in a makeshift litter and Oki put her to bed, smoothing a fresh poultice on her wound and making her drink a brew of steeped leaves.

Later neighbors brought food but neither Oki nor Keva ate. Both moved around the hut dully, caught in the hard weariness of crisis. It wasn't until Lekki slept and Oki finally sank into slumbrous silence at the foot of her bed that Keva remembered she had not stuffed the moss plugs back into Oki's cache. Keva hesitated, wanting only her own bed, then sighed and moved quietly to the door. Oki shifted and muttered but did not call her back.

Mist was gathering upon the stream again, and in the distance Keva heard the hiss of geysers. The damp smell of early evening was heavy under the trees. Keva tried briefly to recapture the urgency of her earlier thoughts, then relinquished the effort wearily. She found Oki's tree deep in shadow. She knelt, gathering up the scattered medicine bundles and stacking them in the tree's cavity.

Hard—there was something hard buried in the crumbled matter that lined Oki's cache. A stone? And with it something that felt like fabric—as if the stone were wrapped in fabric, a fabric so finely woven Keva's fingertips could not distinguish the individual fibers.

Keva sat back on her heels. A stone and fabric, hidden—*as so many things were hidden*. Keva hesitated a moment longer, then closed her hand around the stone and drew it from the tree's cavity.

She opened her hand slowly, breath held, and unwound a

narrow strip of blue cloth. She gazed down, her breath seeping away, her heart thumping softly at her ribs. Par said the women of the mountains—the barohnas—used a black stone called sunstone to capture sunlight. They wore fire-cuffs cut from it and sat upon glowing black thrones. And they used other stones too, which he had not described so vividly. Frowning, she looked down at the stone that had been wrapped in the blue cloth. It was dark blue, many-faceted, and it was mounted in a dull metal setting. Keva rubbed the blue fabric that had wrapped the stone, then stroked the stone itself, cautiously. It was cool to her touch. The fabric was slippery-smooth, the blue of summer sky.

The blue of song. Trembling, Keva smoothed the strip of cloth on the ground and reality shifted from its familiar axis. The strip of fabric was stained and dusty, its edges raveling, but when she touched it she remembered the bluesong as clearly, as achingly, as if she rode behind the bearded man again, clinging to him while their mount carried them—where?

Here? Had they ridden so long only to come here? And had he brought her here only to abandon her? Slowly Keva rose, the sharp sting of tears in her eyes. There was memory, elusive memory, in the touch of blue cloth, and it hurt. *Why* had the bearded man—*her father*—gone and not come back, leaving her only disordered snatches of memory?

Her hand closed on the scrap of cloth, the mounted stone. No one had to tell her these were hers—perhaps the only heritage she would ever have. They were stamped with her father's presence, steeped in it. And Oki had hidden them from her.

Keva's hands trembled. The strip of fabric was just long enough to thread through the stone's metal mounting and tie around her throat. She threaded and tied it and the fabric clung to her throat, blue and cool. Her eyes stung. *Hers*—this was hers, perhaps the only thing she had that was truly hers.

She did not return to Cki's hut immediately. Instead she sat for a while at streamside, watching first moonlight silver the mist that grew on the water. She sat with her knees drawn up, one hand clutching the stone at her throat. She sat until the water was entirely lost in night mist. Her mind worked with cool detachment, her thoughts falling in patterns of geometric symmetry. They were so precisely, so formally structured they hardly seemed to be her own.

At last she stood and returned to the hut. She entered silently and stood looking down at Oki where she slept, heavy, slow, greying. Oki's hair was untidy, her trousers stained. She slept with her mouth open. Lekki slept curled on her side, one plump arm uncovered, her breath faintly rasping. her eyelids were puffy, not from spinner venom but from the salt of tears.

. Keva gazed down at mother and daughter for a long time, her thoughts as remote as they had been at the streamside. Whatever she respected in Oki—her strength, her persistence, her gritty stubbornness—and whatever she loved in Lekki, there was nothing of either of them in her. She was not a weedfisher. She had never been. "I don't belong here, Oki," Keva said with softly stirring anger.

Oki did not respond.

"I don't belong here, Oki," Keva said less softly.

Oki mumbled and moved. Her eyes opened and came to reluctant focus, first upon Keva's face, then upon the stone at her throat. Oki sat, her features registering surprise quickly followed by thick fear. "The stone—"

"I found it in your cache. That's why you were frightened when I saw you this morning. This belonged to my father and you hid it from me."

Oki scrubbed a hand across her eyes and shook her head numbly. "No. Your father—"

"My father left me with you, and he left these things for me. You were to give them to me." That must be how it had been. He had entrusted fabric and stone to Oki for her. They were a message of her heritage, of his love. Perhaps they were even a promise, one he hadn't been able to keep: that he would return for her. "You hid them instead." She didn't try to keep the harshness from her voice.

Oki raised thick-fingered hands to her face. Slowly the fingers closed and she let them fall. "Mountain things," she spat.

So her father *had* come from the mountains. "They belong to me," Keva insisted with muted elation.

Oki thrust herself up from the bed, her eyes taking fire. "Do they?" she demanded, her voice stinging with spite. "And what will you have with them? Ice and stone and fire—that's what you'll find in the mountains. Ice on the ground, stone in your heart, and fire—fire to burn whatever displeases you. Is that the best I've taught you? To make yourself so hard you have stone where your heart should be?"

Keva stared at Oki, the hair at the nape of her neck rising. Ice, stone, fire . . . "I don't know what you're talking about."

"I'm talking about the barohnas. That stone is one of theirs."

Instinctively Keva clutched the smooth-polished stone. "No, the stones they use are black. Par told us. They—"

"Their sunstones are black, the ones they burn with. But they have other stones and this is one of them—just as bad. You have to be stone yourself to use this stone. You have to be as cruel and as hard as stone."

Keva met her vehemence with a tight frown. The stone was a token from her father. She would not have it any other way. "I'm not cruel," she said stiffly.

Oki swelled with anger. "The worse for you then." Her jaw set so rigidly it jutted. "Because there are two kinds of mountain women: those who learn to be hard and become barohnas—and those who don't. The ones who don't learn it die. Is that so much better than being a fisher-woman? Dying in the mountains trying to find some hardness to save yourself with?"

"I—" Nothing Oki said made sense. How could she answer but by returning the attack? "My father—why did he leave me here? Why didn't he come back for me?"

Oki grunted, her eyes blazing with spite. "He didn't leave you here. He left you in my hut three days south. He was riding and you were sick. He stopped at my hut and I gave you brews and nursed you for seven days. Then he went to take his animal to the forest to breed while you finished healing."

Of course—her father had left her with Oki in the southern fisher village where they had lived before coming here. Her father had left her—and intended to come back. Why hadn't he?

Perhaps he had. Perhaps . . . Keva's fingers tightened on the blue stone. She guessed the truth a moment before Oki admitted it. "Oki—"

Hard satisfaction twisted Oki's face. "He thought he could leave you in my hut and come back and find you still there. Well, he came back. He came riding back, but what he found was an empty hut."

Yes. "Because you took me away."

"I took you into the trees the very day he left. I told my neighbors you died and I was gone to bury you. Then we hid by day and walked by night. We hid and walked while he rode away without you. What made him think I was going to nurse you and then give you back? When my mate was drowned in the storm and none of those vixens in the south would lend me a mate to make a child of my own?"

Keva nodded as another piece of the puzzle fell into place. It hadn't been her parents who had died in the storm. It had been Oki's mate. "The bottomweeds—"

"The bottomweeds took him and I had no one. Until *he* came and left you. What did he expect? Why would I heal you and let you go to become one of them? No, I let him ask my neighbors and I let him search for your grave. Finally he gave it up and rode away. He was that kind of man. I saw it in his face the first day he came, when he thought you would die. He was used to losing what he cared for—just as I was used to being lonely. But I ended that."

Keva shook her head weakly. To let her father search for her grave, to let her wonder, to lie for so many years—

"You're the one who's stone, Oki. *You.*"

The muscles of Oki's jaw bunched. Her eyes darted to the bed where Lekki slept. A moment's baffled anger touched her face. "I had no one," she muttered.

"Did he have someone? After you took me?"

Oki's face quivered. She turned away, heavy shoulders set. "I had no one."

The only sound in the hut was Lekki's sleeping breath. Keva stood like stone for minutes, wondering what she must do. She could not stay here. She was no longer a child, to be stolen and hidden. Nor was she an orphan. She had a father, somewhere.

Reluctantly she turned and looked at her sleeping foster-sister. Hard—it would be hard to leave Lekki, and without saying goodbye.

It had been hard for her father to leave her, and then Oki had stolen her from him. He had had no chance to say goodbye either.

Shaking her head, frowning, Keva turned to the hamper where she kept her clothes. She must go, and she must be practical in her going. It was spring now, but it would be cold in the lands beyond the warmstreams. She would need warm quilts and extra clothing. Her hands shook as she bound her heaviest clothing into a bundle and made a second bundle of her bedding.

She refused to turn and meet Oki's eyes. Refused to think of anything but the practicalities of her leavetaking. She would need a few days' ration of food to hold her until she learned to forage in strange terrain. And some extra to carry her through the mountains, where forage would be scant. Silently she stepped across the hut and filled a basket with flatbread and dried berries. Stifling a momentary qualm, she dropped Oki's sharpest digging blade into the basket.

Oki did not speak as Keva slung her possessions over her shoulders and stepped to the door. Keva paused and glanced back, her eyes stinging with regret. She would miss Lekki. Would miss seeing her grow and become a woman. And yes, she would miss Oki too.

But somewhere her father was as lonely as she had been, and he thought she was dead. Turning, she stepped from the hut. Where she would find him she could not guess. Nor could she guess whether he would know her. But she would know him. Even if he had shaved his beard, even if he no longer rode his white steed, she would know him by his searching eyes. She would know her father.

As for what she might learn about her father's kin, about her mother, about the stone—she put those thoughts aside. She was going to find her father. This was not the time for other considerations.

Going, leaving . . . Tears started down her face then, and

she knew that inside the hut tears had started down Oki's face too. She could hear the rough, angry sound of her grief.

More clearly she heard the bluesong, calling her to the search. Clasping the stone at her neck, she ran blindly into the hissing darkness.

TWO
DANIOR

It was morning and the diked fields beyond the palace were faintly green with new growth. The air was warm, touched with portents of summer. Danior stood at his window and watched the season's apprentices follow their masters across the plaza, going for their first instruction in the fields, in the weaving sheds, in the breeding pens. His sense of isolaton was sharp as he watched them go. Some had been his game-mates just a few years ago, until they had reached their first majority and had been sent to mind herds or carry messages. Now they were fifteen, the age of choice, and they had selected their guilds and gone to take their places.

He had reached the same age, but he had been offered no choice. No one had set his feet to a path that would lead him to a place in the life of the valley. Bleakly he paced away from the window, wondering what the response would be if he went to Juris Pergossa and asked to be apprenticed to a guild. Wondered what silent questions her grey eyes would ask before she recorded his request and dismissed him. Wondered how long it would be before his mother called him to the throneroom to suggest he withdraw his request.

Worse, his mother might not suggest he withdraw it. He might be admitted to a guild, but by an unwilling master. What guild master, after all, had ever been called upon to train a child of the palace? There was no etiquette, no convention for the situation. If a son of the halls failed his apprenticeship, there were guidelines to be followed so that no one need be embarrassed. But if the barohna's son were apprenticed and did not train well—

And what promise did he have that he would train well? That he would ever make a place for himself in one of the guilds—when no one from the palace had ever been inducted into a guild? When no barohna's child had ever come to the age of choice without a clear-cut task waiting?

He pressed his temples, trying to stroke away the sense of emptiness that had yawned after him all winter, that threatened to swallow him now. Sometimes this spring he walked across the plaza in bright sunlight and turned quickly to see if he cast a shadow. Other times he stood gazing after hall stewards and kitchen monitors as they went on their errands, wishing he could guess what they saw when they looked at him. Wishing he could tell if the emptiness, the lack of direction, was as apparent to them as it was to him. Occasionally this spring he sat beside his mother's throne while she met with advisers and waited for someone to send him away, as they always had. This year no one did. Because they saw that now he stood as tall as a man? Or because they did not notice him there at all?

His fists closed tight. If they did notice him, who did they see? A dark, tall youth whose presence among them was anomalous? A youth who had no defined place in the social structures of the valley and no path to guide him? Was that why they didn't send him away? Because they had no better idea than he did what was to be done with him?

And if they did not notice him, what did that make him? A product of his own imagination? Thought without substance?

It was at times like that that the restlessness overtook him—as it did today. If he was to have a place, he must find a path. He must build a legend—separate from all the other legends of the valley, of his family. And this was the time to begin to build it. Today. Tensely he turned from the window. His gaze lingered only briefly on the rugged stone wall of his sleeping chamber, hesitated bare moments over the pits and gouges of centuries. He took only peripheral notice of the orange blaze of the stalklamp that grew upon his walls. In his thoughts he was already walking across dike tops to the orchard where the whitemane grazed. He already looked upon its white presence among the trees, promising that if he mounted, if he rode the animal no one but his father had ridden, his legend would be initiated. He would begin to understand who he was and where life might lead him. He had not decided how far or how long he would ride. Just the feel of the whitemane between his legs was what he required.

And if he did not go to the pasture soon, he would think too much and lose nerve. Steeling himself, he slipped from his chamber and down the stalklit hall. The palace was a place where centuries lived in the stones, where history paved the floors and soared in the arched passages. He let none of that touch him today. He deliberately insulated himself against the myths and tales that found permanence in the stones of the palace. It was not his history that lived here.

Not his at all. But if he rode the whitemane, if he did that one deed, perhaps he could make it his.

Reaching the lower floor, he paused in the arched entryway to the throneroom. Light from the mountain lenses blazed from mirrors set high in the walls and made the throne glow. Danior's sisters were curled upon embroidered cushions before the throne, ciphering scrolls. They were younger than he and they were of a kind, delicately made, with auburn hair that hung straight to their shoulders and autumn-gold eyes. Sometimes he looked with trepidation at the fine bones of their wrists, at their fingers that appeared almost too fragile to manipulate eating utensils. Their voices were laughing wisps.

But they were palace daughters and their fragility was a sham. It was he who could not find his way, while his sisters only waited for their chance to take up the sunstone and become barohnas of the sunthrone.

He stood looking at them silently and they did not notice. Then he turned and hurried to the plaza door, before he could lose courage.

He needed fittings: halter of finest white leather, intricately woven reins, an embroidered pad to protect the whitemane's back. He hurried across the plaza and down stone avenues to the shed where the animal's things were kept. There he folded halter, reins and pad into an empty grain bag. He was not surprised to see that his hands shook. If he rode the whitemane, he would not just initiate his own legend. He would usurp a part of his father's legend as well. And while he doubted his father would be angry, the presumption frightened him, as if he offered himself for a task that might prove too large.

He wasted just a moment gazing around at the other fittings, trying to calm himself. Here was the embroidered collar and coat the whitemane wore when he paraded in the plaza at Midsummer Fest. There was the heavy coat that fitted down over his flanks on Darkmorning to protect him from the cold of the mountains. And hanging nearby were a black halter and reins of heavy black leather deeply incised with stylized patterns.

His hands still shook. Quickly Danior slipped from the shed and ran down stone paths, across dike tops, away from the palace and its precincts.

It was a clear bright day, cloudless. Lenses flashed from the mountainsides, beaming thick shafts of light to the great mirrors of the throneroom. Danior paused to trace the heavy shafts to their individual mirrors, then hurried on. When people passed with tools and implements, he evaded their greetings. Finally he left the fields behind. The terrain changed, the ground becoming stonier as he neared the flank of the mountain.

It was not yet blooming time in the orchards. The trees were covered with tight-curled buds and fledgling leaves that rattled as Danior passed. The grasses that grew under the trees were tender and stalky. Here and there Danior found the print of hooves, but they did not form a path for him to follow. He could only search randomly. Once he saw the flash of an Arnimi ship in the distant sky. He watched until it was gone, then resumed his search.

The orchards were wide, but it was not long before he sighted the whitemane grazing near a rocky outcropping. He halted, sucking an involuntary breath. The silky texture of the animal's mane, the glistening white hairs of its coat, the pink transparency of its eyes—there was nothing on Brakrath so heart-stopping as the whitemane. It was a legend living, a legend that had given itself to a man: his father. Now he must take some of the legend for himself or go back to the palace empty.

When he moved forward again, the animal heard his step and raised its head, ears pricked. Its lips pulled back to reveal strong white teeth. On its brow was a black, five-fingered blaze— his father's mark. Unconsciously Danior wiped his palms against his trouser leg and swallowed back apprehension. It had been easier to think of riding the whitemane in his chamber than it was here.

He paused again, gathering nerve. His father talked to the animal—when he groomed it, when he fed it, when he rode it. But words deserted Danior and he approached the whitemane in tight-throated silence. The animal had a light, sharp scent and its whiteness was dazzling. Danior halted and pulled a handful of grass. He held it out. "Come," he urged. His voice was softer than he intended, more plea than command. As if he were begging for what the animal could give him.

The animal studied the wad of grass, the pinkness of its eyes deepening. Danior breathed shallowly, poised. When the animal stepped near he would slip halter and reins from their bag and slide them over the animal's head. He had seen his father do the same thing many times. Then he would strap the pad to its back. And finally he would catch his fingers in its mane and pull himself to its back.

That was what he intended. But when the animal stepped forward, when it bent to nuzzle the clump of grass that dropped from his hand, when he pulled harness and reins from the bag, ready, a force like a quickly tightened fist squeezed his heart. He dropped halter and reins and stumbled backward under the dizzy rise of panic. Because a new thought had come to him, one he hadn't considered before.

Touch the whitemane? *What if he marked it?* He knew by heart the story of how his father had come upon the whitemane as a foal in the forest, of how he had been drawn to it and had put his hand to its brow. When he removed his hand, the mark of his fingers had remained, a black blaze.

What if *his* first touch marked the whitemane too? What if

he seized its mane and turned the silken hair black? What if he touched its neck and left a permanent discoloration? His chest choked shut at the thought. He had no right to ride the animal. What if the very mark of his calves marred its belly?

It was frightening enough that he had come to usurp a part of his father's legend. But to mar the whitemane's gleaming coat—his hands turned cold. His nails, normally pink against his dark skin, were chalk white. Shakily he tried to bring himself under control. His father was the only person who rode the whitemane—but not the only one to touch it. He let other people groom it and feed it when he could not. Every day children stopped beside its pen to rub its nose and whisper to it.

But Danior was not others. He was neither a child of the stonehalls, sturdy and fair, nor a palace daughter like his sisters. He was a palace son, the only one ever born. He had no place, no history, no future decreed by tradition. Who could tell what stain lay in his fingertips?

Or was that just an excuse to abandon his plan? An excuse not to discover that riding the whitemane would make no difference in who he was or in all the things he wasn't?

The grass he had pulled lay wilting on the ground. The whitemane nudged it once, then wandered away, browsing. At last Danior folded harness and reins back into the bag and retreated, walking stiffly, his fingers so cold he could not close them. If this had been a test, he knew bleakly, he had failed. He had come away empty.

Later that day, from his chamber window, he saw his father riding the whitemane back to its pen. The black blaze glistened against the animal's unspoiled whiteness. Danior watched with fists closed tight on nothing.

Later still Danior lay staring up at patches of tangled stalk-lamp and evaluating the sorrowing bitterness that rose in him. Why was he the only one who had no tradition, no place, no way?

Later still, moved by an impulse he recognized as misdirected even as he surrendered to it, he left his bed and went to the stairs. His shadow lost itself in the softer shadows of the stairwell as he descended. If he had no tradition of his own, whose must he live by? If he were a palace daughter, it would be time to stalk his beast and invite the change that came only at the risk of life. Perhaps, he told himself without fully believing it, there was a breeterlik, a crag-charger, a snowminx waiting in the mountains now to test and change him just as his sisters would one day be tested and changed.

It was dinner time and the corridors were empty. Danior's stomach contracted sharply at the smell of roast fowl and fresh-baked bread, but he did not join his family and the palace workers in the dining hall. Instead he turned down the long corridor to the training room.

Despite the scrubbed cleanness of its stone floor, the pains-taking cultivation of the stalklamp that grew bright upon its walls, the training room smelled of years of disuse. Danior paused inside the door. There were tumbling mats on the floor. The wall was hung with protective visors, padded vests, staffs, pikes, targets—everything a palace daughter needed to train to take her beast. Everything was clean and waiting.

Danior let the tall stone door close silently behind him. Waiting—the training room was waiting. It had been waiting since his mother and her sisters had trained here. *Alzaja, Mara, Denabar* . . . He frowned. He could not remember the names of all his mother's sisters, though he heard them each year at feast times. He could easily imagine them, palace daughters all, as slight as his sisters, as fragile.

A chill shivered down his spine. Seven sisters—six had failed in their challenge and died on the mountainside; one had survived and changed and taken the throne: his mother. In a few years his own sisters must come here to train. There were only three of them. If none survived, the valley would die when his mother lost the power of the stones. There would be no one to catch the sun's heat and concentrate it where it was needed. No one to warm the fields and orchards and extend the brutally short growing season. No one to insure that there was grain and fruit.

Danior stared around the training room and tried to guess

how many palace daughters had trained here over the centuries—and still left the room empty; how many had died for each one who lived and changed.

The room was haunted. Danior looked down at his hands and saw that his nails were white again. Handle the staffs and pikes his sisters must train with? Mark them with his fingers, all the things that had only been used by palace daughters preparing for the test few could survive?

Unconsciously he rubbed his fingers on his trouser legs, relinquishing the impulse that had brought him here. He had not marked the whitemane and he would not mark the sparring tools. What could it possibly prove if he went to the mountains and killed a beast? That there had been a beast waiting to give one of his sisters—Tanse, Aberra, Reyna—the power of the stones and he had killed it instead. Stiffly Danior turned and left the training room.

He felt lost in the corridors. He felt as if he had surrendered what little substance he owned, had become nothing more than a wisp of disconnected thought boiling along the floor. He was surprised to find himself in the empty throneroom, standing before the faintly glowing throne. He didn't reach out for its warmth. He simply stood before it in the dark, his thoughts echoing and empty, then withdrew.

Afterward he didn't remember going through the arched door to the plaza, didn't remember wandering down stone-paved streets and lanes, didn't remember hunching against the wall of the whitemane's pen and falling asleep with his knees drawn up to support his head.

His face chilled and his back turned stiff as he slept. He woke with a mumbled protest and realized that someone shook him by the shoulder. "Danior—Danior!"

He raised his head. His father knelt beside him, calling his name. His father: as dark as he, with a smooth strength in his stride and eyes that sometimes seemed to look far and sometimes were turned penetratingly near. His father, who had seen places no other person on Brakrath could even guess at. Tonight moonlight struck the planes of his face and threw shadow in his eyes. Stiffly Danior pushed himself to his feet, trying to see past the shadow. Had he ever seen fully beyond the obscuring veil of legend, he wondered. If he could press the veil aside, if he could learn whether his father had ever felt as he did, lacking, uncertain, alone . . .

His father stood too. "Aren't you cold?"

Danior shook his head, involuntarily measuring his height against his father's, frowning. It was a painful incongruity, being at once nothing and as tall as legend. And he knew he could not ask what he wanted to know. There were no words for questions that lay so close to the heart. Sighing, he glanced up and saw that the night was half gone.

His father misunderstood his glance. "Chia hasn't risen yet. Tanse is still at her window watching."

Danior bit his lip. He had forgotten that tomorrow—today? was it that late?—was Tanse's host day, the first spring rising of her host star, Chia. Everyone in the valley would hum Chia-songs tomorrow and eat foods harvested or prepared on the day of Chia's last autumn rising. Eggs taken from the nest and put into pickling jars on that day, bread baked from wheat harvested on that day, dried berries and fruits—Danior touched his stomach and felt hollowness: for the dinner he hadn't eaten, for the host stones he had not been offered as an infant because they were never offered to males, for all the traditions that had no place for a palace son.

As if to aggravate the condition, his father said, "Word comes from the orchard tender that you borrowed my halter and reins today."

Danior flinched, embarrassed that he had been seen when he thought he had not, anxious that his father thought the matter important enough to seek him out. "I didn't see anyone in the orchard."

His father shrugged, turning to lean against the wall of the pen. "Does it matter? You may ride Fiirsevrin anytime you wish. Tonight if you want."

Involuntarily Danior shrank from his father's questioning gaze. Ride the whitemane now? Did his father think he could intrude that casually upon legend—the legend of the marking, the legend of a steed ridden by no one but his master, the legend of an unbreakable bonding between steed and master? If he rode the whitemane, it would never be at a whim, easily. "No," he said almost defiantly. "I've never touched Fiirsevrin, and I won't now."

That denial brought his father's gaze to tight focus. For a moment his face was almost severe, the dark eyes sharp beneath the arched brows. "Tell me this, then. Do you want to ride him?"

The question was not an invitation but a query, deliberately probing. Danior drew back instinctively. "No." Despite the panic that rose in his throat, he kept the single syllable flat.

But his father heard beyond word and tone. The focus of his eyes grew sharper still, penetrating. "Ah. You went to ride but changed your mind. I have watched you. I think there are many things you have considered this spring, but I haven't seen you do any of them. What will you do, Danior, now that you've reached the age of choice?"

Danior felt his breath quiver. He could not believe his father had asked it—and as easily as if the question weren't a direct offensive against the most tenderly guarded ramparts of his privacy. What *will* you do? Remain in the palace, isolated and without place? Live at the edges of life, trying to subsist on someone else's traditions, someone else's legend? Or hunt a beast to its den and let the beast make his decisions for him?

What decisions? Danior's fists closed. He had no decisions. If Tanse went at her first majority to hunt a breeterlik or cragcharger, its killing of her or her killing of it would have meaning within the legends of the valley. If he went, neither outcome would have meaning. Because who was he?

A palace son. The only palace son a barohna had ever conceived and brought to live birth. The only palace son who had ever taken first steps in a Brakrathi palace. The only palace son ever to stare out tall windows and wonder what path he must take, how he was to raise the courage to find and follow it.

It seemed to Danior that he had no courage. His father's question only underscored the fact.

His hands hurt from clenching them. He stared at his father and felt pain turning in upon itself and becoming anger. If his mother had chosen a man of Brakrath—a herder, a breeder, a gem master—to father her first child, he would have been born a palace daughter or not at all. Instead she had chosen a man from another world. Danior wondered bitterly if she had given thought to the ultimate result of that union, the birth of a child who stood outside all the traditions of Brakrath. "Maybe I'll do what you do," he said, making the words bite. "Maybe I'll be a consort." A man without trade or tools. A man with neither occupation nor profession. And never mind the legends he bore, the tales built around his arrival and presence here. Never mind the place he had made for himself.

His father frowned faintly at the jibe. "Ah, do you think I'm ashamed to be a consort, Danior? Just because there are no others? In that case I'll tell you now—I'm not. The responsibilities your mother carries are heavy. The decisions she makes determine the life of every person in Valley Terlath. And she chose to abandon tradition and give her loyalty to me rather than to a stone mate. She chose to make me the person she talks to, the person she shares concerns with, the person who remains a constant in her life. I'm not ashamed to be that person. I never have been.

"But you shouldn't plan to follow in my footsteps. There will be no consorts after me. The Council made that clear when it sent my brothers away. The barohnas aren't ready to put aside their pairing stones and take permanent mates. Not from among the men of the halls and not from elsewhere either."

Danior shivered and turned from his father's steady gaze, already ashamed of his jibe. He had never known his father's brothers and he had never dared question him about them. But he thought of them sometimes when people laughed on the plaza beneath his window and his room yawned with emptiness. He knew a few things: that there had been four of them; that they had been so like his father and so like each other people said they might have grown from the same egg; that they had come from the stars just as the Arnimi did; that the

Council had sent them back, three of them. The fourth . . . He frowned up at his father. "The Council didn't send all your brothers away. The oldest—"

"No, they didn't send Jhaviir away, though I'm sure they wanted to. We've never discussed any of that, have we—the things that happened before you were born. I've wondered why you didn't ask me."

Danior shifted uneasily. "I thought—I thought you wouldn't want to talk about it." If he had had brothers and lost them— brothers like himself; brothers to understand what he said and to understand all the things he was afraid to say; brothers to go to in the middle of the night when the emptiness was too much—the memory would ache.

His father inclined his head thoughtfully. "There were times when I didn't want to discuss them. It wasn't so hard when the Council requested that the Arnimi send the three youngest to Arnim. Jhaviir was still here. We weren't close, but I felt we would be one day—when we were older, when we had more time to reflect on all the things we had in common."

"Jhaviir was Lihwa Marlath's mate?" Danior probed reluctantly.

"Yes, that's why the Council didn't send him away. The younger three had no ties here. But Jhaviir had already taken Lihwa as his mate, just as I had taken your mother. And she wouldn't peacefully have seen him go—any more than Khira would have seen me leave. That's one of the things that troubled the Council. Barohnas have never taken men as permanent mates. They have always chosen the fathers of their daughters casually, formed a brief liaison—seldom so long as a season— and reserved their loyalties for their stone mates and the other women of the Council. Then we came, my brothers and I, and first your mother and then Lihwa chose to discard old loyalties, old ways. To keep a permanent mate." Absently he reached into his pocket and extricated a worn velvet pouch.

Danior stared at the pouch, at the faceted blue stone his father drew from it. "A pairing stone," he said aloud, surprised.

His father nodded. "Yes. When the gem master heard that Lihwa and Khira had taken their thrones, he cut stones for them. Their mothers had been stone mates, their grandmothers before that. He thought they would be too. He thought they would require stones to link their thoughts, to keep the bond between them strong as they governed their valleys.

"But when he brought this stone to your mother, she wouldn't wear it. We were close, so close she thought it would hurt me to see her hold the stone and share thoughts with Lihwa. She thought I would feel excluded—and angry—every time I saw the stone light."

Danior frowned, wondering how far he dared press his questions. "Would you have felt that way?"

"No. But it's hard to persuade a person who has strong feelings that they aren't common to everyone. She thought I would be hurt and she decided to have the stone destroyed. I felt that someday she would need the stone to share thoughts with someone beside me. Someone who understood better what it is to command the sunthrone: Lihwa. So I asked her to let me hold the stone instead. And she did."

"But Lihwa died," Danior said reluctantly. "And Jhaviir too."

His father gazed down at the stone. He spoke slowly, each word carefully weighed. "I don't know that he did. He rode away, certainly, after Lihwa died, and no one has seen him. No one has heard of him. But there are many places he might have gone where we would not have heard. His training was far more rigorous than mine. He learned to use weapons as a small child. Eventually he learned all the disciplines of a soldier. He was armed when he left and he knew the mountains. He explored them far more intensively than I ever did. At least I tell myself all that when I find myself wondering what became of him. And that's more and more often as I grow older."

So the memory did ache. Knowing, Danior hesitated over his next question. "You were twins," he ventured, "but Jhaviir grew up fighting and you did not." He had never understood why his father and his brothers, so much alike, had been raised differently, by different people.

"No, we were far more than twins. People here called us that because they couldn't accept what we really were. It violated their most closely held feelings about the way life is passed from parent to child, about the sacredness of that process. That, I think, was the second reason the Council voted to send my younger brothers away. They didn't want the institutions of Brakrath and the loyalties of the barohnas to change as rapidly as they appeared to be changing. And they were uncomfortable with what we were, with what they felt when they saw us, so much alike, and knew how we came to be that way. We weren't twins. We were images.''

"Images?" Danior glanced up sharply. What could his father mean? An image was face glimpsed in the looking glass or a sketch quickly drawn with pen and ink. An image—

His father spoke softly, turning the pairing stone in his hand. "We were Rauthimages. Well over a century ago a man named Birnam Rauth left his home world—a planet called Carynon; it lies in the direction of your mother's host star, Adar—to become an explorer. A scientist. He had obtained support to compile a study of little known worlds. Worlds no one had studied or exploited yet. On one of them he encountered several members of a ship-dwelling race, the Benderzic. Without his permission, the Benderzic took cells from Birnam Rauth, placed them in culture, and from each cell they grew a new Rauth. That's what I am, that's what Jhaviir was, that's what all my brothers were, and there were many of them—new Birnam Rauths, identical to the original Birnam Rauth and to each other in every way." His eyes narrowed speculatively at Danior. "Can you accept that? That I'm the rebirth of a man born two centuries ago? His image?"

Danior fought down a bristling reaction at the indignity of the process his father described. "People aren't grown that way."

"But they are, Danior, and in many places. You've seen hall tenders grow stalklamp that way. They break off a piece and place it in a growing medium. After a while it roots and develops and it can be potted to grow on your wall. That's much the way my brothers and I were grown, but in a laboratory on a starship, under far more sophisticated conditions. Then we were left as small children on various worlds, to learn the languages and ways of the people who lived there. In our way, we were explorers too, as Birnam Rauth was."

Stubbornly Danior shook his head. He knew something of starships. He had met the Arnimi who visited the valleys occasionally to record information. They had come to Brakrath by starship and certainly they did not employ children. "No one uses children that way," he said. "They can't be trained. They—"

"But they can be programmed, if you don't care that your techniques leave them little trace of their humanity. And who is a more enthusiastic explorer than a child? Even a child who has been turned into a tool. Who is more curious? Who learns more quickly? That's how we were used, as tools. The Benderzic left us for a few years on one world, then took us to another for a few years. We were used like cultural and environmental recording devices. That's what a child is, after all. A child's job is to learn about his environment, and we did our job very well. Later the information we brought back to the Benderzic was sold to concerns interested in exploiting the worlds that were under study."

"Then—" Reluctantly Danior accepted what his father said.

"That's how Jhaviir came to be different from me, even though we were genetically identical. For some reason, the Benderzic left him for almost fourteen years with the Kri-Nostri, a desert people who lived on a world in the eastern rim of this galaxy. Their environment was harsh, and they were just emerging from a long period of wars. I went to several other worlds, kinder worlds, and then I was sent here. When the ship came to retrieve me and the information I had gathered about Brakrath, it was carrying Jhaviir and three of my younger brothers to new assignments. But it never left here. You've seen the place where it is now."

Danior nodded. The Benderzic ship lay on the plain, crushed under tons of stone. That was part of his father's legend: that his mother had destroyed a starship rather than let him be taken away: that later she had taken him as a permanent mate, over the objections of the Council. He had become her consort and Jhaviir had become Lihwa's; the Council of Bronze had become alarmed and sent the younger three brothers to Arnim; and finally Lihwa had been killed in a snowslide and soon after Jhaviir and their child had ridden away on his whitemane and not been seen again.

"That's why Jhaviir went away," he said slowly, guessing. "He was afraid the Council would send him to Arnim too, after Lihwa died."

"Partly, perhaps. And partly because he was never content to live the palace life. He was an explorer, a Rauthimage. He wanted to see new places, to meet new challenges, to learn new ways. It was in his blood, just as it was in Birnam Rauth's."

Danior's eyes narrowed. Was there wistfulness in his father's voice? He had been created from Birnam Rauth just as Jhaviir had. Was there some restlessness in him too? And if there was, why had he suppressed it? "You—did you ever meet him? Birnam Rauth?"

"No. I heard a recording of his voice once, a long time ago. The Arnimi translated it for me. It was a call for help."

"And did—did someone help him."

Slowly his father shook his head. "I think not. He disappeared over a century ago. No one knows how or where. He had completed his funded studies and gone exploring on his own, in a single-man ship. He resupplied at a small port on Rignar, not so far from his home world, Carynon. But he told no one where he was bound when he left, and he hasn't been seen or heard from since, except for the one message. And that wasn't helpful. It simply said he was being held against his will in a place he could not describe. No one could discover the origin of the message—what world it came from, how he managed to record it. He's dead, I think, and I didn't meet him. But there are many people I've never met. Many places I've never seen."

This time there was no mistaking the regret. Danior pressed his temples, uncomfortable with the knowledge that his father lived with a carefully hidden discontent. "You must have wanted to do the same things Jhaviir did," he said tentatively.

"To ride away and see this world, land by land?" His father's gaze flicked to the distant horizon, lost in darkness. "Yes, I've wanted to do that. I've visited the plain, of course. Khira and I lived with the guardians the summer before she bronzed. But once she took the throne, our scope narrowed. Necessity keeps us in the valley during the warmseason, in the mountain palace during winter. There are other societies on Brakrath but I've never seen how their people live, what customs they've created for themselves, how their thoughts are patterned. I've never seen the lands they live in or the barren lands between."

Danior licked his lips. Did he dare ask? "Why? Why haven't you gone?" His mother could not leave the valley, but his father was not bound to the throne. The life of the valley could continue without him.

His father sighed, rubbing the pairing stone between his fingers, staring down into it. "And leave your mother? Leave you? Leave your sisters? No. When I was very young, the Benderzic left me among a people who called themselves the plain people. They were farmers, people who smelled of the soil. They found me in their fields, an abandoned child who didn't know any human tongue, and they took me in and made me human. Then after four years, the Benderzic came and took me away. They put their helmet on me and drew out all the information I had gathered—the resources of the land, the strengths and weaknesses of the people, their habits and customs. And they took my memory away. They left me empty. After they removed the helmet, I couldn't even remember the face of the man who had called himself my father for four years.

"They set me down empty on another world, this time for five years. A woman found me in the trees and took me home and made me her son. She fed me and clothed for me. She taught me to read and write. And she taught me what it is to care for other people, what it means to be a human among humans. I even found a few stray memories of the plain people before the Benderzic came and took me again. And took all my memories away.

"Finally the Benderzic left me here. They left me in the cold of winter in the palace tower. Your mother found me and this time she was the one who made me human. I didn't have language, I didn't have memory, I didn't have a sense of myself as anything but a tool of the Benderzic. Alzaja, Khira's sister, had died that year on the mountain and Khira was lonely. She took me for her companion knowing nothing about me. She fed me, she protected me, she destroyed the Benderzic ship when it returned for me. Everything I am, she made me.

"But it took me many seasons to find my memories again. I've never found them all. I can remember going to the temple to hear the godsvoice with my second mother but I can't recall the words to the chants—although I dream them sometimes. I can remember helping my father among the plain people sow seeds, but I don't remember what grew from them.

"I've left too many people and too many places in my lifetime. I've learned what it is to wish for a face I know, one I won't see again. I've learned how quickly even memories can vanish, how empty it is without them, how hard it is to call them back when they've begun to fade. Much as I want to see other lands, I want more to stay here, where I know the faces, where my memories still live around me.

"And so I will, until I have to leave."

"Until—" Danior drew an anxious breath. "You think the Benderzic will come back for you? After all this time?"

"It hasn't been that long in the scheme of things. Eighteen years. And they know, just by the fact that Khira destroyed their carrier ship, that there is something powerful here. Something worth their attention. I think they'll make another probe, eventually, probably using some other breed of image. We're watching for them—the Council, the guardians, the Arnimi. Between us we'll see that their second attempt to evaluate Brakrath is just as successful as their first."

Danior's tense shoulders loosened slightly. "Then if you don't think the Benderzic will take you—"

"Why would I have to leave?" He turned his face to Nindra, letting her pale light wash it. "Tanse is old enough now to make her challenge. She'll begin training at Midsummer. If she doesn't bronze, Aberra will begin to train in two years time—and three years later Reyna will train. If neither of them bronzes either—"

Danior shivered involuntarily. "Then the valley will die when Mother loses the power of the stones."

His father shook his head. "No. Your mother has only begun her childbearing years. If she had followed the old ways, her children would have come ten, fifteen, even twenty years apart, over a period of a century—or more. And no two by the same father. Instead she chose to space them closely and to take them all from the same father.

"That may have been a misjudgement. It may be that only a man of Brakrath can father a barohna. If that is true, if none of your sisters bronzes, I must leave so your mother can bear other daughters in the old way. Because I know she won't take a Brakrathi mate, even for a season, while I'm here."

Danior drew a sharp breath, understanding. If his father could not father a daughter for the throne, his mother must look to someone else. And she did not expect his father to take it well. "You'll have to leave—because she would expect you to feel angry if she took other mates."

"Yes. Hurt and angry and abandoned. She doesn't feel by half measures. She doesn't expect me to feel that way either."

Danior pressed his temples, his thoughts running rapidly ahead. "Jhaviir's daughter—" If she were living, she was old enough to have gone to the mountain now, old enough to show them whether the daughter of a Rauthimage could take the power of the stones.

His father understood his unspoken question and shook his head. "She wasn't a palace daughter, not in the way your sisters are. She was like you—so much like you people said you might have been twins. So I'm not sure she would have taught us anything." Absently he placed the pairing stone on the broad wall of the pen. Its polished facets glinted darkly. He stroked it with one finger, seeming to search for words.

Danior didn't wait for them. Jhaviir's daughter had been like him—dark and long-limbed, with none of the apparent fragility that marked a palace daughter. The one person who might have shared his isolation was gone. "She was like me. So she wouldn't have been anyone either," he said, and was immediately ashamed of the open bitterness of the words.

His father raised his head sharply. "Either, Danior?"

It took Danior a moment to recognize the rebuke in the question. It took him another moment to choke back the sense of unfairness it roused. He bit his lip angrily. "I have no place here. I'll never go for a beast. I'll never join a guild. I'll never do anything—because there's nothing for me to do."

"Never? Anything?" The very gentleness of his father's words challenged him. "How can you be certain—when it's entirely up to you, Danior? There are many things to be done by a person willing to do them."

"Then what are they?" Danior challenged. Was he to demand to be apprenticed to a guild? Demand to be taught by a master too courteous to say that he was not wanted? Or was he to go to the mountain and try to usurp a bit of his sisters' legend? Neither course had any meaning for a palace son. "I wasn't born to anything."

"Only because no one like you has been born here before. That doesn't mean there is nothing for you to do. It only means you must find ways of living your life that are as new as you are. Or you must find new ways to do the old things.

"Think, Danior. Your sisters are caught by tradition, bound by it. Perhaps one day they'll die for it. Your mother is caught by it too, bound to the throne. But she set part of her heritage aside and found a new way to live. And I have no heritage at all. I've had to choose my path step by step.

"Now you must do the same. You must put one foot before the other and create your own path, your own tradition."

Make his own legend? As his father had done after the Benderzic dropped him here? But he had no drama to build upon. He was not the rebirth of a man born on another world. He had not been torn from one world and then another. He had not been left without language or memory in the palace tower. He had not even ridden the whitemane.

His jaws knotted. He was overshadowed by his mother, by his father, by his sisters. They blinded him with their light. And now his father told him he must look past the light to find his path. His eyes flicked to the pairing stone. He felt a surge of bitterness. It was as useless as he was. The gem master had cut it to link his mother and Lihwa, but they had elected not to be joined. They had taken the stones from their throats, and now this one was as dark as he was.

Without thinking, Danior reached for the faceted stone. He closed his fingers around it, punishing the stone for his own confusion. Words cluttered his mind, words to wound his father with, words to defend himself by.

The Council should have sent all five brothers to Arnim. Should have sent them before his father had ever become his mother's consort, before they had conceived him. The Council should have sent him when he was born. Should—

"Danior—"

Danior clenched his teeth, shaking his head angrily. There were no words to dissipate the burning helplessness he felt. There were no words so strong.

"*Danior*—" His father's voice was strange, urgent.

Fiercely Danior raised his head, at the same time loosening his fingers. He saw the glow first in his father's eyes, reflected there faintly. Disbelieving, he gazed down. The pairing stone lay in the palm of his hand, a faint light at its depths.

His heart stopped. He forgot to breathe. The pairing stone was alive in his hand. The stone that had been his mother's. The stone that should have lived only at her touch. He felt its warmth. Stunned, he raised his head. The blood had left his father's face. In his father's eyes he saw something he had never seen before, something that struck him with terror.

Find his own path. Create his own tradition. Build his own legend. Those were the things his father urged him to do. Those were the things that could give him the substance and definition of a man. But he couldn't guess how to do them, which step he must take first and in what direction.

He couldn't guess, but in his father's eyes he saw the glow of the stone and the bare beginning of a legend—his own. It lay there like a seed, summoning, and he wasn't ready. He wasn't ready at all. He gazed at the stone and began to tremble.

THREE
DANIOR

It was ten days later when Danior climbed down overgrown mountain trails and descended into the unclouded silence of Valley Marlath. Abandoned trees stood chill-bitten in the orchards, their sparse buds closed against the cold. Dikes waited in stony solitude for repair while weeds bristled in the growing fields. Animal pens stood vacant, rebuking him with their emptiness.

When Danior neared the center of the valley, he found the stonehalls as empty as the animal pens. And he found Lihwa's palace desecrated by the harsh brilliance of overgrown stalklamp. The windows had been left unshuttered when the people deserted the valley after Lihwa's death and stalklamp grew unchecked in every deserted chamber. Its orange light glared from every aperture.

Danior approached the edge of the plaza, wondering briefly why the gem master had insisted they meet in Lihwa's valley. He glanced around uneasily, then stepped across the dark flaggings. The sunstone slab Lihwa had once used to draw sunlight rested at the center of the plaza, its polished surfaces untouched by the debris that littered the flaggings. Danior tensed as he approached it, but the stone remained black. Without a barohna, the sunstone was simply a stone—smooth, inert, dark.

Without a barohna, the pairing stone should have been dark too. Frowning, Danior shoved his hand into his pocket and closed his fingers around the pouch that held the stone. The stone should have been dark, but it was not—not when he held it in the palm of his hand. Then it yielded light and heat, burning enigmatically against the cold of his flesh.

Stiffly Danior drew his hand from his pocket. His father had said he must find his own path. But since he had first touched the pairing stone, his thoughts had become a maze, a series of interconnecting pathways that led nowhere—except back to the pairing stone. Always to the pairing stone. How was he to choose when every path led to the same destination—and all he found there was confusion?

His mother, his father, his sisters had touched the stone and it had remained dark. But for him it lived, and no one in Valley Terlath could say why. Did its response signify that he had some latent touch of his mother's gift of the stones? But that came only in prescribed ways, and he had not done the things a palace daughter must do to become a barohna. He had not trained. He had not gone to the mountain and made a challenge. He had not changed. He was as he had always been, hesitant, shadowed, doubting.

So was the stone's light meaningless? An isolated aberration? Juris Pergossa didn't know. His parents didn't know. Certainly he didn't. But surely the gem master would. His mother had not said so when she suggested he be summoned. His father had not said so when he agreed that it be done. They had said only that the gem master was the best person to evaluate the stone. But if he couldn't say why it lit in Danior's hand, who could?

Danior shivered, rubbing his hands against his trousers, and set across the plaza.

The palace doors stood open, revealing a garishly overgrown foyer. Streamers of stalklamp dangled from matted walls; creeping runners streaked the flaggings with light. Danior studied the foyer floor. There were disturbances in the dust, but no evidence of human passage.

So the gem master had not come yet. Danior hesitated, then stepped through the great doors and passed under the arched entryway to the throneroom. Vines of light encroached from the corridor, crawling across the floor, casting a spectral half-light against the vaulted emptiness of the throneroom. Danior's boots tapped emptily on the flaggings as he approached the dark throne. Even the mirrors mounted high on the walls were dark, their reflective surfaces furred with dust.

Only the sunstone throne was free of ravage. Danior approached it, trying to imagine its clean fiery light in the days when the throneroom had been the living heart of the valley. The clamor of monitors, messengers and advisers; the sound of booted feet on polished flaggings; the smell of bread baking in distant kitchens—all the activities of the valley had converged here. And the life of the valley had flowed from here, from the sunthrone.

Yet all that had died with one person. Danior frowned, stepping near the throne, wondering if he dared touch it. No one but a barohna was permitted to touch a throne that held light. But this throne was dark.

A sound from the corridor distracted him, making him freeze momentarily, his heart leaping. When the sound was not repeated, he slipped to the arched entry and saw a small scampering shadow far down the corridor. An animal, probably one of the tiny seed-gatherers that invaded the fields at harvest time. Now it held title to the entire palace. Danior gazed back at the throne again, then stepped down the corridor, escaping temptation.

Cautiously he explored the palace and found walls matted with stalklamp, floors treacherous with luminous runners, and the smells of dampness and food spoiling in open jars. Yet there were no open jars.

There was nothing in the palace but dust, stalklamp, and the droppings of small animals. The people had taken everything, even the shutters that should have protected the windows. Only one set of rooms remained furnished and Danior did not enter there. He peered in from the door, breath held. Dust-hoared bureaus, time-faded coverlets, scrolls that lay where they had been dropped so many years before—Danior retreated, unwilling to trespass upon quarters once shared by Lihwa and Jhaviir.

Soon afternoon waned beyond unshuttered windows and the desolation of the deserted palace sent Danior to the tower to watch for the gem master. He leaned against slippery stone-work, trying not to think of the pairing stone in its pouch, trying not to worry at the unanswerable questions it raised. A path, a legend, a place—how was he to wrest any of those from confusion and fear? Set one foot before the other, his father had said. But where was he to put the first foot?

Soon after sunset, a figure in leathers and boots appeared at the edge of the plaza. Danior watched, certain the man who crossed the flaggings could not be the gem master. A gem master should be a man of extraordinary proportions or presence, a giant. A gem master should be as tall as the mountains he searched, as imposing as the powers he gave life when he cut and polished the stones he quarried. And the man below was ordinary.

So ordinary in his worn leathers that he might be a worker returning from the fields or a herder who had just settled his flock for the night. Danior watched until he passed through the doors below. Then, the pairing stone heavy in his pocket, a sinking anticipation of disappointment even heavier in his chest, he descended to meet him.

The gem master stood gazing up at the dust-furred mirrors, a stocky man with fair hair and sun-beaten face. Beneath his leather tunic, he wore the roughspun of the halls. When he turned the only thing remarkable about him was his eyes. They were vividly blue, as if he had looked so long at the summer sky that he had captured a part of it—so blue it hurt when he returned Danior's stare.

He was not ordinary after all. Danior knew that when he tried to greet him and his breath rasped ineffectually in his throat.

"Danior Terlath?" the gem master asked.

"Yes," Danior managed finally. "My mother summoned you. About the stone."

"The pairing stone," the gem master affirmed. "Did you bring it?" His voice was husky, the voice of a man of the stonehalls, and the hand he held out was blunt and calloused, with short-bitten nails. But there was nothing of the stonehalls in his manner. He did not nod or speak with careful indirection.

Confused, Danior took the pouch from his pocket and tugged awkwardly at its puckered mouth. "This—this is the stone." It lay on his palm, its faint light driving the moisture from his mouth, its warmth burning against the cold of his skin. He licked his lips, watching for the gem master's reaction.

No expression touched the weathered face. Silently the gem master took the stone from Danior's palm and stepped into the stalklit corridor to examine it.

Danior followed, uneasily. The gem master had said none of the things a man of the halls normally says upon meeting. He had not introduced himself, he had not inquired after the fertility of Valley Terlath, he had not even repeated Danior's name when he addressed him. And his concentration upon the stone was so total Danior felt excluded. "Did you—did you cut and polish it yourself?" he ventured. It was difficult to guess whether the gem master was old enough to have been a master eighteen years before. His face was as creased as his leather trousers but his eyes held a piercing clarity.

The gem master shook his head and continued to examine the stone, turning it to let its polished facets catch and reflect stalklight. At last he straightened and turned his attention just as totally upon Danior. "Tell me what you felt the first time the gem lit for you."

Danior shrank from the vivid eyes, reluctant to share his shock, his elation, his terror. "My hand felt warm."

The gem master nodded as if the answer were not an evasion. As if he had heard what was not said as clearly as what was. "And now? What do you feel when you handle it now?"

Danior hesitated, feeling he might as well try to hide from the sky as from the gem master's gaze. Still he tried. "The— the same thing. My hand feels warm."

"How often do you handle it?"

"Only—only when—" But evasion was no use. The gem master's pupils had contracted to minute apertures—pinholes through which he saw everything. Bracing himself, Danior drew a halting breath and let the words tumble with all the force of his perplexity. "I carry it in my pocket by day. I take it out and put it on my bureau at night. I only touch it when someone wants to see it. I—I don't want to handle it at all. I don't want to touch it. I don't even want to carry it. Not until you tell me—not until—'' Until what? What did he want to hear from the gem master? That the light in the pairing stone was a meaningless refraction? That he could build a modest legend upon it without heavier demands being placed upon him later? That he could handle the pairing stone without the fear that someday he would be drawn to touch his mother's throne and see an answering light there too? A light that could destroy if he wielded it without training, without discipline. A light he was little prepared to tame. He shook his head, unable to frame a coherent demand.

Nodding as if he had, the gem master slipped the gem back into its pouch. "There aren't so many things I can tell you, Danior Terlath. The master who taught me cut this stone and its mate. He gave them to the barohnas of valleys Terlath and Marlath. The barohnas gave them to their consorts, and one of those consorts gave this one to you. It responds to your touch. It gives you heat and light. I can't tell you what it will do if you continue to handle it. Perhaps you will learn to reach into the mind of the person who holds the other stone. Perhaps that person will learn to reach into your mind. Perhaps neither of you will ever do more than make the stones glow.''

Danior's heart missed a beat. *The person who held the other stone?* He had not thought of the other stone, the one Lihwa had given Jhaviir. The suggestion that someone shared his terrifying miracle made his skin turn cold. Made him curl with possessiveness. And misgiving. "How—how do you know someone has the other stone?'' Had Jhaviir carried it when he rode away? Had he dropped it somewhere in his wanderings? Who could have picked it up? Who? Danior pressed his temples, trying to still his thoughts. They tumbled too quickly for him to examine them, to discard those that were meaningless.

The gem master's pupils shimmered, widening. A faint line appeared between his brows. "Perhaps no one does,'' he conceded. "If you were a barohna, I would say it was impossible for one stone of a pair to live if no one held the other. But you aren't a barohna. You aren't even a palace daughter. Yet the stone burns for you. So the usual course of events has been suspended and I have no answers. Have you had unusual dreams since you first touched the stone? Dreams that you were entering someone else's mind? That's usually the first sign that a link has been established!''

"No." But what, he thought with a sudden chill, if someone were using the second stone to touch him? To sample his thoughts as casually as if he had written them upon a scroll and posted them on the wall? His hands tightened against an impulse to dash the stone from the pouch and crush it on the flaggings. For anyone to know how small he was behind the face he wore, how uncertain—for anyone to know his most private thoughts, his fears—

He pressed his temples again, harder, and fastened on something the gem master had said. Fastened on it as if it would deliver him. "You have no answers. You have no answers at all."

"I have none," the man agreed, his eyes rimming with shadow. "I'm only a craftsman. I go to the mountains and find fresh veins. I quarry them. Then, with my tools, I find the living heart of each stone. I cut and polish until the heart is accessible to the barohna who has commissioned the stone. I cut sunstones. I cut pairing stones. Once I cut an eyestone for a barohna who took me for her season's mate. But it shattered when she had it mounted at her winter palace. And no daughter came of our season together.

"I know where to slice a slab, how to cut and facet a stone. But my master never taught me to understand the skills he gave my hands. I don't know why a finished sunstone holds sunlight— or why it holds sunlight only for a barohna. Any more than I know why a palace daughter must take a beast to become a barohna. Why her body requires that stimulation to change. And why the change is so swift and so profound.

"I know that once there were no barohnas. There were no sunstones or pairing stones, until one day a man named Lensar realized something lay at the heart of a block of stone that had broken off the mountainside. When he cut and polished it, when he found what he was looking for and captured it in the facets of a gem, the woman who loved him discovered that she knew what to do with the gem. She knew how to concentrate sunlight in it and call it out later."

"She burned him," Danior said flatly. He did not want to dwell on what came of the unpracticed use of a stone.

"Yes, she turned him to ash before she knew what she had done. Before she realized how fiery sunlight can be when it has been stored in a sunstone. And she never understood how she had known that sunlight could be stored in the stone and released again. Any more than your mother understands the process by which she draws sunlight from the mountainsides each spring to thaw the fields for planting. She exploits the process without understanding it. If she waited until she understood, she would die without ever using the stone." He turned the gazing brilliance of his eyes fully upon Danior. "Do you understand what I'm saying?"

Danior studied the vivid eyes, the weathered face. They were like earth and sky, one worn and eroded, the other so clear it hurt to look directly into them. "You can't tell me whether someone has the other pairing stone."

"I can't tell you."

'You can't tell me why this one lights for me."

"I can't."

"You—you can't tell me anything," Danior realized, caught between relief and disappointent. "My mother summoned you to tell me what to do and you can't."

"But I've told you something far more important."

Danior's shoulders stiffened rebelliously. Something more important than what he must do, where he must put his foot? "You haven't told me anything."

"Haven't I, Danior Terlath? I've told you that many of us go ahead with the important work of our lives without answers. We go with only questions, following them from step to step, learning by what we do. Learning the nature of the world, learning our own natures, learning how the two interact to carry us ahead." For the first time the gem master smiled.

"Usually the first thing we learn is how much more ignorant we are than we ever thought possible. But we press beyond that. We must if we aren't simply to stand still."

Danior stiffened in instinctive resistance, realizing what the gem master was suggesting. That he use the stone without understanding it. That he stroke light from it without knowing where the light would lead. "No. I won't do that," he said. "If I don't understand, if no one can tell me—"

"If Lensar had refused to cut the first sunstone until he knew he would not be harmed, there would be no barohnas in our valleys, Danior Terlath. If Niabe had waited to use the stone until she was certain of her control, she would never have used it at all."

"But I'm not a barohna. I'm not even a daughter. I—"

"Niabi was not a barohna or a palace daughter either. There were no palaces in her day and the people were hungry because there was no one to bring sunlight into the valleys."

"No." The word carried the force of panic.

Shrugging, the gem master reached for Danior's hand and uncurled the cramping fingers. He dropped the pairing stone into the palm, refusing to let Danior draw back. Slowly reflected light grew in his eyes.

Danior gazed down at the stone, his heart thumping at his ribs, a muffled tocsin. The stone's light, its heat—both were more intense than they had been just a few minutes before.

The gem master's words seemed to come from a distance, a pronouncement. "My master said when your father and his brothers came that nothing would be the same in our valleys again. That we would see things never seen before and children born to make them happen. You are one of those children and this is one of those things—a stone that lives for someone who is not a barohna."

Things never seen before. Danior's palm burned. He closed his hand around the stone, trying to hide the sharpness of his fear behind anger—only half succeeding. "I can't use it. I don't know how."

"If you were a barohna, you would wear it on a chain at your throat. You would touch it many times each day, until you became fully sensitive to it. You would feel your way into it, learning with your fingertips, with your senses, with the flesh of your throat how to use it.

"Understand: this is no magical device. It's a tool—but one only a few people are capable of using. And those people learn to use it only by practicing its use. Just as I learned to use my picks and blades by going to the mountains."

The stone burned in Danior's hand. He shook his head in confusion. He wanted to throw the stone down. He wanted to protest, to rebel. But against whom? He was the one who made the stone light.

"I have a chain," the gem master said.

A chain to suspend the pairing stone from. A chain to hold it against the soft flesh of his throat. Danior's jaws bunched. "With you?" The words were whispered.

"Yes."

But the gem master did not move toward his pocket or his pouch. He would not, Danior realized sinkingly, unless Danior requested it. Danior closed his eyes, trying to clarify his thoughts. Wear the stone without answers to any of his questions? Without knowing where the miracle might lead? Stubbornly he clenched his hands at his sides. But his tongue betrayed him. "Let me have one."

"Of course." The gem master reached into his pouch and extracted a thin metal chain. He placed it in Danior's hand, gazing at him almost as if he enjoyed Danior's agony. Then he turned and stepped toward the plaza doors.

He was leaving, Danior realized, and without making anything clear. "*No!* Wait!" Danior ran after him in alarm. "Wait! You—"

The gem master turned back, smiling. "No fear. I'll hear what you do with the stone, Danior Terlath. I'll hear where it leads you. It will be legend in these mountains very soon after it happens."

Legend. Danior halted, torn. He had wanted to be legend. He had wanted to do mythic things. Now they only looked terrifying. He found himself thinking of finding a path instead, of making his way to some goal he could not name. "You haven't even told me why you wanted to meet me here instead of in my mother's valley," he said desperately. So long as the gem master lingered, he would not be alone with the stone.

"Ah. Because the settled valleys cloud over when the warm air rises from the fields. Here I can see the stars. Have you looked at them? They're like stones in the sky—precious stones polished by a hand no one has ever seen. Some night, when the sky is clear, I'm going to reach out and take one." He raised his hand in salute and stepped away through the great doors to the plaza.

Danior stood frozen as the gem master crossed the plaza and disappeared into the deserted avenues. Then he turned, staring down the stalklit corridor. There was nothing there for him but garish light. Choking, he ran into the plaza. Perhaps the gem master planned to sleep in the valley tonight. Perhaps he had already spread bedding in one of the deserted stonehalls. Perhaps—

Danior caught himself at the edge of the plaza, running after the gem master. Grimly he pulled himself to a halt. He was not a child, afraid to sleep alone.

Nor was he afraid to walk mountain trails by night, he reminded himself, though he carried only a pike.

Or perhaps he was simply less afraid to start back to his mother's valley tonight than to stay here with his thoughts. Briefly he stared down at the chain the gem master had given him. Then he thrust chain and stone into his pocket and ran down stone avenues toward the mountains.

He walked until he could no longer look back and see the stalklight glow of the palace. Then he sat with his back to a protecting boulder and let his eyes close. His legs ached, his feet hurt, and his spirit was suddenly as bruised as his body. And still the unanswered questions burned. The maze opened and expanded, confounding him. If he wore the stone, would he step into someone else's thoughts—or would someone step into his? Would he open himself to critical eyes, scornful eyes, belittling eyes? And if no one else held the second stone, if it had been discarded long ago, where would the light of his own stone lead him? Grimly he followed tortuous paths until his thoughts exhausted him and he fell asleep huddled against the rock.

He woke to find the sky fierce with stars and the cold of the mountain upon him. He sat for a long time, pressing himself against the boulder, shivering, thinking of legends and paths and things never seen before.

His fingers felt brittle as he took the pairing stone from his pocket and threaded the chain through the loop of the metal setting. He felt the stone's warmth in his palm. His choice was clearcut. Wear the stone or set it aside. Follow where it led or go back to the valley, to the emptiness of his chambers. What other alternatives were there? Groping, he found none.

But how was he to begin to follow where the stone led? He read no clue in its glow. It offered no guidance, no direction.

He sat holding the stone, his fingers white and cold, his breath frosting the air, until a new thought warmed him. Perhaps his great-grandmother could read something from the stone. She had held the throne of Valley Terlath for over a hundred years before she retired to the plain. What hadn't she seen in that span? Even if she could not answer all his questions, perhaps she could suggest where he must put his foot if he was to follow the stone's vagrant light. Perhaps she could tell him where the path began.

He shivered under the dawning sky, examining his decision. Then he returned the stone to its pouch, the pouch to his pack. Standing, he walked the trail until he found a lens tender sleeping beside his lens. He woke the man and instructed him to send a message to his parents that he had gone to the plain, to Kadura. Then, drawing a deep breath of the cold dawn, he set course toward the plain.

FOUR
KEVA

It was night and Keva crouched near the ashes of her cookfire, her fingers tight on the stone at her throat. She had had her choice of camp spots for the night—a cove of rocks in the roughlands from which she had just emerged, a sheltering tree at the verge of the plain, a grassy hollow beside running water. She had rejected them all for this place, where the ground lay flat and open and her view stretched unobstructed in all directions.

Still the feeling that she was watched prickled at the back of her neck and made her hand close around the stone at her throat. She wanted to whip her head around sharply, to confront whoever—or whatever—watched her.

Each time she turned, her eyes met only darkness.

The very openness of the plain made her uneasy. She had grown up beside the warmstream, where moss-grown trees provided a protective screen against the roughlands that lay beyond. And even the roughlands did not stretch in flat monotony to the sky. The ground's surface rolled and tumbled and was broken by rocks, brush and trees.

Here there was nothing as far as she could see—nothing but grass, an occasional tree, and the sky, a tangible presence that hung just beyond finger's reach. Memory of the bluesong had been very much with her today. All she needed was sunlight and the slippery feel of the blue cloth at her neck and the song returned to her in all its clarity.

She clung to the stone at her throat. Other things came to her with clarity too since she had left the warmstream. Her fire dreams were more vivid than she had ever known, because now the fire was nearer—so near she could feel its heat upon her face, so near that sometimes she glimpsed its source, a tall figure standing against a burning mountainside. So near she seemed to hear a grumbling roar, to feel—

Keva shuddered and stood abruptly, the back of her neck drawing tight. The emptiness around her had grown so menacing even her thoughts had taken an ominous turn. Anything could sweep down upon her here. Quickly she gathered her possessions and slung them over her shoulders. Forcing herself to move deliberately when she wanted only to run, she traced a path back toward the grassy hollow she had passed earlier in the evening.

Clouds cloaked the moons in white lace. Shadows moved over the grass, stealthily. Keva was trembling by the time she reached shelter of the shadowed hollow. Water welled from the ground in a spring and pooled in a rocky basin. The grass itself was fine-textured, thick, soft and green.

Keva sank into the shadows of the hollow and wrapped her bedding around her, as if it could hide her from the eyes she still felt upon her back. She knew there were predators on the plain, preying on the herds of redmanes. She particularly remembered Par's stories of gliding, sharp-clawed creatures with amber eyes and bobbing ringlets who liked to game with their prey before striking. Perhaps that was what watched her now, a plains minx, teasing its appetite by a slow stalking of her.

Or had the guardians who tended the redmane herds seen her and set someone to watch her? Keva frowned into the dark. Each summer the guardians drove their herds across the warmstream on their way to the lakelands. Last year, against Oki's instruction, she had watched from the trees and had seen women who stood tall in their umber capes, forbidding and silent. They had spoken to the fisher-people, but distantly, and they had permitted no one to approach the animals they drove.

Had the guardians seen her and decided she had come to steal redmanes? Keva tried to imagine one of those imposing women moving in silent pursuit, watching. That was not so difficult. In their hooded cloaks, the guardians seemed made for stealth. But it was difficult to imagine a guardian effortlessly slipping into invisibility each time Keva turned to peer around.

She was imagining it—imagining eyes upon her. The fisher-people had never forbidden the guardians passage across the warmstream. Why should the guardians deny her passage upon the plain?

And when she met them and told them why she had come, why shouldn't they answer her questions? Had they seen a dark man riding a white animal that looked as if it had been refined from their own animals: tall where the redmanes were stocky, smooth where the redmanes were shaggy, graceful where the redmanes were heavy-footed? Had they seen him years before with a child? Had they seen him since and what direction had he taken?

There was no reason for the guardians to refuse to answer her. And if they could tell her nothing, then she must take her questions to the mountains. Keva shivered at that thought, wishing she knew which of Par's tales were true and which fancy, wishing she could guess how much of what Oki said about the barohnas was fact and how much spite. Wishing too that she knew why she felt such foreboding dread of the mountains. Was it only because of the things Oki had told her?

Keva rubbed her arms and pulled her bedding close. She did not sleep well that night, despite the slow murmur of running water.

The next morning when she found footprints beside the spring, her appetite deserted her too. They had been made by clawed feet almost as large as her own, but with the six toes widely splayed. There were just two sets of impressions, but there was broken grass in other places and Keva did not know if she had trampled it the night before or if the animal that left its prints had done so.

She did know there had not been prints at the spring the night before.

A minx? Frowning, she sorted through her pack and pouch. She found only a few dried berries, a half-crescent of bread, but that was all there had been the night before. Nor had her extra clothes or bedding been disturbed. So whatever creature had left prints had not stolen from her.

She retreated from the spring, trying to remember what she knew of plains predators. All her information came from Par's tales, and she did not know how much of that was fact. Was it true that a minx would not attack unmoving prey? That it would circle, that it would tease with sharp claws, but would not spring unless its prey twitched or flinched or tried to run?

Was that why the animal had not harmed her? Because she had been sleeping? Or simply because it had not finished its stalking game?

And the other plains predators, the fyurries that ran in hungry packs, the lobbers and wassickers, the things Par said howled when storm clouds dipped low—

She had come this far without a weapon, but she realized now that she should not go farther. Glancing around uneasily, she left the shelter of the rocky hollow.

She had intended to walk into the plain this morning, searching for sign of the herds and their guardians. Instead she turned to the west, to a place where the roughlands embraced the plain. She followed the rolling, tumbled ground as it skirted the plain. When she found a suitable tree, she broke down a sturdy limb and used her digging blade to sharpen one end to a point. It was a crude weapon, but she worked on it ostentatiously, hefting it, testing its balance. If the minx were watching, if it were as cunning as Par said, it would recognize that she was armed.

She walked slowly back toward the edge of the roughlands, carrying her pike self-consciously. If it were indeed a minx that stalked her, she felt its eyes upon her through most of the day, stinging, as the land changed under her feet, becoming lusher, greener. Despite the promise of the terrain, forage was scant, the vegetation unfamiliar, and she found no water. She hoarded the water she had drawn from the spring and saved her bread and berries for later, when she would be hungrier than now.

It was late afternoon when she stood on a rocky promontory and looked down over a distant herd—the first she had seen. The animals were little more than a shadow upon the muted green of the horizon. They were too far for her to distinguish individual animals or guardians. The afternoon breeze brought her neither sound nor scent of them.

Keva clutched the stone at her throat, gazing down. She had come to question the guardians and now they were within a few hours' walk. Yet her feet were reluctant to carry her. What if she approached them and learned things she didn't want to know? That they had not heard of her father. That they had and he was dead.

Stiffly she moved to sit in the shadow of a sheltering rock. *Tonight*. She would go down tonight, while the guardians slept. She wouldn't have to speak to them until morning. With that decision made, Keva closed her fingers around her stone and leaned back against the rock, letting her eyelids fall. The late afternoon sun warmed her to sleep.

It was dusk when she stood, stiffly, and peered down across the plain. The herd had retreated over the horizon while she slept. She could see only an indistinct mottling—scattered animals grazing far in the distance.

Keva's mouth was dry and her stomach cramped with hunger. She turned out her pack and found just what she had found in the morning: a few dried berries and a half-crescent of flat-bread. She ate them slowly, then drank the last water from her waterskin, trying not to worry. The green below was promising. There would be forage and water on the plain.

And there would be guardians. She had been afraid to meet them by day. Now she intended to slip among their herds by night?

Quickly, before she could change her mind, she took up her pack and pike and began picking her way down the rocky face of the promontory, moving hurriedly, before decision could desert her.

The climb was treacherous with loose rock and crumbling clumps of soil. She was halfway down the promontory, stumbling, scraping herself against rock, when the familiar prickling touched her. *Someone was watching. Someone . . .* Instinctively she raised her head—and froze.

A wiry form stood two-legged at the top of the promontory, its wispy golden fur gleaming in the dusk. Keva caught her breath as the creature moved, turning its head from the shadow. Golden fur grew in ringlets from its scalp, curling across its black-muzzled face. Its eyes were bright and pale, gloating.

A minx, just as Par had described. Without thinking, Keva clutched at a clump of coarse vegetation. The grass pulled free and rock slid beneath her feet. She twisted, snatching for a second handhold, then froze in alarm. Motionless—she had to be motionless or the minx would spring. But she was falling. Her hand closed around a thorny plant. She gasped as sharp spikes bit her palm and then, with a smothered cry, she tumbled down the incline. Raw stone scraped her face and scarred her arms. Her ankle twisted and, just before her head hit a protruding rock, she felt something pull in her knee.

It could not have been long before she regained consciousness. The sky was a little darker and no moon had risen. She lay at the bottom of the incline, pain in her leg, her cheeks stinging. As soon as she realized where she was, panic began to hammer in her head again. She lay without moving, hardly breathing. If the minx were nearby, watching, waiting for her to move—

Slowly she rolled her eyes, probing the shadows. She saw nothing. She turned her head, then sat. Unconsciously she put her hand to her cheek and drew it back wet with blood. The other cheek stung too.

Examining herself with careful fingertips, she found wounds on either cheek. She wiped away the blood with shaking hands, imagining the minx hunched over her unconscious body, drawing its claws across her face, trying to tease her into motion.

Perhaps she had only cut and scraped her face on the rocks.

At least the minx was gone. Keva struggled to stand, but the pain in her right leg was so sharp she sank back, gasping.

If the minx returned—

She tried again to push herself up.

It was useless. She lay back, exploring her injured leg with one hand. She was relieved to find no evidence of a break in the bone. Her makeshift pike had fallen beyond reach. Fighting weakness, Keva dragged herself across the ground to retrieve it. Her pack lay a short distance beyond. She pushed herself to a sitting position, then used the pike to maneuver the pack toward her. When she was able to grasp it, she rested for a moment, then pulled up her trouser leg. Her knee had already begun to swell.

With fumbling fingers she tore strips of cloth from her bedding and bound her knee. When that was done, she was able to stand, stiffly, and take a tottering step forward.

But to walk . . . She hiked herself forward awkwardly and pain told her she had no decisions to make tonight. Run? Hide? Walk to meet the guardians? She could do none of those things. She could only rest and hope to be better tomorrow.

She hunched against a tall boulder, pulling the remnant of her blanket around her. Soon stars came to the sky and the first moon rose. Allindra the fisher-people called her, Mist Lady. Keva studied her silver face with distant interest. Seen from here, Allindra was pocked and striated with shadow. The fisher-people never saw her this way because they saw the night sky indistinctly, through the mists that cloaked the warmstream.

With a peculiar, chill detachment, Keva wondered if Oki looked up at Allindra tonight.

And her father—did he see Allindra? From his animal's back? From the mountains? Or from some place she could not imagine?

Later she slept and her father rode through her dreams, his steed's hooves hardly seeming to touch the ground. Sometimes as he rode, his steed raised its head and its face became Allindra's, silver and shadow at once. Other times the animal threw back a fiercer light and became the sun. When that happened a woman came and spread her arms to the animal and its light fled and became hers. The woman burned brightly, but only for moments. Then she was engulfed by a rushing, grumbling darkness. Just instants before she was lost, something spun away from her, a fading circlet of light.

Keva thrashed restlessly, trying to escape the dream, and pain in her leg jolted her awake. She lay staring up at the sky, frightened without understanding why, fists clenched against sleep.

When she did sleep again, pain became fire—fire raised by a woman who stood tall against the sun. Shadow concealed her face and Keva strained to see the eyes that looked into the sun without being blinded, the lips that did not blister, the flesh that did not burn.

Later, much later, she did see the woman's face and she woke with a breathless cry and within moments pushed away what she had seen. All that remained was memory of fire.

Keva woke again soon after dawn, her mouth crusted and dry, her muscles stiff. Experimentally she pushed herself to her feet. The pain in her leg was just bearable as she took a halting step forward. Thoughtfully she balanced there, thirsty, hungry, remembering the herds she had seen grazing in the distance. Where there were herds, there must be water. And surely there was forage. Par said the guardians drank mare's milk. Perhaps she could learn to do that.

Certainly she couldn't stay here. Unsteadily she hobbled across the rough ground.

Her pace was irregular, governed by pain. She covered the rocky stretch at the base of the roughlands and walked among coarse grasses and occasional clumps of large vegetation. Finally at mid-morning, when she still had not found water, she curled in the grass and fell into an exhausted sleep, her entire body aching.

She woke at the soft exhalation of breath on her cheek. Startled, she froze, biting back a cry.

A redmane stood over her, looking down from age-clouded eyes. It was older than any she had seen on the summer drive, its grey coat patchy, its auburn mane tangled. Shoulders and flanks that should have been muscular were flaccid. The animal—

it was a mare—stamped its padded feet, nudging Keva, then turned and padded away to browse nearby.

Keva sat for a moment, fighting the pounding aftermath of panic. Redmanes were not dangerous. She knew that. This one didn't even seem particularly curious about her. And it was old.

So old it couldn't have wandered here from far, and that meant there must be water nearby. Stiffly Keva took her feet. Perhaps the animal was not part of the herd she had seen on the horizon last night. Perhaps it foraged alone or as part of a smaller group. But if she followed it, surely it would lead her to water.

The animal moved away slowly. Keva had no trouble matching its pace. It paused frequently to nibble at the grass, sometimes turning to gaze at her steadily from milky eyes. After a while it seemed to wander less randomly, moving across the plain as if it had found direction, occasionally even breaking into a heavy trot. Keva hobbled after it, biting her lip when her weight fell too suddenly on her injured leg.

It was mid-afternoon when she saw animals grazing ahead, a loose congregation of adults, foals and yearlings. They raised their heads at her approach and gazed at her incuriously. The mare moved among them with a gentle, snorted greeting. As Keva hesitated, a foal approached, its gait loose-legged, and examined her clothing. She touched its neck, stroking the silver-grey fur, and the foal bobbed its head impatiently and cantered away.

Water—there had to be water where there were so many redmanes. Keva hobbled after the mare.

It led her to a narrow strand of water lacing its way through the grass. Keva drank gratefully and splashed her hands and face, carefully washing away dried blood. Then she filled her waterskin and retreated to dry ground, her trouser legs muddy. The mare watched her, cropping at the grass.

Keva sat for a while in the grass, feeling the ache of every muscle and the hollowness of her stomach. Experimentally, she pulled a clump of grass. The roots were long and stringy. There was no sign of an edible bulb. Keva sighed and patted the clump back into the ground. Perhaps later, when she was hungrier, she would chew the unpromising roots. Would range around searching for other types of vegetation. For now she was more tired than hungry. She stretched out for a few minutes in the sun-warmed grass and fell asleep.

She woke with the mare's breath on her face. The animal stood over her, head lowered, gazing at her with disconcerting steadiness. Keva sat, the first chill of evening on her face. "No," she muttered, more to herself than to the mare. It was pointless to walk now, with night coming. Pointless to try to forage. She stood and stretched stiff muscles, then wrapped herself in her blanket and lay down again, huddled around her grumbling stomach.

The mare sighed heavily and tramped away, then returned, lashing its tangled tail. It bent its head and exhaled heavily upon Keva's shoulder.

Keva studied the restless animal, bemused, as it turned away, then approached again. Did it imagine it had established permanent guardianship of her? Did it think it had found a foal, one obliged to follow wherever it led?

Strange foal she was, hardly able to keep up with an elderly redmane. When the mare returned and breathed upon her for a third time, flaring its nostrils, making its breath vibrate loudly in Keva's ear, Keva gave up, rolled her blanket, and followed.

Again their course was slow and wandering. Wherever the mare intended to lead her, the destination was not urgent. Keva followed with baffled tolerance, the ache of her muscles easing as stars came to the sky, as Allindra rose.

When Allindra rose, the mare began to move more briskly, finally trotting, head low, feet pounding. Keva hobbled after her, caught up in some inexplicable sense of purpose. The plain had changed with the moon's rising. The grasses were silvered, and the shadows in the distance offered silent promise. Even the milky film on the mare's eyes was less obscuring. When the animal gazed into the moon, Keva saw dark pupils and a presence behind them far more vital than the body that housed it.

A presence? In a redmane mare who had adopted a two-legged foal?

After a while, Keva heard a whickering in the distance. The mare halted, raised her head and uttered a shrill cry. Then she padded forward again, grunting loudly. Keva hesitated, hair rising on her arms. The mare turned and slapped her tail against her flank. The message was clear. *Come*.

Keva went. Soon she saw the shadowy shapes of several tens of redmanes. They moved restlessly, grunting and whickering as the mare padded among them, then gathering behind her and following just as Keva followed. The elder mare was a personage among the redmanes, Keva realized. A leader, perhaps. No wonder she had expected Keva to follow her.

The mare trotted briskly now, leading Keva to a place where the stream that wandered across the plain briefly broadened into a wide pool. The grass had been worn away from its banks, leaving a broad apron of bare, pounded soil on either side. The mare approached the pool, but instead of lowering her head to drink, she stepped into the water and splashed across.

Emerging on the other side, she shook herself vigorously, then slapped her tail against her flank.

The demand was clear. *Come*.

Feeling foolish, Keva waded into the shallow pool. Water flooded into her boots and her trousers clung heavily to her legs. When she reached the other side, the mare waited while she squeezed water from her trousers and removed her boots to empty them.

The mare planted her padded feet and stood beside the pool, facing the redmanes who gathered on the other side. Keva watched with surprise as more and more animals gathered from the dark. They grunted softly among themselves, pressing closely together, none offering to cross the water.

After a while the mare lowered her head and directed her milky gaze to the pond's dark surface. On the opposite bank, ranks of redmanes pressed still closer to each other, then quieted and stood as the mare did, heads down, eyes upon the water. Puzzled, Keva sat with wet trousers chilling her legs. After a while, when the cold reached her very bones, she bundled herself in her blanket, her teeth chattering.

There was some purpose to the gathering, but she could not fathom it. None of the animals moved now, none drank from the pool. They sent their warm breath against the brisk night air, a susurrus, and they waited, watching the water.

Allindra continued her slow trek across the sky, and still the animals stood. Finally Allindra's reflection touched the pool's edge, silvering the water, then slowly, slowly slid across the water.

The redmanes sighed and the mare snorted once and let her eyelids fall. Keva stared down at Mist Lady's reflection and had the giddy feeling that she peered through the water's surface into another reality. She could not look away. She could only gaze down, falling deeper and deeper, until a breeze came across the grasslands and fluttered against the water's surface. Gently reality rippled and separated.

Reality opened.

Reality—but not the reality of wet clothing and aching muscles, not the reality of chattering teeth and an empty stomach. Another reality entirely rose from the silvered pool as breeze touched its surface. Numbly Keva reached for the stone at her throat. Zan, the second moon, appeared at the pool's edge, her orb smaller than Allindra's, her light sharper, more intense.

As intense as the song Keva had once heard, that song of sunlight and breeze. Keva's fingers closed around the blue stone, then clutched the narrow strip of blue cloth that held it.

The bluesong—she had heard it and it had left traces deep in her memory. But she had never guessed she could sing it. She did now, staring down into Allindra's silver-pocked face, feeling the breeze of a new reality in her hair. She let her lips part and the bluesong came from her throat, sweet, wordless and silent.

Silent. It was not a song of lips and tongue, not a song of vocal cords, not as she sang it. It was a song that came from some deeper place, heart perhaps, or soul. Keva rocked slowly from side to side, clutching cloth and stone, and let the song reach out from her, let the song twist its magic around the night.

Did the redmanes hear it? Did the mare? They stood in silence. Some gazed into the pond, and Allindra and Zan rode upon the surfaces of their eyes, silvering them. Others had let their eyelids drop and they moved as Keva moved, rocking.

She knew from that that they did hear. And she knew from the heaving of the mare's sides that she heard too. The blue-song moved through them all, weaving some alien magic. It fed on sunlight twice-reflected, first from the moons, then from the water. It fed on breeze. But there was a strangeness to it, a quality that was not entirely of this sun, not of the breeze that scoured this grassy land.

The song belonged to some other land then. It came from some distant place where the sun shone hotter but the breeze was softer.

She lost herself in it so completely that she did not notice at first that the redmanes had become totally still, like animals carved of stone. The mare uttered a throaty warning, her body as rigid as the others.

The bluesong slipped away. Keva raised her head and gazed around at the immobile animals, puzzled. The mare's breath rumbled heavily in her throat again. The milky eyes gazed unwinkingly at the perimeter of the gathered herd.

Keva followed the direction of the mare's gaze and saw a wiry form, wispy-haired, its face shadowed. She froze. *The minx.* She had forgotten the minx. Involuntarily one hand tried to rise to her wounded face. She restrained it, knowing she must not move. She could not see the razor claws, but she suspected she had already sampled their capabilities.

The minx slipped among the immobile animals, black-muzzled, furtively graceful. Deep within the silken ringlets that coiled around its face, Keva saw its eyes, mocking amber glints. Grinning, the animal stopped to drive a single sharp claw into a young mare's tender nose. The mare did not move, did not even blink. The minx rocked on its splayed feet, as if in plea-sure, then bounced forward and ripped a buck's ear with finicking precision. The buck did not flinch, did not tremble, did not even roll his eyes. His blood dripped on the pounded soil.

But there were foals in the herd and Keva watched tensely as the minx approached one of them. Although none of the adult animals moved, she sensed their apprehension. The minx bobbed over the silver-furred foal, displaying its claws, chuckling. Keva knew that if what Par said were true, the foal had only to roll its eyes, and the minx would abandon its teasing game and kill.

Keva heard her breath sob in her throat. The sound brought an answering mutter of warning from the mare. Slowly the minx brought its splayed claws down over the foal's head, the two longest claws closing toward the foal's eyes. Keva's eyelids fluttered in spasm.

She could not watch. This was not one of Par's tales. She could feel the foal's fear as sharply as if it were her own and she moved almost without thinking, as if her muscles had life. She scooped up her pike and pushed herself to her feet, ignoring the pain in her injured knee, ignoring the faint voice of reason.

The minx clucked in gleeful response, drawing its claws away from the foal, leaping forward with an elastic bound. Its ringlets shivered and the delight in its eyes was bright, unmistakable. It grimaced across the water at Keva in challenge, waiting for her to move again.

Instinctively she froze, her muscles so rigid they cramped. The minx's reflection fell upon the water, grinning. It chuckled huskily, mocking, and Keva realized that if she did not take the teasing animal, it would choose another victim.

She quaked, her heart turning cold. All she knew of hunting came from Par's tales. She had never stalked anything more threatening than a bark-beetle. She did not even know if she could drive the point of her pike through living flesh.

The minx paced along the streamside on limber legs, not taking its eyes from her, waiting. Impatiently.

Waiting for her to move, waiting for her to signal the next phase of the game. Keva tested her fingers, trying to tighten them on the shaft of the pike. They did not respond. She tried to bend her knees, to flex herself into position to attack. The joints remained rigid.

And then the youngest foal of the herd choked convulsively and began to shudder with the stress of prolonged fear. Keva saw the minx's muscles contract as it turned. This time her reaction came as a result of conscious will. Her muscles knotting, she broke the bonds of paralysis and cried out, splashing into the water. The minx spun, ringlets dancing, amber eyes glinting. It flashed a greedy, sharp-toothed grin of pleasure and sprang for her throat.

Some unsuspected instinct guided Keva's pike. Her thrust caught the animal as it leapt and penetrated the rib cage. The very force of the animal's spring pushed the blunt point through the leathery, resistant skin.

For a moment, Keva thought the minx would not fall, thought it would tear her with upraised claws despite the pike buried in its chest. Then the minx staggered and tipped toward her, uttering a low, angry shriek. Its knees buckled and it sprawled, pressing its black muzzle into the mud.

Keva watched with dry throat as the animal died, writhing angrily, clawing at the pike. For minutes after the death, she was numb. Her first coherent thought was that she must retrieve her pike. But the trembling of her hands, the nausea that nestled in the hollow of her stomach, would not let her approach the dead minx.

If it had not insisted upon its game, she realized, it would be feeding now. Feeding on a foal or one of the feeble older redmanes. If it had not insisted, it could have fed on her the night before.

The gathered redmanes sighed and began to mutter among themselves, the foals shrilling nervously. Grunting, the elderly mare splashed across the water and nuzzled Keva. Numbly Keva turned. The milky eyes regarded her unwinkingly, as if the mare were taking her full measure. Then the mare grunted again and moved through the herd.

Following the elderly mare, the entire herd left the pool and moved upstream, heads low. The sound of their feet was heavy in the dew-damp grass. Keva leaned on the elderly mare, aware again of pain in her injured knee, of the sting of her injured cheeks. And aware of a hard, stony sensation in her chest, as if all the adrenalin that had sung through her bloodstream earlier had begun to crystallize there. She had difficulty breathing around its mass, just as she had difficulty believing what she had done. She had killed a living creature, one that walked on two legs as she did.

But if she had not, she would be looking now at carnage. The herd regrouped a distance upstream. The animals ranged themselves beside the narrow band of water, the elderly mare splashing through the water to face them from across the stream. This time she did not insist that Keva accompany her.

Keva stood lost for a few moments, then settled dully into the grass. Later she didn't even remember pulling her bedding around herself before she sank into a deep sleep.

She dreamed the things she often dreamed: fire, a woman who stood at its center, a face she did not want to see. But tonight she retained a certain waking awareness as she dreamed. Even as images moved and changed, she felt her body press against the soil where she slept. She felt the jarring rhythm of her heart. Felt the breath that rushed and sighed in her throat.

Felt difference. Felt change.

She did not want to change. She tried to put the perception away from herself, but a subliminal awareness remained with her, prickling in the hidden corners of her mind. Exhausted, disturbed, she slept until the mare blew warm breath against her cheek. Moaning, Keva pulled her blanket over her face, but the insistent pressure of the animal's breath reached her through the thick fibers. She rolled to her stomach, hunching her shoulders protectively. If she woke, she had to deal with hunger and the ache of her injured knee. Had to think again of approaching the guardians and perhaps learning things she did not want to know. Had to confront too the strangeness she had felt while she dreamed, a strangeness that did not recognize the barrier of consciousness.

If she woke—

This time the mare nudged her sharply. Moaning, Keva threw back her blanket, reproof on her lips.

She never uttered it. It was mid-morning and the sun shone brightly. The redmanes who had gathered the night before were gone. Only the mare stood beside the stream now.

Only the mare—and the solitary youth who stood on the opposite bank of the stream. Keva caught a sharp breath, her hand closing around the stone at her throat. A youth as old as she gazed across the water at her, gazed with her own eyes, from a face enough like hers to be her own. Except that her face wore an expression of surprise while his wore mute, frozen disbelief. Slowly she stood, wondering from his expression if he would run if she demanded to know who he was and where he had come from. Wondering why he stared as if she were an apparition. Wondering why she had felt change in the night. Wondering.

FIVE
DANIOR

The mountains had always shadowed Danior with doubt. There every moss-grown dike and weathered wall, every crag, every peak, announced that he was beyond the order of things, a person with no place. On the plain the order was broader, more inclusive. The herds, the grasses, the vastness of sky and land made the legends of the valley small. On the plain he walked among the herds by day and sat for the teachings by night. He watched the moons on the water, he heard the voice of the redmanes, and he forgot that he had no place.

Even this time, with the pairing stone at the bottom of his pack and uncertainty his companion, he felt shadows lift when he reached the plain. He spent the first night beside Cnarra's teaching pond, where her herd gathered each clear night for the teaching. Guardians gathered there too, tall in their umber capes, but they did not speak to Danior nor he to them. It was spring, the time when the plains predators had young to feed, and the guardians were listening too closely to their herds to heed anything he might say. After the teaching they went silently to stand among the redmanes, watching, and Danior slept beside the pond.

The second night he sat with a small herd that gathered by a rock-rimmed spring. No guardians came for the teaching, although as he walked southward the next day, he saw them among the herds.

The third night he had intended to spend at Waana's teaching pond. But he stopped in the afternoon to help a pair of guardians attend a difficult foaling and slept in their campment instead.

The next morning when he reached Waana's teaching pond, Waana and her herd were nowhere near. He found only a plains minx impaled upon a crude pike, its dead eyes glaring. He circled the creature, chilling, and realized the pike was nothing more than a tree branch sharpened to a point, not a guardian's weapon at all. He stared down at the stiffened corpse, disbelieving, and tried to imagine standing against a minx with a sharpened stick. Certainly someone had, but he couldn't guess who. After a while he went on, glancing uneasily over his shoulder.

He followed the stream and by mid-morning he began to see members of Waana's herd, grazing. When they recognized him, they raised their heads and muttered low greetings, foals and yearlings running to meet him with gawky grace. He paused and stroked their necks, then walked on, letting the earthen perfume of the grasses, the unchanging sky lull him. And so he was unprepared when he approached a bend in the stream and found Waana standing sentinel over someone who slept.

He was still more unprepared when Waana nudged the sleeper and she woke and stood. He stared across the narrow band of water for moments that seemed to stretch into all time and thought he would not be able to speak. Thought he would never find use of his tongue, his throat, his vocal cords again.

He knew who she was, of course—knew at a glance. Jhaviir's daughter. She was so much like himself, who else could she be? Dark, her hair heavy and smooth, she had the same arched brows he had, the same pink nails against bronze skin. And the stone she wore at her throat, the stone . . . His fingers contracted on the strap of the pack where he carried his own stone.

But much as she was like him, she was also unlike him. She was taller by several fingers' breadth and there was a deepness in her eyes, a darkness, as if she glimpsed something she had not yet permitted herself to see fully. And the proportions of her face were subtly different from his, each feature stronger, more prominent. As if—

He caught his breath sharply. As if the scratches on her face had come from a minx's claws. As if she had taken the animal in challenge—and changed. But not completely. If she had changed completely, she would have been taller. The deepness in her eyes, the strength in her features, would have been pronounced. And her gaze would have been as distant as his mother's. *Eyes that see fire,* valley people called a barohna's eyes.

Instead there was passing uncertainty in her eyes, although she kept it from her voice. "Who are you?" The words were very nearly a challenge. Her fingers pressed the stone at her throat, whitening on it.

The stone did not light at her touch and Danior's shoulders eased. For the first time he noticed her clothes, the long, full trousers, the boots strapped tightly at the ankles, the padded jacket. All were in shades of grey, woven—he realized—of vegetable fiber. He licked his lips, knowing there would never be another moment like this one, distressed that he had so little idea how to respond to it. "I'm Danior Terlath. You've come from the warmstreams," he said finally, surprised that the words sounded so commonplace, that they conveyed so little of the confusion he felt. He had found her, Jhaviir's daughter, and what his father said was true. She was enough like him to be his twin. Yet she was a stranger, startled by his presence, by his appearance. A stranger, and as uncertain as he.

It showed in the way she stiffened, her brows contracting. It showed in the wary challenge in her voice. "How did you know?"

"My great-grandmother has told me how warmstream people dress," he said, his thoughts racing ahead. How had she come to be among the fisher-people? Had she lived with them only long enough to outfit herself? Or much longer? And her father— "She's seen them when she crossed the stream with the herds."

Color washed from her face, but she regathered her composure quickly and shook her head, frowning. "You're not a guardian. There aren't any men among the guardians. They don't bear sons. I know that much."

It was his turn to frown. He had told her he was Danior Terlath. Didn't she even know what his use of the two names in conjunction meant? That he was Danior of the barohnial family of the Valley Terlath?

But if she had lived long beside the warmstream, perhaps she didn't know the conventions of the valleys. It was said the fisher-people were reclusive. That they were seldom seen beyond the geyser streams. "My great-grandmother lives in retirement with the guardians. My grandmother too," he explained. "I spend part of every summer in their campments." If the girl had been living with the fisher-people, he wondered, did her father live there too? His father would like to know, if it were true. His father would like to know that Jhaviir was alive, would like to know what had happened in the years since he had ridden away from Valley Marlath, where he had gone, what he had seen.

Before he could frame questions, Waana waded across the narrow band of water to him. Deserted, the girl took a limping step forward and halted, frowning in pain and hesitation. "You've hurt your leg," Danior realized, forgetting everything else. That, he guessed, must be why the mare had been standing sentinel over her. "Waana must have been waiting to lead you to Tehla's campment when you woke. To be treated."

"Waana?" For a moment confusion showed behind the girl's mask of wary composure.

The mare shook herself and let Danior scratch the patchy fur of her neck. "She's eldest mare of this herd. She teaches to the animals that graze out here. You may have passed her pond. She—" He broke off, remembering what he had found beside Waana's teaching pond just a few hours earlier. He glanced involuntarily at the wounds on the girl's face. "The scratches on your cheeks—"

"I fell," she said quickly, not meeting his eyes. "Night before last. I ran out of food and water. I was climbing down a bluff, trying to reach the plain to forage, and I slipped. She came the next day—the mare—and I thought if I followed her, she would take me to water. And to food."

She hadn't eaten since the day before? At least he knew how to deal with that. Quickly he stepped into the stream. "I have food—plenty of it. And I'll show you how to forage for more." If she was so poorly acquainted with the plain that she had gone to sleep hungry, he had much to teach her. And while he taught her, perhaps he could reach beyond her wariness, her uncertainty—and his own confusion. Perhaps they could learn to be at ease with each other.

The girl stepped back, keeping her distance, but when Danior opened his pack and laid out cheese and bread, glancing up at her anxiously, she joined him and accepted a portion without argument. While she ate, he dug honey-bulbs from beside the stream and peeled them with his knife. "I'll show you how to find string-grass too," he promised. "And poppers, when the season is right." He sat beside her peeling the honey-bulbs, pleased to share the small ceremony of a meal with her. In the halls people said that to share food was to share much. And it was obvious that they did share much. If he could come to some understanding of what it meant to be so much like someone when he had never been like anyone before—

She was clearly aware of the likeness too. Hungry as she was, the girl glanced at him covertly as they ate. He knew because he glanced at her the same way, fascinated by the familiar proportions of her fingers, by the way she used her hands, by the texture of her skin. It was as if he had found himself in another person, as if he might guess her thoughts without questioning her. He could tell by the tautness of her features, by the tight, contained frown between her eyes, that she did not understand why he so closely resembled her and that she was uncomfortable with the resemblance. But she did not question him, although he could not tell if that was because she thought it would be discourteous or because she simply had no better idea than he how to frame her questions. Perhaps it was simply part of the etiquette of the warmstreams not to question. Almost any inquiry was permitted in the halls, but only if it was presented with careful indirection, so that no one would be embarrassed if no answer was forthcoming. Perhaps she simply didn't know how to speak so.

Not knowing the customs she had been raised by, he couldn't guess what to say to put her at ease. Nor did he feel free to question her, however artfully. They sat eating together as if they did so every day, but he didn't know why she had appeared on the plain wearing warmstream clothes, didn't know where she had been all the years since she had ridden away with her father, didn't even know if the scratches on her cheeks had come from a minx's claws. If the pike that had killed the minx had been hers—He retreated to fill their waterskins from the stream, wondering. Wondering at the implications if it had been.

Finally they finished and the girl tossed the hair off her shoulders and stared down at the ground. She spoke softly, as if apologizing for her slowness to identify herself. "My name is Keva. Keva-by-Oki, but she wasn't really my mother. She—" She glanced up, brushing the hair back from her face, frowning. "She adopted me when I was small. And now I'm trying to find my father. I'm hunting for him."

Danior glanced up in quick surprise. Jhaviir? She was hunting Jhaviir? "You don't know where he is?" He was startled by the sharp sense of dismay he felt. How could he take news of Jhaviir to his father if the girl hadn't seen him either? And if she hadn't, where could he be? How had they become separated?

"No. He's—" She frowned, wrapping her fingers around the stone at her throat. "I haven't seen him since he left me at the warmstream. He—he's dark like I am. Like—" She hesitated, then went on hurriedly. "He was riding a white animal. If you've seen a man who looks like—like me, riding—"

"A whitemane," he said quickly. At least he could tell her that much. "It's called a whitemane. My father has one too."

She drew a sharp breath, looking up at him with sudden, frozen wariness. "Your father?"

He drew his arms around his knees, suddenly uncomfortable with her tense watchfulness. What would she do, he wondered uneasily, if he told her what he knew? That her father and his had been replicated on a starship from cells taken from a man who had disappeared over a hundred years ago? That they had been used as tools by men eager to exploit other worlds? That they had remained on Brakrath only because his mother had destroyed the Benderzic ship with a hail of stones? If she had grown up in the isolation of the warmstream, would she believe him? And if she did—

He frowned at a new thought, one he hadn't considered before. If their fathers were brothers grown from the same tissue, what did that make them? Brother and sister? Cousins? Or were they of some order of kinship that had never been named—because they were the first to share it. And if so, what was the etiquette of that kinship? What were the implications that rose from it?

"Your father has a whitemane?" she probed.

Danior nodded, biting his lip, realizing he didn't know what to tell her. That they were kin? That his father could as well have been hers? That their mothers should have been stone mates; that their grandmothers had been? There was too much to be conveyed and he didn't know how she would accept it, any of it. He didn't know what to ask her either. The minx, and the shadow in her eyes . . . Aware of her gaze, he said cautiously, "He found it in the forest. Years ago, before I was born. He named it Fiirsevrin. It means cold fire." But not in any tongue of the valleys. In a language he had learned on another world.

Kadura. His mind churned desperately. *Kadura would know what to tell her.* Certainly he did not, and the unspoken questions in her eyes only added to his confusion. He stood. "I'll take you to Tehla's campment," he said with quick decision. "It's not far. She'll treat your knee and we can stay the night." And then tomorrow they could go on to Kadura's campment. Kadura would know how to answer her questions. Kadura could guess just from what she read in the girl's face how much of the truth she must have and which portions of it would be too disturbing. And Kadura could help him understand better what their kinship meant, what it meant that they were like each other and strangers at once, that they both held stones.

He half expected the girl to refuse. She studied him, frowning, biting her lip, then glanced across the water at the grazing redmanes and stood. They crossed the stream and Waana joined them. At first Keva refused to ride the younger mare who also elected to accompany them. But after a while her lips grew white with pain and she let Danior help her to the young mare's back.

There was excitement among the herds today, but Danior was too preoccupied to notice. He was aware of all the questions Keva still did not ask, aware of his relief that she withheld them. He was aware of her shrinking tension when they passed the first guardians standing among the herds. Aware that she stiffened when a group of guardian daughters came laughing through the grass, then stopped and stared. Aware that the campment itself, when they reached it in mid-afternoon, was alien to her eyes: a collection of patted mud structures overgrown with grass, narrow lanes winding between them.

Guardian daughters ran ahead of them, laughing with particular shrillness, and by the time they reached Tehla's kefri, she had heard of their arrival and was waiting at the door. She stood head and shoulders taller than either of them, her coarsely streaked hair hanging upon her shoulders. Her face was so creased and weathered she seemed as old as the land, but her heavy brows were still dark. She clasped both Danior's hands, her voice rough, little used. "We thought you wouldn't come to the plain this year, Danior Terlath."

They thought he wouldn't come because he had reached his second majority this year and was no longer a child, to summer on the plain. He wondered momentarily what the guardians had expected him to do instead. Wondered what future they thought awaited him. But there was no time for that. He turned as Keva slid from the young mare's back and leaned stiffly against Waana. "I'm going to visit Kadura. This is Keva. I told her you would treat her leg. She fell." He hesitated, gazing up at Tehla, wondering briefly how much to tell her. When she did not speak, he plunged ahead. "She—she's been trying to find Jhaviir."

Keva raised her head sharply, staring at Danior, then turning to meet the spent power of Tehla's gaze, her voice disbelieving. "You know my father?"

Tehla folded lean brown arms over her chest. Time had marked her features so deeply her expression was unreadable. But Danior knew by the cautious tenor of her words that she had noticed his hesitation. "Many of us knew him on the plain," she said carefully. "He spent his first summer here and he rode here sometimes after he took the whitemane. Let me examine your leg and we will talk."

But Keva did not move. Her lips grew white and her fingers twisted in Waana's mane. "Knew . . . Is he dead?" She glanced quickly from Tehla to Danior, her eyes bright with dismay.

He stiffened at the tension in her voice, at her sudden pallor. His impulse was to reassure her, to tell her that her father was not dead. But how could he say that when he didn't know?

"No one knows," Tehla interceded. Strangely, when her dark brows gathered into a frown, some of the austerity was dispelled from her face. "He's been gone since the drought year. No one has seen him from that time. But there are lands beyond the plain. People live in some of them. And Jhaviir was restless."

"The drought year?"

"Twelve years ago. But this is not the time for discussion. I can see you're almost too tired to stand. Come, let me look at your leg." Tehla turned back to her kefri.

Keva hesitated, then ducked her head to follow. Danior rubbed Waana's neck, then entered the kefri after them.

Keva stood by the door, her eyes taking in the curved mud walls, the hard-packed floor, the implements and tools that hung from ceiling and walls. Beside the fire pit were two platforms with rolled bedding. Stiffly she sat on the stool Tehla placed for her. She licked her lips, gathering courage. "If you knew my father, you knew my mother," she said slowly, as if she were afraid of the answer.

Tehla's hooded eyes flashed. "Oh yes. I took my plow teams to her valley often when she was a child. Before she took the sunthrone. Her mother lived in this campment for three seasons after her retirement. Waana carried her bundles when she and

Tiahna moved to Vendana's campment." Tehla's hands were rough, the fingers blunt. They moved briskly as they rolled up Keva's trouser leg and probed the swollen flesh of her knee. "Does it hurt when I press here?"

Keva stared at her, hardly seeming to hear the question. "No." Numbly.

Tehla peered at her face as she probed again. "I can see very well that it does."

Keva met her eyes and shuddered. "It hurts," she admitted tautly. "My mother was a barohna. That's what you're telling me." The words seemed to give her more pain than Tehla's probing.

Tehla weighed her response carefully before answering. "She was, yes. But her valley isn't cultivated now. Our teams don't turn the soil there anymore."

Keva spoke flatly, from stiff lips. "Because she's dead."

"Yes. For many years," Tehla said at length, nodding to herself. "And you have done yourself damage, Keva Marlath. Danior, crush pagnyon berries for tea. We will have that while I soak chatter-leaves for a dressing." The words were almost brusque. Tehla rose from her stool and busied herself with a bundle of dried leaves from her storage net.

Danior hesitated. It didn't seem right to turn his back when all the color had gone from Keva's face, when she looked as if she had taken a heavy blow. But she held her lips tightly pressed and would not meet his eyes. Obviously she did not want to be burdened with his sympathy. Reluctantly he turned and took down the mallet and pounding board.

He was much aware of her tight-lipped silence as he worked. But when he served tea, it came to him that it was not grief for her mother that made her pale. She did not seem so much bereaved as frightened by what she had heard of her mother. She accepted the earthen mug with shaking hands and drank silently while Tehla applied the herbal dressing and bound her knee with clean cloth. Puzzled by her reaction, Danior poured her a second and third cup of pagnyon tea. She drank those too, just as silently, although her color had begun to return.

Then of course she was drowsy, as Tehla had intended. She

didn't protest when Tehla unrolled bedding and led her to a sleeping platform. Danior sighed and let the single mug of tea he had taken work at his taut muscles. When Keva's eyes closed, Tehla studied her for some moments, then stooped to leave the kefri. Danior followed.

It was late afternoon and guardians passed silently in the overgrown lanes. Guardian daughters ran and shrieked, auburn hair flying, the gawky grace of foals upon them. Danior frowned, slowly recognizing the special quality of their excitement. He raised his head and sampled the air, trying to catch the scent of pollen. "It's time for the running," he said. He should have guessed from the dancing of the yearlings they had passed on their way to Thela's kefri, from the shrill laughter of the guardian daughters. But he had been too preoccupied with Keva and with his own thoughts.

Tehla nodded, studying the sky. "Tomorrow. Or the next day. The sky will be clear for tonight's teaching."

The special teaching that prepared the yearlings for the running. But Danior had more urgent concerns. "Tehla, I found a minx. This morning. At Waana's teaching pond. It was dead. Killed."

"With a guardian's weapon?"

"No, with a sharpened limb."

Tehla's eroded features disappeared into the folds of her hood. "The marks on Keva's face are much like claw wounds," she said after a while.

"But she's not a barohna," Danior said, perplexed. At least she was not a barohna like any he had seen before. But of course there had sometimes been barohnas who did not change profoundly, particularly in the early days. And there had sometimes been barohnas with maverick powers, barohnas who used the stones to do things no barohna had done before or since.

The pairing stone had lived in his hand, and he was not a barohna.

But he had not killed a minx. Perhaps if he had, perhaps if he could find courage for that—

Go for a beast? A palace son? He pressed his temples, trying to discipline his thoughts, but they escaped control. Reluctantly he recognized that the day had been long, that he was too tired to deal with the growing disorder of his thoughts. "I'm going to have another cup of tea," he said.

Tehla nodded from the depths of her cape. "Do. But remember to wake yourself for the teaching."

"I will." Danior turned back to the kefri, rubbing his temples, trying to stroke away the ache of confusion. Keva slept quietly, one hand on the stone at her throat. Moving silently, he opened his pack and stared down at the velvet pouch that held the other stone. Then he poured himself a second and third cup of tea. Soon drowsiness loosened his muscles and quelled the disorder of his thoughts so that he could sleep.

When Danior woke, oil lamps burned in the kefri but Tehla was gone. He moved stiffly, throwing off his covers. Had he slept too long? Quickly, he went to the door.

It was dark in the campment. The narrow lanes were deserted, although Nindra barely touched the horizon and Zan had not risen. Danior rubbed a hand across his mouth. He had not overslept. He even had time to wash and eat before the teaching. And he must wake Keva. He hesitated, reluctant to disturb her. But when he turned, she was already awake. She lay on her platform, watching him with a steady, cold gaze.

"Tehla has bread and cheese if you're hungry," he said uneasily when she did not speak. "And milk pudding. There's always milk pudding in the spring."

Keva sat, pushing her covers aside. "And tea?"

Her inflection made him wary. But why would she be angry? "If you want it. But then you'll be sleepy again and miss the teaching."

She nodded, her gaze narrowing. "You put something in the tea that made me sleep."

"It was pagnyon berry tea," he said, surprised at her accusing tone. "That's why people drink it, to sleep. I drank some too."

"Not as much as you gave me. And you didn't tell me what it would do."

Was that why she was angry? Because she hadn't expected

to sleep? "I—I thought you knew. Tehla wanted you to rest. You were upset. It upset you to talk about your mother." He frowned uncertainly. "I think you knew she was dead—before Tehla told you." The query was blunt, but this was not the time for indirection. Not when she looked at him with such cold anger.

Her eyes narrowed. "I guessed it. And you knew too. You knew my mother was dead. And you knew she was a barohna."

He eased across the room, but her gaze followed him. Was that what had disturbed her? Learning that her mother had been a barohna? Or was she angry because he had known and hadn't told her? But how was he to guess what she knew and what she didn't know? He couldn't find the sense of the situation, of her anger. "I—yes, I visited her valley just before I came here. I went—" But he sensed dangerous ground and decided not to mention the pairing stone. Not now. Not until he understood better. He averted his eyes, surprised that someone who had seemed so much like himself could make him so uncomfortable. It was a special kind of alienation, one he wasn't prepared to meet.

"You knew my father's name too," she said with the same core of anger in her voice. "I'd never heard it until you used it this afternoon."

"I—his name is well known. Many people know it."

"But I don't know anything about him. I don't know where he was born, where he grew up. I don't know who his family was. I don't know if he was a barohna, if—"

He glanced up sharply, frowning. "Men are never barohnas." Didn't she know that?

"Then he wasn't a barohna," she amended quickly. "But he must have been their kin if he lived in the mountains. Because he was dark, and there are only two kinds of people in the mountains. Serfs and barohnas. Oki told me, and so did Par. The serfs are fair. They—"

Danior stiffened, stung that she used the old term, the belittling term. "No one holds serfs now. Not since the Seventeenth Cycle of the Council. The people who live in the halls are called freeworkers. They have guilds and associations. They—"

"But your people treat them as serfs, even if you don't call them that. They do the work and you—the barohnas burn them if they refuse. They—"

"That's not true!" Danior protested, wounded. Where had she heard those things? From the fisher-people? Was that why they, were so reclusive? Because they still told the old tales among themselves? "No one has done anything like that since the troubled times. No one even speaks of it anymore. You can't even find the scrolls from those days in the public rack. You have to ask the scroll keeper to bring them from storage if you want to cipher them. And my mother—"

"Your mother is a barohna."

"*Yes.*" But how could he convey what that meant when she had heard the wrong things? How could he make her understand the control a barohna must have, the strength, to use all the power of the sun yet never scorch a single seedling? How could he explain what it meant to the people of the halls that a barohna held the throne? If she could see her mother's valley now, the dikes standing in disrepair, the orchards frost-bitten, the fields rank with useless growth—

"Come to your mother's valley with me," he said impulsively. "I'll show you. The people had to leave when she died. They had to go to other valleys because there was no one to draw the sun. No one can live there now, not until another barohna comes. If you see—"

Her shoulders stiffened. "I'm not looking for my mother. She'd dead."

"Your father lived there too, in the palace. I've seen their quarters. The people took everything else when they left, but your parents' quarters are still furnished. If you come, if you let me show you—"

For a moment he thought she would agree, but she shook her head. "No. He doesn't live there now. I won't find him by going there."

"You won't find him anywhere," Danior snapped, and

regretted it immediately. Color drained from her face, leaving only anger and pain. He extended a placating hand, but she drew away. "I didn't mean it," he said in an agonized voice, sorry he had not guarded his tongue better.

"Do you know that he's dead?"

"*No*. But no one has seen him, Keva. And he'd be recognized anywhere in the mountains or on the plain."

She raised one hand, pressing her temples. When she spoke again, her voice shook but her decision was clear. "Then if he isn't there, he's gone somewhere else."

To the uncharted lands beyond the plain? To all those places where people had wandered since the first-timers had been stranded on Brakrath? Wherever they had gone, little news had come back. No one knew how many of those people had survived, except for those who had gone to the warmstream and the desert.

If Jhaviir had gone to the warmstream, Keva would know.

If he had gone to the desert—Danior frowned, remembering what he knew about the desert clansmen. Sometimes desert traders wandered into the plain, hungry and sly, to offer worthless objects in trade for cheese and bread. The guardians fed them but would not take their wares. Usually the guardians discovered when they had gone that any unguarded objects— pikes, capes, cooking pots, tools—had gone with them. Lately he had heard that the clansmen came to the forest for the running, to steal redmanes. And he had heard of the clan wars that bloodied the desert, of the angry rivalries and the vendettas. If Jhaviir had gone to the desert, had he survived?

"He's gone somewhere else," Keva repeated.

Danior heard the desperation in her voice. He sighed, conceding the argument. "Somewhere else," he said without conviction. "And if we don't eat, we're going to miss the teaching."

She frowned at his unexpected capitulation, her shoulders still rigid. "The teaching?"

If she had just reached the plain, she probably didn't know. "The herds come to the teaching ponds when the nights are clear and the mares teach them about the plain," he explained. "About how to live. How the herd lives. If you were with Waana's herd last night—"

"They stood beside the water," she said slowly, "but nothing happened. They just stood there."

"You didn't hear because you didn't know how to listen. You have to press the ground with your hands and close your eyes and listen in a particular way. I'll show you. If you're going to travel on the plain, you need to sit to the teachings." Few people beyond the guardians ever heard the voice of the herds. Few people ever learned what the redmanes had to teach. If he could not answer her questions, if he could not give her news of her father, at least he could give her this.

He thought she would refuse. But after a moment's silent resistance, she nodded. He went quickly to fetch bread and cheese, eager to share the teaching with her, eager for her to understand he had not meant to hurt her.

The teaching pond was in an area of hard-pounded soil beyond the campment. It stretched grassless in every direction and sloped gently to a shallow basin filled with spring water. The guardians had already gathered, silent in their heavy night-cloaks. Their daughters laughed and ran, auburn hair flying. The herd gathered on the other side of the pond, the yearlings and foals as eager as the guardian daughters.

"We sit here, at the top of the slope," Danior instructed Keva. "The guardians and their daughters sit nearer the pond."

Keva weighed the situation with a taut frown. Danior thought for an anxious moment she would refuse to sit to the teaching after all. But finally she pulled her cloak tight and sat.

Nindra already touched the edge of the pond. Moments after Keva and Danior arrived, the elder buck appeared from the dark and approached the water, his auburn mane ragged, the coarse hair of his tail tangled. But by Nindra's light his haunches seemed more powerful than fat and he ignored the night wind that tore at his heavy grey coat.

He stood for a while beside the spring, gazing up at the assembled guardians and daughters. When the last shrilling foal, the last restless daughter settled quietly, the buck lowered his head to drink.

"Put your hands to the ground now," Danior whispered.

Keva did so, frowning. "I don't hear anything."

"It hasn't started yet," he assured her. He could see the resistance in her muscles, the tension of all the things she didn't understand: what the redmanes had to teach her, whether the things he had told her were true, where her father had gone. "You have to put your palms against the ground. Don't press hard. Just let them rest there. And let your thoughts go. Take a deep breath, and when you let it go, let your thoughts go with it, so there will be room for the teaching. It isn't hard."

Reluctantly she uncurled her fingers and breathed deeply, but Danior could see from the tense set of her face that she had not emptied herself.

Perhaps she wouldn't be able to do so this time. Perhaps the questions that preoccupied her were too immediate. Perhaps the teaching was too far beyond anything she had known before. He curled his own hands in sympathetic tension. But that would solve nothing. Sighing, he let his palms rest against the soil as Tarla, eldest mare of the herd, padded to the spring to join the buck. She was older than he, but her body held memory of a younger time, of bondings and matings and foals. She moved with pondersome grace. She grunted in answer to the buck's muted greeting, then bent her head to drink. Danior relaxed and released himself to her, grateful to escape his own thoughts for a time.

Behind her all the redmanes of her herd stood with heads lowered, eyelids drooping. The eldest mare raised her head and for a moment seemed to peer directly at Danior. His muscles tightened in a moment's instinctive resistance. Then, almost without his consent, his breath seeped away. His eyelids closed and his head fell forward, the level of his consciousness sinking with each sighing breath. He forgot Keva, forgot the pairing stone, forgot everything as the teaching began.

It came to him like a possessing consciousness, first reaching tentatively into his mind and senses, then dominating them, a welcome force.

Listen, my herd. The peace of our herd is greater than any in this world. It must be preserved in each of you. So mind me, foals. Pondwater smells different when stingmadders nest in the rocks. It smells this way . . . this way . . . When it smells so you must not drink or you will surely be stung and the madness that follows will destroy the peace of the herd.

Listen, my herd. The strength of the herd is greater than any in this world. So mind me, mares. There are years when you must not foal. In those years the egg has formed improperly and your offspring would be so malformed as to hinder you and detract from the strength of the herd. You will know you must not conceive by the tightness of your abdomen when your mate approaches you. It will feel to you . . . this way . . . When this happens, you must turn from your mate and walk alone, for the strength of your offspring is the strength of the herd.

Listen, my herd . . .

The teaching continued, monotonous, soothing. Danior roused himself after a while and saw that Keva had pressed her hands to the soil, that she had bowed her head and closed her eyes, that she appeared to be listening too.

Listen, my foals. We all dwell together in the strength of our herd, which is yours to preserve. Near the end of summer, you must eat certain barks and leaves to balance the nutrients you have taken from the fresh grasses. At those times, there will be a sensation at the back of your throat that will feel to you . . . this way . . . You must learn to heed this signal, for the strength of our herd lies with us all.

Take care, young bucks and mares. Soon will be the time for choosing mates. Our peace is precious, yet there are some who would disrupt it. You will know them by their inattention to the teachings and by their careless behavior as they pass among us. It is not ours to drive them away unless they openly violate our peace, but you must not mate with those careless ones. They will give you foals who carry the same heedless qualities. Our peace lies in the wisdom we share. You must preserve it always.

Heed me, mares . . .

Keva was listening. Danior could tell from the waxen immobility of her eyelids, from the slow measure of her breath. He raised his head and gazed around for a moment, then bowed his head, relieved. Because if the teaching touched her as it always touched him, washing away inner barriers, perhaps the awkwardness, the hesitation that had come between them today would dissolve and they could begin to know each other. Could begin to understand what it meant that they were alike, that they had found each other. That neither of them was alone any longer. He glanced covertly at her, wondering if that could ever mean as much to her as to him—not to be alone. Sighing, he slipped back into the teaching.

SIX
KEVA

The teaching was as it had been the night before. The mare stood stolidly, the redmanes let their shaggy heads droop, and the moons moved upon the water. And Keva did not understand. What was she supposed to hear? What did a redmane mare have to teach her?

That her dreams of fire were only dreams and not a foreshadowing? That nothing irrevocable had happened when she killed the minx? That the sense of change that had come in her sleep was only a product of fatigue and the strangeness of the plain?

That the tales Par had told of barohnial daughters who killed beasts and took their mothers' powers—to draw fire from the sun, to make stones dance—were fantasies, centuries removed from reality?

That she would find her father?

Instead of opening and resting against the soil, Keva's hands knotted. She could feel the haft of her makeshift pike against her palm again, could feel the resistance of the minx's leathery skin. Then the rupture and the plunging entry.

Her mother had been a barohna. Must she become a barohna too? Had she already begun to do so? She shivered, wondering if she had any will in the matter. Wondering what other things she had yet to learn that she did not want to know. All day she had been aware of levels of complexity proliferating just below the surface of her understanding. She had met Danior, she had eaten with him and talked with him and felt that the ground was about to open and reveal a web of relationships and possibilities she had never suspected.

She had felt the web was about to draw her in, that there was nothing she could do to free herself from its adhesive strands.

Danior, Tehla, her mother, the dead valley—

She glanced at Danior. He had drawn up his knees so the soles of his feet pressed the ground, as did the palms of his hands. His eyes were closed, his face still. He seemed to have gone somewhere else entirely.

Keva caught her lip between her teeth, then drew up her own knees and placed her palms to the soil. If there was another place to go, a place where her thoughts might be stilled for a while, then she would follow Danior there. Gazing across the pond, she saw Waana among the redmanes, watching her from cloudy eyes. Sighing, Keva closed her eyes and let her head fall forward. She let her breath seep away, taking thought with it.

At first she heard only a thin, distant stirring. The wind? A voice? It played upon her consciousness, and she breathed more deeply and let the world slip away entirely.

She was aware of memories first, stretching back over time. Memories that had been passed from mare to mare yet were still fresh. Memories of all the warmseasons the herd had ever known. Memories of the sunrises of centuries.

Then the focus of her awareness narrowed and she moved deeper into the teaching mare's consciousness. The mare's senses became hers. She felt the pain of the mare's arthritic joints. She felt the acids that worked in her stomach. She felt the mare's enduring strength.

But beyond that Keva became aware of all the experience the mare had gathered in the years of her life. The mare's memories became hers: the sunlight of her youth, the birth-shrill of her first foal, tens of years of moonlight bondings and matings. Keva let her breath sigh away and she sought out fresh grazing lands with the mare and tasted lush grasses. She chewed pungent barks. She tossed her head and loped across the plain with the herd, her feet making the soil pound like an earthen heart.

She took the mare's wisdom for her own. *Listen, my mares. When it is time for you to deliver, there are leaves you must chew. You will find them growing near the streams and ponds. When your time is near, you must go to the water so that you may feed on them. If foaling time finds you elsewhere, your labor will be hard and your foals will be damaged. And they will detract from the strength of the herd.*

Listen, bucks. Your instinct is to guard the herds. But we have human guardians among us now, as we did not when your instinct was forged. If you see predators stalking, you must not give your lives needlessly. You must shrill the warning abroad. You must broadcast alarm to every mare and every foal, and the guardians will hear it. They will come and the predators will go without taking your foals and without taking you. They will go because they have learned to fear our guardians more than they fear hunger. And you will be preserved for the strength of us all.

Listen, foals—

The teaching continued, enveloping, enfolding, instructing. Giving herself to it, Keva learned how to recognize the best grasses, where to find the barks that provided the necessary acids when the grazing was too sweet, how to discipline a spirited foal. She learned how to distinguish good water from tainted, how to recognize when storm was coming, how to contribute to the peace and strength of the herd. Then the mare's voice faded and Keva was aware of the shuffling of feet, of the shifting of bodies. She was aware of anticipation. Her own? The mare's?

The mare's voice returned, fuller, deeper. *And now, my herd, we have come again to a time that is as old as our herd. You have felt the southwinds today. You have tasted in them pollen from the flowering trees of the forest. Here the days have been cool with light morning rains, but to the south the days have been warm and dry—until now.*

Listen, my herd. Now the spring rains have come to the

forest. They have washed the dust from the trees and brought the flowers bursting from their bud-cases. And with the pollen comes the time of the running. We have cherished the yearlings among us. We have protected them and taught them and guided their feet.

Now something else must guide their feet, something older. Now the pollen calls them and they must run to the forest—as we once ran. They must run with pounding feet and bursting lungs. The pollen calls and they must test themselves. They must establish which among them are strong and which weak, which wise and which foolish, which generous and which selfish. Only in the running can they learn their places in the herd.

And you, mothers; you, fathers; you, grandsires and granddams and elder siblings—you must release them to the running. You must let them find their places, even though some you love will find their hearts are not as strong as they must be, even though some you cherish will learn they are not fit to give their herd foals, even though some will fall from exhaustion and others will fall to the predators who are called by the pollen just as our yearlings are.

Listen, my herd, the running serves the strength of our herd. We must make its rule our rule. However we love the weak, we cannot permit them to be ranked along with the strong. However we cherish the foolish, we cannot permit them to find mates and bring more foolish ones among us. We have guardians to stand among us and watch with us for predators. We have guardians to help us in many ways, and that is good. We did not always have these women among us.

But even with their guarding presence, we must serve our own strength. For only in strength will we find peace and only in peace can we continue as we have these hundreds of centuries.

Listen, my yearlings—

With effort, Keva withdrew from the teaching, the stone tight in her hand. *The forest.*

Her father had gone to the forest. Gone to take his whitemane for mating. Oki had told her so. Now the yearlings were going there too, running in some kind of test of fitness. She did not know where the forest lay, except southward, but if she could follow the yearlings . . . She pressed the stone too tightly and it cut her palm. She released it and pressed her hands to the soil again, reaching for what she could learn.

When at last the moons passed from the surface of the pond and the mare's voice faded, Keva emerged slowly from the teaching. She came as if from a strange land, wondering. She looked up to find Danior gazing at her.

Gazing expectantly with her own eyes. The serenity of the teaching began to slip away almost immediately. The web opened before her. All the questions, all the inexplicabilities returned. *Danior.* So like her he could be her twin. She could read every mood that passed across his face. The tension of muscles, the tautness of flesh, the hooding of eyes—she had a sense of what emotion lay behind each small alteration of expression, just because he was so much like her.

But she didn't know why he had gazed at her as if at an apparition when they first met. She didn't know why he seemed eager to tell her certain things, yet withheld others. She didn't know why they should be so alike.

Ask him? Something prevented her. Perhaps simply a reluctance to exploit the eagerness she saw in his eyes when she was thinking of slipping away without him and going to the forest. Of searching for her father there.

"You heard? The teaching?"

She touched probing fingers to her temples, realizing she didn't want to talk. She wanted to think, about the running, about the forest, about what she must do. "Yes," she said shortly and was immediately sorry for the disappointment she saw in his eyes. Would it be a betrayal to slip away, to leave him? What claim did he have, beyond their disturbing resemblance?

The claim of one person who had fed and helped another.

It made her feel no better than he drew back at her tone and didn't press. Didn't even study her as she knew he wanted to do, from the corner of his eyes. Didn't try further to assess her mood and its causes. They joined the guardians who walked silently back toward the campment. Tehla had left an oil lamp burning. She already slept on the platform nearest the fire pit. Danior insisted Keva take the other platform. He unrolled his bedding on the floor near the curved wall.

He soon slept. But Keva lay on the padded platform with eyes open, trying to sort her thoughts. Finally, too restless to lie still, she got up and slipped from the kefri.

The lanes of the campment were deserted. The moons hung low in the sky. As Keva moved away from the kefri, Waana rose from the shadows and followed, snorting softly. Beyond the campment, bucks and mares slept in the grass, their younger foals curled beside them. But the yearlings moved restlessly, running, dancing, feet pounding. Moonlight touched their silver coats, washing away colt-gawkiness, endowing them with fleeting grace.

Keva watched them, shivering when she realized she saw the gleaming coat and restless grace of her father's whitemane in the yearlings tonight. The yearlings could only be distant cousins of the whitemane, if that. But tonight they seemed to offer a promise, one she did not understand. Keva clutched the stone at her throat and let her thoughts take their course. Her father had taken his whitemane to the forest. That had been years ago, but perhaps there was something to be learned in the forest anyway, even now. Perhaps he still returned there sometimes. Perhaps she would find some sign there—or meet someone who had seen him. She caught her lip between her teeth, undecided. Go when there were so many things she didn't understand here? So many unanswered questions? So many facts she couldn't fit into a coherent whole? Go when she knew Danior would be hurt?

Waana stirred against her. Pensively Keva began to walk again. Eventually her feet led her to the teaching pond. She descended the sloped bank and stood beside the water. Wanna bent to drink, and Keva knelt beside her.

She cupped water in her hand, intending to drink, but never raised it to her mouth. Instead she stared down, suddenly unable to move. Her reflection gazed at her from the surface of the pond. Her reflection, but with a difference. Because this was not the face she had glimpsed so often when she bathed in quiet pools. Unbelieving, she leaned over the water and saw a new depth in her eyes, a subtle new proportion to her features. They were bolder, stronger. Her nose was more prominent, her mouth wider. Her eyes were set deeper. Yet the actual physical alteration was so subtle she almost wondered if she imagined it.

She had not imagined she had killed a minx. Had not imagined she felt some change later as she slept: And her mother had been a barohna. She could not argue that when both Tehla and Danior told her it was so.

Those stories Par had told . . .

Disturbed, she retreated from the water. She hugged herself, suddenly cold. Cold and frightened. And decided. Grimly decided.

She couldn't stay here. Reality was slipping away from her here, taking identity with it. Quickly she slipped her fingers through the strip of blue fabric at her neck. Surely when her father had left her with Oki, he had left the stone and the bit of fabric not just as tokens but as a message. And not a message that she was to wander mountains and plain learning things she didn't want to know, changing in ways she didn't understand. A message that she was to find him if he did not come back for her.

Or did she tell herself that because she was afraid of the face she had seen in the pond? Afraid of what might lie behind the altered features?

Danior—but she didn't think he would understand if she told him she was going. He would try to dissuade her. Or perhaps even insist upon accompanying her.

And so she wouldn't tell him. Quietly she slipped back to the kefri and gathered her possessions. Furtively she slipped bread and cheese into her pack. Neither Tehla nor Danior stirred. She paused briefly at the door, looking back. Another leavetaking, this one not so wrenching as the last. Quickly, before she could have second thoughts, she stepped into the lane.

The pad of feet told her Waana followed. Keva paused, wondering how much the old mare understood. The redmanes opened their lives to the guardians through the teachings. Did understanding flow the other way too? Did Waana have any inkling of where she was going or why?

"If you come along, are you strong enough to carry me when my leg hurts?" she asked softly, rubbing the mare's neck. Waana snorted softly and continued to follow.

As they passed beyond the campment, Keva found a pike some guardian daughter had left lying. She took it and walked southward from the campment, anxious to leave the campment as far behind as her feet would take her.

Later, when her knee began to ache and Waana nudged her repeatedly, she climbed onto the mare's back. She rode, tired and aching, until well after dawn. The grass was damp with dew and the sky tinted delicately pink when she pulled the old mare to a halt. Twisting awkwardly, Keva peered back in the direction they had come.

There was no sign that anyone had seen them go, that anyone followed. Guiltily she wondered how long it would take Danior to realize that she had not just wakened early and gone to explore the campment. Would he guess where she had gone? From what clue? Would he try to follow her?

She rode until she couldn't keep her eyes open longer. Then she slid clumsily off the mare's back. "We'd better sleep," she said huskily. Sighing, she spread her bedding in the damp grass.

She slept uneasily, her knee aching, her muscles tender. Her only dream was of tall trees and long shadows. Tossing uneasily, she wondered if the trees were fabrication or memory. Wondered if she had visited the forest as a small child, with her father. She woke at noon, not to the sound of running feet but to their jarring rhythm in the soil. *The running*— She pushed herself up in quick alarm, expecting to see a line of yearlings bearing down upon her.

She saw only Waana standing beside her, dozing. There was no sign of the yearlings, even in the distance. Lowering herself, she pressed her ear to the soil and heard the sound of feet again. The soil, she realized, acted as a giant drum, transmitting distant sounds, making them seem near. Reassured, Keva rolled her bedding, then poured water from the waterskin and splashed her face.

She was extracting bread and cheese from her pack when

Waana shuddered awake. The old mare shook herself and flexed her neck, as if the muscles ached. Then she stood with feet planted wide, eyes closed. Keva knew from the quivering of her eyelids that she felt the running too.

Keva walked through the early afternoon, Waana following. She paused and gazed around frequently, studying the horizon in every direction. Sometimes the vibration of the soil grew heavier and she seemed to hear a faint grumble from the distance. Other times the soil carried no sound at all.

And then, to the south, she saw a receding grey line—and she saw another dark line approaching rapidly from the west. She halted, pressing herself apprehensively against Waana, her fingers catching in the mare's auburn mane.

The vibration of the soil became pronounced, pervasive. It reached up through the soles of Keva's boots. She felt it in Waana's prominent hip bones, in the muscle of her haunches. But Waana did not seem alarmed, so Keva forced herself to set aside her own trepidation.

Gradually the dark line from the west resolved into individual animals, yearlings running silver-coated in the afternoon sun, tossing their heads, slapping their tails. They ran eagerly, snorting and squealing and darting at each other, then dodging away.

The yearlings grew from indistinct shadows to individual animals, racing across the grassy plain. Some ran a zigzag course, cutting buoyantly back and forth in front of others. Others ran doggedly, as if the effort were already costing them. Some faltered and choked on their breath. But all ran.

All ran south. Toward the forest, where flowering trees cast pollen on the air. The yearlings lunged past, silver coats gleaming, and then they were gone. They left only trampled vegetation and pounded soil.

Keva was surprised to find that the rhythm of the running persisted in her heartbeat long after the yearlings were gone. She leaned on her pike, using it as a walking stick, and continued in the direction the yearlings had taken. She felt, as she walked, that she partook of a rite, one she comprehended more with heart than mind. Occasionally the earth shuddered and she saw other dark lines on the horizon. Once a wave of year-lings from the direction of Tehla's campment passed. Later there were animals from the more distant regions of the plain. They passed with sweaty flanks and foaming mouths, passed with less and less of the joyousness of the early runners. They had come farther, their reserves were slimmer.

Some will fall . . . A cloud crossed the late afternoon sun and Keva thought of the night shadows of the forest, of the predators that waited there, attracted by the same pollen that called the yearlings. Keva curled her fingers in Waana's mane, beginning to wish she had not brought the elderly mare with her. Wishing she knew how to send her back to her herd.

She wished it more keenly a short time later when she found the first fallen yearling in the trampled grass, padded feet twitching. She hurried to its side, frightened by the way it lay, by the involuntary spasms of it muscles. Its breath was faint, its heartbeat weak when she pressed her ear to its chest. Yet there was no sign of injury.

She cradled the young animal's head in her lap, rubbing its fur, trying to rouse it to drink from the palm of her hand. Instead its legs stiffened in a final spasm and its head lolled, the eyes glazing. Keva stood with angry tears in her eyes, her stone clutched tight in one hand. Soft silver fur, eager feet—if the foal had stayed with its herd, if it had not pressed beyond its strength, running—

Waana nudged her, snorting softly. Keva turned and found something in the mare's eyes she could not understand, some painful understanding. But instead of honoring it, Keva turned on the mare with all the anger she could not loose on the dead yearling. "Go back! I'm not your foal! Go back to your herd!" She didn't want Waana's company if the journey to the forest was too hard for the old mare, if she might fall as the yearling had fallen. Keva stamped her foot. *"Go—get!"* Quickly she turned and hobbled away, tears streaking hotly on her cheeks.

Despite her admonition, the old mare followed, head hung, milky eyes dull again.

At last it was dark and Keva approached a barren tumble of rocks that seemed fury-flung across their path. She paused, leaning heavily on her pike, her knee aching. Two jagged pinnacles of rock stood against the evening-grey sky, their rough contours reflected in a clear pond at their base. Surrounding the pond were hundreds of boulders and jagged rocks, scattered as if someone had thrown them down in anger.

Keva turned and looked around uneasily. Shadow lay heavily behind the tumbled boulders. Anything could inhabit those shadows. Anything . . .

Waana picked her way to the water, shoulders sagging with fatigue. When finally she raised her head, nostrils quivering, Keva watched tensely, grateful she had not turned back. Waana's eyes were filmed but if there were predators, she surely would smell them and give warning.

The old mare gave no sign of alarm. Shuddering with fatigue, she turned back to the water, dipping her muzzle again. Reluctantly Keva sat beside the water, clutching the stone at her throat. Something about the air of this place disturbed her, some lingering mood. It almost seemed to bear a residual anger, as if something had happened here that could never be undone. She did not want to spend the night here. But her knee ached and Waana was exhausted.

Rousing herself, Keva took food from her pack but found she could not eat. She was too tired, her muscles too painful. Finally, when the sky was as dark as the shadows cast by the tumbled boulders, she unrolled her bedding and stretched out stiffly. Sleep overtook her quickly. She seemed to hear pounding feet in her dreams. Once she heard a shrill scream in the distance and lay with eyes wide, knowing the cry was no dream.

Nor was it a dream later when Waana's voice wakened her. Keva shivered free of her bedding and sat, pressing her hands to the soil. Waana stood by the pond, the light of the risen moons in her eyes. *Hear me, foal. This is the time when I can speak to you. Our herds have been upon the plain for more centuries than any can remember. The peace and strength of our herds are eternal. They are forever.*

They are forever because we have learned how we must preserve them. We have learned what things we must eat, what signs we must watch for, how we must honor one another. More, we have learned to teach our young these things so that our strength lives in each generation as in the last.

And beyond that we have learned that we are one. We walk the plain in separate bodies and those bodies are endowed with different gifts and intelligences. But the spirit that animates us is one, not many. We are not divided. We are joined. The benefit of each is the benefit of all.

So too the weakness of one is the weakness of all. We cannot be strong and weak at once. Nor can we live in peace if we permit weakness among us. And so there are tests and trials to winnow the weak from the strong.

You have watched the running and seen that some will die. Some with weak bodies, some with foolish minds will fall. We send them to fall not because we have no care for them but because they are imperfect receptacles for the spirit of our herd. We cannot achieve strength and peace if our spirit is bound to weak vessels.

The running is for the benefit of all, my foal. It is for the benefit of weak and strong alike, wise and foolish. There are those distinctions among us, but there are no divisions. The interest of an individual cannot be separated from the interest of the herd.

And so you must not be troubled as you continue on and see sad things. You must trouble yourself only with your own safety. Because if you continue as today, there will be dangers for you too. And I have no other foal like you.

No other at all like you . . .

Keva opened her eyes and gazed at the still pond, wanting to respond. If she could speak to Waana as Waana spoke to her, in the silence of her mind . . . Impulsively she pressed her hands to the soil. Rough particles gritted against her palms. For a moment she thought she couldn't do it, thought she couldn't deliberately reach out to Waana.

But Waana had heard her once, when she sang the bluesong. She was sure of it. If she could just project her thoughts, float them upon the water's surface . . .

Her voice, when it came, startled her with its silent clarity.

*You're going to leave me. You're going to go back to your herd,
Waana.*

*I must. The running is for the young, who must test them-
selves and learn their places. I am old and I will fall another
way.*

And your herd needs you.

*No, that is not why I must leave you. There are others to
teach when the moons are on the water. We all carry the same
memories, the same lessons. And some among us understand
your kind more clearly than I do. I came this far because I
wanted to protect you. But now I have become more understanding of you, of what is in you, and I know that I must let
you find your own way, your own place. I must leave you, foal.*

*But if there are predators, Waana, are you strong enough to
escape them? If they follow you, if they attack—*

*No, no, they are hunting tender meat, foal, and I'm stringy.
But you must be alert for them as you near the forest. They will
not venture far into the trees, not the rock tigers, the dune
lobbers, the plains and sand minx. But they will be hunting
nearby. And there are men from the desert clans who hunt the
forest at running time. You must watch for these men, foal.
They live in a hard land and it has made them hard.*

I should never have brought you here, Waana. Regretfully.

*You didn't bring me. I came. And I will go. But if I can hear
you teach again as you taught that night at my pond, before
you learned to listen, it will make a lesson to be passed to
many generations. A lesson many will enjoy hearing. We have
lessons like that, taught only to pass a moonlit night, to please.*

She wanted to hear the bluesong again. Keva clasped her
stone, uncertain she could teach it at will. It was elusive, a
thing of reverie and dreams. *I'll try.*

She took a deep breath and let her pupils widen to accom-
modate Allindra's silver reflection, hoping the light would touch
deep and release the bluesong. For a time nothing changed.
Then reality shivered, parted, and the bluesong came. Sunlight
and breeze and some other force brought it living to the night.
Unconsciously Keva fingered the strip of slippery cloth at her
throat and let the song rise from the deep place where it lived.

The bluesong . . . It fed on sunlight twice-reflected. It fed on breeze. It cast its alien spell. Keva lost herself in it, in its silent notes and living colors.

At last she grew tired and the song slipped away. Keva shuddered back to awareness. Her body had grown stiff, her hands cold. Waana's voice came to her lightly. *There are bright things in the song, foal, but there are dark things too—behind the light.*

Keva clasped her stone, pressing one hand to the soil. *Dark things?* What dark things could there be in the bluesong?

Dark things, Waana said, lidding her milky eyes. *But they are not real.*

Keva nodded, not understanding, too tired to think. She stretched out to sleep again.

When mid-morning sunlight woke her, Waana had gone. Keva sat, licking dry lips, feeling very much alone. She rolled her bedding and slung her pack on her back. Leaning on her pike, she picked her way among the tumbled boulders.

She soon realized there was something here she had not seen the night before. Some boulders were strewn randomly across the ground. But many were heaped together, and beneath them, crushed and mangled, she saw the dull glint of a metal body. It was larger than anything she had ever imagined, an elongated shape. Frowning, touched with sudden chill, she picked her way around its perimeter, climbing precariously from boulder to boulder.

A large metal vessel—many tens of paces long, crushed. She gazed up at the two rocky pinnacles that stood beside the pond, realizing there must have been others once, companion formations. And some force had pulled them apart and flung them at the metal body. She didn't think, from the pattern they took, that the fall had been natural.

Her entire body was cold. Her arms were stiff with gooseflesh. She could not stay here. Too much anger lingered in the air. As quickly as she could, she picked her way clear of the field of boulders. When she reached its edge, she paused, looking back, pressing her stone—wishing there was someone to tell her what had happened.

Perhaps she didn't want to know. Shivering, she turned away.

A shadow lay upon the day. Bright morning sunlight could not dispell it. Nor could the occasional flurry of running yearlings. Because now as she walked, she came across more and more fallen yearlings. Some were still warm, others cold. Twice something had torn their throats and she found tracks around the mutilated corpses. The tracks of a minx.

She began to watch as she walked. And she walked as briskly as her knee would permit. Each time she saw a shadow, a smudge ahead, she thought she would find a fallen yearling, and dread made her chest tight, her breath shallow. A lone runner stumbled past, its mouth foam-flecked. Keva watched it and wanted to call it back, to send it back to its herd. But it could not test itself there.

Late in the afternoon she reached a grove of tall trees. She took their shade gratefully. It was too early to stop for the night. The forest still lay somewhere south. But her knee was throbbing and she was light-headed with hunger and all she had seen. She would rest, then continue by night.

She ate, then found a place where brush formed a protective screen and fallen leaves lay deep and soft. Exhausted, she curled up to sleep.

She slept dreamlessly and the trees darkened around her, throwing their shadows in a broad gridwork. When she woke, it was at a faint sound. She sat, her mouth dry, her heart thundering. Moving cautiously, she peered out through the screening bushes. Moonlight fell through the trees, casting as many shadows as it dispelled.

As she watched, a dark shape detached itself from the trunk of a tree and moved with hunched shoulders to the shelter of another tree. It moved upright, on two feet.

A minx? Perhaps the very one that had savaged the yearlings she had found that afternoon. Keva chilled, straining for a better view of the animal. It was stalking something now, she realized. Something that moved deep in the trees, something that picked its way carefully, its coat gleaming by moonlight.

A yearling. Keva's hand clenched on her stone. A yearling separated from its running mates and wandering in the trees.

She did not pause to think. She took her feet, her fingers cramping around the haft of her pike, steeling herself to utter the cry that would turn the minx's attention to her.

The yearling was receding into the trees. Its pursuer slipped after it, moving from shadow to shadow with predatory concentration. Keva hesitated momentarily, then left the brush and stepped silently after predator and prey.

She glimpsed no more of the minx than an indistinct silhouette as it glided from shadow to shadow. She saw the yearling more clearly: the proud carriage of its head, the lanky grace of its stride, the rich glint of its coat. It moved with unexpected delicacy, pausing often to listen. Keva clutched her pike. It didn't matter what Waana had taught. She could not turn away and leave the yearling to the minx. At least she had a pike to defend herself with. The yearling had nothing but delicate hooves.

Her heart stopped. *Yes,* the yearling had stepped into a patch of moonlight and its feet were capped with hooves. For a moment Keva felt slack with shock. *Hooves.* Unbelieving, she crept forward again. The yearling paused in a shaft of moonlight, gazing back the way it had come.

She could see it clearly now. Could see that moonlight did not glint from the silver-grey fur of a redmane yearling. This animal was white, its coat sleek and shining. Even its mane was white, lying like strands of silk upon its graceful neck. Its eyes—she was near enough now to tell—were pink. They had a translucent quality, as if she were not seeing the color of the irises but of the blood vessels behind them.

This animal was a yearling, but not a redmane yearling. It was a whitemane.

And it knew it was followed. Keva saw that in the quivering alertness of its nostrils, in the prick of its ears. Keva glanced toward the shadows where the minx hid and her stomach turned. She had seen what the minx had done to the foals that had fallen in the running.

Her throat tightened. Her hand rose and closed around the stone. She pressed it, trying to find courage to distract the minx.

Before she could move, before she could cry out, the minx

stirred, its feet making a barely perceptible shuffling sound. The yearling heard and danced backward, hoofed feet tapping a nervous rhythm, gathering itself to flee. And the predator uttered a piercing cry and lunged.

For a moment all Keva's responses were frozen. She was plunged into vaccum, into timelessness. The pike dropped uselessly from her hand. A dizziness spun into her head, and her respiration slowed, as if her body had suddenly begun to burn some fuel other than oxygen, some fuel manufactured from its own cells.

What came next seemed to Keva to happen more slowly than any event of her life. Later she was only able to remember frozen images: the minx throwing itself at the yearling, body arched; the yearling's eyes glaring with helpless fear; her own body moving forward into the moonlight. The dizziness spread until it consumed her, bending her awareness into new configurations. Then came the shaking of the soil, the rumbling of the earth, the grinding of rocky sublayers against each other. Soil erupted and was flung into the air. The stony strata that lay below the topsoil shook. Rocks and boulders tore free and flew through the air.

Flew at the minx, which forgot its prey and flung itself against a mossy trunk, mouth gaping.

Human mouth gaping. The flying stones did not arc toward a minx but toward a wiry youth scarcely older than Keva. His dark hair was knotted behind one ear. His dark eyes stared, his thin-lipped mouth gaped. He wore clothes like she had never seen before, flapping robes over loose trousers. And at his waist—

At his waist were two colored sashes, one vividly blue, the other red.

Sashes like her father had worn, although coarser, less brilliant. Staring, she saw that they were knotted as her father had knotted his, loosely, so that they hung low over one hip.

Stones hung in the air and then dropped heavily to the ground short of their target. Dark eyes stared into hers, the pupils wide with shock. And it had happened so quickly that the youth's cry still echoed in the trees. As the last stone dropped, Keva saw that he did not hold a weapon. His knife still hung at his waist. He had thrown himself at the whitemane yearling unarmed.

Why? But there was no time for questions. They turned as one and saw the yearling flee, hooves pounding. The youth stared after it for a bare moment, then overcame his paralysis. His face twisting with fear, he ran in the opposite direction.

Keva gazed after first one, then the other. Slowly the tension ebbed from her muscles and she stared around her, trying to ground herself in reality again. Soil was torn from its place and thrown everywhere. Approaching the raw gash in the earth, she peered down numbly. Moonlight did not reach the bottom of the gash from which the rocks had been torn.

The stones . . . she stared at them where they lay. She might have persuaded herself that they had erupted into the air of themselves. But she knew better. She had flung them. Somehow. Something in her had changed when she had killed the minx and something had changed again tonight. And she had opened the earth and the rocks had flown. Not at her command but in execution of her will, of her anger. If she had not seen in time that they flew at a human rather than a minx, the rocks would have crushed the youth.

Keva shook her head, trying to overcome the growing numbness of shock. She had to think. She had to understand. Were Par's tales true? Had she become a barohna when she killed the minx?

Wouldn't Danior have recognized it if she had? Wouldn't he have told her?

But he had not told her he knew her father's name, not intentionally. He had not told her he knew of her mother, not until Tehla spoke of her. And his manner had been halting, cautious. Because he recognized what she was?

Her mind worked numbly. If this was what it meant to be a barohna, would she tear the earth apart again? If she were threatened? If she were startled? Or angry? If someone approached from behind without speaking, might she unwittingly crush him before she had time to deliberate?

Her entire body began to tremble. Weakly she sank to the ground and let her head fall back against a tree trunk. She clutched her stone as talisman against confusion, but confusion reigned free. She sat, her body boneless with shock, her mind staggering. She sat while the stars crossed the sky and woods creatures moved warily around her. She sat and did not cry, although she wanted to. She was afraid the tears would petrify on her cheeks.

"*Oki, I'm not hard,*" she whispered aloud. "*You were wrong about me. I'm not hard at all.*" And if she was not hard, how could she be a barohna? She tried to find comfort in the question, but it was lacking.

SEVEN
DANIOR

I t was mid-afternoon before Danior admitted what his heart knew——that Keva had gone. He stood at the edge of the camp-ment, feeling the vast openness of the plain like a knot in his stomach, like an ache in his head, like a hungry, nauseous, frightening emptiness. No one had seen her go. No one knew what direction she had taken or when she had taken it. But she had gone and she could be anywhere.

She had gone to continue her search for her father. He was certain of that. She had learned that her father had not been seen in the mountains or in the plain. So she had carried her search elsewhere.

But where? She hardly knew the plain. How did she expect to find her way safely beyond it to other lands?

And what other lands were there? The warmstream, the roughlands, the lakelands, the desert. He licked his lips and rubbed the back of his neck, where the muscles had clenched tight. The roughlands, the lakelands——no one lived there. Did she know? But the desert——would she have gone to the desert? Did she even know where it lay? And had she heard of the clansmen? His fists knotted. If only he had warned her. But how was he to know she would go without telling him, just go and leave him wondering?

Wondering? No, this yawning sense of dread was certainly more than that. Frowning, he groped through the complex tracery of his thoughts. She had not given her knee a chance to heal, so she would travel slowly, even if Waana had accompanied her. He could overtake her if he knew what direction she had taken.

But he did not know. And the plain lay vast in every direction. He gazed around, squinting against the sun. It was quiet in the grazing grounds. The yearlings had gone earlier in the afternoon, shrilling and stamping. Only the adult redmanes and the younger foals remained. The scent of pollen was no more than a subliminal tickle in the air. Why, he wondered with quick bitterness, was it so important to know where she had gone? To be with her?

Obviously she didn't consider it important to be with him. Otherwise she would not have gone—and without a word's parting. So that was the other side of what he felt at her leaving: a hard, lonely anger, like a fist knotted in his chest. Tensely Danior rubbed his temples, trying to bring his thoughts to clearer definition. They had met, they had walked together, he had taught her how to listen to the teaching. And she had gone.

It wasn't enough. They had hardly touched. He had hardly begun to understand what it meant that they were at once so much alike and so different. What it meant that she had killed a minx, that he could make a pairing stone burn, that they had lived so long in ignorance of each other and then met. By chance. Only by chance.

Use the stone? What other way was there, when she could have gone in any direction? How long could he stand here frightened and angry, doing nothing? Still, he hesitated, his head aching with unresolved questions, before he left the grazing ground and returned to the campment.

Tehla had not gone to the herd today. She worked in the milk kef with three other guardians, their lean arms wet to the elbows with creamy milk, tubs of milk pudding steaming around them. Danior went there when he had fetched his bedding and his pike from the kefri. "Thank you for the shelter of your kefri, Tehla," he said formally. "I must go on my way now."

"You won't stay for the night's teaching, Danior Terlath?"

asked Mirala, youngest of the four guardians. She had been a guardian daughter a year ago, and much of the laughter was still in her eyes. She teased him with it, showing gleaming teeth.

"No," he said shortly. "I'm going to my great-grand-mother." A lie, and he knew from Tehla's impassive nod that they all recognized it. His face reddened. Why couldn't he tell them the simple truth? That Keva had gone and he must find her. That he had things to learn from her, that he intended to learn them. Something kept him from saying any of it. He turned away sharply.

But before they would let him go, he had to stuff cheese and freshly baked bread into his pack. And Mirala told him in laughing tones that she would meet him in the orchard when she brought her first plow team to Valley Terlath next year and his face reddened even more fiercely. Though why it embarrassed him that she suggested he father her first daughter . . . He snapped his pack shut and left the hut hastily, running down the narrow lanes of the campment.

He knew he had no hope of finding Keva's prints in the grass. The yearlings had trampled everywhere before finally going south. But since he had to go in some direction, he chose to go south too. Perhaps it was only the faint musk of pollen that drew him. Perhaps it was instinct.

He did not open his pack until he was well beyond the campment. Did not remove the stone from its velvet pouch until there was no one to see. Then he held the stone in his palm and felt a wracking shudder of doubt. He had seen barohnas wear pairing stones that glowed so brightly the light hurt his eyes. His gave only a small light, as if it could not find the vitality in his touch to burn with full radiance.

Perhaps he could not even learn its use. Perhaps it would never do more than faintly glow. He dropped the chain over his head anyway and placed the stone at his throat, his hands shaking, his throat dry.

Nothing happened. The stone lay against his flesh, faintly warm, and nothing changed. With a moment's surge of nausea,

Danior closed his pack. He had only the gem master's words to encourage him. The pairing stone was a tool. If he was to learn to use it, if he was to find Keva with it, he must wear it, stroke it, become sensitive to it. He must find his way to its heart with his fingertips, with the flesh of his palm.

He closed his hand around it and because he had no idea what else to do, he continued walking south. The musk of pollen became perceptibly thicker as he went. Occasionally he saw yearlings running, individually or in groups. After a while, he began to feel like a yearling himself, called to a test. One he didn't understand but could not turn from.

He walked until dark, sometimes holding the stone, sometimes only stroking it. Then he spread his bedding near an outcropping of boulders. He sat for a long time pressing the pairing stone to his palm, trying to find something more in it than faint warmth. When he held it before him, it illuminated his hand, throwing the creases and folds into relief. But nothing more happened. Finally, discouraged, he rolled into his bedding and slept.

His dreams were confused, discolored by the day's events. He searched endlessly for things he could not find, reached for things he could not touch, mouthed words that held no sense. And he clutched the pairing stone. Even as he slept, he felt it grow warm and then hot against his palm. Vaguely he remembered what the gem master had said. That sometimes the link was forged in sleep. With barely focused effort, he tried to reach into the stone, to breach its crystal facets and press through to another place. He tried with all the power of dream.

Then he was not dreaming at all. The flesh at the base of his throat warmed and began to burn. He stirred uneasily and struggled to sit, rubbing his eyes. He shook his head, trying to clear it, trying to understand. He seemed to sit in two places at once. The boulders he leaned against were interpenetrated by others. He gazed up and saw the moons, but they were four, as if he saw Nindra and Zan twice, from differing perspectives. Anxiously he peered around and found the edges of reality blurred, eroded.

From nearby he heard a familiar voice. Waana's voice, he realized—teaching. But where was she? With Keva? Had he linked with Keva? Anxiously, he tried to capture the words of the teaching. They eluded him, distant, wispy. But the smooth succession of visual images—of the herd, the plain, of familiar places—was clear now. He might have been sitting beside the teaching pond.

Instinctively he tightened his clasp on the pairing stone and made a deliberate effort to reach out. The effort made the flesh of his throat burn, as if nerve centers there blazed alive.

He reached but it was not Waana who taught now. Keva's voice came to him instead and was quickly succeeded by another, one he had never heard before—one that made a chill race down his spine.

The voice was not human. And it did not teach with words. It taught with a bright-hued song and with visual images, not sharp-edged but shaded, as if shadow overlay them. Frowning, he attempted to bring them to focus and the breeze of another place moved into his mind. Shadow pulled back and sunlight fell hard and clean from a sun he had never seen. Confused and compelled at once, he realized that he did not see it now, but he felt its power in the song that sang blue.

The song Keva taught was at once energy and substance, light and sound—all those things caught up in an enveloping silkenness. It wrapped slippery fingers around him, reaching for him. It coiled around him and carried him to another place. He went willingly, barely aware of the burning of the pairing stone in his palm.

Another place. Silently Danior struggled to orient himself. There was land behind the bluesong and there were trees. He saw their reaching white stalks, saw moving shapes on the ground beneath them. Swift, clever shapes. Caught, he fell deeper into the bluesong. He became totally drenched in its light, and a face emerged. Glinting yellow eyes, obliquely set— predator's eyes. Yet the face was not threatening. It was clad in glossy chestnut fur and it smiled toothsomely, its pink tongue flicking out mischievously.

A rock-leopard? No, something gentler, playful. But it didn't play now. Danior brought his attention to tighter focus and saw that the creature had begun to groom itself, pulling its pink tongue over the chestnut fur, lingering until the fur lay clean and damp. Moving closer, Danior saw that the creature rested not upon the ground but in a bower of brilliant silks. They were of many colors: scarlet, amber, noon-yellow—chartreuse, emerald, crimson. And blue, the blue of sky, so brilliant and clear it hurt to see.

But Danior did not withdraw his attention. He thrust himself deeper into the spell, deeper into the realm of color and song.

He thrust himself deeper and then there were the dark things. Nightmare images growling out of nowhere, casting sticky arms around him, tearing him with razor claws. They clutched at his mind, trying to drag him into their nightmare pit. They tangled their claws in his hair, they tugged and tore—

The stone! They reached for him through the stone! Gasping, he tore the chain over his head and threw the stone away from him.

It fell in the grass, but the scream was still in his throat, a raw cry, as he shuddered free of the pit, of the bower, of the strange song Keva taught. He glared around in shock, expecting to see the dark things come boiling after him.

He saw only moonlight and grass. And his pairing stone, fading to darkness.

He wrapped his arms around his drawn-up knees, trembling. He had reached out through the pairing stone. Reached out into some strange place Keva knew. Someplace where there was a yearning blue song and a hot sun and a predator that slept on brilliant silks and groomed itself with a pink tongue.

But the dark things—he tried to summon back the faces of terror, so alien to anything he had ever experienced. The terror did not lie just in the images but in the sense of being caught, of being drawn in.

Into what? He could not formulate a clear answer. The dark things were alien, their threat incomprehensible.

The only recognizable image he salvaged from the episode was of the pinnacles. Keva was spending the night at the place where his mother had torn down the rocks to destroy the Benderzic ship. He rubbed shaking hands across his face. At least he knew that Keva had gone south, that instinct had guided him well.

Numbly he retrieved the pairing stone from the grass and placed it around his neck again. He did not touch the stone with his fingers, did not stroke or clasp it. Shaken, he rolled back into his bedding and stared up at the stars.

It was near dawn before he slept. It was midday when he woke. His mouth was stale, his hands tremulous. The water he splashed on his face felt icy, although the morning was not cold. He could barely bring himself to eat. He sat for a long time staring at the horizon before he got to his feet and began to walk south again.

He walked slowly, stopping often to lean on his pike. He felt as if the stone had drained him of energy, as if it had fed on him. His thoughts ran a slow course, monotonous and undemanding, yet in some way alien to any thoughts he had had before. Because now he had used the stone and he had seen the dark things.

He hardly saw the occasional yearling who passed. He stopped before dusk beside a small pond, knowing it was useless to press on to the pinnacles tonight. He wouldn't find Keva there now. And tomorrow he would travel more quickly. Sighing, he sat and opened his pack. This time the smell of bread and cheese at least teased his appetite, although he found he could not eat much.

He had almost finished his meal when he heard a shuffling sound. Slowly he stood, peering into the gathering shadows. A predator? He closed one hand around his pike, the fingers cramping.

The shuffling neared and, with a surge of relief, Danior recognized Waana. She picked her way through the grass cautiously, her gait hobbling, painful. "Waana," he said softly, not wanting to startle her. Had Keva turned back? He peered anxiously beyond Waana but did not see her.

So it was not to be that easy, finding her.

Waana raised milky eyes, studying him silently as he made

his way to her. When he reached her, she bowed her head. Danior studied her more closely, concerned. She stood as if she were not just tired but in pain. Quickly he bent to examine her, raising her padded feet one by one.

Even in the dusk, he could see the gash on her left hind pad. The wound was caked with dirt and dried blood. "You've torn your pad. If you'll let me wash it and bind it—" He hesitated, not certain that she understood speech. Some mares understood well; others understood no better than most valley people understood the silent communication that passed among redmanes.

Waana grunted and moved to the water. Painfully she lowered herself to her side and gazed up at him.

At least she understood he would care for her. Quickly Danior sorted through his pack. He carried little beyond food, a waterskin and a few extra clothes. He selected a roughspun tunic, tore it into strips and wet it in the pond.

Biting his lip, he flushed the wound with water, cleaning out caked dirt. He had nothing to sew shut the gash, but he bound it as tightly as he dared. She had probably cut herself on the jagged rocks of the pinnacles.

"Now if you'll sleep," he urged, "you can walk tomorrow."

The mare grunted and did not attempt to stand. Relieved, glad to have her company, tired, Danior spread his bedding nearby and slept almost immediately.

When he woke later and found the moons on the water and Waana standing beside the pond, he pulled his bedding closer and refused to join her. "You shouldn't put your weight on your foot tonight."

But she continued to stand teaching to no one. Finally, when he could not fall asleep again, he sighed and left his bedding.

She taught as she always taught: how to find the required foods, how to sense the presence of danger, how to treat herd-mates, how to live. She taught everything Danior would need to know were he a redmane. He sighed again, more deeply, and released himself to the teaching. Gratefully he felt some of his energy return, moving from his fingertips to his arms, from his arms to the base of his neck, warming him.

She taught at length, until the moons neared the edge of the pond. Then her voice changed. *Listen, valley foal. Sometimes we take lessons from other plains creatures. Sometimes we take lessons from our guardians. Now I have learned a new lesson that is not a lesson at all. All the herds will want to hear it, although it will contribute nothing to their peace and strength, only to their pleasure. It is a lesson full of light and shadow, a teaching from a place we don't know.*

Instinct told him what Waana wanted to teach. He tensed, his fingertips chilling again. He wanted to raise his head, to break the spell of the teaching. But more he found he wanted to walk under the white-stalked trees again. Wanted to look more closely at that strange place. With only a moment's hesitation, he raised his hand and clasped the stone.

Listen, Wanna admonished. *You will hear light things and they will make you glad. And you will hear dark things, but they can't hurt you because they aren't real. Listen, valley foal.*

Then the song came, smooth and silken, and lights moved behind Danior's closed eyelids. They took many colors and many degrees of brightness as Danior watched, as if alien moons shone on changing surfaces. Then there were strands of silken cloth, some free and flowing, others stretched tight into translucent sheets of color. There were trees, their trunks reaching into the surrounding darkness like tall white stalks. There were pink bodies, hunched and fearful, and long sinuous bodies with dark fur. Stalking creatures large and small turned glinting eyes to the light, then fled. Danior reached for it all, the stone burning his fingers, its light stinging his eyes.

The song continued. The many lights fused into one and picked out faces from the backdrop of darkness. Pink fleshy faces, dark-furred faces, yellow-fanged faces—Danior groaned as the faces became feral.

The light narrowed to a searing pinpoint, then widened again and Danior gazed into a dark-furred face with oblique eyes. It was thick-muscled at the jaw, supported by a heavy neck. He recoiled, his heartbeat rising from a distant drumming to an anxious clatter. It was a bestial face, a threatening face, yet there was something about it, something . . .

Curiosity drove him and he reached for more detail. This face was duller than the one he had seen the night before. The eyes were sulphurous, muted. The teeth did not smile. Still, upon closer examination, this animal was much like the other he had seen, grooming itself in its bower. He concentrated on the burning patch at the base of his throat and looked more closely.

Shadow peeled back, light spread, and he saw a heavily muscled body with matted chestnut fur. Saw a pink tongue that hung laxly from between stained teeth. And he saw pain. Saw it clearly.

Was the animal injured? Lost? Danior expelled a long breath and light spread again. The animal stood among tall white trees with veined black leaves. It stood with its matted head raised, gazing far up into the trees.

Danior followed its gaze. High in the trees he saw a bower of brilliant silks. Moonlight shone through them and emerged stained many colors: chartreuse, emerald, crimson—scarlet, amber, noon-yellow. Narrowing his eyes, he saw a shadow against the silk panes. He turned and saw that the heavy-jawed animal on the ground gazed up at the bower in mute pain.

It was the bower he had seen before. And the other animal was there again, grooming itself. Danior frowned, trying to find the sense of the scene. A bower of colored silks in the trees. One animal within it, pulling its tongue through its dark fur. Another animal staring up at the bower with eyes that held no spark, staring up in pain—as if at something it knew well, yet could not attain. Danior watched the brutal face, trying to find something in the dull eyes that would tell him more.

He was afraid to reach too deeply. There were shadows just below the surface of the dull eyes. He was afraid of what might live in the shadows.

Dark things. Images of terror. Incomprehensible terror.

Waana said the dark things were not real.

But the animal that stood looking up at the bower seemed real. Real somewhere. Confusion made Danior's neck draw tight, made his head ache. Confusion and the bare beginnings of panic. He exhaled heavily, trying to breathe away the heat at the base of his throat, where the pairing stone rested. Immediately he found himself moving away from the animal in the trees, from the bower. He exhaled again and shadow flowed among the white-stalked trees. The strange, wordless song Waana taught faded.

Trembling, Danior extricated himself from it entirely. Regained the reality of the plain, of stars that glittered overhead, of solid ground beneath him. He sat for a moment, numbly triumphant. He had that much control. He could reach into that other place, then extricate himself from the terror before it began.

If he could do that . . .

Shakily he stood, running his fingers through his hair, trying to understand. Last night he had worn the stone and it had taken him into Keva's consciousness. That was how the stone had been intended to function, after all. It had been created to link one mind with another.

But how had the images that accompanied the bluesong—the colored silks, the white-stalked trees, the chestnut-furred animals—come to be in Keva's mind? Had she even been aware of them? Or had she only heard the song? And why hadn't the linking of minds been mutual? Why hadn't she been aware of his presence, his thoughts? Did the pairing stones only work for him?

Waana at least had reached past the song to the white-stalked forest. How else could she have warned him that the dark things were not real? And did her warning mean that the other things were real—the trees, the bower? He had no way to ask her. Frowning, he touched the pairing stone with a single fingertip, then drew back when the stone began to glow. A tool, he reminded himself. The stone was simply a tool, one he understood imperfectly. And the ony way he could perfect his understanding was through practice. Through reaching down into its heart.

Practice. He must practice. The moons left the water. Waana sighed and lay down in the grass to sleep. Danior sat for a while, staring at the dark water. Then he raised his hand and closed it around the stone again. He reached for its core, for the place where it lived. He knew when he touched it because the stone took light, casting a cloudy blue radiance against the surface of the pond. Reach—he must reach, as he had done the night before while he slept, as he had done tonight, going deeper and deeper into the stone, into the white-stalked forest. Instinctively, he drew a deep breath and held it, pressing his eyes shut. The node of warmth at his throat grew, intensified. He thought of Keva and he reached for her, reached for her heart, for the thoughts that framed her consciousness.

Quietly, almost effortlessly, he stepped into her mind. At first he touched only memory. He smelled the sulphur tang of geysers and felt mud under his toes. Reaching nearer—*reaching,* that was what he must do—he saw the surface of the water. There were yellow-throated plants floating there. Other stalks reached up through the water—to take sunlight, he understood, drawing upon what Keva knew.

He explored the warmstream for a time, then reached into other pockets of memory. And then the warmth at his throat spread and he stepped into present time. It took him moments to recognize it for that because Keva was dreaming. He felt the pressure of her body against the soil where she lay and traced the quick, confusing passage of dream-images: a tall woman who stood against fire, a bright circlet that flew into the grumbling darkness, confusion, fear, uncertainty. Danior stirred uncomfortably, wishing Keva would waken.

But when she woke, it was to see a dim shape stalking a whitemane yearling. Confused, Danior tried to ground himself in her thoughts, tried to reach through her rising alarm to find and define his own response. A minx? Surely she wouldn't go against a minx with just a pike? Surely—

And then, before he could fully orient himself, she was tracking the minx and rocks flew. The earth tore, boulders rose in the air, a frightened face stared—and when the whitemane and the terrified youth had both fled and Keva was alone,

Danior was caught in the same shocked numbness Keva experienced.

Jarred by the intensity of the experience, frightened, he pulled his hand free of the stone. Keva's thoughts slipped away and he retreated from the pondside, shaking. She was a barohna. If he had had any doubt before, it was gone now. Keva was a barohna. She had torn up the ground. She had pulled stone from the earth and made it live. Only a barohna could do that.

And the youth who had stalked the whitemane—Danior's thoughts ran rapidly in an unwelcome direction. The youth had been a desert clansman. He knew that from his coloring, from his features, from the robes he wore. But the youth's bright-colored sashes, the way he wore his hair, knotted tightly behind one ear—Danior had never heard of a clansman who dressed so.

But Danior had glimpsed Jhaviir in Keva's dream, and he had worn a colored sash—the bluesong—and he had worn his hair knotted behind one ear. Was the desert youth dressed in imitation of him? But why imitate Jhaviir—if he had not seen him? And recently?

Danior's throat tightened with alarm. Did Keva realize that the youth had been a desert man, a clansman? That his dress, his appearance had been unusual? If she knew anything of the desert people and how they costumed themselves—

Quickly he took up the stone and inhaled deeply. He reached.

Numbness, terror, bewilderment, doubt. A reluctant recognition of what she had done and its significance. With relief, Danior found Keva wasn't thinking of the youth at all. She was thinking only of herself.

But later, when she did think about the youth—Danior released the stone and retreated to his own thoughts—when she did think about the youth, about the details of his appearance, she would recognize the same thing he did. That the youth was dressed in imitation of Jhaviir. That he must have seen Jhaviir. Recently.

And then, if she learned the youth was a clansman—Danior didn't pursue the thought further. There was no time—no time for thought, for question, for doubt. No time for hesitation. He rolled his bedding with trembling hands and left Waana without a word's parting. Quickly he began to travel south, half-running. If Keva learned the youth was a desert clansman, if she decided to go to the desert in search of her father—Danior thought of the stories he had heard of the desert people, of their raids, their wars, their savagery, and he chilled. He ran faster, urgency driving him, knowing he had to reach Keva before she decided to go to the desert. Before she decided to go among the warring clans without even guessing the danger.

EIGHT
KEVA

K eva walked slowly the next day. The herbal dressing Tehla had applied to her knee had lost its potency and her knee swelled against its bindings. The minx wounds on her face itched. But she was so preoccupied that she hardly noticed those things. If she refused to think about what had happened the night before, she told herself, if she refused to hear the grinding of stone upon stone, if she refused to admit the fear that yawned before her like a pit—

But of course she could think of nothing else. She walked numbly, hardly seeing the trampled grass, the occasional trees, the yearlings who ran and fell. Now more than ever, she realized, she must find her father. Danior had kept things from her, for whatever reason. Her father would not. He would tell her why the earth had torn. He would tell her why stones had grumbled in the air. He would tell her how to reverse the changes that had come in her, the differences she had seen in her face, in her eyes, the other differences she had not seen but had felt.

What had Oki told her? That there are two kinds of mountain women: those who learn to be hard and become barohnas. And those who don't—who die.

Keva clutched the haft of her pike. Were those the only choices she had? To be a barohna and hard. Or to die. Couldn't she reject both alternatives and find another course? Or was she helpless against forces she didn't understand? Forces within herself, bred there, developing now toward some inevitable end?

It was no use tormenting herself. She would find her father and he would tell her what she needed to know.

Late in the afternoon she began to pass clumps of trees, thickets of brush, and she knew the forest was near. The smell of pollen was in the air, heavy and musty-sweet.

At last she saw the forest ahead, dark and towering, stretching dimly from horizon to horizon. And she saw a field of grey. Yearlings—hundreds of yearlings sprawled in the grass to rest. As she came near, sentries at the perimeter of the herd snorted softly. Keva picked her way among the sleeping animals and felt the warmth of their gathered bodies. Soon her own eyelids began to droop. Giving in to the heavy weariness that had followed her all day, she spread her bedding and stretched out.

She slept without dreaming, gratefully leaving her preoccupations behind. But when she woke it was dark and the youth she had seen the night before was in her mind again. She had only glimpsed him by moonlight, but she remembered the structure of his face: long, narrow eyes set above high, sharp cheekbones; thin lips; narrow nose with nostrils sharply flared. She remembered his clothing too, the wide, dust-stained robe caught at the waist by bright sashes, the loose trousers. His feet had been bare, the toes long, the nails caked with dirt. He had worn his hair in a knot behind one ear.

He had to be a desert man. Certainly he was not from the mountains, not from the warmstreams, not from the plain. And there were no people living in the roughlands or the lakelands. Hadn't Waana warned her that men from the desert clans hunted near the forest during the running?

But the way he wore his hair, the sashes at his waist—their texture was coarser than the bluesong's. The fabric was harsher, the color duller. But the youth had worn them as her father had worn the bluesong, knotted to hang at one hip. Was that how all men of the desert dressed? Had her father found the bluesong in the desert? Had he taken it from the clansmen?

Or had he been a desert man himself? Slowly Keva opened

her eyes, staring at the darkness of the forest. Danior—he was so like her, they might have had the same father. But he had come from the mountains. How was it that her father wore his hair like a desert man, yet had lived in the mountains with her mother, a barohna? Her mother was dead now, but if her father's place had been in the mountains, why had he gone away?

To return to the desert? To his people there?

She shook her head, trying to clear it. Trying to separate the important questions from the irrelevant. It didn't matter where her father had come from or why he had left the mountains. The thing that mattered was that she find him. And if he had not been seen in the mountains, on the plain, at the warm-stream, then she must go to the desert.

It didn't matter that she knew nothing about the desert people except that they hunted redmanes at running time. And that the youth she had encountered had been gaunt and dirty. After her days' travel, she was not particularly clean.

The desert. She must go to the desert.

And to find it, she realized, she must continue to the forest and find the desert youth or some other desert person to direct her.

She gazed up at the moon which had slipped higher above the trees. Around her sleeping yearlings began to stir. One shook vigorously and nudged her with a curious nose. She rubbed its soft ears, but it granted her only a moment's attention. The forest musk had grown stronger, sweeter, and the yearling was impatient to go. Anxious to join others who were stirring, awakening, greeting each other with gentle snorts and subdued whickerings.

Keva stood, rolling her bedding, slinging it on her back. Taking up her pike, she picked her way among the yearlings.

By the time she reached the edge of the herd, yearlings danced and shrilled around her, tossing auburn manes, padded feet pounding. She paused briefly to watch, then continued walking.

She had not gone far before yearlings overtook her and the ground jarred with the pounding of their feet. They passed in a long grey wave, celebrating noisily. Then came successive waves, until she walked alone again and the animals ran ahead. Soon she didn't even hear the sound of their voices as they spread and lost themselves in the shadow of the forest.

She came upon the forest gradually. Isolated trees appeared and were succeeded by small stands. Those thickened into taller, denser stands and finally she knew she had entered the forest. The trees stood tall and widely spaced, with broad trunks and sparse limbs. They threw a gridwork of broad shadows. The forest floor was spongy with fallen leaves. It gave silently under her feet, tugging at the butt of her pike when she leaned on it.

And the smell of pollen—Keva coughed at its concentrated musty-sweetness. She paused for a moment, staring up into the trees, and a pale face loomed down at her. She jumped back with a gasp, instinctively thrusting with her pike.

There was no body behind the face. It was a fleshy white blossom. It bent toward her on a rubbery stalk, reaching out for—what? Confused, she backed away and the blossom slowly retracted, drawing back up into the shadows.

She moved ahead cautiously, trying to find some familiarity in the trees, in the texture of their bark, in the dry smell of their leaves. Trying to find some memory. Perhaps she had been here before, with her father. Perhaps they had ridden through the forest together on his whitemane. But tonight she felt only strangeness, and fleshy white blossoms continued to reach down to her, mute faces carrying the choking sweetness of pollen.

Once as she groped through the gridwork of shadows, she heard a scream in the distance. She froze, her fingers whitening on her pike. It was repeated, then shrank away through the trees.

The silence seemed heavier then. She put her feet down carefully, trying not to disturb the silence, and stopped often to listen.

Finally she heard shuffling sounds ahead, heard the faint snort of a redmane. She hesitated, then continued ahead. Redmane yearlings moved in the moonlight, lifting soft noses to the blossoms that groped down from the trees. They pressed their noses deep into the blossoms and drew them out coated with yellow pollen. Keva halted and watched as they progressed from flower to flower. Occasionally one of the yearlings sneezed softly and shook its head. Behind the yearlings, the pollinated blossoms drew back and pulled their pale petals shut. Slowly they retreated back up into the trees.

Insects. The yearlings were doing the work of insects, she realized with slow-dawning surprise. The trees that grew by the warmstream were pollinated by soft-shelled crawlers who carried the yellow grains from tree to tree on their sticky legs. These blossoms used redmanes to carry their pollen. The yearlings moved from tree to tree with none of the shrilling excitement of the earlier evening. Moved docilely, as if this were what they had come for.

Experimentally Keva approached a hovering blossom. She reached into it and found a velvet head. When her fingertips tingled, she drew them back yellow. The blossom pulled away, its petals still open. Not knowing what else to do, she slipped ahead and plunged her fingers into a second blossom, stroking pollen into it. The blossom hovered for moments, then drew back, closing its petals upon her hand.

The caress was cool, satin. Carefully Keva extricated her hand and watched as the blossom furled tight. She moved on with a peculiar satisfaction, moonlight creating dappled avenues before her. She had made the running. She had survived the journey to the forest. And she had fulfilled the imperative of the blossoms.

Now that she was here, she must find someone to direct her to the desert, and she couldn't guess how that was to be done. But something in the pollen, in the soft whicker of the yearlings, put concern from her mind. She spent the early hours of night as the yearlings did, meeting the demand of the blossoms.

By the time the moons passed zenith, the perfume of the forest had grown fainter. Hundreds of pollinated blossoms retracted into the trees and hoarded their scent behind closed petals. The yearlings began to move briskly again, kicking up their feet, nipping at each other's flanks. Keva selected a small group and followed them. The yearlings seemed not to mind her company. Occasionally one or another of them turned and gazed back at her, then darted ahead after its companions.

Keva had almost forgotten to think of predators when the yearlings began to move warily, ears cocked, tails held high. Keva slowed, tightness coming to her chest. The yearlings— there were seven—halted, stamping their feet nervously. Keva saw fear in their bristling manes, in their rolling eyes. Reluctantly she joined them.

Blood spattered the forest floor, its smell thick on the air. Nearby a plug of grey fur was ground into the leaf mold. Keva gripped her pike, her eyes following the dark trail of blood into the trees. One of the yearlings looked up at her anxiously, shrinking against her.

The yearlings lingered a moment, then snorted nervously and altered their course. They drew closer together as they padded through the trees.

After a while they forgot their fright. But Keva continued to watch the shadows until she saw that the trees were thinning, that they approached the edge of the forest. She rubbed her eyes and wondered when the yearlings would stop to sleep, wondered if they would gather by the hundreds as they had before. Wondered how she was going to find the desert youth or one of his kind. Wondered—

She was so preoccupied, she noticed nothing—no sound, no shadow— until suddenly the forest exploded. Loud cries, crouched forms, running feet—Keva was caught at the center of yearlings. She froze, her eyes recording a flurry of images: running men, flying ropes, savage faces. The startled shrills of the yearlings mingled with the harassing cries of the men. The yearlings were pressed in upon themselves. Ropes dropped over their heads and tightened upon their necks. The smell of fear was heavy.

Keva did not regain use of her muscles until she felt a rough noose fall over her shoulders and tighten around her arms, pinning them to her sides. She spun around, caught between shock and anger, a hoarse cry in her throat. Stained teeth gleamed at her from mud-smeared faces. The rope that bound her jerked sharply and she lost her balance, her pike dropping from her hand.

She struggled against the noose as she was pulled across the ground. A panicked yearling lunged and caught her leg with its padded foot. She cried out; her hands opened and closed futilely. She could not raise her arms to push away the rope.

Worse than helplessness was the rising bile in her throat, the dizziness, the sense even as she fought the rope that she was moving into a timeless place, a place where the earth would part at her will and stones would fly.

No! She swallowed back the bile and took a gasping breath, refusing to let control slip away. She heard a burst of guttural speech and a sweating face loomed over her, white teeth flashing. A dark man with narrow eyes and sharp cheekbones pulled her to her feet, swiftly looping his rope around her again and again, binding her tight. He wore soiled robes and loose trousers, his feet bare. His hair was cut bluntly to fall in a heavy black cap around his head. Before she could do more than record a brief impression, he pushed her aside, casually knocking her to her knees, then to her stomach.

Gasping, she rolled over and struggled to sit, pushing herself up against the rough trunk of a tree. The screams of the yearlings were terrible. The men—there were five of them, perhaps six—threw them to their sides and bound their feet. They worked with practiced swiftness, as if they had done this chore times before, as a team.

As if they had hunted redmanes many times before. Desert men—she had found her desert men.

The finding did not reassure her. Keva pushed against the tree trunk, struggling to take her feet, but one of the men felled her with a swift shove and dug his bare toes into her ribs, grunting angrily.

She fought back tears of pain and bit her lip, fighting the dizziness, the whirling sense of timelessness again. And wondering why she did so. If ever there were a time when she needed to be hard, when she needed to be cruel—she clenched her teeth and imagined the earth parting and its rocky foundations grumbling through the air, pounding at the dirty men in their baggy robes. She imagined their screams, their blood.

She choked back the images. She could not question them about her father if she stoned them. And she did not want to see blood, theirs or anyone's. *My father is a desert man,* she would say when they turned from their brutal handling of the yearlings. *I've come to find him. I've come to be with him.* And they would untie her and take her to him.

Watching the callous way they handled the yearlings, she doubted it. She squeezed her eyes shut, trying to escape confusion.

When she opened her eyes again, the seven yearlings lay bound under the trees. The desert men prodded at them, measuring the firmness of their muscles, the girth of their bellies. Keva shuddered. One of the yearlings raised its head and pleaded with its eyes, begging her help.

But what could she do, short of tearing up the earth? The heaviest of the men turned. His eyes narrowed speculatively and he rose and advanced toward her. She cringed involuntarily, unable to speak. He was older than the others. His face fell in deep furrows, the skin weathered by sun and wind. As he approached, she realized there was something in his eyes she had never seen before, not by the warmstreams, not on the plain, not in her nightmares: an angry hunger, directed at her.

Keva stiffened, unwilling to think of him as the same kind of man her father was. He did not wear a sash; his robes were caught at the waist by a rope. He did not wear his hair knotted. The darkness of his skin was different too. It came from years of harsh weathering, not from natural pigmentation.

His hands were calloused and thick. He extended them like weapons he would take pleasure in using. No, she decided desperately, if her father was a desert man, he was not this kind of desert man.

Keva stared at the man's rough hands, licking her lips. She had heard stories of men who used force. Not the laughing force of a playful lover, but angry force, a force that did not admit the humanity of the woman it was directed against. By the warmstreams, if a man debased himself so, he would be sent away, to live and die alone. Keva licked dry lips, understanding how such men must look to their prey. She pressed herself against the tree, trying to make herself small.

But where was it written that her choice was to kill him with stones or to deliver herself to him? Or that if she did deliver herself, she must yield him spirit as well as body? Keva's jaw stiffened. Grunting, she struggled to her feet. Her knee cramped with pain but she bit back her cry. Raising her head, she met the desert man's eyes directly, with a will. She would not stone him—not if she had control. But let him look into her eyes and he would see that she could. Let him look and he would see what was latent in her.

See it, she urged him.

He took another step forward and faltered. The steeliness in his eyes wavered. Then his gaze dropped to the stone at her throat and the pupils narrowed so swiftly they shrank to hard black motes. He uttered a harsh word, not to his mates but to himself.

Test me. But he was staring so intently at the stone, at the strip of blue cloth that held it, that he did not see the challenge in her eyes. Keva frowned in confusion, pressing herself against the tree.

The desert man grunted, then reached with a knotted hand and snatched the stone from around her neck.

But it was not only the stone that drew him, Keva saw immediately. It was the cloth. The desert man rubbed the slippery fabric between thumb and forefinger, his face greying. Then he held the stone to his eye and peered through it. His mouth clamped shut with a snap. He glanced back up at her, appetite dying from his eyes, leaving only dregs—not of cruelty, not of anger, but of fear. He inhaled heavily, then drew back one hand, as if to redeem himself by striking her.

Keva found voice. "Test me," she hissed, challenging him.

He did not meet the challenge. The desert man's hand rose, then fell back to his side. He struggled to break free of her gaze. Jerkily he backed away from her, perspiration suddenly shining on his face.

Keva choked back elation and stood free of the tree, looking past the first man to the others.

They had turned from their work to watch the encounter. The first man stumbled to them, the strip of blue fabric trembling in his hand. He muttered guttural words. The other men examined the stone and fabric and gazed at Keva with dawning wariness. They began to talk rapidly among themselves, gathering close, as if for protection.

From her. They were afraid of her. She was bound and helpless and they feared her so sharply she could smell it. They fingered the cloth. They fingered the stone. And they muttered and grunted and backed away.

What did they take her for? A barohna? Were they as frightened of the barohnas as Oki had been? She released a slow breath, wondering how much she could make of their fear if she could hide her own. "Your ropes are hurting me," she said, keeping her voice firm and clear. "Untie me."

Even those few words heightened their fear. Sharpened it.

"Let me loose," she said, pressing her advantage. "And let my animals go. I won't have them stolen." When they did not respond, except to clutch closer to one another, she took a step forward, careful not to betray herself with a limp. "Untie me."

With a grunt, one of the men slipped a long-bladed knife from his waist. Its blade glinted dully. The other men hissed in alarm, their faces turning the color of ashes. One seized his arm and twisted until the weapon fell from his fingers. He protested, the cords of his neck bulging, but the others stilled him with a series of deep-throated utterances.

The advantage was hers, Keva saw, her heart leaping so hard against her ribs it left her breathless. She would be foolish not to press it. Steeling herself, she stared at the muttering men and stepped toward them again. She said nothing. She simply walked, deliberately, firmly.

Later she marveled that none of them saw that she was as frightened as they were. Marveled at how swiftly they disappeared. She took six even paces and abruptly the men groaned and scattered into the trees. The one who had dropped the knife dodged forward and snatched it up. Glowering at her with a moment's bravado, he snatched up her pack too and ran after the others. She heard the swift pad of bare feet, heard one voice raised, and then she was alone.

Alone with her arms bound and seven yearlings tied at her feet. They hadn't even left her the digging blade from her pack. She hesitated, evaluating her situation with a momentary sense of letdown. She had frightened away the clansmen, but she could not reach the knots that bound her.

The yearlings—if she could bring her hands together in front of her, perhaps she could at least release the yearlings. Frowning, she pressed against the ropes, trying to find some slack, but there was none. She could not slide her arms together. And that meant she could only use one hand at a time.

She must act quickly, she knew, if she was to do anything. Her fingers were growing numb. Soon they would be too clumsy to grapple with the coarsest knot.

Painfully she dropped to her knees beside the nearest yearling. It thrashed and reared its head, trying to gain its feet. "No, no. Lie still. I'll try to untie you," she coaxed. "Lie still."

She could tell by the roll of the yearlings's eyes that he didn't understand her words but was reassured by her tone.

She maneuvered to bring her right hand within reach of the knots that bound his hind legs. Her position was awkward, half-crouched, her hand bound tightly against her side. She could not see what she was doing without arching her neck so sharply her back cramped.

She fumbled at the knots. The rope was loosely woven, and that acted in her favor. When she found the free end, she was able to compress the rope enough to work it through. The effort partially restored circulation to her fingers, but left them sore and quivering. And there were more knots, many more.

Working painstakingly, trying to ignore the pain in her knee, the cramping of her neck and back, the increasing tenderness of her fingertips, she eventually freed the first yearling. It took its feet uncertainly, stumbling a little, and stepped back from its companions. Keva watched with held breath, afraid it would flee into the trees. She did not trust the silence of the forest.

The yearling edged away from the group, then returned, sniffing its companions thoughtfully. It bared its teeth at the ropes that bound them.

If it would chew the ropes—but the yearling turned away and lay down a short distance from the others, obviously troubled and uncertain.

Working with bleeding fingers and cramping muscles, Keva freed the yearlings one by one. None abandoned the group. Even when the last yearling stepped from its ropes, the yearlings remained clustered under the trees, gazing at Keva from solemn eyes. She tried to imagine what they were thinking. Did they understand she could not free herself? Or were they waiting for her to throw off her ropes and lead them out of the forest? They were accustomed to human protection.

She looked around uncertainly. It was not far to the edge of the forest. But Allindra was approaching the horizon and Zan followed. Soon it would be dark. Dark until dawn. And Waana had said that most predators did not venture far into the trees. Better to pass the dark hours deep in the trees than exposed where there was less protection.

Keva pushed herself against a tree trunk and struggled to her feet. Her fingertips were sticky with half-dried blood. "Come," she said. "Come with me." Clumsily she stumbled into the trees. She clutched and unclutched her hands as she walked, trying to keep her fingers from numbing.

The yearlings padded after her, heads hung in weariness.

They could not be more tired than she was. She hardly saw the occasional unpollinated blossom that bent inquiringly as they stumbled through the trees. She walked until her knee began to buckle with every step and the yearlings staggered. Then she selected a place where three young trees grew closely spaced and sank to her knees. Carefully she took a sitting position, her back against the broadest of the three trunks. The yearlings settled nearby, grunting and sighing.

Keva closed her eyes, wanting only to rest until it was light enough to walk again. She knew that if she slept, her fingers would numb completely. She might not be able to restore circulation again.

Despite her intentions, her breath grew thick and she slept, her head sagging.

Her dreams were fleeting, tainted with disturbing snatches of familiarity. She saw Oki's face, she saw the curved walls of Tehla's kefri, she saw Danior at the teaching, his eyelids pressed shut. She saw places she had glimpsed through Waana's teaching, saw redmanes running. Confused, she tried to reach after the disparate images, tried to order them into coherence. Sometimes she thought she stood and walked across a familiar plain, only to have the grasses disappear from underfoot. Sometimes she thought she lay asleep in Tehla's kefri.

Sometimes she thought she didn't dream at all. She thought she had wakened and was about to leave her bedding. She had only to kick off her covers, stand . . .

It was during one of these intervals, when she thought the forest around her was real and not a dream, that the white yearling appeared. Keva gazed into the trees and saw a faint brightness. She groaned, trying to bring her eyes to sharper focus, and the brightness stepped nearer and took form: smooth white flanks, delicate hooves, silver-white mane. It approached, stepping lightly. As it neared, the redmane yearlings stirred and raised their heads, their eyes dull with sleep.

The white yearling extended its neck and pressed its smooth pink nose against Keva's cheek. The flesh was warm, the animal's breath soft. Keva moaned, expecting in her confusion to be free at the animal's touch, expecting the ropes to fall away.

They did not. She remained tied, her hands numb, her arms aching. She tried to reach out to the animal but could not. Keva sank back against the tree, squeezing her eyes shut in disappointment.

When she opened them again, the white yearling had withdrawn into the trees. He stood poised for a moment, then turned and cantered silently away. Keva shut her eyes and passed back into the full confusion of her dreams.

Sometime later a sound brought her swimming awake. She opened her eyes and drew breath sharply. This time she was not dreaming. The image was too clear, too sharply delineated.

The desert youth stood over her. She could see the pores of his skin, could trace the line of his hair where it was pulled sharply back, could smell the sweat and dust that stiffened his robes. The knife in his hand was real too. Even without moonlight, she saw the cutting sharpness of its blade.

She saw those things in a fraction of a second and knew, as he bent nearer, that she did not have time to react. She didn't even have time to catch her breath as he brought the knife up and then down in a sure, clean stroke.

It took her a moment to move past shock and realize that the knife had not slashed at her throat, at her chest, at any vital organ. Instead the youth made one swift slash at the ropes that bound her, partially severing them. Then he jumped back, his face white, his eyes glittering.

He hardly seemed to breathe as he watched for Keva's reaction. Clenched muscles stood clearly defined in his forearms and his jaw. After a moment, he lowered the blade. His lips worked stiffly. "See? I would not hurt you. So you will—you will let me untake the ropes." His voice was low, the words wary and boastful at once. When she did not answer, he said, "I speak mountain talk, see? I will unfasten you with ropes."

Keva shook her head dumbly, shock still binding her throat. Surely she imagined him. Or dreamed him. Surely—

"Wrong?" the youth demanded with a subdued flash of anger. "Unfasten you from ropes? Those are the mountain words?"

She did not imagine him. The anger told her that. Keva forced herself to catch a deep breath. "Yes," she said, measuring out the syllables, careful not to betray herself with a hysterical sob of laughter. "Yes, unfasten me from the ropes. Those—those are the words."

"I knew they were," the youth boasted, studying her with frowning intensity. He was as she remembered, wiry, his cheekbones sharp against his wind-burned flesh, his eyes narrow and dark, frowning. Although his robes were soiled, the two strands of fabric at his waist were clean, as if he washed them even when he didn't wash himself.

The youth caught the direction of her gaze and bared his

teeth. "You see my sashes. They show I am of the family Magadaw and of the Greater Clan, which is led by the Viir-Nega. So I am both his clan-kin and his soldier. And you are his kin too. I see it in your face. I saw it when you made the stones dance. Your skin is like his, your brows. But your eyes . . ." He frowned. "He told us he had kin in the mountains. Women."

Keva stared at him, trying to read the glinting intensity of his eyes. The Viir-Nega? She was his kin? *Her father?* Her eyes flashed to the youth's bright sashes. Her father *was* a desert man? He called himself the Viir-Nega? This youth was a member of his clan? And the other desert men, the ones who had pulled the stone from her neck and then fled in panic— perhaps they hadn't been frightened because they took her for a barohna. Perhaps they simply took her for her father's daughter.

Certainly the youth seemed impressed by the kinship. Instinctively she spoke sharply, determined to use the awe she saw in his face to best advantage. "Yes, the Viir-Nega is my kin. Untie me now, please."

Although the youth lost color at the sharpness of her words, his voice quickly regained its boasting edge. "I will. And then I will take you to the Viir-Nega and we will see what he says of me for finding you."

Keva had a moment's misgiving. Was she making a mistake, claiming kinship to a man she had never heard of before today? What might be the price of her presumption if he denounced her? Still she managed to say haughtily, "He'll thank you, I'm sure." But would he? Could the Viir-Nega really be her father, or was he someone else entirely? And how much trust should she put in the youth with his knife and his boasting gaze?

But what choice had she? The youth was her only resource, however governable or ungovernable he might be.

The youth darted her a swift glance, eyes glinting. "Yes, I will take you and he will thank me. And to make public his thanks he will give you to me for my marriage. All I have to do is ask. I am that well-regarded among my people. Then I will have a wife who can draw fire and make stones dance and later I will have a sash with voice and a whitemane to ride beside the Viir-Nega's when we parade to clan-call. I will have all those things with you.''

Keva glanced up sharply, biting back the impulse to a sharp response. Certainly she had no intention of becoming a part of his ambitious plan but she could make that clear later, when her hands were free. "Untie me," she said with all the authority she could summon and was relieved to see fear brighten in his eyes again at the sharpness of her tone.

NINE
DANIOR

The pounding of his boots against the soil, the surging pressure of his blood against his ear drums—Danior ran across the plain to a rhythm of drumming urgency. He hardly noticed the cramping of his legs, the burning of his lungs. He felt only the need to reach Keva before she placed herself in jeopardy. There were so many things she didn't know, so many stories she hadn't heard, and ignorance made her vulnerable. Even if she could tear the soil and make stones fly, she was vulnerable. And he felt her vulnerability as his own.

He ran until the sun rose, until a tight band closed around his chest and he could run no more. Then he stopped and slept, heavily, his fingers curled around the pairing stone.

When Keva woke he woke too and pushed himself again, trying to narrow the gap between them. He had traveled to the forest before, riding there with the guardian daughters to fetch knots of resin to be melted for caulking. Now he stopped occasionally to press the pairing stone and take his bearings from what he saw through Keva's eyes. He recognized rock formations, small groves and stands of trees, brooks and ponds. By mid-afternoon he realized he could not overtake her before she reached the forest. Several hours still separated them, his thighs were weak and cramping, and his eyes were grainy from lack of sleep.

Still he pressed on until the hour after dark. Then the ache of his legs, the pounding of his temples was too much. He spread his bedding under a clump of trees, promising himself it would be for only an hour.

He tossed uneasily, hardly falling asleep before he was drawn into a series of half-waking dreams. His throat burned and he saw tall trees, Nindra and Zan caught in their reaching arms. Then he was beneath the trees and white-faced blossoms reached down. Redmane yearlings moved through a gridwork of moonlight and shadow and he heard them whicker and shrill. He smelled the soporific sweetness of pollen. He sighed under its influence, slipping back into the full darkness of sleep, only to emerge later, wandering the forest again. Vaguely he realized that he clasped the stone, that its light penetrated his closed eyelids. He realized he wasn't dreaming at all. He tried to rouse himself but failed, the heaviness of exhaustion upon him.

Still later his throat began to burn and for a few moments he was caught in a welter of images: mud-smeared faces, glaring teeth, ropes. He stirred in half-waking alarm and struggled against an unaccountable sense that he was bound, his arms pinioned to his sides. He shuddered, shaking himself fully awake, only to have the dream—if it was a dream—end abruptly with the image of a reaching hand. Danior sat, staring into the dark in confusion. Keva? Had he clasped the stone in his sleep again? Had something happened to Keva? His heart hammered with half-apprehended panic. Anxiously he clutched the pairing stone, but nothing came. Confused, disoriented, he lay down again. Perhaps he had only dreamed. Perhaps . . . His thoughts ran no farther before he fell again into exhausted sleep.

It was first light when he woke, his muscles aching, his mouth dry. Instinctively his hand moved to the pairing stone. He pressed it and felt it warm against his palm. But when he reached tentatively for Keva's thoughts, the stone brought nothing. Troubled, he shrugged off his bedding and gazed around uncertainly.

He reached again when he had eaten and could not raise even the stir of memory. Sleeping. She must be sleeping, too tired to dream. He tried to assure himself that it was so. But he was anxious as he rolled his bedding, snapped shut his pack, and set out.

The morning was clear, the air only faintly scented with pollen. As he walked, Danior met yearlings returning to the plain. Their coats were matted and their eyelids drooped. Their noses were smeared yellow with pollen. They scarcely grunted in passing.

By midday, when his stone lay warm in his palm and he still could not touch Keva's thoughts, he was able to reassure himself no longer. He passed the place where the yearlings had slept the evening before, where Keva had slept. A few yearlings slept there again, but there was no sign that Keva had returned from the forest with them.

Something had happened to her. The thought, repressed through the earlier hours of the day, came to him with grinding clarity. Otherwise he would be able to touch her thoughts, would be able to see what she saw, hear what she heard. Instead there was only silence.

Troubled, he ran toward the trees.

The soil of the forest was trampled. Blossoms hung drunkenly from long stems, furled tight. Danior hesitated, gazing around, wondering what he must do, where he must search. Reluctantly he thought of predators and desert clansmen. Remembered the confusion of dreams from the night before: ropes, mud-smeared faces, a reaching hand. Remembered the unfounded panic that had made his heart pound. Had it been Keva's instead of his own?

Disturbed, he threw off his pack and crouched under the trees. Perhaps he simply had not tried hard enough to reach her. Perhaps he had let fatigue raise barriers between them. Quickly he took the stone in hand and inhaled deeply, putting every other thought away. The stone warmed immediately and he felt the heat of active nerve centers at the base of his throat. He held the stone before him, staring into it, trying to find his way into Keva's thoughts. If he reached deeply enough, if he extended himself fully—

He breathed deeply, investing himself entirely in the stone, in its growing light. Losing himself in it. He let its brilliance fill his eyes. His throat began to burn. He reached.

For long moments he was aware only of the blaze of the stone. Then alien memories began to take form: far stretches of a harsh land, a sun that burned too brightly, empty cooking pots, quenched fires, hunger. Frowning, he reached deeper and had a confused impression of a sweaty body, of crusted finger-nails, of brooding anger compounded by fear and a stinging sense of injustice. The forest floor lay underfoot and there were companions nearby, the sweat of fear upon them. And they were angry too, as angry as himself. He could read it in every dark face, in every burning eye. He—

He . . . Danior pulled back, stung to panic. *Where was Keva?* And why had the stone taken him into a stranger's thoughts? Danior swallowed down the sour rise of fear—fear that could only erect further barriers. Disciplining himself, he pressed his eyes shut and forced himself to take several steady-ing breaths before reaching again. As he reached, he held an image of Keva in mind: her face, the arch of her brows, the deepness of her eyes.

Effort. He was aware of effort, of his throat first cooling and then catching fire. And then the memories came, of hissing waters and coiling weeds and a heavy-limbed woman who hovered possessively. A man sat beside the streambank spin-ning tales, another man rode a whitemane, a bluesong reached out for sunlight and breeze.

Danior pressed his eyelids tighter, trying to reach past memory to the present.

Suddenly he had a wavering vision of a dark face: narrow eyes, hungry cheekbones, lean jaws—the youth who had leapt at the whitemane yearling and narrowly missed being stoned. Alarmed, Danior let the vision waver. Then, catching himself, he drew a deep breath and held it, clarifying the vision. The youth sat under the trees, a knife buried blade-first in the soil beside him, his hand clenching and unclenching on its handle. He was speaking, but although he strained, Danior could not hear what he said.

Keva—he felt her presence now. She sat near the youth, eating. Bread, cheese—he felt the food on her tongue but could not identify it. Nor could he hear what she said when she spoke or fathom the emotion that lay behind the words. It was the desert youth who came to him most clearly. A complex of emotions played across his lean face: wariness, uncertainty, fear. He tried to hide them behind arrogance and only partially succeeded. He played with the knife constantly, pulling the blade from the ground, then tossing it with a sharp flip of his wrist, burying it again.

They sat, eating, talking, while Danior struggled to bring the scene to clear focus, to hear what they said. Before he was able to do so, Keva and the desert youth stood, packing their possessions, and began to walk.

Danior lost the vision then. He sank back on his heels, his face wet with perspiration, his hands trembling. It was minutes before he was able to stand, quivering with relief.

He had found Keva and she didn't seem to be in immediate danger. Though why had it taken so much more effort to reach her today than ever before? He rubbed his throat, puzzled. The distance that separated them was less now. And he was more practiced.

Perhaps the fact that he was tired and anxious, that she was distracted by the desert youth's presence made it more difficult to reach her. At least now he knew she was in the forest. And from the slant of light through the trees, he knew the direction she traveled.

Toward the southern perimeter of the forest. Toward the roughlands and the desert that lay beyond.

He frowned, remembering the snatch of memory that had come when he first tried to use the stone. A desert man's memory. Had he somehow reached past Keva's thoughts into the desert youth's mind?

No, the person he had reached had had companions—desert men like himself. Angry and seething with injustice.

And they were in the forest too. Quickly Danior slung his pack over his shoulder and took up his pike, a fresh sense of danger fueling his stiff muscles.

He used the stone to guide him. Each time he reached, he found the distance that separated him from Keva and the desert youth less. By late afternoon he began to recognize individual trees she had passed earlier. Once a straggling group of redmane yearlings stumbled past, tossing tangled manes, yellow pollen still clinging to their noses. Eventually Danior found the print of Keva's boots and the desert youth's bare feet and followed their trail.

It was near sunset when Keva and the youth abruptly changed direction, veering eastward. Danior halted, peering at the forest floor, and quickly realized why they had done so.

There were hoofprints in the soil, a single line leading eastward. Danior studied the prints, something that had troubled him suddenly coming clear.

The youth had been tracking a whitemane yearling when Keva first saw him. He had stalked it through the trees and lunged without rope or weapon. Now, staring down at the track of hooves, Danior realized why. He had been trying to mark the whitemane.

Danior frowned, considering that conclusion and its implications. The youth wore his hair knotted as Jhaviir had worn his. He tied colored sashes at his waist—and now he was tracking a whitemane. If the youth were trying to emulate Jhaviir, then Jhaviir must be alive—in the desert. He must have influence. Position. Legend.

Legend to be carried back to his father. Tales of places Jhaviir had ridden, people he had seen. Danior's hand tightened on the haft of his pike. For the first time, he recognized the stirring of Birnam Rauth's blood in himself. He felt it in the rising beat of his pulse, in the fresh eagerness that toned his muscles. He wanted to see strange places and alien people too, wanted to quench his curiosity with them—a curiosity he hadn't even guessed he owned. Quickly he turned to follow the tracks in the soil, hardly noticing this time that his thighs ached and his calves cramped as he ran.

He didn't use the stone again. Soon he was near enough to hear the faint sound of Keva's and the youth's feet, near enough to see them slipping among the trees. They walked single file, the youth leading the way, studying the whitemane's tracks, Keva following with her pack and the youth's bundled possessions. Danior tracked them cautiously, keeping his distance, occasionally moving near enough to reaffirm his impression that Keva accompanied the youth willingly, without constraint.

Eventually the sun slid below the horizon and the forest grew dark. The youth hissed and he and Keva halted and sat to eat. Danior moved nearer, barely able to glimpse them in the shadows. They talked, a low murmur, but Danior was wary of moving close enough to understand. Then their voices fell to nothing and Danior guessed they were napping until the moons rose.

He moved nearer, tensely, wondering if he should try to wake Keva, to let her know he was near. She slept curled against a tree, just a few paces from where the youth slept. If he moved quietly enough, if she didn't cry out when he touched her, when he shook her—

The youth drew a sighing breath and shifted, muttering to himself, and Danior retreated. He would catch her attention later, when she woke. He crouched behind a nearby tree, wondering if she would be relieved to see him, or if she would be angry that he had followed her. Wondering why the stone did not take him deeply enough into her thoughts now to guess her reaction. He hugged himself against evening chill and soon, without intending it, he slept too.

The moons had risen when he woke—woke to a sense of presence. He opened his eyes warily, half expecting to find the desert youth standing over him. Instead he saw a whitemane stallion poised among the trees, moonlight shimmering on its smooth, snowy pelt. Its mane lay like silver upon its arched neck and its eyes were pink transparencies. *Fiirsevrin* . . . but there was no five-fingered flame upon this whitemane's brow. It moved through the trees with unconquered aloofness.

Had it come for him, as Fiirsevrin had once come for his father? Cautiously Danior took his feet. He held his breath as the animal approached, pleased that it did not seem afraid, that it seemed simply curious. He exhaled gently, standing very still, letting the animal come nearer. If the stories he had heard were true, if the whitemanes were descended from animals the first-timers had turned out because they could not feed them, then perhaps he held as much fascination for the whitemane as it held for him. And if he could touch it, if he could place his mark upon it—

The animal came near enough for him to catch its scent, light and dry. Near enough for him to feel its body heat. Slowly, with a sense of unreality, Danior raised one hand. But before he could extend it, the whitemane pricked its ears and took a wary step back, raising its head sharply.

The desert youth emerged from the shadows of a tall tree. Moonlight touched his staring eyes, silvering them. His prominent cheekbones thrust at the thin flesh of his face. His lips drew back, leaving his teeth unguarded. He seemed not to breathe. Keva stood behind him, her face shadowed.

Danior caught a steadying breath, reluctantly shrinking back into the shadows. If the whitemane had come for anyone, it must be for the desert youth. He was the one who had tracked the animal. He was the one who had faced the hail of stones, yet come back to try again. And he was the one whose eagerness glittered in his eyes, rasped in his throat.

Jerkily the youth extended one hand. Danior was not surprised to see that it trembled as the youth took a single step, then another toward the whitemane. As he slipped closer to the animal, he slowly raised his extended hand. The whitemane retreated nervously and the youth froze. Then the animal stepped forward again and extended its head, nostrils flaring.

The youth's hand trembled so violently Danior was afraid he would frighten the animal away. But the whitemane was curious. It bent to smell the youth's loose trousers. And the youth thrust out one thin, dark hand and pressed the animal's brow.

For moments only the whitemane moved, casually sampling the admixture of odors the desert youth carried on his trousers. Only the whitemane breathed, snorting softly. Danior, the youth, Keva—all stood frozen. Then, slowly, reverently, the youth drew his hand back.

The whitemane's brow remained white. The youth's fingers left no mark.

Danior wished afterward that he had not even glimpsed the youth's face in the moment after that. Wished he had not seen the swift, fiery desolation. The youth took a single step backward, his face drained of color, his lips twisting. Then, the muscles of his jaw knotting, his hand fell and he twisted his knife from his waistband. Startled, the whitemane raised pink eyes to him and retreated a few nervous steps.

Before Danior guessed what he intended, the youth flung himself at the animal, tangling the fingers of one hand in its mane. He caught the blade of his knife between his teeth, freeing the other hand, and with it seized at the whitemane's neck. Grunting, he clawed his way to the animal's back.

The alarmed animal backed away, then began to rear, screaming with fright. Its delicate front hooves thrashed the air. It arched its neck and quivered. Then it arched its back and began to buck and heave, its breath coming in heavy gouts. The desert youth clung, eyes glinting, sashes flying.

Danior pressed himself against a tree trunk, trying to avoid flying hooves. The whitemane rolled its eyes and scraped the youth's legs against the trunk of a rough-barked tree. When he still clung, the animal pounded away through the trees, bucking and rearing, shrilling angrily. Danior gasped, seeing the downward flash of the youth's knife blade as the animal carried him into the trees.

Then the youth flew from the animal's back, arms helter-skelter. He smashed to the ground and lay struggling for breath. The whitemane fled, hooves beating a drum rhythm.

Danior and Keva ran to the desert youth. His eyes stared and his mouth gaped painfully as he fought for breath. A trickle of blood ran from his nose. In one hand he clutched a swatch of the whitemane's mane. Keva bent over him, helping him sit.

"My knife—" he choked when he was able to draw breath.

"Over there. You dropped it."

Following the direction of Keva's glance, Danior retrieved the knife without thinking and placed it in the youth's hand—and realized from the sudden frozen immobility of the youth's features that his attention had been so concentrated on the whitemane that he had not noticed Danior until now.

The youth heaved himself to his feet, the cords of his neck standing out, his fingers white-knuckled on the knife handle. His eyes darted from Danior to Keva and back again. He uttered a sharp demand in a language Danior did not know.

Before Danior could guess how to respond, Keva caught his arm. "Rezni, this is my kinsman, Danior—Danior Terlath. Danior, this is Rezni, the Nathri-Varnitz—Bold Soldier of the Viir-Nega."

Danior's glance flickered to the youth's knife, then back to his rigid face. How could Keva speak so calmly when the youth seemed poised to leap? How could she nod with as much composure as if she had just introduced one friend to another? As he hesitated, her fingers tightened on his arm again. And this time he realized, with a start, what she intended the light pressure to tell him. That he must follow her lead. Must not let the youth see that he was frightened or confused. Must respond as calmly to the introduction as if the youth did not hold a raised knife. Danior steeled himself to offer the traditional welcome to strangers. "My valley warms at your approach, Rezni. I hope you leave yours green."

The youth's eyes narrowed, but the knotted muscles of his jaw relaxed slightly. "You are kinsman of the Flame? What—what degree is this kinship?"

The Flame? Before Danior could let doubt show, Keva squeezed his wrist again. "The Nathri-Varnitz is taking me to meet our kinsman, the Viir-Nega: Savior of the Greater Clan. He has honored me by offering me marriage and a place at his back during the next clan-call. Under the circumstances, you can tell him the degree of our kinship."

Marriage? Danior darted a startled glance at Keva. Surely she had not agreed to marriage with a desert man. Not in the short time since they had been separated. "You haven't—"

"How can I accept when I already have obligations to the throne of Valley Marlath?"

"The Flame of Marlath can burn in my *han-tau* despite all her encumbrances," Rezni interjected fiercely. "There are more places than the mountains for a woman who can make stone live."

So she had not agreed. But something in the flicker of her eyes when she met his startled glance, something in the continued pressure of her fingers on his wrist told Danior he must speak carefully. Told him she followed some considered strategy with the youth. Danior licked dry lips. "Of course there are," he agreed. Was she simply trying to confound the youth, to immobilize his aggressive instincts by impressing him with her importance? Was that why she called herself the Flame of Marlath, why she claimed to hold her mother's throne? He spoke carefully, hoping he guessed her intent correctly. "But the Flame—the Flame has heavy encumbrances. She has the responsibility for all the people of her valley. For the success of their crops, for all the food they eat. I know because I am— I am her Rauth-brother."

The youth frowned suspiciously, glancing from one to the other of them. He spoke stiffly. "I don't know that kinship."

"It means our fathers were the same man once," Danior said, extemporizing. "Though they are no longer, of course."

The youth stared at him. "Of course," he muttered, as if he understood. But it clearly angered him that he did not. His voice took a hostile edge. His eyes narrowed. "You frightened away my whitemane. You were hidden here and you startled him."

"Danior wasn't hidden at all, Rezni," Keva contradicted him immediately. "I saw him."

"Perhaps you did, but I didn't. And my whitemane ran. If he had stayed, if I had touched him again—"

Danior recoiled at the youth's accusing tone, his thoughts taking an intuitive leap. "No, he—he was too old to be marked," he said with as much authority as if he knew it to be true. His father, after all, had marked Fiirsevrin when he was little more than a foal. Jhaviir, or so legend said, had marked his steed when it was a yearling. But this whitemane had been an adult stallion, too old perhaps to bond himself to a master. "You— you have to find a younger animal, one who hasn't come into his final growth. And you must never frighten a whitemane by riding him before he knows you."

"If I hadn't taken his back, I wouldn't have even his hair to show," the youth retorted bitterly, flourishing the swatch of gleaming white mane. "I would have nothing."

Nothing. For a moment desolation burned in Rezni's eyes again, and Danior realized with quick surprise that he understood the desert youth. Apparently the desert was a place of legends just as the mountains were, and Rezni had none. He had come to the forest hunting a whitemane to mark, but the first animal had eluded him and now the second one had run away. He had offered marriage to Keva and she had spun him a tale of responsibilities in far places. By rights—if Danior correctly understood the mores of the clans from tales he had heard—the youth should simply have taken her, but she had shown herself too dangerous for that. And now Danior had come and spun more confounding words Rezni could not admit he didn't understand.

Rezni had nothing as surely as Danior had had nothing before he touched the pairing stone. And the society of the desert clans must be far less kind to a man who had nothing than the society of the mountains.

"We can track him if you don't believe me," Danior said.

Rezni stared at him suspiciously, licking his lips. Finally he shook his head, hostility abating. "No. I promised the Viir-Nega I would return to Pan-Vi in time for clan-call, even if I found no whitemane. There is no more time left for tracking."

"The call is in three days," Keva explained quickly to Danior. "And of course the Viir-Nega will want to present us to the clan at that time."

Danior hesitated momentarily, then nodded. The Viir-Nega. Pan-Vi. Clan-call. So many things he didn't understand, but apparently Keva did. And apparently she knew some reason why they should accompany Rezni, why they should trust him. Unconsciously his hand rose to his throat. If he could use the pairing stone to touch Keva's thoughts . . . Unconsciously he flicked a glance at her throat.

Her neck was bare. Surprised, Danior glanced toward her pack. Had she hidden her stone from Rezni? Or had the desert youth confiscated it? "Your stone," he said, touching his own lightly, with his fingertips.

Keva rubbed her bare neck, shrugging. "It was stolen. Last night."

"And she refused to raise the earth," Rezni expanded immediately. "She is a barohna from the mountains. She can make stone live. With the right stone, she can call down fire from the sun. But she let men from one of the small-clans tie her and take her jewelry. If she had thrown the same stones at them she threw at me—"

"I don't—I don't do that unless I have to, Rezni."

"Against me? It was necessary to do it against me and not against the small-men? When I'm a soldier of the Viir-Nega?"

Danior recognized an argument that had been aired before. But he had no time to reflect on Rezni's grievance. Keva's stone had been stolen—the night before. Yet he had reached into her thoughts today.

Not easily. Not well. But he had reached them.

He had reached someone else's thoughts too. Those of a desert man with dirt-caked nails and an angry hunger. *The man who had stolen Keva's pairing stone.*

But the stones were not supposed to work that way. He should not have been able to touch anyone's thoughts but Keva's—and hers only when she wore the stone.

He should not have been able to reach behind the bluesong either and see yellow-eyed predators prowling an alien forest. Dizzily he raised a hand to his throat, then realized Rezni had stopped speaking and was staring at the stone. Danior knotted his hand, drawing it away—but not before he felt the first vagrant warmth of the stone. "If we have only three days, we'd better walk before we sleep tonight," he said quickly.

Rezni's attention was not so easily deflected. His narrow eyes contracted to slits. "That stone—it's like the jewel Keva described to me. But you've made it light."

"I—" Danior darted an uncertain glance at Keva. But what guidance could she give him? She had worn the other stone in ignorance, considering it simply a piece of jewelry, a keepsake from her father.

Now she stared at the stone he wore. "You didn't have that the last time I saw you," she said slowly.

"I was carrying it in my pack." If only he could speak to her alone, without Rezni. If only they could spend just a few minutes answering each other's questions—

Rezni's eyes darted from one to the other, his face suddenly darkening with angry comprehension. "*I know that stone.* The Viir-Nega has described stones like that to us. You carry a thought-stone and you thought I would never recognize it—as if I were an ignorant man of the small-clans instead the Nathri-Varnitz, given that title by the Viir-Nega himself." He turned on Keva. "And you told me it was a piece of jewelry the small-clansmen stole. You said it was an ornament you wore on a ribbon. You didn't even raise the earth. You let them take a thought-stone and now they can see everything we do. When we reach Pan-Vi, they will see into the heart of our campment as if—as if they stood there in the flesh. They will hear everything the Viir-Nega plans. They will watch when we go to quarry fire-coals. They will attack when we are most poorly guarded and shatter our panes and let our gardens die."

"No, the other stone is useless to the small-clansmen," Danior assured him quickly. "Keva's the only person who can use it. In anyone else's hands, it's only what she told you—an ornament."

Rezni's eyes narrowed. "You tell me that? In truth?"

"Yes. If you know about the stones—"

"The Viir-Nega has told us everything about the stones," the youth said sharply. "And we have tales of our own about them too. Every clan has tales of the atrocities that drove them out into the hard-lands. There are stones that see far distances—"

"Eyestones," Danior confirmed. "The barohnas used to mount them on their palace towers, to keep watch over the valleys. They're seldom used now. My mother has never commissioned one."

"Stones that hold sunlight and loose it and burn everything."

"Sunstones. They're used to heat the valleys so crops can grow. They were used for—for other things during the troubled times. But no one uses them that way now. No one—"

"Thought-stones," Rezni continued relentlessly, nodding at the pairing stone. "Stones that carry thoughts from person to person."

"But only among certain persons."

"You have one."

"Yes, it was paired to Keva's stone. But the men who stole her stone will never be able to use it. They don't have barohnial blood. The power of the stones is inherited."

Abruptly Rezni relented. He squatted and pegged his knife blade-first into the ground. He watched it quiver there. "They can't spy on our campment with it?"

"No. It's impossible."

"But if the stones are paired—can they spy on you? Since you hold the other stone? Can they use it to enter Pan-Vi through your thoughts if I take you there to present you to the Viir-Nega?"

"No," Danior assured him, distractedly, as something Keva had said earlier struck him. *Our kinsman, the Viir-Nega.* Did she think—

But Rezni reclaimed his attention, drawing his knife blade free and thumping it into the earth again. Small muscles tightened under his eyes. "Can you use your stone to spy on them?"

Danior shuddered, feeling the intensity of his gaze like a blade. "I already have."

"Ah, because you have barohnial blood, as Keva does." He gazed at the stone, his pupils contracting to dark points. "My family-clan, the Magadaw, came from the mountains a long time ago. In the time of atrocities. My father and my father's father have told me what strains our blood carries. Not all the children of the barohnas were raised in palaces, you know. Some were turned out to live with the slaves who worked in the fields."

Danior read the direction of his thoughts immediately, from his words and from the speculative covetousness of his gaze. Anxious to dispell any dangerous misconception, Danior took the chain from his neck and displayed the pairing stone on the palm of his hand. It glowed softly, then became more brilliant, staining his fingers, his wrist, with light—staining Rezni's face when he bent near. "You take it," he said.

Rezni's pupils widened. He took the stone with lean fingers and dropped it to the palm of his hand. It darkened immediately.

"An ornament," Danior said, relieved the stone had not betrayed him. "For me it's a thought-stone. For you it's an ornament."

For a moment disappointment darkened Rezni's lean face. He stared at the stone, trying to will it to life. When it did not respond, he returned it to Danior with a rejecting shrug. "So I will bring the Viir-Nega a barohna from the mountains and a stone that will take us into the camps of our enemies. It's enough. Even the whitemane is a small loss."

A small loss to the legend that would accrue when he returned bringing powerful allies. Danior hung the pairing stone at his neck again and exchanged a long glance with Keva. He found no hint that she was reluctant to be taken to the Viir-Nega as the Bold Soldier's offering. No hint that she wanted to turn back, with or without Danior's help.

Because she thought the Viir-Nega was her father? Could it be? And if it was—

Danior bit his lip, thinking again of the pairing stone. He had accurately described its function to Rezni. What he had not told Rezni was that it was not functioning as a pairing stone should. He should not have been able to use it to reach the clansman who had stolen the other stone. He should not have been able to reach Keva when she did not wear her stone. And the bluesong—

A tool. The pairing stone was a tool, one that behaved differently for him than it would have for another—because he was different from any person who had used a pairing stone before. He told himself that firmly. He had taken the stone in hand, he had practiced its use, and he had learned what he could do with it.

He had taken the stone in hand and it had brought him here. And now it was going to take him to the desert with Keva and

Rezni. To a place he had never thought to see, perhaps to Jhaviir as well. He touched the stone and felt a quick surge of anticipation.

As if reading his acceptance, Rezni stood briskly. "You are right, Danior Terlath. We have only three days. There is no time to sleep."

TEN

KEVA

They walked through the hours of moonlight, Rezni setting the pace, pausing anxiously each time Keva or Danior lagged, as if they were precious acquisitions that might slip from his grasp. Twice they heard movement in the trees. Each time Rezni called a halt, pressing a finger to his lips. "Men from one of the small-clans," he announced. "Listen—you can tell from the way they stumble. No man from the Greater Clan walks so heavily, not since the Viir-Nega taught us silent-stalking. We move as silently as moonlight."

Keva listened to the faint brush of bare feet. When the clansmen passed and Rezni took his fingers from his lips, Danior peered into the trees. His voice was low. "How many parties come for the running?"

"Many. They come from most of the fifty-three small-clans—and the three larger clans send several parties."

"And the Greater Clan? Does the Viir-Nega send men to steal redmanes?"

Rezni snorted disdainfully. "The Viir-Nega knows how little redmanes are worth in the hard-lands. He brought one to us once, a mare, and had it talk in our minds, those who could hear it. Now we understand why it is a waste to bring them to the desert. We can't give them the right foods. And they can't live without their herds. They die."

"But the small-clans apparently find some use for them," Danior persisted.

"The small-clans take them so they can brag about how many they have captured," Rezni retorted haughtily. "They try to make them work, but they die too quickly. So all that's left are the hides and the meat. A dishonor to eat that if you have ever heard a redmane teach. But of course the small-clansmen have not because they have no Viir-Nega to teach them to listen."

"The Viir-Nega spent time on the plain when he was younger. He lived with the guardians for a summer when he was a boy," Keva explained, wondering if Danior understood what she was trying to tell him: that she suspected the Viir-Nega was her father. If she could only speak to Danior directly, without tailoring every remark for Rezni's ears—

But it had seemed important earlier to claim long acquaintance. How could Rezni look at the two of them and guess that they had only met once? That she didn't know the actual degree of their kinship, couldn't guess why Danior had followed her here? What Danior had said about their fathers, that they had been the same person once—was that why he had come? Why he had put aside his initial wariness of Rezni to accompany them to the desert? She shook her head, confused. How could their fathers have been both the same person and different persons? Surely that was simply something Danior had thrown out to confound Rezni.

As they resumed their trek, she thought of other things Danior had told Rezni: that the stone the clansmen had stolen had been paired to his stone, that the two stones had been created to link the thoughts of the two people who wore them. Unconsciously her hand rose to her throat. Was that why he had followed her, how he had found her? Because of the stones? But her stone had never glowed as she had seen his do earlier.

Perhaps only Danior had the use of the pairing stone. She shivered and hoped it was so.

They walked until the moons set and there was only starlight to guide them. By that time they neared the edge of the forest and her knee throbbed. The trees were sparse. Thorny bush encroached. "We'll sleep here," Rezni said. "Under the bushes, where none of those stumblers will trip over us."

Danior glanced around doubtfully, some of his earlier wariness returning. "If the small-clansmen did find us—"

"Then they would cut our throats for what we carry. That's how it is among the small-clansmen."

"And among the Greater Clansmen?" Danior spoke softly, probing.

"The Viir-Nega's principles of honor teach that stealing is dishonorable. So if we stumble across small-clansmen hiding out here, I will cut their throats simply to prevent them from cutting ours, but I will not touch their possessions. Here— don't let the thorns scratch you. They're venomous at this time of year."

Danior paled at the contrast between Rezni's casual callousness and his concern for their comfort. Keva slid under the bushes and squirmed against the soft soil, guessing how doubtful he must be. Because she shared his reservations. But if she did not go with Rezni, she would never know if the man who called himself the Viir-Nega was her father.

She expected, from the tired ache of her muscles, to sleep immediately. But she found herself thinking instead, wondering what she would find when they reached Pan-Vi—the Greater Clan's desert settlement. She stretched stiff muscles, considering all the things Rezni had told her, about himself, about the Viir-Nega, about his own family, wondering how many were true. Wondering to what extent he was even to be trusted. He was boastful, he was suspicious, he was callous, but he had untied her, he had rubbed her limbs to life and fed her, he had ridden the whitemane.

And he was taking her to the Viir-Nega. She shifted, peering through the shadows, hoping to find Rezni's face unguarded in sleep. Instead he watched her as he would watch a treasure he feared would be stolen, his eyes gleaming wakefully. Keva sighed and turned away.

The next day they crossed the roughlands that lay between the forest and the desert, walking silently, alert for sign of small-clansmen. Keva's knee hurt less than it had the day before; she had thrown away the soiled wrappings and it was little swollen. Occasionally they saw redmane droppings in the thorny vegetation. Once they found a dead yearling. Danior knelt beside it but could not say what had caused its death. "Every year the small-clansmen take animals and every year they die," Rezni observed. "They eat too much mutton. It makes their minds as small as their clans."

Later they found three clansmen sprawled in the brush, scowling at the afternoon sun with fierce, dead faces. Their throats had been slashed, their bodies stripped of everything but their loose trousers. Rezni kicked their stiffening legs and studied the ground for prints. "Thieves steal from thieves," he observed this time and walked away.

Keva met Danior's eyes and saw that he was as sickened as she.

But in other ways the journey stirred something in Danior Keva had not seen before. After they left the forest, he questioned Rezni closely about vegetation and land formations, about game animals and water sources. He made Rezni show him the burrows of small seed gatherers, insisted that Rezni point out tracks in the rough ground, and when he learned that Rezni had trained to spar with pikes, Danior cut down a tree limb and engaged him.

Renzi had not been trained to show quarter and Danior emerged from the encounter bruised, with a bleeding lump on his forehead. But in some way Keva did not understand, the episode cemented a comradeship between them that excluded her. Much of the time after that, she walked separately from them and listened to their talk without giving it full attention. She had thoughts of her own to preoccupy her, and Rezni and Danior seemed to have much to discuss.

They reached the desert the next day and Keva quickly learned she did not like the long, harsh-lit distances, the crackling dryness of the sparse vegetation, the hissing of the wind. But Rezni's eyes glinted with pleasure as he dug bare toes into the fine granules that drifted across the ground in many places and piled against the dry vegetation. "Silica sand," he told Danior.

"We saw no use for it until the Viir-Nega taught us to melt it to make glass. Now we join our glass panes and make *han-taus,* so we have homes and gardens in one, and you will see how well we live with this sand to help us."

Danior scooped up a handful of sand and watched it trickle between his fingers. "You grow crops? I didn't think there was enough water in the desert for that."

"There is if your *han-tau* is well sealed and if your Viir-Nega has shown you how to dig wells and how to develop forage plants into crop plants. There are methods for everything, uses for everything, once you learn them, and now we have. We mix the soil, we plant the seed, we water them. When the seeds sprout, they take up the water and when they have used it, they exhale it again. It clouds on the panes at night, when the air outside is cold, and drops back to the soil in the morning. That's why we're stronger than the small clansmen, because we know these things. The small-clans live on stringy mutton and forage, but the Viir-Nega has taught us to grow green food all through the year."

Danior nodded thoughtfully. "Has he ever told you where he learned to grow crops under glass?"

"In a place no one on Brakrath knows but him. A place so far away he can never go back. He brought our clan language and the principles of honor from the same place and gave them to us. He can never go back to his rightful people, so he has made us his people."

Keva sharpened to attention. Was that why her father had ridden so far—because he was trying to find his people? And if that were so, who were his people? "But he won't teach the small-clansmen how to make glass and grow gardens?" she said doubtfully. Was that like her father, to hold knowledge so closely, to refuse to share it, whatever its source?

"He'll teach anyone who pledges to the Greater Clan. But the small-clansmen would rather come and break our panes than learn. Just as they rip each other's tents and steal each other's women. Their minds are small. They don't have the Viir-Nega's principles of honor to discipline them."

So it was not the Viir-Nega who was small-minded. Keva gazed around, and decided it was not so surprising the clansmen were brutal, with the silica sands slithering underfoot and the wind hissing from every direction.

It was hot on the third day of their journey. Keva's clothes, heavy-woven to repel streamside mists, clung. The watering spots Rezni showed them were brackish and the forage he found left her mouth sour. When he trapped a small animal and wrung its neck, she shuddered and could not eat. After Danior and Rezni had eaten, she trudged behind them and thought of sweet, cool bulbs harvested from the mud at the bottom of the warmstream, of pungent, juicy root strands, of weed stems dried, salted and braided into chewy ropes.

She kicked at the ground, sweat damping her hair and trickling down her back, and was not aware of much beyond her wandering thoughts when Rezni's lean fingers suddenly closed on her forearm. She started, too surprised to protest as he pulled her down behind a clump of brittle vegetation. Danior already lay on his stomach.

"There—small-clansmen," Rezni hissed. "Don't raise your head. They have redmanes. Walking Adder Spring is just ahead. They're taking them to drink."

Keva stared through dried branches in the direction he indicated. The clansmen were some distance away, indistinct shapes, but she could see that they drove their small herd of yearlings almost directly toward the brush where she, Danior and Rezni lay. "They'll see us," she said in sharp alarm.

"Not if we're still." Rezni squirmed against the sandy soil. "Push yourself down into the sand. Don't raise your arms or legs. Just brush them back and forth until you've made a hollow and the sand trickles in." Quickly he demonstrated, rocking back and forth until the loose grains yielded a hollow for his body and filtered in to cover it.

Danior and Keva followed suit, burrowing into the warm sand. Sharp grains worked between Keva's clothing and her skin, making her itch.

The clansmen neared. Soon she heard their voices, heard the

reluctant clump of padded feet. Peering through the dried brush, she watched a dozen yearlings labor through the warm sand, heads hanging, eyes dull. Five clansmen in soiled tunics drove them, beating their flanks with knotted ropes. The clansmen wore their hair loose and long. Their faces were weathered dark, their voices as harsh as the land.

"Gothni," Rezni hissed.

"You know them?" Danior whispered.

"Well." Rezni's lean face drew tight with scorn.

The clansmen were too preoccupied with the march to notice three pair of eyes watching them from the brush. But as the yearlings drew near, the most alert raised its head and halted, testing the air. The tallest clansman kicked its flanks, muttering angrily, but the yearling refused to move. It shrilled, then cocked its head, listening. Finally it lowered its head and broke free of the group, sniffing the sandy soil.

Rezni muttered angrily as the yearling followed its nose toward the brush, a single clansman yelping after it, flailing with his rope. Keva pressed her face to the sand, but when she heard the clansman's sharp exhalation, she knew they had been seen.

Before she could react, Rezni heaved himself free of the sand, knife in hand. Danior followed suit, shoulders tense, face ashen, one hand closed around the haft of his pike. Uncertainly Keva stood, shaking away sand, remembering all the things Rezni had said of the small-clansmen. Surely he had exaggerated, painting them meaner than they were.

Surely. But the men she had met in the forest—

The single clansman retreated one step in surprise, then flung his rope aside and snatched the knife from his waist. The long blade flashed. His kinsmen froze. Then they too were crouched, blades in hand, advancing warily. Keva stared at their bared teeth, their narrowed eyes, her pulse suddenly racing with remembered fear.

Before she could respond, Rezni seized her arm, addressing the advancing clansmen sharply in a language of harsh consonants and sputtering vowels. They halted and looked from Rezni to Keva uncertainly. The nearer clansman licked his lips nervously, eyes darting.

"*Now!*" Rezni hissed into Keva's ear. "Now or it will be too late. I've told them you are a barohna from the mountains."

"You've told them—" Keva twisted to stare at him, not understanding. The clansmen gaped at her, nervous pulses beating in their bare throats, the smell of fear on them. Fear, she realized, because he had told them she was a barohna. She turned, staring at Rezni's strained face, realizing what he wanted of her.

What Danior wanted too. "Keva—" he urged softly.

They wanted her to tear up the earth. To break loose its stony foundation and throw it in pieces at the small-clansmen. Rezni thought he could use her like a weapon, and Danior thought she must let herself be used so. She shook her head angrily, pulling free of his grasp.

And the clansmen, seeing her confusion, moved. The tallest uttered a vengeful series of syllables and backed away, seizing the nearest yearling by the mane. Swiftly he pulled the startled animal's head back and plunged his knife into its throat.

Immediately the other clansmen retreated, throwing themselves at the grunting yearlings, knives raised. Keva's heart closed tight in shock. She stared, unable to move, to understand.

"*Now*—or they'll kill them all," Rezni hissed. "They'll leave nothing but carcasses."

"They—" Keva couldn't believe what she saw, what she heard. It happened too quickly, overwhelming her. The screams of the yearlings, the stained blades, the blood—it came in a crimson spray, and suddenly her chest felt heavy, as if she were drowning. As if her lungs were filling with the yearlings' blood.

No, not blood. It was an agent manufactured deep in her own cells that filled her lungs, excluding oxygen. An agent that made her reel dizzily, reaching numb fingers toward her temples. She groped for control but a floating sense of timelessness overtook her and she could not even raise her hands to press staying fingers to her pounding pulses.

Time. It had become a tangible stream. It buoyed her, carrying her beyond the present moment and its imperatives, beyond anything she understood. She fought helplessly against its current, against its eddies and undertows, against the vortex she knew

lay ahead. But the struggle was useless. She already felt herself
drawn into the black maw. She already heard the grating sound
of sand being whirled into the air. Hundreds of sharp granules,
thousands, countless millions, lifted and boiled. Before she
could call them back, they formed a spinning funnel that reached
abrasive arms for the clansmen. It enfolded them, muffling
their screams, obscuring their thrashing limbs. It grew, becoming so dense the air seemed solid. Solid and moving at once.
Grinding.

At last Keva's reaching fingers found her temples. She pressed,
trying to establish control. If she were the one who held the
sand in the air—

And she knew she was. Because as she pressed her temples
and gasped for breath, as she sucked oxygen into her lungs, the
vortex slowed. Grains of sand began to spin free and fall back
to the ground. She continued to draw shallow, panting breaths
and sand rained from the air. It fell away until the vortex was
an ephemeral thing, a spinning scarlet tracery, a veil.

And the things the veil hid—no, it did not hide them. It
pulled away and revealed them. Grotesque things that had been
men and now were only masses of raw flesh. Keva stared
disbelievingly as the last of the blood-stained sand fell from
the air.

The yearlings had dropped to their knees, instinctively huddling
together against the abrasive sand. Their thick coats had been
sheared away, their auburn manes shredded, their ears scrubbed
to bloody stubs. They shivered violently, but they were alive,
those the clansmen had not killed before the sand rose.

The clansmen were dead, skin and muscle eaten by the
whirling sand.

Keva stared at them. This was her work. She had called up
the sand. She had made it spin. Now she clutched her throat,
trying to hold back nausea. "I—I don't understand," she said
when she could speak. "I don't understand why—why they
killed the yearlings." That, of all the things she didn't understand, she could articulate. Only that.

Rezni clutched her forearm, his fingers like claws. His dark
eyes stared, as if the slaughter left him numb too. "Did you

think they would leave them for us? That's the clan way—to destroy property rather than see it fall to the enemy.''

Keva swallowed back the acid rise of sickness. Property? The yearlings were property and not living creatures, capable of caring and sharing? "And they—the clansmen were enemies?" Or had their reaction, their swift slaughter of the yearlings, been simply a reflex action, a thoughtless presumption of hostility conditioned by the harshness of the desert?

"All the small-clans are our enemies. They're afraid of us because we have changed our ways. But these—the Gothni—were my special enemies. They came to Pan-Vi two seasons ago when we were gone to fetch fire-coal and broke the panes of my father's *han-tau*. They let the dry air in to kill our gardens. And they took a woman who was kin of mine." He managed a smile of bitter satisfaction. "She's a widow now."

"She—what kin was she?"

He regarded her with brief suspicion, then shrugged. "My sister. The tall one, Parni, the first to sink his knife—he's the one who took her. But he'll never have a child from her now. Not a child to raise as a Gothni. Parni, Ned, Tarlin—there isn't a brother left from Parni's tent. Tethika will return to my father's *han-tau* before ten days pass."

Keva shook her head, not believing any of it. A stolen sister, the dead yearlings, the bloody remnants that had been living clansmen—suddenly she felt cold. Her teeth began to chatter. She hugged herself and stumbled away to vomit.

They agreed, when Keva could talk, that they could not leave the seven surviving yearlings to find their way back to the forest. There would be other small-clansmen traveling the desert. And the yearlings were too disoriented to undertake the journey alone.

"I have a few green things in my *han-tau* for them," Rezni agreed finally. "And our well has water for them. We will slaughter a few sheep to compensate. We need the mutton for clan-call anyway. We can return the redmanes to the forest after clan-call."

Keva acceded numbly and they resumed their journey. She saw that Danior was silent, pale. He glanced behind anxiously as they walked, as if he expected to see a vortex of sand rise in their wake. The redmanes stumbled, the patches of abrasive sand irritating their pads. Even Rezni was subdued, the muscles of his jaw knotting spasmodically with some private tension. Keva was grateful that he didn't talk, didn't boast of her rout of the Gothni, of his part in it.

Instead he watched her solicitously and tailored his pace to hers, occasionally insisting they stop to rest. "The hard-lands make hard people," he offered the third time he called a halt. "You will learn to be hard too, Keva, in time."

Hard. The same word Oki had used. "No," she said without inflection. She would never be hard. Not if hardness meant not caring for the harm she did, not if it meant swallowing back her fear of what she might do next. Today had taught her that.

"But you will. You have the substance. You're a barohna from the mountains."

He was trying to reassure her, she realized—even to console her. Instead his words only underscored the bleakness of her mood. "No," she said and refused to discuss it further.

They lost one of the yearlings in the afternoon. It lay down and refused to move, and after a while it quivered, stiffened and died. Rezni and Danior kicked sand over the corpse, although they had left the bodies of the clansmen exposed. "We want men from the other small-clans to see what became of the Gothni," Rezni explained. "The Zollidar—the men who took your stone—are already boasting by now that they stole a stone from a barohna. When the Gothni are found, it will be apparent that you are not such an easy victim after all. That you must be approached with care by anyone who wants to live. But there's no purpose in leaving this carcass to be seen. It carries no message."

Keva shrugged and walked on in silence.

Then it was sunset. They stood on a low bluff. Rezni touched her arm and pointed toward the southern horizon. "Pan-Vi," he said—without arrogance, without boast. With something Keva had not heard before: reverence.

Danior dropped his pack and bedding and gazed in the direction Rezni indicated. "There, Keva. Beyond the band of thorn bushes. You can see the sun on the panes. If you look closely, you can pick out individual structures."

"Yes, look to the eastern perimeter and you will see my father's *han-tau*. It's the round dome—you can see it beyond the two rectangulars *taus*. They belong to Pesta and Frinz, who were Sisserle before they pledged to the Greater Clan. My *tau* is hidden from here, but you will see it later."

Danior nodded. "How large was your family-clan before you joined the Greater Clan?"

"The Magadaw? We brought thirty-seven men and fifty-eight women to the Greater Clan. That was five years ago."

"You were one of the men? You were that old when your clan joined?"

"No, I made my initial vow two years ago, at autumn clan-call. And tomorrow at clan-call we will all renew our pledge. That is done each season."

Danior gazed toward the distant settlement. "Does anyone ever decide not to renew?"

Rezni snorted. "Every call there is someone who covers his mouth when the pledge is taken. Then the Viir-Nega must give him a private audience and a private pledging."

"They don't ever just go away? Leave?"

"Where would they go? Where could they get panes to build new *han-taus?* The furnaces are here. The glassworkers are here. No one is permitted to remove panes from Pan-Vi. They would only be wasted—broken by the small-clansmen."

"And no one wants to live in a tent again?"

"No one wants to go back to the old ways, no matter how much they complain," Rezni said staunchly.

Keva listened to their talk absently and gazed at the distant structures, wishing she felt more than a pervading numbness. If the Viir-Nega were her father, he lived behind the glass panes that glinted in the distance. She would meet him before she slept again. Her search would be finished.

But if the Viir-Nega were not her father, she would still meet him. And she would learn that she need not have made the journey. Need not have seen blood spray in the air. Need not have made a vortex of sand and scrubbed the living flesh from five screaming clansmen.

Feeling sick, she sat with her head on her knees until Rezni and Danior were ready to walk again.

The air cooled after sunset and she was grateful for her heavy clothes. The yearlings raised their heads and padded more briskly, grunting among themselves. They descended from the bluff and the terrain changed, pockets of sand giving way to hard-baked soil. Soon they reached a solid wall of densely grown vegetation, every branch armed with long thorns. "Our guard maze," Rezni explained. "The small-clansmen burn it, but we water it from our wells and it grows back. And we cut new paths. Walk in my footsteps. The thorns are at their most poisonous at this time of year."

He walked ahead, picking a route through the bristling vegetation. The yearlings entered the maze reluctantly, gazing up balefully at the surrounding walls of vegetation. One tried to sample the oily foilage and was pricked on the nose. He shrilled angrily and Keva and Danior had to hold him by the shreds of his mane to keep him from blundering blindly through the venomous bushes.

Then they emerged from the maze and moonlight lay on hundreds of glass panes. Keva caught her breath and felt Rezni press her arm. When she glanced up, he was smiling—without bravado or boast, a smile of pure pleasure.

"It's beautiful," she told him, surprised at her answering pleasure. Structures of every conceivable shape and size, formed from thick glass panes, were gathered on the barren soil. Small lamps burned inside them, flickering. The shadows of lush interior foliage patterned the panes. Even by first moonlight, Keva could see that some panes were clear and others tinted. "Beautiful," she repeated.

"Now you see why I boast," Rezni said. "Come—the Viir-Nega will be in his tent."

"I—" Suddenly the anticipation she had not felt earlier caught her, twisting her heart, making her breath catch. Making her suddenly apprehensive of what lay ahead. She stared up at

Rezni dumbly, trying to find some excuse to hold back, to delay confronting the Viir-Nega.

But Rezni caught her arm, drawing her quickly ahead. They hurried down lanes of pounded soil, the yearlings grunting with excitement at the smell of moisture. Watchful shapes appeared from lamp-lit structures, then withdrew when Rezni identified himself.

She was dirty, she realized with belated distress, stumbling. Her clothes were caked. She had not combed her hair since morning. And they were going to meet the Viir-Nega. Quickly Keva drew her fingers through her hair, brushed at her face, tried to straighten her clothes. Danior, she saw, was going through the same hurried grooming process. She suspected her efforts were as useless as his.

"Here," Rezni said when they stood before an oblong *hantau,* the panes so thick they distorted view of the interior. He tugged at a rope and glass chips tingled somewhere inside. "The Nathri-Varnitz comes," he called into the open doorway. "He brings kin of the Viir-Nega."

Shadow shifted behind glass panes. Feet shuffled and a child appeared. Large, dark eyes. Arched brows. Smooth, dark hair. He stood in the doorway like an apparition, staring up at Danior and Keva, then turned and disappeared without word.

Next a woman appeared and studied them from obliquely set eyes. "I bring kin of the Viir-Nega," Rezni said, repeating the salutation in his own language.

If the woman felt any surprise, she didn't betray it. She nodded tersely, summoning them in.

Keva had no time to glance around as they brushed through the hanging panel of an interior door and entered a room where the air was thick with moisture. Because as they entered, a man appeared from another chamber and Keva could only stare.

Raked soil, the earthen smell of growing plants, the dim light of a lantern—she noticed none of those things. Nor did she hear what Rezni said. Not even the tone of his voice registered. She saw only her father, as unbelieving as she, staring at her from eyes she remembered. Dark eyes, searching eyes. But this time it was not the distance they searched but her face, as if it were some half-remembered terrain, one he had not thought to see again. Slowly, disbelievingly, he raised one hand, the nails like hers, pink against bronze skin, and touched her cheek. The bluesong hung at his waist, knotted. The fabric was as slippery, the color as brilliant as she remembered. Her father even smelled as she remembered.

The only thing different was the ingrained lines around his eyes, as if he had peered into the distance so long watchfulness had been etched into his very flesh. And the polished stone wristlet he wore. Keva had not seen that before. "So the woman lied to me," he said finally, the words glad and angry at once.

Keva laughed. What she heard in his voice was so much the same thing she felt: angry that they had been separated, relieved that he was alive, that she had found him. "*Yes*. She told you I was dead but I wasn't," she said, her tongue beginning to work again—too quickly, spilling out words untidily. "She—she just wanted a child. Her mate had drowned and none of the women would let their mates share her mattress. None of the women in that settlement. So she took me to a settlement three days' walk downstream. She—" Tears stung her eyes. "She let you hunt for me. For my grave. She—"

He placed one finger lightly against her lips, stemming the tide. "Stay. We don't need to say everything at once. Some of it we'll never need to say. I can read your face as clearly as I ever could. And the woman—was Oki her name?—must have told you the truth eventually. Or you wouldn't have come here. With my Bold Soldier."

Keva glanced at Rezni and almost laughed at the fierce pride in his eyes. "She told me. I made her. If I hadn't, I would never have known. But—"

"But you do know and it is as well this way," her father said, pulling her to his chest, touching her hair. "It is as well, Keva Marlath, because I rode in hard places after I left the warmstream. I rode in places no child could have survived. I met men who would have quenched you before I knew what they intended. They came close enough to quenching me, before I finally realized I must stop riding and start building instead."

He held her at arm's length again. "Do you know how many times I've wished I had learned that lesson before I lost you? Before I pushed through winter storms and made you sick when we could have taken shelter in the valleys, in the plain, in any number of places. But now I haven't lost you at all."

She laughed, inappropriately—she couldn't help it—and felt tears begin to streak freely from her eyes. She wiped them away impatiently. She had arrived. She had found her father and he was as glad of it as she was. This was no time to cry.

Her father didn't seem surprised. He held her until she had wiped away the last of her tears and conquered the weak laughter that kept rising in her throat. Then he glanced beyond her at Danior. "And this?"

Danior started, caught off guard. "Danior Terlath—I'm Danior Terlath."

The Viir-Nega brows rose. "Of course. Who else could it be? You've brought news of your valley, I hope. News of my Rauth-brother?"

"My father—yes."

"And your mother? And Fiirsevrin?"

"Everything," Danior promised, his gaze flicking briefly to the sash at the Viir-Nega's waist.

The Viir-Nega nodded, glancing at Rezni. "And in addition to news, you have sand in your boots and dirt in your hair, all of you. Keva, Danior—Maiya will take you to the wetroom to wash and she will find clean clothes for you. That will give me time to talk with the Nathri-Varnitz so he can return to his *hantau*. His wives are beginning to be anxious."

Wives? Keva darted a startled glance at Rezni. He scowled at the floor, a dark stain rising in his cheeks, and refused to meet her eyes. He seemed relieved when the woman who had met them at the door reappeared and gestured for them to follow.

The wetroom was a small chamber, and when Keva glanced up, she saw that its panes stained the stars deeply blue. There was a large round tub half-filled with water recessed into the graveled floor. A species of plant that seemed, by lantern light, to have foliage of the deepest violet grew profusely against the curved glass wall. Maiya silently laid out lengths of absorbent cloth and said, "Clothes—later."

When they were alone, Danior turned and studied the room. Then he glanced back at Keva, apparently uncertain of her mood. "I think we're supposed to sit in the tub," he said finally. "And scrub with leaves from the plants."

Keva studied the violet foliage doubtfully, grateful that at least the tendency to tears and laughter had begun to subside. "Rezni told you that?"

"He told me his wives grow purple star for their wetroom instead of redleaf soap-plant because it isn't so likely to irritate the skin." He bent to unlace his boots, then glanced up uncertainly. "Do you want to bathe alone?"

"No, there's room for two," she assured him. "You knew Rezni had wives?" There at least was a subject that did not threaten her fragile composure.

"He told me. But he thought if he told you that you wouldn't be first-wife, that there were two before you, you would refuse him."

Keva stared at him in amazement. "I refused him the first time he asked. I told him—" Tales—carefully calculated tales. That she was barohna of Valley Marlath. That she was traveling to visit her kinsman, the Viir-Nega. That she must return to her people when she had seen him.

"Yes, he thought that was a good sign. It lessens a woman's worth if she agrees too quickly. His other wives come from very strong family-clans. He's made good alliances by taking them, but he's decided to give them to his younger brother if you accept him. Then of course you would be first-wife."

So Rezni had already plotted her future. She wondered briefly what else she had missed in not listening more closely to Rezni and Danior's talk. She repressed a moment's impulse to laugh, guessing tears would follow. Obviously many things were different here, but she would not think about them tonight. Her mood was too fragile. Tonight she must put everything aside: unanswered questions, unexplained relationships, inexplicabilities—and images of sand whirling in the air.

Sand and blood. She shivered, choking back nausea.

Danior noticed and caught her arm. "Are you all right?"

"I felt cold," she said weakly. Cold and sickened and confused, even though she had found her father's roof and was safely under it. And from what she had seen of the desert, it was clear she had come to an alien place, clear there would be other moments when she felt cold, many of them.

But not tonight. She had completed her search. She had found her father. Tonight she would put away disturbing thoughts.

Tonight.

ELEVEN
DANIOR

D anior had many things to think about as they bathed. The stories Rezni had told him of plundering small-clansmen. What Keva had done that afternoon and the mark it had left on her. Jhaviir: the place he had made for himself among the clansmen, the sunstone wristlet he wore, the bluesong. Danior had a sense of discoveries and events following so quickly upon each other that he had scant time to reflect, to wonder where he must put his foot next. He had taken the first step, and broad avenues had opened to him, drawing him from event to event.

Now they had brought him to a land he had never expected to see, to people he had never expected to know. Had brought him to friendship with Rezni, to reunion with his father's brother. More, they had brought him to an anxious sense that he had come here to be tested. Not in the traditional way of a palace child, by going to the mountain to kill or be killed. But in a more complex way, in a way no one had been tested before. In a way, perhaps, that he would not even understand until the test was done. And the danger, he guessed, was not that he might die, not even that he might fail, but that he might turn away.

He had wanted to today, when the sand fell and he saw what it had done to the Gothni. He had wanted to run—back to the forest, back to the plain, back to the valleys, where the forces of the stones were leashed and harnessed by centuries of tradition.

But Keva could not turn back. She was caught, bound—not

by tradition but by the very forces tradition had evolved to guard against. She had no mother to set an example for her. No Council Elder to instruct her. No stone mate to share her bewilderment and her doubt. She had only Danior and her father.

And Danior had a full sense of his own inadequacy. What could he tell her? How could he guide her? He could only stay, offering his presence. Perhaps that was part of the test: accepting his own helplessness.

When they had finished bathing, they pulled on the loose robes and trousers Maiya had brought for them and made their way back to the front of the *han-tau*. There they found a low table spread with food. Cushions were arranged around it and half a dozen children sat cross-legged, waiting. When Keva and Danior entered, they turned and stared with a bold-eyed curiosity that made Danior stiffen self-consciously.

The oldest boy stood and gestured to the vacant cushions, speaking rapidly. Danior sat, Keva beside him, and glanced around cautiously, wondering what to expect. A formal dining; a family meal; a ceremonial? He didn't know the desert etiquette for any of those occasions. But perhaps there was none. The younger children were already picking at the food, snatching tidbits from the serving bowls, protesting loudly when the oldest tried to discipline them. Keva, he saw, barely noticed. She watched the doorway with barely veiled anticipation. Some of the color had returned to her face. Her eyes were brighter than they had been since afternoon.

By the time Jhaviir appeared, the children were openly warring. "My young clansmen," he said deprecatingly, striding into the room. He had dressed in fresh robe and trousers and reknotted the bluesong at his waist, but Danior saw he no longer wore the sunstone wristlet. "They'll quarrel over a shadow on the sand. I've seen them do it. That's the desert way."

Nevertheless Danior noticed that the children jumped to their feet and came to order immediately at his appearance. They only sat again when he selected a cushion beside Keva and crossed his legs.

When the children were quiet, he said, "I've already told the children we will use only mountain language at the table tonight, which will give us some peace since only Tedni and Resha—'' he indicated the two older children ''—have begun to learn it.'' He smiled reprovingly at the impatient children and said, ''Yes, you may eat now. Here, Keva, Danior—fill your platters quickly or you'll have nothing.''

A small melee ensued, from which everyone finally emerged with a filled platter. Danior hesitated at first, then decided that if this was the etiquette, he would observe it rather than go hungry. When he sat again, he tried to identify what he had snatched from the confusion and recognized almost nothing. Fruit, meat, roasted seeds and pods—all unfamiliar except the mutton. But it took him only a few bites to realize how hungry he was.

Keva ate more cautiously, glancing around the table doubtfully. ''Doesn't Maiya eat with you?'' she asked finally.

Jhaviir's arched brows rose. ''No, no, neither Maiya, Ramari nor Kliya. They like peace with their meals, so I eat with the children and they eat with themselves. In fact, Maiya suggested you might prefer the women's table, but I told her that you would not mind eating with us tonight. I wasn't wrong, I hope.''

''No. Of course not,'' Keva said quickly. But Danior noticed that she stared down at her plate, her face flushing. He studied her covertly, realizing she had not guessed her father followed the desert custom. Though why it should make her uncomfortable that he kept three wives . . . Perhaps she held strong feelings, as his mother did, and could not imagine sharing a mate.

Later Danior gathered from the loud protests of the younger children and the frowning annoyance of the eldest that the children were not normally dismissed from their father's presence so early. Tedni, the eldest boy, lingered, arguing, until his sister Resha tugged him away.

When they had gone, Jhaviir excused himself and groped in the vines that grew along the wall for a small flask. ''Now we will drink,'' he announced, pouring amber liquid into hand-blown glasses and seating himself again. The planes of his face gleamed by lantern light. ''*Hi-basa*, made from a tuber I discovered in the roughlands and brought here. Drink slowly or you will regret it. In fact, you will probably regret it anyway, but we must observe your arrival with something more than a hasty meal."

Danior accepted a glass, studying Jhaviir, trying to understand how he could be both so much like his father and so different. His facial structure, the proportion of body and limbs, the shape of his hands—all those things were identical. But Jhaviir moved differently, every motion broader, more emphatic, as if he deliberately called attention to himself. And there was something in his eyes, in the way he spoke, that seemed directed to the same end. He carried himself, he spoke like a man who has placed himself upon a stage, who expects to engage every eye. Danior watched him and wondered whether his own father's reserve was cultivated or whether Jhaviir's more commanding way was a deliberate manner. Carefully Danior raised his glass.

The *hi-basa* had a resinous taste that made his tongue burn. Aware of Jhaviir's weighing gaze, he took several swallows anyway. At the fourth, blood rushed to his head with vengeful speed. He set the glass down with a clatter and was immediately embarrassed by his sudden clumsiness.

"Very slowly," Jhaviir cautioned. "And now, before any more time escapes us, there are things we must learn from each other. Rezni tells me, Keva, that you are barohna of Valley Marlath, that the valley is peopled again and you serve it. But I know that if that were so, your flesh would be burned dark at this season, so soon after the thawing. And I observe that it isn't."

Keva flushed, meeting his gaze reluctantly. 'No, I—I don't even remember Valley Marlath. I only heard of it when I met Danior. I left the warmstream—'' She glanced at Danior uncertainly. "It was eleven or twelve days ago. I went as soon as Oki told me what she had done. That she had stolen me. I was going to the mountains to find you, but I met Danior and he told me no one had seen you there. So I decided to follow the redmanes to the forest to see if I could learn anything there."

"Ah. And you met Rezni in the forest. And showed him how a barohna makes stone live."

"*No.* I—I don't know what I did. He frightened me. I thought—it just happened." She stared down at the table top, her lips tightly compressed, tears standing at the corners of her eyes. "I don't know how," she whispered. "It just happened."

Jhaviir gazed at her at length, frowning. Then he leaned across the table and took her hands, holding them palm-upward in his. He studied the fingers one by one, as if they could tell him something. He sighed deeply, suddenly seeming neither emphatic nor commanding. Suddenly seeming only tired. "Pardon me for insisting when we should only drink quietly and speak of inconsequentialities. But the things we must discuss are important. Have you thought of going to Valley Marlath and taking the throne? The people have scattered, but they would return. Gladly, I know, if you want it."

Keva pulled her hands back as if he had burned them, color washing from her face. "*No.* I'm—I'm not—*no!*"

Jhaviir studied her pleading face, then took his fingers and gently curled them shut. Again strain showed in the fine lines around his eyes, in the bunching of muscles in his jaws. His words seemed reluctant. "I appreciate that you have just arrived, Keva. I appreciate that you should have time to rest before we talk like this. But you've come at an important time—on the eve of spring clan-call, and at a period when the small-clans are at their most hostile. You are obviously a significant personage—both of you are significant personages. You presented yourself so to Rezni and by now—just in the time it took you to bathe—word has gone around Pan-Vi. So has word of the way you terrorized the Zollidar and left five Gothni dead on the desert. And since you caught the Gothni near Walking Adder Spring, very soon word will be around not just here, but all over the hard-lands. Dozens of parties pass Walking Adder at this time of year. It is one of the places where neutrality has been declared among the small-clans.

"And so I must make a request I realize you won't welcome. No more do I welcome the fact that I must make it. But I must ask that you permit me to present you to the clan tomorrow during the ceremonies both as my daughter and as a barohna—

a barohna who has come to ally herself for a while to the cause of the Greater Clan.''

Keva raised her head sharply, staring at him. "*No*," she protested with open horror. "No. *Please*. I only came here to find you. I—"

"I know that," he said, obviously sorry for the pain his request caused. "And I would like to be able to give you the time you need. But you must understand what a fragile social organism I have created here, Keva.

"I don't know how much you remember of the stories I used to tell you of my own childhood. Not a lot, I expect. Some of them, I see now, were only worth forgetting.

"I grew up among a people called the Kri-Nostri. They were a rigidly disciplined people who lived a carefully structured life among harsh circumstances. Their discipline, in fact, was the only thing that saved them from falling victim to recurrent drought and warring neighbors. That and the reputation they built for themselves as soldiers who turned back from nothing. I learned how to be strong from the Kri-Nostri. Just as important, I learned to give the appearance of strength even in my weak moments. And I learned to love adversity. I measured myself against it every day and let it make me stronger. That was the Kri-Nostri way.

"Then I found myself here, a Kri-Nostri soldier plunged into the society of the valleys. Everytime I rode down stone avenues, I felt diminished. Because nothing I had been trained for was of any use in the valleys. There were no enemies, no wars, no need to be strong or vigilant. No need for any of my soldier's discipline. There wasn't even the simple physical hardship of pitting myself against a harsh land. The barohnas have tamed the valleys.

"So I rode out of the valleys to find hardship. And not just that. I rode to find the sense of myself hardship could give. The sense of strength, of control.

"I rode long past the time when I should have learned better. I rode until I realized that hardship was no longer making me strong. It was only making me lonely. I began to recognize that—belatedly—after I lost you, Keva. I recognized that it meant nothing that I rode through the worst weather without flinching, that I pushed myself when I was tired and sick, that I carried the skins of minx and rock-leopard and had brought down breeterlik and crag-chargers. I had no people. I was alone.

"I had passed through the desert several times and seen how the clanspeople lived. Among the Kri-Nostri, it would be said they are like children: without discipline or principle. In truth, even a Kri-Nostri child is better disciplined than most clansmen. Certainly a Kri-Nostri child, left to himself, would devise a better way to live.

"Perhaps that's what decided me. I had just lost a child, or so I thought, and the desert was full of children, hungry and dirty and ignorant—waiting to be shown a better way to live. And hardship—they offered me hardship in full measure. I saw quickly that here I could use everything I had learned among the Kri-Nostri: strength, vigilance, cunning, persistence.

"And so I elected to stop here, to make the clanspeople my family. Because I had finally recognized the need for family and society, for constance. Something that would extend beyond my own lifetime if possible. And the land was familiar. Sometimes at sunset I walk a distance from Pan-Vi and I can imagine that I stand on the silica sands of Grenish again. The colors in the sunset sky are like those I knew there, harsh and red. The heat, the dryness are the same. This place says home to me. And it uses me fully. More than fully sometimes. Certainly it required all my strength and all my bravado to establish myself among the clansmen.

"I won't tell you all the things I went through to make a family of these people. I will tell you that when I came here, the people who now live as the Greater Clan belonged to twelve small-clans and two larger ones. They were nomads, hungry and hostile, living in ragged tents and speaking six different languages. Their women were haggard and beaten. Their children more often died during their first year than not. And their men slaughtered each other upon the pettiest of pretexts.

"I measured myself against them as I once measured myself

against physical hardship and I welded them into a social unit. I gave them a common language, a language no one else on Brakrath speaks. I gave them agriculture and technology. I gave them principles and social organization. I fed their self-importance by offering them titles and honors. And I brought them symbols. This for instance." He indicated the bluesong. "This is a magic no one else on the desert commands. Only the Greater Clan has a singing silk. And of course I've given them a leader who holds the silk and has claim to important associations. Myself.

"Now you have come and affirmed my claim to important associations. You are my daughter and you have done things only a barohna can do. But if I don't present you in a suitable manner at clan-call, your presence won't support my position at all. It will undermine it.

"Reticence isn't respected here, Keva. A man—or a woman—who doesn't flaunt his advantage is asking to be dismissed as a weakling. That's simply the way of these people. I'm sure they will seem like braggarts to you. To them, a person who doesn't boast must be hiding weakness. And weakness is no more well-received than reticence. It is a matter for shame. So as their leader, I must proclaim myself more loudly than anyone else. Or lose their confidence. And I dare not lose their confidence.

"What we have built here is still too fragile. We're still raising the first generation of children who will remember no loyalty but to the Greater Clan. If I don't show myself strong, their parents may very well sink back into disorder. And then everything will be lost and the small-clans will overwhelm us. There will be no mark of my work here but broken glass and wilted crops. Do you understand me, Keva?"

It was apparent to Danior that she did, that she understood why he must present her to the clan as a barohna. Her lips had begun to tremble. She spoke in a reluctant whisper, avoiding his eyes. "What do you want me to do?"

Jhaviir sighed deeply, passing one dark hand across his face, pressing his temples in a familiar gesture. Danior studied him, guessing he seldom let anyone see him like this, tired, regretful, subdued. "Nothing difficult, Keva. Ride with me to clan-call. Listen to a lot of rhetoric in a language you don't understand. Conduct yourself as you instinctively did with Rezni, as a person of position. My people will be impressed simply because they want to be impressed. They want to have strong allies."

When Keva continued to stare at the tabletop, saying nothing, Danior said doubtfully, "The small-clansmen—when they find the Gothni, when they realize what happened to them—"

Jhaviir gazed down into his glass, swirling the amber liquid, sighing again. "I have achieved two distinct things in my years here, Danior. I've united a group of quarreling clans into the Greater Clan. And in the process, without intending it at all, I have also partially united many of the other small-clans—simply by offering them a common enemy."

"The Greater Clan," Danior said softly, understanding. The very existence of the Greater Clan had forged tentative bonds between the smaller clans. Not bonds of friendship but bonds of common fear.

"Yes. They have lived in the old way—wandering, fighting, plundering each other's camps—so long that they have no understanding of any other way to live. Nor do they understand that we *have* found another way to live. They see us growing stronger year by year, and they think it is only a matter of time until we move against them. And so every year, they draw closer together. They fight each other less and press us harder. And now—" Jhaviir's eyes flickered to Keva, who still stared at the table, lips tight. Brows arching, he raised his glass in a shrugging gesture.

Now. Danior glanced at Keva and saw she did not realize what Jhaviir had left carefully unsaid: that when the small-clans learned a barohna had joined the Greater Clan, they would feel even more threatened. They would unite even more firmly—more savagely—against their common enemy. "How quickly does news travel on the desert?"

"Very quickly now. The small-clans still fight and steal among themselves, but they have commissioned couriers who are permitted to pass without harassment. By now they are already running."

Carrying the news. Danior touched his pairing stone, troubled by the picture Jhaviir had drawn—of a fragile union, of savage enemies, of people who could easily slip back into chaotic ways. And there seemed nothing he could do. "Do you want me to come to clan-call too?" he ask uncertainly.

Carefully Jhaviir placed his glass on the table. He glanced at Keva, then turned his full attention back to Danior. "As my Rauth-son? Yes, it is important that you come. In fact, I would like you to lead Ranslega, my stallion. Rezni will march with you carrying the songsilk—the first time I've permitted another person to do that. I would like to bestow a ceremonial title upon you—and perhaps another on Rezni, for guiding you here. For your part, all you need do is put on a soldier's face, like a man aware of his own strength."

Like a man with a legend in his own land.

Because that was what Jhaviir was telling him—was telling them both. That legend was important among the desert people, far more important than in the mountains. It was legend that assured strong allies, that provided protection against rapacious neighbors—that insured survival. While he was here, he must behave like a man secure in his own legend. Even if that legend were totally ephemeral. Even if behind it he remained the same person he had always been, doubting and uncertain.

Certainly the fact that Jhaviir had revealed his own vulnerability took some of the sting from Danior's doubts. If Jhaviir, who had ridden in places Danior had never seen, who had welded an unruly people into a small nation, must put on a public face, how could Danior's uncertainties make him small? "I will," he said.

"Good. You understand—and we can turn to lighter matters," Jhaviir said, raising his glass.

Relaxing, they sipped the resinous *hi-basa* and let it dissolve the last barriers of reticence. Gradually Keva's face took color again and she spoke of her life by the warmstream, of Oki, of Lekki, of a young fisherman who teased her from his boat.

Danior related what he could of people Jhaviir had known in the valleys: his mother, his father, Juris Pergossa, others. Jhaviir told them of lands he had explored during the early years, while Lihwa was in her winter palace—lands Danior had not guessed existed. And he told them of the morning he heard an alien song and discovered a length of brilliant blue silk caught in the branches of a tree, blown there from the nearby wreckage of a small star-trader.

Danior gazed at the blue sash at Jhaviir's waist and stirred to full attention, casting off the growing fuzziness of drink. "Where—do you know where it came from? What kind of place?" Had Jhaviir seen silken bowers in white-stalked trees and pink-tongued predators too when the silk sang? Or was he the only one?

"No." Jhaviir shook his head regretfully. "I don't know where the ship traveled from or why it wrecked itself there. I suspect it flew by an automatic system that failed. Perhaps it was an accident much like the one that stranded the first-timers on Brakrath—except that I found no sign of a crew. The other cargo it carried—I had no use for it. I left it."

Danior sighed. So he was the only one who had reached beyond the bluesong. The only one who had seen yellow-eyed predators in an alien forest. "You only took the bluesong?"

"Ah, I took songs of other colors too, Danior. But I never showed them to Lihwa. She was unhappy with my restlessness. She wished me to winter with her in her mountain palace, though she understood me too well to insist. So I hid the silks and only wore the bluesong after I left Valley Marlath. Then later, when I was separated from Keva, I went back and retrieved the others. And hid them again when I settled here. The Kri-Nostri call that the principle of *karnikile-karmaka*. The hidden treasure-weapon—a very loose translation. I learned as a boy always to keep something back."

Danior nodded thoughtfully. "Your people—they know about the other songsilks?"

"I've dropped hints—hints that one day I will confer them upon the most diligent as symbols of special recognition. One day when we reach a certain point in our life together." Quickly

Jhaviir emptied his glass and turned it upside down. "And now the drinks are enough and you are tired. It is time we slept, daughter, Rauth-son."

Danior wanted to protest, wanted to talk more, but his tongue was growing thick. Jhaviir showed him to a cushion in the chamber where Tedni and his younger brothers slept. Danior stretched out, his mind full of half-formulated questions, half-digested insights. There was much he could learn from Jhaviir, he realized—much no one else could teach him.

More, perhaps, than he could learn from Keva. Perhaps there were even things he could teach her, if she would let him, just as he had taught her to listen to the teaching. Sighing, he clasped the pairing stone, thinking of the couriers who ran between the small-clans. By now word had already gone out that the Greater Clan harbored a barohna. And only he and Jhaviir knew the barohna was untrained and unwilling. He pressed his pairing stone, trying to guess what he could do to help guide Keva past her fear. He remembered too well his first fear of the pairing stone.

But use of the pairing stone was a small gift compared to the power Keva had unleashed. And what could he tell her? To walk the path, to learn from doing seemed dangerous advice, although it might be the only advice he could give. Because if she did not explore her gift, if she did not practice its control, it would rule her.

Uneasily he closed his eyes and sought sleep.

He woke in the morning to find Tedni, Jhaviir's oldest son, standing over him frowning fiercely. And to find that his head throbbed dully. He sat, rubbing his eyes, hoping water would wash the foul taste of the night's drinking from his mouth. Morning sunlight poured through heavy glass panes. The younger boys had gone.

"You slept in your clothes," Tedni said, the words heavily accented, accusing. "Now Maiya will have to get you clean ones and you will have to wash those." Impatiently the boy brushed dark hair back from his sharp-boned cheek. "It was my place to lead Ranslega to clan-call before you came, you know. I lead him every year because I am the Viir-Nega's first and strongest son. Now my father tells everyone you will lead him.''

Slowly Danior stood, pressing his palms against his aching temples, trying to comprehend Tedni's grievance. Apparently Danior had usurped a valued ceremonial chore. "Why don't we walk one on either side of Ranslega?" he offered without thinking. "We can share the privilege."

Tedni's pupils contracted sharply and his lips thinned to a narrow line. "If you will walk three paces behind, we will share," he agreed haughtily.

Danior's face colored. "The Viir-Nega didn't ask me to walk behind anyone." It wasn't hard, given the ache of his head and the boy's scowling arrogance, to put a sting in the words.

Tedni drew himself up on the balls of his feet, scowling more fiercely than before. When Danior did not respond, he abruptly bared his teeth in a flashing grin. "I'll speak to my father," he said and dodged away.

Danior looked after him with a shrug, then brushed at his clothes and ventured to the wetroom to splash his face. Either *hi-basa* or fatigue had left his eyes dull and dark-rimmed, his complexion sallow. His muscles felt leaden, his movements poorly coordinated.

He washed and ate with the others, jostling for food, his head throbbing. Jhaviir's edict that mountain language be spoken at the table had apparently applied only to the night before. Today the children squabbled in their own language. No one made any allusion to Danior's rumpled clothing.

When he ventured outside to where Jhaviir was grooming Ranslega, he saw no trace of the night's drinking on Jhaviir. He raised one hand in greeting and said, "I've told Tedni he can walk at Ranslega's left side if he remains five paces behind you and doesn't touch the halter strap. He's old enough this year to walk at the front of the procession."

So Tedni's grievance had been manufactured. "He told me he always leads Ranslega to the clan-call," Danior said without much surprise.

Jhaviir bared teeth in a broad smile. "He would tell you that. And he'll tell you many other things about his importance here if you give him the chance. Keep him in his place if you want to be his friend. Otherwise you'll just be someone he uses. Here—you've probably braided Fiirsevrin's mane a hundred times. Do Ranslega's for me.''

Danior retreated a step, wanting to refuse, but Jhaviir had already handed him the comb and left him with the animal. Danior hesitated, then laid a cautious hand on the whitemane's shoulder. The animal's flesh was firm and warm. When he raised his hand, it left no mark. Relieved, he began parting and combing the silver-white strands.

Keva joined him after a while, standing silently in the harsh morning sun, her eyes darkly ringed, her face pale. She watched, then took the comb from him when she recognized his total lack of skill.

"Did you eat?" he asked, worried by her pallor, wondering if it came from *hi-basa* or lack of sleep.

"No," she said shortly, deftly working the stallion's mane into plaits.

He could see she didn't want to talk. Withdrawing, he found brushes on the ground nearby and silently began brushing Ranslega's coat. Occasionally he stopped to gaze uneasily around. Jhaviir had erected his paned home at a distance from the others, so that it commanded a view of the desert. Beyond it, the land rolled away to the south in barren hillocks. Brown-dried vegetation stood sentinel. Peering back in the direction they had come the night before, Danior saw the guard maze, its thorny growth incongruously green against the dun of the desert. By daylight, it was not so imposing as he remembered it. It made little better than a half-circle around the gathered structures, leaving the perimeter unguarded in every other direction.

He searched the distance, frowning against morning sunlight. By daylight the Greater Clan's settlement seemed frail shelter against the barrenness of the desert. Glass panes sheltered the gardens and conserved the precious moisture that fed them. Barefoot men and women with sun-hardened faces gathered for clan-call, their children squabbling in the dirt lanes. And beyond lay sand, wind and the small-clans.

Danior darted a glance at Keva and saw that she too peered uneasily toward the desert.

After a while Rezni appeared, padding down the lane barefoot, his robe and trousers blazing white, his hair freshly knotted. He carried both knife and spear. He paused to survey the state of Ranslega's grooming, then said with measured self-importance, "I'll get the riding pad and the halter." When Keva did not look up from her work, he tapped Danior's arm, raising his brows questioningly.

Danior lifted his shoulders in a noncommittal shrug. Certainly he wanted no part in Rezni's suit for Keva.

Soon the whitemane stallion stood braided and saddled, his neck proudly arched. People pressed near, staring at Keva and Danior, muttering in clan-language. Tedni appeared, ducking beneath the whitemane's belly, and addressed Rezni with a long, boastful harangue. Rezni answered him sharply and the boy dodged away, shooting back a rejoinder over one shoulder.

"He wants us to understand that all these people have come to watch him lead off the procession," Rezni remarked. He turned, his eyes sweeping the watching people haughtily. "They have, in fact, come to see me carry the bluesong." He raised his head, baring his teeth. "So?"

"I don't think so," Danior answered but saw from Rezni's darting glance that the boast had been addressed to Keva. When she did not respond, Rezni's eyes sparked with intensified interest. But before he could try again to command her attention, Tedni returned, loosing imperious instructions in every direction. Rezni snapped his bare heels together. "The Viir-Nega comes. I will assist you into the saddle."

Keva met his eyes for the first time, distantly. Deliberately, she put aside the grooming comb, seized the whitemane's mane, and pulled herself to his back. "I don't need help."

Rezni's dark eyes glittered and the watching people sighed as Keva caught the whitemane's reins and raised her chin. She looped the reins in her right hand. Her face was pale, every muscle so tautly controlled she might have been carved from stone.

Danior stepped forward quickly, taking the whitemane's halter strap, trying to assume some of the same poised control. For that was what Jhaviir wanted of him: a manner. He even managed to echo Rezni's haughtiness. "What route must we follow, Nathri-Varnitz?"

Rezni gazed up at Keva, his dark eyes brightly calculating. "I will walk to your left and show you," he said. "And if the brat presses closer than five paces, we will stop and throw him into the thorns. A few scratches will improve his appearance."

The people in the lane began to shout and Jhaviir strode from his *han-tau*. He wore robe and trousers bleached a dazzling white, a braided rope at his waist. More, he wore an air of command that took every eye. His oiled face gleamed. On his outstretched hands, he carried the bluesong, folded. Danior gazed at him and could see no trace of the tired man who had spoken to them the night before.

He raised his arms, addressing the people in clan-language. From their sudden, hooting cry, from the stamping of their feet, Danior guessed his words carried some ritual challenge. Jhaviir met their response with a cry of his own. And then the procession began, Jhaviir and Keva riding, Rezni bearing the bluesong on outstretched hands, Danior leading Ranslega, and Tedni jostling for position, pressing forward so insistently he stepped on Danior's heels. Rezni hissed at him without breaking stride. By the time the procession had wound its way through all the lanes of Pan-Vi, Rezni had taught Danior a number of expletives. Tedni accepted them as tribute, grinning fiercely, and pressed harder, until even Keva had difficulty repressing a pale smile.

By the time the procession reached the edge of the desert settlement, every man, woman and child marched with it. Some wore bleached robes, some only stained and soiled trousers. All wore a blue sash and a sash of another color: scarlet, gold, emerald, violet. There were knives at every waist, spears in every hand. One group of men and women hobbled separately from the others, wearing robes splashed with dried blood. "Those who have taken the enemy blade and lived to tell,"

Rezni informed Danior. Another group, men, women and children, carried half-burned garments. "Those who have lost a warrior since last clan-call." Their number made Danior chill, since he knew the clan assembled for call each new season.

Finally they emerged from the lanes and stood upon a shallow elevation, looking down over the gathered people. Danior peered around and saw a single small tree, its limbs severely pruned, the soil at its roots damp. There, he guessed, the bluesong would sing.

But first there was rhetoric. Jhaviir began with a long, posturing harangue that made the people mutter and stamp and glower across the barren lands. He was followed by the leader of each affiliated family-clan in turn, by impassioned citizens who simply wanted to speak, even by children who seized the opportunity to posture at the Viir-Nega's side and shout slogans. Once a girl who looked hardly old enough to be a mother urged a toddler forward. The child was so surprised to find herself standing beside the Viir-Nega's stallion that she could only stare in open-mouthed wonder. Finally Tedni coaxed her away and returned her to her mother.

Then Rezni shuffled his feet and thrust back his wiry shoulders and Danior guessed it was time for his part in the ritual. Danior glanced uneasily at the songsilk. Warmth gathered at the base of his throat, where the pairing stone rested.

Control. He drew a deep breath and exhaled it in a series of shallow pants, discharging the heat.

But when the blue sash hung in the tree, when Rezni stepped aside and the breeze caught the shimmering fabric, when the strange song began, Danior's hand rose to the pairing stone and found it warm. Trembling, his fingers closed around it. *Control.* He could dismiss the node of heat that grew in his throat. He could listen to the bluesong as everyone else did, with only his ears. But now, with the strange, bodiless voice in the air, he did not want to listen that way. The bluesong caught sunlight and breeze and created a caressing, wordless melody from them, and Danior did not want to draw back. He wanted to let the heat grow. He wanted to walk under white-limbed trees again. Sighing, he let his eyelids fall shut. The heat in his throat intensified and he extended himself, reaching beyond the robed clansmen, the glaring sun.

It was dark under the white-limbed trees. A single moon hung in the sky and Danior was alone. There was no sleek-furred form with yellow eyes, no coarser form with swollen muscles. There was only soil that yielded softly underfoot and trees. And the bluesong. He listened and it came to him from deep in the trees. It summoned, light and sound inextricably interwoven, softly beckoning. Hesitantly he experimented and found he could move toward the source of the sound.

The song did not grow louder as he approached. It simply grew sweeter, more yearning. And as he moved, Danior had a growing sense of light, although the trees remained dark. Dimly he felt Rezni's fingers dig his forearm, heard the stirring of feet, and then heard another song from the distant trees.

Not blue. This song was not blue. It was another color, brighter, lighter, trilling. Danior drew a deep breath and moved forward again until he stood looking up at a bower of bright silks. A noon-yellow length of silk reached out on the soft night breeze, casting a wordless song against the shadow. Danior stared up, spellbound, until the silk was drawn back, secured, and a dark face peered down at him from the bower.

Oblique yellow eyes, chestnut fur, delicate pink tongue licking nervously at sharp white teeth. Did the animal see him? Danior tried to raise his hand, tried to call out, could not. Somewhere high in the trees a small creature shrilled.

The yellow-eyed creature drew back until he saw only its shadow against the silk panel. It manipulated the silks, releasing a new panel. The silk rippled and sang a crimson song, sweet and brooding, deep-throated.

Caught, Danior stood under the trees and listened to songs of every color. Stood under the trees and tried without effect to raise his voice. Stood under the trees and wondered where his reaching power had brought him, what place, what world, whether it was real or fantasy. Had he reached into some untapped part of his own mind? Or did a forest like this exist somewhere, with songsilks and a creature who released them to sing in the moonlight?

The dark things—they had been unimaginably alien. How could they have come from his own mind? Remembering them, he drew back into the trees.

The dark things did not reach for him tonight. Instead the yellow-eyed creature bound the last of the colored silks to the framework of the bower and then released the single silk that had not sung. It twisted violently in the moonlight, ivory entwining itself with silver, although the breeze was mild.

And it did not sing. It spoke. It caught at moonlight, seized at breeze, and pleaded with Danior in a hard-edged masculine voice. He didn't understand the words it used. They were of a language he had never heard before. But their pressing need was clear. The voice begged him.

And it was a voice he knew. A voice he had heard from childhood.

A voice he had heard today.

Confused, Danior caught a deep breath and held it until the kernel of heat in his throat grew so large it threatened to choke him. The effort did not bring him any nearer the white silk. Did not make its pleading words any more comprehensible. Danior staggered backward, his entire chest burning. He coughed, trying to clear blocked air passages.

Quickly the forest slipped away. Trees darkened, the moon faded. But still he heard the insistent voice.

Danior shuddered, dispelling the last of the burning mass in his throat. Jhaviir stood with one hand on his shoulder, the fingers digging hard. "What did you see? Danior—what did you see?"

Danior shook his head, too shaken to speak. "I—"

"Our enemies!" Tedni hissed, trying to push between them. "Your stone burned so bright it made your face blue. You saw our enemies!"

"No. I saw—something else," he finally managed, the words painful. "A white silk. A white songsilk." He stared into Jhaviir's startled eyes, begging him to understand, to tell him what it meant, that familiar voice pleading in a foreign tongue. "Is there—do you have a white silk? Hidden?"

Tiny muscles contracted beneath Jhaviir's eyes. "I have one."

"Have you—have you ever listened to it?"

Strain was clear on Jhaviir's face now. He darted a glance at the people of the Greater Clan, who pressed near, hands on their weapons. "Yes. Once."

"Did you hear—your own voice?"

Jhaviir frowned, releasing Danior's shoulder. His voice was crisp. "I heard my voice. My brother's voice. Someone lost."

Lost. Distressed. Danior pressed his temples, aware that the Greater Clan watched. What had his father said? That there had been one message from Birnam Rauth since his disappearance over a century ago. A message to the effect that he was being held against his will in a place he could not describe. Danior pressed the pairing stone with testing fingers. Had the message his father heard been recorded in a songsilk? Had his father found a white songsilk—either here or on some other world? And today—how had he reached beyond the bluesong to hear Birnam Rauth's voice? If it were Birnam Rauth's voice. The pairing stone—

He didn't understand how he had done what he had done. Perhaps he would never understand. And the people of the Greater Clan were beginning to stir, to mutter among themselves. Apparently they thought, like Tedni, that he had used the pairing stone to glimpse their enemies. Danior dropped his hands to his side. "Tell them—tell them their enemies are still sleeping," he instructed Jhaviir. "Tell them I will have to use the stone again when the sluggards have wakened. All I see now are their dreams."

Jhaviir nodded, baring his teeth appreciatively at Danior's quick recovery. "Their cowardly dreams," he amended. "And I'll add further embellishments. And later, when we are done here—"

He didn't have to complete the request. "I'll use the stone to look into their camp," Danior agreed. Surely that could be no more jarring than what he had just heard and seen.

"Yes." Jhaviir strode back to his place and raised his arms. Danior's statement and Jhaviir's embellishments rang grandly across the hard-lands. The Greater Clanspeople closed calloused hands around their weapons and shouted and stamped with derisive pleasure. Tedni beamed up at Danior.

Mercifully the next part of the ritual was a sharing of plenty. Tedni suddenly heeled away to join a group of older children. They returned carrying platters of fruit and meat and jugs of water. Danior sat gratefully and ate. Jhaviir squatted a distance apart while the clanspeople were served, solitary, his oiled face distant, unreadable.

And the sun burned down.

The sun burned down and Jhaviir resumed his oratory. Tedni returned and translated hoarsely. "He's telling them about the barohna now. About how she came all the way from the warm-stream searching for him, about how she will stay so long as she is respected here, about the things she might do if we are brave enough, if we are strong enough." Tedni shot Danior a challenging gaze, his lean fingers closing on the knife at his waist. "You have seen that we are very strong here. We are very brave. And we work in our gardens."

"I've seen the gardens in your *tau*," Danior assured him, watching the intent faces of the Greater Clan.

"Stay and you will see my very own garden. And he is telling them that he thought to give his Rauth-son—you—a token of his esteem, but no token can shine as brightly as the thought-stone." Tedni licked his lips, his gaze falling keenly on the stone. "If I am truly your brother in some degree—"

"I'll let you hold the stone. Some other time."

Tedni's eyes flashed with satisfaction as he continued his half-whispered translation. "But Keva Marlath, Flame of Marlath, has no thought-stone to blaze at her throat. She let the Zollidar steal hers so we could have eyes in the camp of the small-clans. She tricked them and they carried the stone away unsuspecting. So she has no jewel left.

"And so he is pleased to give her something that has been his own all these years, something small that comes from his heart. He gives it with the people's pledge that they will be deserving of her and of any power she chooses to exercise on their behalf. He gives it—" Tedni jerked and stared up at Danior in pain as Danior's fingers bit his forearm. "Brother—" he protested.

Danior loosened his grip, his mouth half-open in protest. Because he knew even before Jhaviir reached into his robes what he would bring forth. What he intended to give Keva, publicly, where she could not refuse it. He should have guessed sooner, but he had been distracted, only half-listening.

Did she know what it was, the carved stone wristlet he had seen on Jhaviir's wrist the night before? Did she know her mother had carried the sun in it? Had melted snow and ice from an entire valley, creating spring flood waters so deep the growing fields had to be diked to prevent the soil from washing away. Did she know the token Jhaviir bestowed upon her was one of the most powerful tools of a barohna?

Instinctively Danior rose to the balls of his feet, but a quick glance at the gathered people froze the warning in his throat. Jhaviir knew the danger as well as he did. But Jhaviir did not show the people any uncertainty. As Danior watched, clinging hard to his own composure, Rezni escorted Keva forward. Jhaviir took her arm, drawing her to him, freezing Danior with a warning glance. *Not here—say nothing here.*

Danior stared at the breathless people. His hands balled tight and his stomach turned to stone as Jhaviir first displayed the wristlet and then slid it over Keva's hand. Miraculously his hand did not even shake. And Jhaviir had lived in Valley Marlath. He knew that no fledgling barohna casually slid wristlets over her wrists for the first time while people stood near. Knew that instead she met the gem master high in the mountains to accept the wristlets he had carved and polished for her, then waited until he was an hour gone before she ever touched finger to them.

Knew that she practiced their use in solitude until she was ready to wear them among people.

Jhaviir knew the same things Danior knew. But the wristlet was in place and he held Keva's arm aloft for all to see. Danior watched in fascination as the sunstone quickly took life. Within moments the dark band became a blazing circlet of light. Keva gazed up at it, her face paling, her body sagging.

Jhaviir slipped off the wristlet and began speaking again, still holding Keva's arm. Tedni nudged Danior. "You—you're going to hold the sunstone for her. You're going to carry it," he hissed, his eyes wide. "He wants you."

Danior was so relieved to see the sunstone darken in Jhaviir's hand that he did not object. He moved forward automatically, without thinking. He hardly noticed Rezni's avid stare, hardly saw the belated tremor of Jhaviir's fingers as Jhaviir slipped the wristlet over Danior's wrist. He stared down at the stone cuff, holding his breath in brief anxiety. If it brightened for him too—

But it did not.

Slowly Danior raised his head, daring to breathe. He met Keva's eyes and saw fear and rebellion—and shocked disbelief. Gradually, through his own confusion, he became aware of a waiting silence. He looked out over the gathered clan and realized they expected him to speak.

Legend. He must be a man with a legend. Because he was Rauth-son to the Viir-Nega, holder of the sunstone. Numbly he raised his wrist, exhibiting the sunstone wristlet. Tapping some reserve of nerve, he proclaimed in a carrying voice, "I accept the office of guardian of the sunstone."

Then, although no one understood his words, the people of the Greater Clan began to shout and pound their feet. Danior held his arm stiffly aloft, and hoped no one noticed the perspiration that coursed down his face and damped his robe. Unconsciously he raised his other hand and touched the pairing stone. If there was to be a testing, its time had surely come today. It had surely come now. Because he wanted nothing more, at that moment, than to turn and run. To flee the desert, to flee the fire he had seen in the sunstone, to flee the paths that continued to open before his feet—and Keva's.

TWELVE
KEVA

If her memory had once been disordered and indistinct, there were events seared there now Keva knew time could never soften. She would always remember the silent warning in her father's eyes when he slid the carved stone cuff over her arm. Would always remember her startled terror when the cuff blazed alive, the suffocating sense that she was about to be drawn so far beyond anything she understood that she would never find her way back. Would always remember Danior's bloodless pallor when her father took the band from her wrist and placed it upon his—and the moment when she understood what had so briefly circled her wrist: a barohna's fire-cuff. That was when her knees weakened and she almost fell.

But some instinct had stiffened her and she had played out her role—because what else could she do with all the Greater Clan watching? She had stood with chin high through the rest of the rhetoric, the muscles of her scalp and neck rigid and cramping. Had not even cringed when the ceremonies ended and people surged forward, shouting words she didn't understand.

There were so many other things she didn't understand that words no longer troubled her.

She didn't understand the changes that had come to her. Didn't understand the things she had done—in the forest, on the desert, today. Didn't understand how she could have come to find her father and found a barohna's fire-cuff instead.

That was what hurt most. That her father had placed the fire-cuff on her wrist before hundreds of people without telling her what it was or what he intended. As they rode back through the lanes of the settlement, she seized blindly on that wrong and tried to build a wall of anger to block out the fear and confusion that threatened to engulf her. Anger, at least, was hard and clean. The others were formless, suffocating.

But her anger was as weak as she was. She trembled, wanting only to hide—from the people who pressed around her, from the demands they made, from her own thoughts. When they neared her father's *han-tau* and he pulled Ranslega to a halt, she slid quickly from the whitemane's back before anyone could reach to help her down. "I want to be alone. I don't want to talk to anyone," she said in a half-strangled voice, and ran into the paned structure. Then, because she didn't know where else to go, she ran to the wetroom and threw herself down on the rim of the tub, giving up the effort to hold back tears.

Later, when she could cry no more, she took down a jug and drank, then splashed her face and bathed her hands and arms. Trembling, she studied the brown ring where the fire-cuff had rested against her skin. There was no blistering, no rawness, no pain. The texture of her flesh had not changed. The skin had simply darkened. She rubbed it and felt a last tear streak down her face. Would she ever again be the person she had been? Or must she always live with the feeling that she had become a stranger? The band of dark flesh seemed a stigma, one that set her apart—even from herself.

After a while dusk came. She heard subdued voices from the rest of the *han-tau*. Once the door panel folded aside and Resha peered in. When Keva did not speak, the girl dropped the panel and slipped away.

A little later Keva thought she smelled food. Her stomach contracted hungrily, but before she could decide whether to end her seclusion, the door panel was pulled aside again. A shadowed face peered in.

"You come. Come to the women's table." The words were halting, heavily accented.

Keva stood uncertainly, trying to remember the names of her

father's wives. Maiya, Ramari . . . She couldn't remember the name of the third, the one she had not yet met. She hesitated. Anger, fear, confusion—everything was still fresh and painful. But she was hungry too and she couldn't hide herself in the wetroom forever. "Yes," she agreed.

The face withdrew and Keva stepped from the wetroom.

She expected to be led to the front of the *han-tau*, to the room where her father's wives ate. Instead she followed the shadowed woman down a short corridor and out a rear door. When they emerged, the woman turned, looking back uncertainly. "You come," she repeated. "Women's table."

She was little more than a girl, Keva realized, seeing her clearly for the first time. Hardly older than herself. Her face was plump, with round, anxious eyes. And she was pregnant. Keva frowned uncertainly. "Where is the women's table?" Not outside, surely.

"You come."

Keva glanced back, hesitating. Why would her father's wife lead her away from his *han-tau*? Did neighboring women eat together in some other *tau*? And why lead her anywhere so furtively, glancing anxiously back over her shoulder? She discovered quickly that it was no good to ask. The girl seemed to have only a few words of Keva's language, apparently learned by rote, and Keva had none of hers. For a moment Keva thought of turning back. But what harm could this girl offer her? Shrugging, Keva followed.

They threaded dirt lanes and the girl brought her to the back entrance of a domed *han-tau* with vividly colored panes set among the clear to form a bold pattern. Its interior was lit by a solitary lantern. Keva hesitated. The woman enjoined her to come again, then led her through darkened garden rooms to the source of the light.

A low table sat among growing vines, spread with food in glass bowls. Four platters sat at the end of the table. Silently a young woman stood from her cushion on the floor. She was years older than the girl who had led Keva here, her face harder, more weathered. Her eyes were narrow, watching. She stared openly at Keva.

"You are welcome to Rezni's *han-tau*," a proud voice said, and Keva turned to see Resha, her half-sister, sitting at the far side of the table. "We are to eat first and then it will be time to talk."

Rezni's *han-tau?* Keva's eyes darted around the room. But she did not see Rezni. Only Resha, the pregnant girl, and the hard-faced young woman. "What—why did she bring me here?" she demanded, biting back her first impulse to indignation.

Resha drew herself up importantly. "Women's talk. They brought you for women's talk. There are matters to discuss, and I will make their words into mountain language so you can understand. But first they want to give you food."

Keva's gaze shot back to the two women. They studied her intently, straining for the words they could not understand. Rezni's wives—they could only be Rezni's wives, she realized. The wives he proposed to set aside for her. And they had summoned her here, not Rezni? What did they have to discuss with her? She shifted uneasily, but she could find no anger in their eyes. "I don't know their names," she said, stalling.

Resha flashed bright teeth. "Tinata—this is Tinata, from the family-clan Kranich," she said, presenting the plump-faced younger woman. "And Aeia, from the Baanta. Two strong families."

The two women inclined their heads, still watching intently for her response.

"Did Rezni know they were going to invite me here?"

To her surprise, Resha grinned broadly. "Oh no. He has gone to eat with his brothers. And taken his son. He has had his chance to speak. Now is their chance."

So Rezni had a son. Something else he had not mentioned. Keva sighed, realizing she would only meet prolonged argument if she tried to leave. And she was hungry. "Please tell them I'll be honored to eat here." At least neither young woman appeared angry, although the older studied her so closely it made her uncomfortable. She rubbed her wrist, then realized that Tinata was offering her a cushion. She sat.

The meal was conducted with none of the confusion of the

meals she had experienced at her father's table. Tinata, Aeia and Resha served each other and addressed themselves silently to the food, eating methodically. Keva followed their example and found herself hungry for the first time since reaching the desert. As she ate, some of the emotional residue of the day dissolved. She began to feel more relaxed. Began to feel she could deal with strangeness and confusion, at least on this level.

Then the meal was done. Resha piled their platters together at the end of the table and squirmed on her cushion, her eyes flashing with expectation. In a manner that suggested ritual, Tinata and Aeia reached beneath their robes and extricated long-bladed knives. They laid these on the table before them, then turned to Keva with expectation.

The moment extended uncomfortably. "What do they want me to do?" Keva demanded finally.

"Offer your blade," Resha said. "It's part of the talking."

Part of the talking to place weapons on the table? To demonstrate trust? To show that nothing was hidden? The only blade she had ever owned was a digging blade, and that had been stolen in the forest. "I don't carry a blade," she said finally, wondering if it was the wrong thing to say. Would they take her lack of a weapon as a sign of weakness?

Resha quickly translated and to Keva's relief, all eyes turned to her with awe. Aeia spoke rapidly, her sun-chafed face intense.

"You are very strong, to need no blade," Resha translated. "But of course you are a barohna from the mountains. No other woman in these hard-lands would dare go unarmed. Tinata and Aeia are pleased to negotiate with you."

"I—" Keva groped in fresh confusion. "Please—what are we to negotiate?"

Resha's teeth flashed in a quick smile of triumph. "Tinata and Aeia wish to negotiate the matter of the marriage. Rezni came to them last night and told them they must go to his brother so he could make you first-wife of his marriage. No lesser status would be suitable and his brother is a skilled glassworker already, although he is only fifteen. He would make them a good marriage. But Tinata and Aeia have considered this proposal and have prepared a counter-offer, since the obligation cuts with two blades."

Two blades? The two blades on the table? And was Rezni so sure of himself—of her—that he had already discharged his wives? But they didn't appear angry or dispossessed. Keva pressed her temples. One thing was clear, and that was that she did not intend to become Rezni's wife. "Resha, please tell them that I don't intend to—to upset their marriage. I've told Rezni that I don't intend to become anyone's wife. I—"

"But this would be a very good alliance," Resha contended immediately, without direction from Tinata or Aeia. "We have discussed this among us, since I am your eldest sister. I am a year older than Tedni, you know, and he will be twelve this season. Tinata comes from a very strong clan. The Kranich wear the scarlet sash. You saw how many scarlet sashes were worn at clan-call. It is a powerful alliance for you. The Baanta are not so numerous, but they are very cunning. They are hard workers too. Aeia has the gift of soil-working. Everyone knows she is the best gardener in this entire quarter of Pan-Vi. No one will be hungry here. And she has already given a son to the marriage. And Tinata will give a child too, very soon."

"Yes, I see that," Keva said faintly. "I—"

"So the obligation is there, both blades. They cannot leave Rezni, since they have borne him children, and he cannot discharge them for the same reason. Not without their consent. Not even to his brother.

"And so this is what they have decided will be best. They will permit themselves to be discharged to Dari for one night, so that you may have that night to become Rezni's first-wife. Then they will reenter the marriage the following day. You will gain the rank of first-wife and strong alliances, and they will have a marriage stronger than any in the Pan-Vi. And of course there will be a feast like hasn't been seen for many seasons, since you are the Viir-Nega's eldest daughter."

Keva gazed at the two silent women, beginning to understand at last, struggling not to express her surprise in laughter.

It wasn't only Rezni who proposed to marry her. Tinata and Aeia were proposing the match too, but with slightly different conditions. And Resha, as her eldest sister, felt competent to advise her. Even, from the self-importance on her lean young face, felt privileged to do so.

Keva's first inclination was to refuse immediately and unequivocally. But she had learned enough of desert ways to guess that a blunt rejection would only make her a more desirable candidate. And so she must find some other way to deal with the proposal, although she couldn't guess what that might be. "Is this the way marriages are always made in the clans?" she asked cautiously.

Resha translated quickly, then said, "This is what the principles of honor prescribe. This is how marriages are made among the Kri-Nostri, who handed down the principles of honor to the Viir-Nega. Among the small-clans the way is to steal a woman from some other clan. Aeia was stolen once, when she was very young—younger than I am—but she put the knife to him."

"She killed him?" Keva glanced uneasily at the older of Rezni's wives.

Resha nodded. "She is a Baanta. Very cunning. And Tinata—" Resha turned to the younger wife and spoke rapidly. Tinata snatched up her knife, narrowing her round eyes, and slashed at the air. Resha bobbed her head emphatically. "Tinata is very brave, even though she is not so strong as Aeia. We have already decided that Tinata will be guard-sister to you until the marriage is agreed upon. I will stay here to take her place and she will go to my father's *tau* with you. She will carry her knife for you to demonstrate the strength that will come with the marriage."

Tinata intended to guard her? When she was little more than a child herself, and clumsy with pregnancy? Keva chose her words carefully, anxious to refuse the offer gently. "Please tell her I appreciate her offer, Resha. And I appreciate the service you have done us all, by making our words clear to each other. But I—I'm used to being the oldest sister. I'm used to being the one who protects the other. I would be uncomfortable if she left her home to—to guard me.''

"But it is her obligation. Everyone knows Rezni has asked you to be first-wife and that Tinata and Aeia will be proposing a counter-offer. People will say she has no principle."

"But we all know she does. It—it's obvious even to me, and I've just met her. And she should stay here. Her baby—"

"It is not due for another season."

Keva bowed her head, aware of Tinata's gaze, of Aeia's. "Is this—guarding me—part of the principles of honor?"

"It is an ancient custom the Viir-Nega brought from the Kri-Nostri. It is called the principle of *nishana nishata*. Two against the threat. Tinata will be very ashamed if you refuse her protection."

Keva shook her head, wondering how she had come to this, accepting protection from a pregnant girl? But how could she refuse and make Tinata ashamed? "I haven't even said I will join the marriage," she pointed out. "My father—"

"He will understand when he sees Tinata with you," Resha said with finality. "Everyone will understand that you are considering the marriage. And everyone will tell you the advantages."

Keva tried to argue further, but to no avail. The very fact of her reluctance made Resha argue Tinata and Aeia's proposal with greater insistence. And so Keva found herself in the lane a little later with Tinata at her side, knife ostentatiously drawn, her round young face set in what was apparently intended as an intimidating scowl.

Had it been Aeia, Keva would have shrunk from the glint of the blade. Fortunately Aeia, as first-wife, had to remain to tend the gardens. Keva rubbed her arm, grateful for that. And grateful that she had passed the early part of the evening without thinking of the fire-cuff and all the other things that troubled and confused her.

They followed a route she didn't recognize back toward her father's *han-tau*. The moons had already risen. Their light glinted from hundreds of glass panes. Lanterns glowed and growing plants cast nodding silhouettes. Keva wondered in passing where the redmane yearlings had been quartered, who was feeding them.

Then Tinata held out one arm stiffly, hissing. Keva halted and heard feet pounding in far lanes. Heard the shout of a single voice, then answering cries. Finally heard the pounding of many more feet. She turned to Tinata. "What is it?"

Tinata answered in clan-language, turning and peering down the lanes, listening intently. Then she caught Keva's arm and began to run, dragging her back the way they had come. She hissed a single word. "Yarika!" Keva could not tell, from her blazing eyes, whether she was frightened or excited.

By the time they neared the edge of the settlement, other people ran with them, and Keva heard the same cry. "*Yarika!*"

"Keva!"

Keva turned in confusion. Tedni and Danior materialized from the darkness, the stone at Danior's throat casting a faint blue radiance. "The Yarika are coming," Tedni proclaimed with a fierce grimace. "They're coming with torches to burn our maze, but we're ready for them this time. Because Danior saw them with his stone. They robbed the Zollidar and took the thought-stone, and we're ready for them. We'll cut them to meat."

Keva glanced quickly at Danior, her stomach tightening with quick fear. "You aren't going?" To fight marauding clansmen with knives? When he had no training? She was surprised at the sharpness of her reaction, but she remembered the bruising he had taken when he had challenged Rezni to spar with pikes.

He shook his head briskly. "Only to the edge of the campment."

"So he can tell us what he sees," Tedni declared. "With his stone, he doesn't even have to know the Yarika clan-language. He understands everything without knowing their speech. So he will use his stone to see what the Yarika are doing, to hear what they say among themselves, and I will pass word of what they intend to the others."

Tinata caught Keva's arm. She spoke rapidly, jabbing the air with her knife for emphasis, her round eyes blazing.

"She says that if you go to the fighting, she will go before you," Tedni translated. "She will defend you. She will show you that no one harms a wife of Rezni's *han-tau*."

"I—"

"That is the strength of Rezni's marriage," Tedni continued. "She is of the Kranich clan, you know. Her people wear the scarlet sash. You saw at clan-call—"

How many wore the scarlet sash. Keva pressed her temples with both hands, trying to bring some order to her thoughts. Did women go to the fighting as well as men? Was she expected to go? To confront the Yarika, who had stolen the pairing stone from the Zollidar? To—but she did not want to think of it. It made gall rise in her throat.

And the excitement she saw in Tinata's flashing eyes, heard in Tedni's boasting words—how much of it was anticipation and how much fear? Her eyes darted to Danior. "My father—"

"He wants you to wait in his *tau*," he said quickly. 'He only wants to turn the Yarika back. They're one of the smallest of the small-clans. If he turns them back, the others will take the thought-stone from them. Then he will have an ear with the larger clans. The ones that are uniting against him."

"But then the others—" Keva frowned, wishing she had listened more closely the night before, when her father had talked of the small-clans.

"He wants you to go back to the *tau*," Danior repeated.

Keva shoved her fingers through her hair. What choice did she have? Tinata was anxious to prove herself, but Keva was sure that part of the fire in her eyes was fear. For good reason. What chance did she have, clumsy with pregnancy, against skirmishing clansmen? "Tedni, tell Tinata. Tell her we aren't going to the fighting. We have to wait in my father's *tau*."

Tedni spoke rapidly. Tinata argued briefly, her blade wavering mid-air. Then she put it away with a grumbling show of reluctance.

"She wants you to understand she only goes because the Viir-Nega orders it," Tedni said. "She wants you to know she will always stand between you and the enemy. She—"

"I understand." Impulsively Keva seized Tinata's hand. "I understand."

Tinata's round eyes grew. She squeezed Keva's hand, nodding eagerly. Then she turned and led the way back toward the Viir-Nega's paned hut.

No one remained but the younger children and Maiya. They bombarded Tinata with questions, the children lacerating the air with imaginary knives and taking militant stances, kicking and grunting. Isolated by her lack of common language, Keva sat on a cushion in the room where she had eaten the night before. After a while the children went to bed and the paned structure became quiet. Tinata dozed, curled up on her cushion, her eyelids quivering. Maiya came and spoke a few words Keva did not understand and disappeared.

The single lantern guttered and extinguished itself. Keva let herself fall into a peculiar, drifting state of consciousness, her thoughts wandering and vacant, as if she deliberately put away any thought of the fighting on the desert, as if she were willing to think of anything but that. Eventually those thoughts caught up with her anyway. She shivered, staring up at the stars that shone through the glass panes. Trying to shake a rising anxiety, she padded to the front door and looked out into the lane. She saw no one, heard nothing. There was only moonlight and silence.

She was about to retire again when she thought she heard the faint shrill of a redmane. She hesitated, reluctant to leave Tinata. But there seemed to be no danger here. And she knew she would not sleep. Not until her father and Danior returned. Quickly she slipped down the lane, listening for the shrill to be repeated.

She wandered randomly through the dark settlement, thinking of the desert beyond, of its vastness. Thinking of the vulnerability of glass panes and sleeping children.

Thinking of anything but her father and Rezni fighting in the dark.

The redmane shrilled again, from nearby, and she found her way to the sheep pens where they were quartered. The yearlings whickered and grunted excitedly at her approach, pushing their way through the protesting sheep to the low walls of the pens. Keva pressed their enquiring noses and rubbed their necks, laughing at their eagerness, until a small form materialized from nearby shadows and hissed at her.

She started. A girl of perhaps eight glowered up at her. The child spoke rapidly, pointing to the penned animals, gesturing forcefully. Keva frowned. Was the child telling her that she was caretaker of the yearlings? That she slept here, watching the pen? Or was she spinning some verbal extravagance? Keva nodded as if she understood and the child puffed her chest haughtily but continued to glower possessively.

Sighing, Keva turned back into the lanes. She wandered randomly for a while, until she reached the edge of the settlement and peered across the moonlight desert, her chest tightening again. Suddenly it seemed that the night had become very long, that it had been many hours since she and Tinata had heard the first warning cry. Tedni dismissed the Yarika as one of the smallest small-clans. But that didn't make the bite of their knives any less deadly. She gazed around uneasily, wishing she knew what was happening on the desert. If she could find Danior and Tedni—

Tedni had said they would be somewhere at the edge of the settlement. Probably, she guessed, near the guard maze. She glanced around, taking her bearings, then began skirting the settlement, calling their names softly until the guard-maze loomed. She peered into its shadows. "Danior?"

No response. But somewhere in the thorny vegetation, she heard a coughing sound, a low voice. She peered into the wall of green. The moons were low now, ready to set. If she could find her way into the maze, if she could see just well enough to pick her way down its venomous corridors—

The voice she had heard before grew louder. She hesitated. "Tedni?"

"Keva?" It was Danior's voice, muffled.

"Here. I'm over here."

It was several minutes before they emerged from the maze,

Danior stumbling, his face bone-pale. Tedni tried to support him, but they had hardly emerged from the maze before he fell to his knees, vomiting violently. Tedni held his shoulder, then ran to Keva.

The first thing she could think was that something had happened to her father, that Danior had seen it with his stone. "My father—" she said breathlessly. Had he been injured? Killed?

"No, no—we don't know. They're coming back. They're coming back now," Tedni said. He was as pale as Danior, shadow carving deep hollows in his lean face. "But it was bad. It was bad, sister. Danior—" He turned back, concerned. "Can you walk, brother?"

Danior took his feet shakily, his lips white. For the first time Keva noticed that he didn't wear his stone. Instead Tedni carried it, the chain spilling from one hand. Keva drew back. "What happened?" she demanded, wondering if she wanted to know. Wondering what could be so bad it had driven all the color from Danior's face.

"The man who was wearing the other stone—the man he was seeing through—" Tedni gasped, gazing up at Danior with frightened awe.

"The stone—I was there," Danior said finally in a dry croak. "I was there when they skirmished. When they fought. I was there when his brother was killed. I was there—" His voice choked away.

Keva's stomach squeezed sourly as she understood what he was trying to tell her. "You saw everything," she said in a harsh whisper. The stone had taken him to the heart of the fighting and he had seen it all.

"Everything—but I didn't just see it. I felt it. I *felt* everything." He glanced quickly at Tedni. "Those people, the small-clansmen—"

"They're animals!" Tedni spat.

Danior shook his head. "They're—no, they're not animals, Tedni. They—they know you're here, Keva. They've already heard. They think—they think the Greater Clan will push them off their ranging lands now, the lands they need to feed their sheep. They think the Greater Clan will take their women and kill their children. They—''

''Because I'm here?'' Keva shrank back, not wanting to believe.

''Because—*yes*. They don't understand. That's what Jhaviir meant last night. That's what the small-clans would do if they had a barohna. They would drive the other clans off the land. Kill them. Keep only the women to breed with.

''They're hungry. That's how they live—hungry. Every bite they take means someone else has to go hungry. Every bite someone else takes means they go hungry. If they had a barohna, they would use her to drive everyone else away.''

''But my father—'' Her father wasn't a small-clansman. He had drawn people together, not driven them away. He had taught them to work glass and grow gardens. His people were fed.

Yet involuntarily she remembered something Rezni had said at the beginning of their journey from the forest. That if they met small-clansmen on the trek, he would cut their throats but leave their possessions undisturbed. Because stealing was against the principles of honor.

Was killing an enemy without provocation against the principles of honor? Or was the very existence of an enemy provocation enough?

''No,'' she said, and realized from Danior's strained look that he didn't follow her thoughts. ''My father wouldn't—'' He wouldn't kill the small-clansmen if he had the power to do so simply to insure the security of the Greater Clan.

''They fought,'' Tedni said, glancing back toward the bristling maze. ''The Yarika have never fought like that. They're thieves—not soldiers. But my father couldn't drive them back. They threw themselves on his knives.''

Hungry. Starving. Driven hard by a hard land. They had thrown themselves on her father's knives because they expected to die anyway. Because the Greater Clan had a barohna.

Her mouth was suddenly dry. Because she had come to find her father, people had died. She had pressed her search and now five Gothni were dead. The Yarika were dead. Probably even the Zollidar, from whom the Yarika had stolen the pairing stone. All because she had come to the Greater Clan's settlement. She licked her lips, knowing her face had grown as pale as Danior's.

And there was only one thing she could do. "When—when will my father return?" she demanded. She felt as brittle as glass in that moment, ready to shatter under the driving assault of emotion: horror, sorrow—and stronger than either of those, anger. Rising anger.

Tedni stared up at her, vertical creases appearing between his eyes. "By dawn. Maybe sooner."

Her father would return by dawn and soon after she would leave. She would go away and try to forget she had ever ridden a whitemane and heard a bluesong, had ever known a dark man with searching eyes. She would go, but not through any decision of her own. Her right to remain with her father had been taken from her. By the Yarika. By the Gothni and the Zollidar. By all the other desert clans.

Because even if her father did not intend to destroy the small-clans, even if he only intended to defend Pan-Vi, people had died because she had come here. And if she remained, more would die. Men and women. Perhaps even children as young as Tedni and Resha.

She turned, bitterness suddenly welling in her throat. "Tell my father I'll be with the redmanes," she said, and ran quickly back toward the paned settlement before Danior and Tedni could see that she cried. Before they could see the blind, burning anger behind her tears—and the helpless confusion it hid. She had come to make a search and the clans had turned it to carnage. They were hungry, they were driven—but they were driving her from her father when she had just found him.

Animals, savages—no, they were neither. And she knew she must not hate them for what they were: flawed human beings who made her responsible for their lives and their deaths. But she was flawed too, and in those moments she did hate them.

THIRTEEN
KEVA

"K eva! Keva!"

Moaning, Keva groped through a barrier of fire toward her father's voice, then shuddered and tried to turn back. She didn't want to wake, even from her dreams of burning mountains. She didn't want to grapple again with everything that had happened the night before. She pressed her hands to her eyelids, resisting, but her father touched her forearm and everything came spilling back anyway. The Yarika. What Danior had seen with his stone. The people who had thrown themselves on the Greater Clan's knives. Her anger.

"Keva, you've slept on the ground. Your arms are cold as the mountain. Come—get up and I'll have Maiya warm the tub."

Sobbing, she opened her eyes. It was early morning, barely past dawn. Her father crouched beside her, barefoot. He was freshly scrubbed, dressed in spotless robe and trousers. But looking up, she saw something in his face that water could never wash away. A stain: blood. And he wore a bandage on one arm.

She pushed herself up stiffly, surprised to find Tinata curled against her, her white robe soiled. Keva dislodged her carefully and glanced around in confusion. Reluctantly she remembered coming here, to the pen where the redmanes were confined, hoping to find some reassurance in their familiar presence. Just as reluctantly she remembered she had found none. Quickly she put away the last confusion of sleep. "You're hurt."

"I have a few cuts. Some bruises. We had a hard fight."

He spoke with full gravity, and she recognized almost unwillingly that the stain in his eyes was not blood but pain. "Did you lose many from the Greater Clan?" People she had seen at clan-call yesterday, shouting and triumphant—how many were dead now?

"A few. Most of the dead were from the Yarika."

Yes, because the Yarika had come expecting to die, quickly by knife and spear or slowly, driven from their grazing lands. Her fists clenched. She turned away and caught a deep breath, trying to find strength in it. "I'm leaving," she said—quickly, because telling him that was the hardest thing she could imagine. Everything beyond would be easy. Painless.

He rocked back on his heels, his arched brows contracting with surprise. "No." The protest seemed involuntary, something that escaped despite his better judgement.

And that made it that much harder for her to go on. "Yes. I only came to find you. To find if you were alive, to tell you I was. To tell you Oki lied. And now we—we both know and I have to go. If I stay—" She shook her head, not wanting to cry again, not wanting him to see her anger, her fear, her confusion.

He laid a staying hand on her arm, but before he could argue, Tinata's round eyes flew open. Gasping, she sat and groped in the dirt. She snatched up her knife, speaking rapidly, pleadingly, to Jhaviir.

He nodded, quieting her. "Please—she wants me to tell you how ashamed she is that she guarded you so poorly," he explained. "She should never have fallen asleep and it will not happen again. Her knife will protect you even through the hours of night. She—"

"Oh, please—tell her no one else could have guarded me as well," Keva protested, wondering guiltily when Tinata had found her, how long she had slept curled uncomfortably on the bare ground. "She needs to sleep."

"She needs to bathe and eat and sleep, all those things," he agreed immediately. "And she won't do any of them without you. Come back to the *han-tau* and let us fill the tub. You can both bathe. And then we can talk, quietly. Privately."

Keva wanted to argue. But her father was already helping her to her feet, brushing at her clothes. Tinata's fingers were blue with cold. And people were gathering, men with bandaged arms, women with spears and bleak faces. This was not the time or place to talk.

She held her tongue while she and Tinata bathed, while they ate—quietly, from the women's table—while Tinata was persuaded to sleep. Then she returned to the room where they had eaten the night she arrived. Danior sat cross-legged on a cushion, the thought-stone on the table before him, the fire-cuff on one wrist. Keva hesitated, then sat beside him, surprised to see how old he looked. Years older than the youth she had met at the teaching pond just a few days ago, his face ashen, a distracted frown gouging creases between his brows.

Her father joined them soon, taking a cushion opposite them. Early morning sunlight fell through glass panes, scoring fine lines in his face, revealing a bruise near his left ear she had not noticed earlier. He studied Keva silently, rubbing his neck, as if he could stroke away fatigue. Finally he said, "I believe Danior and Tedni told you in better detail than I did about the fight we had last night."

Keva drew a deep breath, wishing she had gathered her possessions and gone the night before. Wishing she hadn't prolonged her leavetaking. Because all the things she had tried to put back were returning, rising to the surface. Her voice shook with them. "Yes. And they told me why the Yarika fought so hard. Because they thought the Greater Clan would drive them off their lands. That's—that's why I'm leaving. Because if I stay—" She stopped, catching a tremulous breath. Surely she didn't have to say more. He already knew as well as she did what would happen if she stayed. Slaughter.

His pupils narrowed. Small muscles tightened, pulling his features taut. He spoke sharply. "You're leaving because the Yarika, who have been invited to pledge themselves to the Greater Clan many times, chose the old ways instead? Because they were so frightened by the stories they heard that they used our knives to kill themselves with? They could have joined us anytime. They could have built *han-taus* among ours and taken the seed we offered them. They could have come to clan-call yesterday and shared the plenty with us.''

Keva shrank, not wanting to hear him speak so harshly of the dead. "But they didn't.''

"No. Because they didn't choose to live by the principles that apply here. That we don't steal. That we don't fight among ourselves. That women aren't stolen and children aren't beaten. The Yarika chose the old ways instead.

"Not because they were evil. Just because they had lived too long by the old ways to trust anyone but their own clan-mates.

"And now they have died with their clan-mates, by the old ways. They chose the time and they chose the weapons. And it has nothing to do with you. What happened last night was not your decision or mine. It was theirs.''

Theirs, but a decision they would not have made under different circumstances. Keva stared at the fire-cuff on Danior's arm and felt angry tears rise in her eyes. She should have gone the night before, before he had a chance to argue with her, to confuse her further.

Her father leaned across the table, catching her hands in his, pressing them until she met his eyes. "Do you remember your mother, Keva?''

"I—I think so," she said, stiffening at the abrupt change of topic. "I remember a woman standing against fire. And not burning. I remember—'' She shuddered and her voice hardened. "Oki told me about the barohnas. About the things they did when the fisher-people still lived in the mountains. About the burnings, about—'' She stopped, the words drying in her throat. The anger she had felt the night before, against the Yarika, the Gothni, the other small-clans—was that what warring barohnas had felt when they unleashed their fire?

They were driving her away—the small-clans were driving her away before she even had a chance to know her father. Her hands closed to fists. She bit her lower lip.

"Oh yes, there was a period when the barohnas abused their

powers. But it was very brief, Keva. Less than three centuries. And there have been twenty-three centuries of peace since. I don't think you can hold the actions of a few confused women against hundreds of women who have lived only for their people's benefit."

Confused? *She* was confused—and wherever she looked for answers, she found only more questions. Keva shook her head helplessly, trying to draw her hands from his. He would not release them. Nor would he release her eyes. "You don't understand," she said. Didn't understand the caustic anger she had felt last night, still felt today. Didn't understand how heavily the deaths of the Yarika and the Gothni weighed on her. Didn't understand how those deaths had already poisoned the desert for her. The small-clans were ready to kill because a barohna had come to the desert, yet she knew she could never be as Oki said a barohna must be. She shook her head angrily. "I'm not like a barohna. I'm not hard."

"Hard?" His brows rose sharply. "What do you mean—hard?"

"I—what happened to the Gothni. I can't stop thinking about it. I dreamed about it, last night, this morning. I remember it when—when I'm eating, when I'm bathing. I—"

Her father pressed her fingers, forcing her to meet his gaze again. "If you felt any other way, I wouldn't want you here among my people, Keva. In the mountains the people say a barohna is stone where she lives. Rock. But understand—that doesn't mean a barohna is uncaring. Unfeeling. It means that she is strong enough to hold steady against her own impulses. Strong enough never to use her power lightly, without thinking. A barohna must be hard in just that one way. She must be as firm as a rock in her control."

Keva shook her head stubbornly, remembering Par's stories of the power of the sunstone. "I—I don't think anyone has so much control." Certainly she did not.

He shrugged, releasing her hands, leaning back. He pressed one hand to his eyes and looked briefly inward. "Keva, has anyone told you how your mother died?"

"No." Hoarsely. No one had told her, she hadn't asked, and

she didn't want to hear it now. Because that wasn't what they were discussing. That—

But he ignored the rebellion that crossed her face. "Then it's my privilege to tell you. There aren't so many people who know the whole story.

"Lihwa was already a barohna when I met her. A girl of fifteen trying to meet a woman's responsibilities, beginning to regret that she had assumed them so many years sooner than she need have. She went to the mountains to take her beast early, the very day she reached her first majority, and her mother lost the power of the stones almost immediately. So Lihwa had hardly two hands of days to return to the mountains and practice the use of her cuffs. Then the valley was hers to maintain, hers to govern. It became her responsibility to draw sunlight late in winter and use it to thaw the growing fields for early planting. Her responsibility to make cold summers warm. Her responsibility to hold back the frost in autumn until the crops were done. Her responsibility to make all the decisions expected of a barohna.

"The responsibility sat heavily. She began to wonder why she had gone to her beast so soon. Why she had pressed to become a barohna when she could have been a palace daughter for years longer.

"I met her in the first summer she governed the valley, the first summer I spent on Brakrath. A warm day. She wasn't needed in the valley so she went to the mountains. I had been living in the plain with the guardians, but I left and went exploring, trying to find my way in this new world. I was angry and a little lost because I wanted to return to the Kri-Nostri and it was impossible.

"I regretted a lost people, a lost culture. She regretted a lost time—the youth she had put behind too soon. That created a bond between us very quickly. We traveled together for two days, and when she went back to the valley, I went with her.

"I soon found the people of Valley Marlath weren't the Kri-Nostri, any more than the guardians had been. They were disciplined, but in an entirely different way. They had no need for a Kri-Nostri soldier and I wasn't prepared for the life they did offer. I felt that if I could not be a soldier, I was no one. I stayed for a few hands of days and left. But the bond with Lihwa had been created and I returned. I soon became her consort—her wandering consort.

"In the winter when Lihwa went to her winter palace in the peaks, I spent some of the cold-time with her. I spent more of it traveling across Brakrath, measuring myself against this world—never taking what I wanted from it because I wanted the wrong things.

"You were born in the second of the four years we had together. After your birth, Lihwa made me wear her pairing stone and take one of her wristlets each time I left, thinking they would bring me back to her. It isn't usual for a barohna to retain a mate beyond one season. But what we had was different from what most barohnas have with their mates. A permanent bond rather than a passing liaison. I wish I had honored the bond better, but I didn't know how.

"She wore the second cuff herself. It was enough for her use. She could store enough sunlight in a single cuff to do all she needed.

"We reached late winter of our fourth year. I had marked Ranslega the year before, in the forest, and that winter I returned to the mountains with him. Lihwa had kept you with her, and the three of us spent several hands of days together in the winter palace. I was less restless than usual. It was a good time—for all of us, I think. I remember I envied my brother Iahn—Danior's father—then because he never seemed to be torn between the need to go and the desire to stay. But of course his experience before coming to Brakrath had been very different from mine.

"Then one morning we saw the smudge-pot burning in the palace plaza, signalling that the people had wakened from wintersleep. It was time for Lihwa to go for the spring thawing.

"That afternoon we walked together to Misana's Cropping, a rocky overlook two-thirds of the way down the mountain. From there Lihwa walked alone, so she could let her wristlet blaze and the people would see she was coming. The Spring Coming is one of the large celebrations in the valley. Everyone gathers on the plaza. Parents pile their children on their shoulders so they can see the barohna as she walks down the mountain, her cuffs blazing. So they can see the long cold time is over again.

"I waited on the cropping with you. The people waited in the plaza. The sun set and Lihwa walked in the dark, her wristlet blazing—blazing so brightly she seemed to walk at the center of the sun. Perhaps that's what you remember—your mother walking down the mountain that day."

Keva frowned, trying to draw the scene fully into memory. A figure silhouetted against fire, the mountain—but there was more. She remembered a cracking, grumbling sound, a shaking. And fear. Did she remember fear? "I—don't know," she said, her muscles tensing. In anticipation of what her father would tell her next? Or in memory?

Jhaviir nodded, sitting back on his cushion, seeming to withdraw into time. "I remember—every detail. The way the rocks of the cropping ground under my boots. The glint of moonlight on the snow. Ranslega's restlessness. Perhaps he felt what was coming. The mountains that cup the cultivated valleys are stable. Occasionally there are rock slides, but not often. Snow slides are far more common, particularly at that time of year. While we watched from the cropping, a mass began to move on the upper mountain. It swept down to the east of us. Swept down directly toward Lihwa."

Keva drew back, memory becoming sharper. The ground shuddering underfoot. A sense that the darkness of the mountain itself was tearing apart, that it was bearing down. And fear—yes, sharp, breathless.

"She had just fractions of a second to recognize what was happening and to decide what she must do. Just fractions of a second to find and weigh alternatives. To realize that she had enough energy stored in her cuff to turn the snow to steam. To boil it away—and scald the people waiting on the plaza. The slide was so heavy, it had caught her so near the bottom of the mountain, and there was no time for the people on the plaza to flee. And no place to flee to.

"I didn't appreciate all this at the time. I only understood later, when I had time to think. At the time I heard the avalanche, I looked up and saw moonlight on a moving mass of snow, I looked down and saw Lihwa staring up. She was too far away for me to see what was in her face. But I saw what she did. She pulled off her wristlet and threw it away. And then the snow swept down and crushed her. She must have died instantly.

"She—" Keva saw the scene so clearly it took her breath. The snow grumbling down the mountainside, the lone figure, the dying brightness of the fire-cuff. A dream . . . memory . . . reality. Something wrenched in her chest, bringing tears to her throat. "She threw it away so she wouldn't use it," she whispered.

"Yes. She was afraid that if she kept it, she would forget herself at the last instant. She would lose the control she had spent four years building and save herself."

And scald the people waiting on the plaza. Keva pressed trembling fingers to her temples, not knowing what to say. Not even sure she could speak.

Her father sat erect again, addressing her with a weighing gaze. "You know, the first night, when you came looking for me, I hoped to hear you had come looking for your mother too. I'm sorry you didn't."

Keva stared down at the table top, sorry too. Sorry she had been so eager to dissociate herself from the person she feared her mother to have been, so afraid of what she might learn that she had not troubled to ask anyone—Tehla, Danior, her father— who her mother had in truth been. A woman who ruled with fire, cruelly, or a girl just a few years older than herself, with responsibilities she had never imagined. She glanced at the fire-cuff on Danior's wrist and tried to accept what she had learned, tried to accept without guilt the fact that she had not asked sooner.

But knowing who her mother had been, how she had died, did not change what had happened since she had come to the desert. Reluctantly her thoughts turned back to the Gothni. "The men I killed—"

"There were other ways you could have dispersed them. But you had no way of knowing. And you had no one to guide you." Reaching across the table, he slipped the fire-cuff from Danior's wrist. He toyed with it, dark fingers rubbing its polished surfaces. "The man who cut this for your mother was one of the most accomplished gem masters on Brakrath. When he presented it to her, he told her it was a tool, simply a tool. One she must learn to use just as he had learned to use his stone-cutting tools. She must learn what she was capable of doing with it, must learn how to control herself in the use of it, how to use it without harming the people around her.

"All the gifts of the stones are like that. They are tools you must learn to use. But you didn't have a chance to learn before you met the Gothni. You suddenly found yourself with an ability you didn't know you possessed. An ability you had never witnessed or experienced in anyone else. It's not surprising that you didn't use it as well as you might have."

Keva sighed, gazing reluctantly at the fire-cuff. Would she ever dare touch it again? Ever dare intentionally draw the sun with it? Ever dare try to make controlled use of that and the other gifts of the stones? "I—I don't even know how the stones work," she said. "I don't understand how anyone can catch the sun in a stone."

Jhaviir nodded. Reaching into the growing beds behind him, he broke a single leaf from the vines. He placed it on the palm of his hand. "Tell me how this plant takes sunlight and water and turns them to green plant tissue. Tell me how Lihwa and I danced and laughed together in our quarters after Midsummer Fest and here you are sixteen years later, a person in your own right. Separate from either of us, although if we hadn't come together that night, you would never have existed."

"I don't know," Keva admitted. She couldn't explain any of those things.

"Neither do I know. But there is order to life and there are rules that govern its processes—and the processes of the stones as well. Someday we will understand them. The fact that we don't understand them now doesn't mean that the rules don't exist. That we can't explore them and benefit from the processes."

Danior roused himself. "You have to practice," he said. "To

learn about the stones, you have to use them. If you don't, you won't learn—anything.''

Keva nodded, remembering how she had called back the stones she had hurled at Rezni without knowing how she did it. How later she had managed to bring the sandstorm under control too.

But she had brought it under control too late. The Gothni were dead.

And Danior—he had used the thought-stone the night before. What had it taught him? How fear felt when it coursed through another man's body? The shadow of what he had learned was still in his eyes. She frowned, remembering Tedni's awe, his solicitude. "The man who carried the other stone—" she said impulsively, frowning.

Danior's lips twitched. He refused to meet her eyes. "He—died.''

A cold hand closed on her heart. He had died while Danior held the stone that linked them. And he need not have. If she hadn't come here—

But it had been the Yarika's choice not to join the Greater Clan. His choice to live in the old way. His choice to join in the attack on her father's people.

Keva bit her lip, her thoughts running confused in every direction. If she stayed, other people would die as the Yarika had, for the same reasons. Because they knew—wrongly—that if they didn't destroy the Greater Clan, they would be driven from their lands, extinguished.

But if she didn't stay, if she left and the small-clans learned she had gone, knew there was no longer a barohna in Pan-Vi—

"If I leave," she said, groping, "what will the small-clans do?''

Her father frowned, stroking the fire-cuff absently. "Keva, the small-clans have pressed us from the beginning. They have stolen women, they have stolen goods, they have destroyed our *han-tau*—they have killed our children. If you stay, they will almost certainly join against us. Soon, I think—maybe very soon—hoping to destroy us, and you, before we grow any stronger.''

"But if I leave—"

"Then they will press us too. I don't know how quickly or how hard. But they will press. They always have."

Keva touched anxious fingertips to her temples, trying to find some relief from the disorder of her thoughts. Her decision to leave the warmstream and find her father had been so simple. Her decision last night to leave the desert had been equally simple. Now it had become so complex she didn't think she could deal with it.

"Danior—what will you do?" Strangely, she realized for the first time that she didn't even know why he had come to the desert. She had accepted his presence, his company, without question. Not even wondering.

He stroked the thought-stone with one fingertip, then carefully coiled the chain around it, creating a nest of metal links. "I don't know," he said. He looked up at her and shrugged helplessly. "I don't know. I thought I would stay. But now I have to think again. Last night—"

Last night he had become old. Last night he had died in another man's mind. Keva nodded. They sat for a long time without speaking. From other parts of the *han-tau* Keva heard children's voices, smelled food cooking. Beyond the glass panes, the sun cut a slow arc. Looking up, she saw that the fine lines around her father's eyes seemed more deeply etched than they had been just a few minutes earlier. As if he contemplated a hardship more severe than any he had met before. He frowned, rubbing the back of his neck.

Finally he turned his hand palm up and rapped the table once, a gesture that seemed almost ceremonial. "Keva, we have an institution we call *tarnitse*. I won't even attempt to translate it for you. I brought it from the Kri-Nostri. When there is a decision to be made, a new project to be undertaken, and our thoughts are frayed, we go to *tarnitse* to bind the strands together again."

Something that would help her sort through confusion and deal with everything she had learned? Was it a rite—or a place? "Where would we have to go? Does it happen here—in Pan-Vi?"

"No, we've built our *tarnitse* hut south of here, over a spring. We go there and fast and take silence. The only voice allowed to speak in the hut is the voice of the water. After a while, if you listen carefully, the *tarnitse* water can tell you things you would never guess otherwise."

Keva pushed her fingers back through her hair and thought of the times she had gone to streamside to think when she was young. Certainly she needed to the think now. Needed to send confusion away on the moving waters. "I'd like to go," she said.

Danior shifted and took up his pairing stone. With a decisive gesture, he placed the chain around his neck. The glowing stone nestled against his throat. "I'd like to go too."

"Of course. The traditional time to begin the journey is two hours after dawn. It's too late today, but Tedni will be honored to guide you there tomorrow. He'll know what you need and pack it." He rubbed a tired hand across his face. "And now I think we all need to sleep. Danior?"

Danior nodded and rose. Keva stood too, realizing from the ache of her muscles how little she had slept the night before, how tired she was. She accepted a handclasp from her father, then made her way to the room where Tinata slept. Her mind was brimming with images—of flying sand, of grumbling snow, of a woman who stood against fire, arms extended, reaching back to be remembered. But she had been eager to forget rather than remember. Tears wetting her eyes, she found a cushion and curled up, hoping to sleep without dreaming.

FOURTEEN
DANIOR

Danior stirred in his sleep, trying to shield his eyes from the sun that glinted off the sand. The cushion where he slept shifted against his belly as he crawled forward, one fist knotted so tightly on the handle of his knife the knuckles ached.

No. His fingers were closed around his pairing stone; he had clasped it in his sleep. Someone else's fingers ached against the bone handle of a knife. Someone he recognized as little older than himself but leaner, harder, someone whose thoughts came to him as clearly as his own even though they did not share a common language. Garrid was his name and bravado and curiosity drove him forward, crawling flat on his belly.

He wanted to run. Wanted to put the Yarika and their dead, staring eyes far behind. Uneasily he raised his head and glanced back to where their sprawled bodies lay, blood blackening the sand. His throat closed against the acid rise of fear.

But he had not come so far out of his way to turn back now. And the pendant he had taken from the dead Yarika—that would protect him. He was sure of it. He had hesitated over taking it. But the cut and polish of the stone was so shining, the workmanship of the chain so intricate, it had to be more than a simple ornament. And while it had not protected the Yarika, certainly it would protect him.

He was not a Yarika, after all, dirty and hungry and ignorant. He was a Fon-Delar, member of the largest clan on the desert and the most prosperous.

Largest, most prosperous and strongest—except for the clan that had pitched its glass tents below. The clan that had slaughtered the Yarika.

A thrill of envy made him shiver in the hot sunlight. His uncle, Kanir, was headsman of the Fon-Delar. But Kanir wasn't half so well known as the Viir-Nega—headsman of the deadliest fighters, the most skilled knifesmen on the desert! Even the women of the Viir-Nega's clan carried knives, and that doubled the clan's fighting strength. Certainly no one among the Fon-Delar would trust a woman with a weapon.

Garrid squirmed forward, remembering the night the woman his brother Pelar had stolen from the Vernica had snatched a knife and slashed Pelar's scalp, slicing off his ear. And that only because Pelar had ducked before she could drive the blade into his throat. Garrid had decided that same night that he would never steal a wife from the Vernica. Some other clan, perhaps, less savage.

And now that the time for establishing his own tent came nearer, he even toyed with the idea of arranging a ritual stealing. That would diminish his stature, certainly, but he wouldn't have to constantly guard his back. He had a few sheep of his own. He could offer those for the bride and perhaps his uncle would sponsor a wedding feast. A rich wedding feast commanded almost as much respect as a good stealing.

He had reached the thorn-maze, crawling on his belly. Cautiously Garrid took his feet and studied the thorny wall. When he found the entrance, he made his way down narrow paths cut through the woody vegetation. It would be simpler just to skirt the edges of the maze and look down on the campment from another perspective, but the dense leaves offered him cover. And there would be sentries mounted at the perimeters of the campment today, so soon after the engagement with the Yarika.

Eventually only one thickness of thorny vegetation separated him from view of the glass-paned structures of the Viir-Nega's campment. He peered through the oily leaves as he had so often before. It seemed strange to him, planting permanent tents in one place, instead of following the sheep across their ranging lands. It seemed strange, growing food plants instead of subsisting on mutton, game and forage. It seemed strange, making all the promises one had to make to live as the people of the Greater Clan lived. Promises not to go armed against each other, not to steal women, not to take from each other. Although as youngest brother, he felt a certain sympathy with that stricture, since he was always the one things were taken from.

Yes, many things seemed strange, but the glint of glass panes by sunlight fascinated him—as it always did when he detoured in this direction. The notion of burying seeds and watering them and watching brilliant green plants spring from the soil fascinated him. Unconsciously he touched the stone he had taken from the dead Yarika. That fascinated him too. He stared into it and tried to decide, from its flawless clarity, if it could be glass instead of stone, made by the craftsmen below. Craftsmen who had once been ordinary clansmen. It would be all the more valuable if that were so because then it was a token of what men could do if they just knew how.

So many things fascinated him. Sometimes when he passed this way, he stood in the maze and thought of walking into the Greater Clan's settlement with his hands in the air, signaling that he would not touch his knife, and talking with the people who lived this new way. Often he gazed down and wondered what it would be like to watch sunlight from inside one of those glass tents, to see it stained by colored panes. He wondered what it would be like to stitch a new robe and not have to surrender it to Pelar, only to get it back two seasons later torn and stained. He wondered what it would be like to wear the pendant he had found openly, with no fear it would be stolen.

New ways. But his thoughts were tinged with fear. There was no enemy so bitter as a brother abandoned. And all the men of Fon-Delar were his brothers, although the strength of the blood-tie varied. He stepped back into the maze, frowning with a new thought. Did his uncle know the Yarika were dead? Garrid frowned, wondering why they had committed themselves to an assault to the death, why they had died when they could have skirmished and run. Everyone knew the Greater Clan seldom pursued its enemies. It simply fought them back and returned to its glass campment. Weakness, Pelar said, but Garrid suspected the Greater Clan behaved so because they had found more important things to do than fight.

Creating glass from sand could be more important, once you learned the secret.

Planting seeds could be more important too.

But he dared not suggest those things to Pelar.

And the Yarika were dead. Perhaps there was something he didn't know. Something new. He had been gone for seventeen days, scouting for new range lands. He had spoken to no one but a messenger for the Hensi, and that fourteen days ago. Perhaps there was a new war he hadn't heard of.

He turned and picked his way back through the maze, concerned now. Anxious to reach camp and learn what had happened in his absence. He put disloyal thoughts—dangerous thoughts—behind. But as he emerged from the maze again, he tucked the stone pendant under his robes, where no one would see it. Especially Pelar.

As Garrid started back across the desert, Danior pulled his hand from the pairing stone and sat, pressing his temples to dispel a momentary confusion. The Fon-Delar—one of the two large-clans on the desert, their men respected for their bravado with knife and spear. Rezni had told him that much. But Garrid's thoughts had been so much less fiery than the Yarika's. He had not been filled with hysterical fear, with the vengeful need to sink his knife.

Perhaps that would change when he heard of the barohna. And he would hear soon if messengers were already running.

Danior found Jhaviir in one of the growing rooms, cultivating seedlings, working with such concentration that he might have been observing a solemn rite. He looked up at Danior's approach, then stood when he saw Danior's expression. "Yes?"

Danior gave the news reluctantly. "Someone else has taken the stone."

Jhaviir's fingers closed on the tined tool he used. Tension scored vertical lines between his brows. "Tell me."

Wishing he did not have to, Danior told him what he had seen, what he knew. When he finished, Jhaviir rocked back on his heels, nodding thoughtfully. "A nephew of Kanir. Garrid, Pelar . . . I don't recognize the names. But close to Kanir. So my decision to leave the stone on the neck of the Yarika who wore it was well-taken. We will have a well-placed ear in the camp of the Fon-Delar when this young clansman reaches home. Tomorrow, probably, late in the day."

Danior nodded, feeling neither triumph nor elation. How could he when they intended to use Garrid's fascination with the glass-working skills of the Greater Clan against his people? He pressed his temples, wishing he could learn to use the pairing stones without developing rapport with the wearer of the other stone. Wishing he could step coldly, impersonally into another mind and emerge untouched. He frowned, a new thought striking him. "Do you want me to stay here tomorrow? When Keva goes to the desert?"

"When she goes to *tarnitse?*" Jhaviir stood, brushing his hands on his robes. He paced away, picking his way thoughtfully among the seedlings. Finally he shook his head. "No. You will be traveling south and any attack that comes within the next day or two will come from the north or east. So you will be in no immediate danger. I will ask you to break *tarnitse* occasionally to monitor the stone. If there is urgent news, send Tedni with the message immediately. And follow with Keva and Tinata."

"Tinata?"

Jhaviir shrugged. "Tinata has pledged her knife to Keva."

Yes, and Danior had seen how enthusiastically Tinata's protection had been accepted. "Does Keva know she's coming?"

"She's probably guessed by now. And you—have you eaten? No? And you haven't had much chance to explore Pan-Vi either. You'll want to see the furnaces and the special nurseries where we're hybridizing seeds. Find Tedni and tell him it's time he showed you around. Then even if you never leave Brakrath, you'll have seen a bit of another world. A bit of the Kri-Nostri culture.''

A bit of Kri-Nostri culture surrounded by sand and wind and hostile clansmen. But of course the Kri-Nostri culture had evolved in just such a place. Danior touched his stone and for a moment ran across the hard-lands with Garrid, hurrying to reach his people. A worm of fear grew in Garrid's stomach as he ran. Danior released the stone, feeling the same worm grow in his own stomach. But he was not afraid for his safety but for Garrid's. And there was nothing he could do. If only he could use the stone to project a plea to Garrid, to call him back to the Greater Clan's campment . . .

Fleetingly he wondered if he would be able to speak to Garrid in his own language if they met face to face. Could he use the pairing stone to tap Garrid's sense of the Fon-Delar tongue, to learn how individual words and phrases felt in his throat, on his tongue, to learn what images accompanied the sounds? If he could teach himself to speak the Fon-Delar language simply by monitoring the pairing stone—

Distracted, he went to find Tedni, who was pleased to show him how the furnace turned desert sand and its impurities to glass of many colors. Later Danior saw the carts used for hauling fire-coals from quarries located far to the west and saw the special nurseries where common desert plants were culled and bred to produce the most desirable seeds for cultivation. Tedni plunged so enthusiastically into his duties as guide that he scarcely noticed Danior's preoccupation.

Danior touched the pairing stone at intervals through the day, searching Garrid's memory for clues to the spoken language of the Fon-Delar, mouthing the words and phrases he found there. He clutched the stone when he slept, making Garrid's dreams his own. And he touched the stone again the next morning when Tedni woke him shortly after dawn. Garrid was traveling south again, running, the worm in his stomach a coiled serpent now because of what he had learned from the messenger he met at dawn. A barohna in the hard-lands, housed in the glass campment he had looked down upon yesterday. A barohna, woman fire-warrior from the mountains. His few sheep—he imagined them reduced to blackened bones and terror made his heart race. There would be no arranged stealing if he had no sheep. There would be no wedding feast. If he had no sheep, there would be nothing.

Fire-warrior. He imagined her laughing as she threw bolts of sunlight at his sheep and he ran faster.

Danior had expected some argument when Keva learned that Tinata was to go with them to the *tarnitse* hut. But she simply shrugged, accepting Tinata's company, and Danior realized she was as preoccupied as he.

They ate and made farewells and then they stepped upon the desert, Tedni leading the way, Tinata following, her dagger ostentatiously at the ready. Occasionally as they walked, Danior caught an anxious glint in her eyes, but she did not abandon her protective pose.

The *tarnitse* hut was located two hours' walk south of Pan-Vi, a small structure of dried grasses tied to a framework of sturdy poles erected directly over a small spring. A trickle of water cut a channel beneath one wall of the hut and ran briefly into the desert, a tracery of green marking its path. Danior studied the structure dubiously, wondering what he could learn here. Not to touch so deeply when he read from the stones? Not to care? Perhaps he could learn nothing. Perhaps it was impossible to use the stones and remain untouched.

"My father has instructed you what to do here," Tedni said importantly. "You are to eat now and then go into the hut when the sun is at its highest to begin the fast. Tinata and I have the office of guarding you while you listen to the water."

"Yes, he instructed us," Danior said absently. Perhaps it was impossible.

Tedni nodded with satisfaction and made a show of setting out the customary seeds and dried fruits and mutton strips.

Then the sun stood high and Danior and Keva approached the *tarnitse* hut. Danior peered through the narrow doorway. Needles of sunlight pierced the loosely thatched roof and glinted on the water that bubbled from the center of the floor. There were no furnishings, no implements or tools, no embellishments of any kind. There was only the bare floor and the slowly bubbling water.

Self-consciously Danior entered and lowered himself beside the tiny spring. Someone had pressed shards of glass into the damp soil that surrounded it, creating a tiny, jeweled basin. Keva avoided his eyes, guarding her thoughts. But he did not need the stones to guess what they were or to know the pain they brought. Was she to go or stay? There would be bloodshed either way. Bloodshed because she had come—because they had come. Sighing, he gazed around, letting his eyes grow accustomed to the dimness, trying not to feel stifled by the sense of enclosure.

He sat as Jhaviir had instructed them, cross-legged, one hand lying palm-down on each knee. He closed his eyes and let his head drop forward, making a conscious effort to empty himself, as he would have for a teaching. He breathed evenly, trying to send one troubling thought away with each measured exhalation.

But there was no teaching voice in the *tarnitse* hut. There was no voice at all. There was only the ache of his legs and the faint sound of water. And gathering heat. The early afternoon sun beat down on the hut. After a while, when his thoughts continued to drum anxiously at his awareness, Danior knelt and drank from the spring. The water was cool, faintly sweet.

But it told him nothing. Sweat ran down his back and made his skin itch. His calves and thighs began to cramp. His thoughts, he found, ran in chains, each successive thought leading to others, none new, none helpful. Remain in Pan-Vi? Hold the pairing stone through skirmish after skirmish? Follow more frightened, hungry men into death? He pressed his eyelids shut, feeling nausea rise in his throat.

Go then? Leave Jhaviir, Rezni, Tedni, the others to fight their battles unaided. Battles more fierce for the fact that he and Keva had come. Could he do that?

If only there were some alternate course, some third path. But he found none.

After a while he remembered he had promised to monitor Garrid's thoughts. Anxious to break the monotonous chain of his own thoughts, he clasped the stone and reached out. Immediately the ache of his legs changed, becoming harsher.

Garrid had run so hard he thought he would cry out from the cramps in his calves. And he saw as he limped into the campment that he need not have pushed himself. He saw that news of the barohna had already come. He knew that immediately from the air of barely repressed hysteria among the tents. Men stalked grim-faced on hurried errands, fingering their knives, thoughts of starved sheep and rent tents clear in their faces. Women gathered possessions and supplies, packing to flee. Children stared with hollow eyes, as frightened by the adults' fear as by what they heard of the barohna.

Garrid ran seeking his uncle, but no one could tell him where Kanir had gone. Messengers had come, and then Giddon and Sonkar of the Tyuna had come into camp with hands raised. Later delegates had come from the Pazniki and the Ternar clans too. And they had all retreated, leaders of rival clans plotting together as if they were long allies. Because—did he know?— a barohna had burned the Yarika. Had left their seared bones scattered on the desert in a pool of melted sand. Fortina and Simar—and others in the campment too—had seen the moons dim when she did it. They had been wakened by a sudden screaming darkness in the middle of the night and had known immediately that disaster was upon them all.

Disaster: a barohna serving the Greater Clan. A barohna come to drive them deeper and deeper into the hard-lands, where there was no forage—where there were only alkali beds and the skulls of wandering beasts. Garrid listened to the stories and before he reached Pelar's tent almost believed he had seen the burned bones of the Yarika himself, instead of men dead by knife and spear. Almost believed he had seen a pool of melted sand instead of glass-paned structures sitting peacefully under the midday sun.

Finally, when there were no more stories to be heard, Garrid went to Pelar's tent to scrub away the worst of the grime and to change to clean robes. Instead he lay down for a moment and fell heavily asleep, oblivious to the chaos in the campment and the ache of tortured muscles.

Danior sighed, slipping free of Garrid's mind. Certainly there were no answers there. He flexed his legs briefly, searching for a more comfortable position, and tried again to let the voice of the spring speak to him.

Nothing. Stray thoughts darted through his mind. Impressions of places and people he had never seen. Garrid's fear. His own. Unconsciously he mouthed words from Garrid's clan-language, wondering if they would be comprehensible to a Fon-Delar.

Afternoon passed and the light in the *tarnitse* hut faded with the sun. Keva passed into shadow, head bowed, eyes closed. Danior gazed at her restively, at the pinched set of her eyelids, at the tension in her jaws, and realized that she might have been in another land, for all he could guess of her thoughts. What did she hear in the water? Was she finding answers? Or was she simply hungry and stiff, as he was? He wondered a while longer, feeling empty and alone, cast out. It seemed an invasion to reach for her thoughts with the stone. But after a while he did it anyway.

Dry throat, aching back—and irresolution. Keva tried again and again to center her awareness upon the sound of the spring. Instead her thoughts scattered to every quarter and took her feelings with them. Guilt at what had happened simply because she had come to the desert. Anger when she thought of leaving her father. Fear of the fire-cuff and of her own anger. Wishful memory of a time when everything had been simpler. Danior sighed and released the stone, realizing she had found no more direction than he had.

Perhaps if he tried harder, perhaps if he reached for the voice of the water as he had reached for Keva's thoughts . . . Certainly he had nothing to lose by the effort. He bowed his head and tried again to set aside the chatter of conflicting thoughts. Deliberately he loosened tight muscles and let his head fall forward loosely. He reached out for the faint sound of the water. Reached as it bubbled its incomprehensible tongue, speaking to the earth in a language all its own.

Language. The pairing stone had taught him a language more potent than any individual tongue. He had linked his thoughts with the Yarika, he had linked them with Garrid, he had linked them with Keva, and he had learned that they all felt the same things: fear, confusion, uncertainty, anger. He had learned that those things were universal, that they drove everyone—palace son, barohna or clansman.

But what could he do with that understanding? It was useless if he sat here while the clans gathered for war. But if he went to the small-clans . . .

Startled by that half-formed thought, he pulled his head erect, staring at the darkened walls of the *tarnitse* hut. If he went to the small-clans, he could do nothing. What could he tell them when he didn't speak their tongues? But if he went to the Fon-Delar—

If he went to Garrid's clan, perhaps he could make himself understood. Perhaps he could tell them what he knew: that their fears were baseless; that Keva had not come to drive them off the desert; that the old ways and the new could live side by side. Not happily, perhaps, but bloodshed wasn't necessary.

Quickly he bowed his head again, wondering. Could he do it? With Garrid's awareness to guide him, could he coax the Fon-Delar language from his untrained tongue and throat? Could he speak to the Fon-Delar?

If he could . . . The Fon-Delar was the largest of the small-clans. They were respected—feared. If he could talk to Kanir, their headsman . . .

He rubbed his temples, trying to think clearly. By now the desert would be teeming with clansmen and messengers. But he had learned things—tricks and ploys—from the Yarika and from Garrid that would help him make his way unnoticed.

And what options did he have? To wait for the clansmen to converge on Jhaviir's settlement? Frowning, he clasped the stone again, hoping to find Garrid still sleeping.

Instead Garrid was stumbling across the desert again, trying to keep pace with his clan-brothers, his legs trembling with fatigue. The shouts of his clan-brothers were in his ears, and the shouts of the Pazniki, the Ternar, the Widebolt and the Kessermin too. Five clans, running together, their knives pledged to each other against the Viir-Nega and the barohna. Five clans—

But the things they shouted—maybe what they said of how the Gothni had died was true. But he had seen the Yarika; they had not been burned. And he had been walking on the desert at the time they died, and he had not seen the moons dim.

What if there was no barohna? What if they were running to smash the Viir-Nega's campment for no reason? What if—

Garrid stumbled and Pelar bellowed at him angrily. Quickly Garrid pulled himself up, fighting the cramping pain of his calves. How could he drop back, even if there was no barohna in the Viir-Nega's glass campment? How could he lessen himself in the eyes of his clan-brothers when he must rely upon them each day for protection, for support against the hard-lands? He seized desperately at images of burned sheep. There was no other way he could keep running.

Burned sheep, burned sheep, burned sheep . . . He synchronized the pounding of his feet to the terrifying syllables. The others synchronized their feet to different syllables. Angrier syllables. *Kill the barohna, kill the barohna, kill the barohna* . . . Garrid gasped for breath as he ran. If the tales he had heard of barohnas were true, he couldn't guess how they would accomplish that. He couldn't guess how anyone could kill a barohna. But he ran anyway to the rhythm of his own private chant, his heart bursting.

Danior broke the link, trembling, but the rhythm of running feet persisted. It pounded in his heart, heavily. And he knew he could not sit here any longer. Could not sit here waiting. He must try to reach the Fon-Delar. Try to turn them back. A hopeless cause, perhaps, but he could think of no other.

Keva had not opened her eyes. Cautiously Danior stood and moved to the door of the hut. Outside it had grown dark. He saw only the light of the first stars. Tedni and Tinata were talking in low voices. He listened until their conversation became more desultory and finally tapered to nothing.

He peered out. Tedni slept sitting upright, propped against the side of the structure. Tinata had curled up a short distance away, her knife falling loosely from her hand. He hesitated for a moment, then stepped silently from the structure.

The night air was cool. His stomach growled irritably and he was thirsty. But he decided not to risk trying to extricate food from Tedni's pouch. And he did not pause to drink. He must try to reach the Fon-Delar, try to turn them back. Try to tell them in their own tongue that their offensive against the Greater Clan was misconceived. He pressed the stone and looked at the rising stars through Garrid's eyes and took bearings. Then he began to run.

FIFTEEN
KEVA

O nce or twice, as she sat in the early evening shadows of the *tarnitse* hut, Keva thought she was about to hear some soft insight, some quietly spoken direction. Once, after it had grown dark in the hut, she saw her mother's face, young, laughing. She clung to the smiling image and tried to understand how her mother could have been so many things in such a short time: a caring mate, a loving mother, a barohna—and a girl who had taken responsibility too soon and suffered its weight.

Keva was just a few years younger than Lihwa had been, but she had neither lover, child nor people. And she was afraid to touch the fire-cuff.

Worse, she couldn't even guess if courage lay in taking the fire-cuff and using it against the small-clansmen—frightened men fighting for survival—or in turning her back while her father's people fought the small-clansmen. How could she justify that kind of courage if her father died? If Rezni were wounded? If Tedni or Resha were scarred or crippled?

She sighed. She had brought her dilemma to the *tarnitse* spring and the water told her nothing.

Nor, apparently, did it speak to Danior. She opened her eyes at a faint sound and saw he had moved to the door. Surprised, she watched as he peered out for long minutes, then slipped from the hut. She hesitated, expecting to hear him speak to

Tedni. When he did not, she stood stiffly and moved to the door too.

Tedni and Tinata slept. And, dimly, she saw Danior disappearing into the dark, running. She caught a startled breath. Had he learned something from the thought-stone? Was he going back to Pan-Vi to warn her father?

But if he was going to Pan-Vi, why did he run to the east, deeper into the desert, instead of south? And why was he going himself, instead of sending Tedni? Keva hesitated, watching him. He didn't move like someone simply stretching cramped muscles. He moved purposefully. And quickly. Soon she would not be able to see him at all.

She turned, gazing back toward the spring. But she had already learned there were no answers there. And it made her apprehensive to see Danior disappearing into the dark. There were clansmen on the desert and Danior carried no weapon. All he carried was the thought-stone. Deciding, she slipped from the hut and followed him.

The air was cool, the sky lightly dusted with stars. Keva's stiff muscles welcomed activity as she ran in the direction Danior had taken. Once she thought she had lost him, but a few minutes later, stopping to catch her breath, she saw his thought-stone glow a short distance ahead.

She hesitated, wondering momentarily if she had been right to follow him. He had left secretly. He might not be pleased to see her.

But if the stone had told him something, she must know too. Instinctively she called his name softly, as if the desert had ears. "Danior!"

He turned slowly, the stone fading. "Keva? You followed me."

He wasn't angry. He was dismayed. "Yes. You left without me. Where are you going?" When he shook his head and avoided her eyes, refusing to answer, she caught his arm. "Where, Danior?" What had he learned? And why keep it secret from her? Surely they could share everything now.

He licked his lips, obviously reluctant to confide. But his reluctance only made her more determined, and she refused to release his arm. Finally he drew a sighing breath and said in such a low voice she hardly understood, "To the Fon-Delar."

"The—" She stared at him, momentarily confused. The young clansman who had taken her thought-stone from the Yarika—he was a Fon-Delar. Her father had said the Fon-Delar was one of the largest clans on the desert.

She understood that much. "But—why? You don't even know where to find them. And if you did—" What did he intend? To walk into their camp unarmed? Offering what? Saying what? "You'll be killed."

He shrank from her gaze. "No. I'm going to talk to them. I can take my bearings from the stars. From the moons when they rise. I'll find Garrid and make his uncle—his uncle is headsman of the Fon-Delar—understand that they don't have to attack Pan-Vi. That you don't intend to drive them off their grazing lands. That you won't harm their flocks."

She stared at him incredulously, wishing suddenly that she had the other thought-stone, that she knew how to use it. Perhaps then she would know if he believed what he was saying. If he believed he could talk to the Fon-Delar. "You don't know their language," she protested. "You—"

"I've heard Garrid use it. I know how the words sound, how they feel on his tongue, what they mean. I—"

She drew back. He couldn't believe what he was saying: that he had learned the Fon-Delar language through the thought-stone. He had been linked with Garrid for less than two days. Had he even heard the Fon-Delar clan-language spoken aloud in that time? And to go to their camp—"They'll kill you! If you go into their camp—"

"They're not in their camp. They—Kanir has gathered four other clans. They're coming."

Coming—Keva's mouth went dry. She felt her hands begin to tremble. "Coming to attack Pan-Vi," she breathed.

"Yes. Five clans."

Including the Fon-Delar, which was almost as large as the Greater Clan. And they stood here talking. "We have to tell my father," she said quickly. "We—"

Danior frowned, hesitating. "I didn't want to wake Tedni. I

was afraid he would follow me. But if you'll go back to Pan-Vi—''

Go—and leave him alone on the desert? "*No*. You're the one who has the thought-stone. You're—''

He shook his head violently. ''*No!* Keva, there's no time. It took Garrid a full day to travel from Pan-Vi to the Fon-Delar camp. By the time he got there, his uncle had already heard about you. About the Yarika. The clans left the Fon-Delar campment at dusk. They'll reach Pan-Vi by dusk tomorrow. But I can catch them halfway if I travel fast enough. I can intercept them early tomorrow.''

And make some doomed effort to speak to them? Using a language he had never spoken? Telling them things they would never believe? Because if the Fon-Delar had a barohna, would they want simply to live as before—quietly, without disturbing their neighbors?

No.

Then why should they believe that the Greater Clan chose to live that way?

But if she went with Danior, if she met the Fon-Delar on the desert and showed them she intended none of the things they thought—reluctantly she followed that line of thought. They would never believe Danior if he told them her father did not intend to drive the small-clans from their lands. But if she confronted them and let them return to their camps unharmed—she hesitated. There was so much she didn't understand. So many things that were unclear. Some she hadn't even thought of until these last few days. ''I—I don't even know why you came to the desert,'' she said haltingly.

''Why?'' Danior pressed his thought-stone and blue light briefly stained his fingers. ''Because you were coming. You were looking for Jhaviir and you didn't know about the clans. I was afraid you would be hurt.''

''And you never stopped to think you might be hurt too?''

He stared down at the ground, as if reluctant to admit a weakness. ''I thought about it.''

''But you came anyway.'' Why? If she could at least understand that—

He was long in answering. When he did speak, the words seemed to challenge her. "I wanted to learn something from you. Something—" He met her gaze and shrugged helplessly.

He had come to the desert to keep her from harm. And to learn something he couldn't name. That, she realized when he didn't go on, was the best he could tell her. "I'm coming with you," she said, knowing there was nothing else she could do.

Danior looked up at her sharply. "No. They'll try to kill you."

"That's why they're coming to Pan-Vi—to kill me."

He licked his lips anxiously. "Yes," he agreed finally, reluctantly.

"Then I'll meet them on the desert. With you." And if they would not listen to Danior, if he could not speak to them as he thought he could . . . She combed her fingers back through her hair, putting those thoughts aside. "If you won't come back to Pan-Vi, then I'm going with you."

"Your knee—" he protested.

"It's healed. I won't slow you. I'm coming, Danior." He had, after all, come with her: to protect her, to learn from her. Perhaps she had something to learn from him. Certainly it would be better than sitting beside the *tarnitse* spring, listening for a voice that never came.

He sighed heavily, accepting her company with open reluctance. He paused to take bearings again, and then they ran together. As they ran the moons rose, silvering the desert, and the air grew chill. After a while they slowed to a steady half-run. Gratefully Keva let the pounding rhythm of their feet anesthetize her against thought.

They had traveled for perhaps an hour when Danior faltered and called a halt. "Keva, there—" he said, pointing to the west.

Keva pressed one hand to her chest, gulping for breath, and peered to the west. A small arc of the horizon was tinged orange. Above it, a heavy cloud blotted out the stars. Keva's heart jumped against her ribs. "The maze." One of the small-clans had set fire to the guard-maze.

Danior's eyes glistened in the dark. "Rezni said the small-clans burn the maze every spring. It grows back."

And there was nothing they could do now if this was more than a torching of the thorn bushes. Her father had assigned sentries to the perimeter of Pan-Vi. Everyone had carried weapons this morning, even the children. If one of the small-clans had mounted an offensive, they would be turned back.

But if it were an aggregate group, several clans united—

It was useless to speculate. They ran again, covering ground so swiftly by moonlight that they seemed to glide across sand and soil. After a while Keva ran without looking at the ground, trusting instinct to keep her from stumbling. The growing ache of her muscles seemed unimportant, someone else's pain.

Later, when they stopped to rest, her legs trembled and her hands shook. She gulped dryly for breath, wishing for water. Water in any quantity, tepid, stagnant, stale. She squeezed her eyes shut and imagined food spread before her. The effort brought only a small trickle of saliva. But when Danior had monitored the stone and was ready to run again, she ran too.

The moons stood halfway up the sky when they reached a small spring, little more than an ooze of water that disappeared quickly into the soil. Kneeling, cupping their hands, they caught enough to quench their thirst and to splash their hands and faces. Then they sat back, laughing with relief. "If any of this is edible,—" Keva speculated, studying the green vegetation that surrounded the spring.

Danior studied a cluster of thick stalks and uprooted one. "This is," he said, rinsing a fat white bulb in the spring. "Rezni told me about it. Peel the outer skin first." He passed the bulb to her and pulled another for himself. "And that—the grassy stuff. It stings your gums, but you can eat it. The leaves. The roots. Everything."

They made a small feast, drank again, and when they took their feet, Keva ran almost light-heartedly.

Her mood fell again when the moons set. They paused, Danior losing himself in the stone. When he released it, he was frowning. "Garrid is sleeping."

"The others—"

"I don't know if everyone has stopped for the night, or if he dropped behind." He gazed up at the darkened sky. "It's hard to plot our course without the moons. We're so close we see the stars from almost the same perspective."

That close. Unconsciously Keva raised her hand to her throat. "Danior, when we met them—" What did he plan?

Danior rubbed an anxious hand over his forehead. "I've been practicing as we ran. He hasn't spoken much while I've been linked, but I can touch his memory. I've—I've found all the words I need there."

Words he could reproduce intelligibly? Keva remembered how Tinata had laughed when she had tried to speak a few words of the Greater Clan's language. A simple error of inflection could alter the meaning of an entire conversation. And what could Danior have learned of inflection when he had never heard the Fon-Delar language spoken aloud?

But it was too late to turn back. Keva studied Danior's set face and guessed it had been too late from the moment he had slipped from the *tarnitse* hut. "We may as well sleep too," she said. "Until Garrid wakes."

Danor nodded distractedly and they burrowed into the shallow drift of sand beneath a clump of dried vegetation. Danior closed his eyes, but Keva saw that the light of the thought-stone seeped from between his fingers. Was he dreaming Garrid's dreams?

Had he once dreamed hers? She wondered if it need disturb her if he had. Wondered how it felt to walk through another person's mind.

Surely it felt less lonely than living with no thoughts but her own. Tired, uneasy, she closed her own eyes and eventually slept, sand gritting against her skin.

She dreamed with haunting intensity, dreamed scenes, emotions, exchanges she realized must be long-repressed memories. Her mother climbing a rocky trail, stopping to curl snow into a ball and throw it, laughing. Another occasion: her mother's voice, raised, and her own anxiety that she had displeased her. Jealousy when her father came riding a tall animal and went to greet her mother first. Terror when the snow grumbled down the mountainside. The wordless fear that somehow she had made it fall, with her jealousy.

And incomprehension when her mother failed to brush the snow aside and continue her walk down the mountain. Incomprehension and growing fear of the silent mountains that stood witness to what she had done.

But she had not called down the snow. That was simply a child's misapprehension, one she had never realized she harbored. Until now. *A misapprehension*. Sleeping, dreaming, she examined it, saw the damage she had done herself with it, and absolved herself.

She woke at dawn, choking on unshed tears. Woke with the feeling that decisions had been reached while she slept, corners turned, changes accepted. Sitting, she glanced around. Danior was curled in the sand, his eyes pressed shut, the stone tightly clasped. She stood and brushed away sand and looked up into the rising sun. The same sun that had always looked down on this land.

The same sun barohnas had always drawn their fire from. Licking dry lips, she knelt beside Danior and studied the fire-cuff. She wondered what he would think if he could read what she was thinking now: that it was time she wore the cuff.

After a while he woke, drawing a deep breath, his eyes opening. "He's awake. Garrid's awake," he said.

"And the others?" Her voice didn't seem her own. She had made a final rapprochment with herself while she slept. Had accepted her innocence in her mother's death. Had recognized that to be angry did not mean to destroy. And in so doing, she had stepped out of herself and into some new phase of life, some new readiness. She wondered, in her new detachment, what that readiness would bring.

"They're waking too, the other Fon-Delar." Danior sat, scrubbing his face with one hand. He gazed at the sun and briefly clasped the stone again. "They're near," he said when he released it.

Near. But the clansmen had been near since the night she had killed the minx. They had been waiting unglimpsed on the horizon of her life since then. Perhaps even before. "I want the cuff," she said.

She spoke with such lack of emphasis he didn't understand at first. "They're—what?"

"I want the cuff." She wanted to wear it and feel the sun blaze at her wrist. Wear it and do what she had to do. Because that was what barohnas had always done—what they had to do. Her mother had had to throw her cuff away. Now she had to assume hers.

Danior's pupils contracted to points. His lips whitened. "You—you don't know how to use it."

Of course she didn't know how to use it. She had scarcely touched it. She permitted one fingertip to hover over its polished surface, surprised at the sense of detachment she felt. Fear, confusion, anger—all those things had dropped away, leaving only certainty. "Today I will learn to use it."

"*No*. I'm—I'm going to talk to them. I've learned the words I need to know. I know how to tell them that we don't intend to burn their sheep. I know—if you use the sunstone—"

She met his anguished gaze with distant surprise. After the things he and her father had told her, after the assurances they had given her, did he expect her to take the cuff and burn the Fon-Delar? Before he even made his attempt to speak with them? She frowned with a weary, detached patience. "Did you and my father lie to me? In all the things you told me about barohnas?"

He shook his head numbly. "No."

"Then I want the cuff."

He shook his head again, mouth working, but whatever argument he tried to muster would not come. She wondered abstractedly what it might be, even as she silently disallowed it. She extended her hand and let him see that she would not be denied. He licked his lips and then, with fingers that suddenly seemed very stiff, he slipped the cuff off his wrist.

It glided over Keva's fingers and seated itself on her wrist with an almost sensual coolness. Keva touched the polished surfaces with her fingertips and with catching breath felt them begin to warm. Within moments the stone cuff took fire. She held out her arm, caught by the brilliance of sunlight captured in stone. If she gazed long enough into the blaze of the stone, she realized, she might gain a vantage point from which she could look back over all her lifetime, over the lifetimes of all the women who had preceded her.

"It—it takes in light by itself," Danior said. "You don't have to do anything but wear it and it gathers in the sun, although if you want, you can make it draw faster. But to discharge the energy—"

"Yes?" His voice seemed to come from a distance. She gazed into the fiery stone and saw the world in broken images, as if she looked at many different worlds at once. The world of her mother, of her grandmother, of her great-grandmother, of the first barohna who had ever drawn the sun's fire. She wondered who that woman had been, what she had felt the first day she had captured the sun.

"You have to learn to discharge the light without burning anyone. You have to practice. You—"

Something in his tone, some agitation, briefly caught her attention. She nodded, remembering what her father had said. That her mother had had barely two hands of days to go to the mountains and practice the use of her cuffs before taking the throne from her own mother.

She did not have any days to go to the mountains. Not now. Was that why Danior kept licking his lips, why his face was so ashen? Was he afraid she would use the sunstone carelessly?

Not a baseless fear when she had no one to tell her how to take care with the sun.

Uncomfortable time passed between them, Danior frowning, biting his lip, she absently stroking the bracelet with her fingertips. Finally Danior said, "We'd better walk." His voice was pitched high with unsuccessfully repressed fright.

They walked, stopping once at a tiny spring, drinking sparingly. Danior touched the thought-stone often, frowning, muttering to himself in what Keva realized must be the Fon-Delar tongue. She wondered if he knew what he was saying or if he was just echoing something Garrid said.

The sun rose in the sky, separating itself from the horizon, becoming round and rosy-gold. They walked farther and the hair stirred at the back of her neck. She caught Danior's arm, pulling him to a halt. The western horizon was no longer a stable, dark line marking the separation of earth and sky. Instead it moved, as if in a series of slow muscular contractions. "The Fon-Delar," she said, pointing.

Danior stiffened, clasping his stone. After a moment he released it. "Yes. Keva—"

"Yes?" She asked—unnecessarily. She already knew what he was going to say.

"Don't use the cuff."

"Not unless I have to," she agreed—and saw by his face that he knew better than to ask more.

They saw after a few minutes that they needn't continue walking, that the Fon-Delar were traveling directly toward them. They halted, Danior holding himself stiffly, his features blanched, Keva gazing at him dispassionately, wondering if he would be able to speak the Fon-Delar language, wondering if he would even have the chance to do so. The fire-cuff blazed at her wrist, rivaling the newly risen sun. Looking down, she saw that the band of brown flesh had widened.

The detachment that had brought her this far began to slip when the Fon-Delar came nearer and she saw individual figures: lean men with dark hair, running. With a warning twinge, she remembered the Zollidar, who had caught and bound her before she could react, the Gothni, who had slashed the yearlings before she had realized what they intended. These men were of the same stock, hardened by a hard land. And their intent was to kill her. Could it be done? If they acted quickly enough, before she guessed they had the courage to try?

The Fon-Delar did not run in an organized phalanx. They simply surged across the sand in a wave, long knives at their waists, spears in hand. And there were hundreds of them, she saw, carried forward by the momentum of rage.

"Danior—" Involuntarily she recoiled, her voice losing body. Could the Fon-Delar stop to listen even if they wanted? If the men in the front ranks tried to halt, they would simply be pushed forward by all the hundreds behind them. And she began to see individuals now, none of them with the look of men who would stop to listen to anyone.

Yet she had to stop them. Her mind worked dizzily. She hesitated, reluctant to call the sand into the air. But was there another way?

She didn't have time to devise one. The first Fon-Delar had seen her and instead of slowing had begun to shout hoarsely. Quickly she pressed her eyes shut and caught her breath. She had only to think of a blood-mist rising in the air and the result was swift. Her throat closed, cutting off oxygen, and her lungs began to fill with that other substance. That intoxicant that drove her quickly beyond the bounds of time. She became aware of the slow surge of blood in her veins. It drummed at her ears and eddied in the large vessels of her abdomen. The running Fon-Delar slowed to a peculiar, fluid crawl.

Danior shouted something that she did not hear. Because now sand rose in a tall column. It peeled from the desert floor in sheets and spun into a towering, glistening vortex, the sharp-edged granules catching the early morning sun, glinting with its rosy light.

Keva distinguished faces among the front-runners now, dumbstruck. Sun-hardened flesh turned pasty, fiery eyes stared in startled shock, mouths gaped. Quickly Keva seized for full control of the sand and sent tendrils reaching lazily for the astonished clansmen. She set the sand upon them with calm deliberation. Because if they knew what had happened to the Gothni, if they understood the warning in the sting of sand—

Lightly. She scoured them so lightly she drew only threads of blood from sun-beaten cheeks. The nearer clansmen threw their arms before their eyes, shouting in terror.

But they kept running, driven by the men behind them, driven by their own momentum. Running with spears raised, shouting in ragged unison now. Shouting—she could not understand the words, but she knew they were directed at her.

And they did not stop running. Clansmen—they were clans-men. She would have been stopped by less than this, but what was she? A warmstream fisher-woman. She had never been hardened by hard-lands and hard ways, not as these men had.

"Stop!" she cried, knowing it was useless. She and Danior had miscalculated. They had come to reason with men who were beyond reason.

The first bone-tipped spear flew so close she felt its breeze on her arm. It quivered into the ground close behind her. The second skimmed her leg and Keva felt her blood rise dizzily, singing shrilly in her ears. Her first angry instinct was to call up every grain of sand within reach and scour the flesh from the men who raised spears against her. *Savages. Animals.* But she heard Danior shouting—screaming—in Fon-Delar, saw him clutching the thought-stone, and knew she must not. She must be hard too, in a barohna's way. She must be stone where she lived—proof against her own intemperate instincts.

"Run!" she screamed to Danior, but he only stumbled a few steps backward. *"Run!"*

How could he run when spears came cutting through the glistening vortex of sand, when they buried themselves in the ground everywhere—when one buried itself in his shoulder? Keva stared, momentarily unbelieving, thinking irrationally of the small animal he and Rezni had snared when they crossed the desert. Danior's face didn't register pain or surprise. He simply staggered backward, his eyes staring in shock. His mouth worked, but she could not read the words.

Perhaps he was telling her now what he had wanted to learn from her. Why he had come here.

Perhaps he had come simply to join the loneliness of his confusion to the loneliness of hers. She spun around angrily, instinctively raising her arm to the early morning sun. It was red-gold, light and fire. It sat fat upon the horizon. Fat with the very fuel she needed.

The very fuel she must not use.

She sucked a harsh breath and drew the sun into her fire-cuff anyway. Drew it without knowing how she did so. Her heart leapt against her rib cage. Her lungs caught fire, and the cuff blazed so brightly she could hardly see the storming sand, the clansmen. Could hardly see Danior where he had fallen, blood on his robes. If he died, she would never learn to share thoughts with him. Would never escape the lonely bonds of her own mind.

She caught a second breath and held it, and her sense of time became so distorted that she looked down at Danior and saw him do a slow, writhing dance in the sand. His body rolled. His hands rose. They grappled with the spear, uselessly. His legs beat the sand—but slowly, so slowly. He stared helplessly at the fiery blaze of her fire-cuff. Then, still more slowly, he rolled to his side and pressed his face to the sand.

She spent precious moments gazing down and wondering why he tried to bury himself. After a while she guessed it was because of the blaze of her cuff. He had seen her rage and he thought it would spill over him in flames.

She knew she must not spill rage upon him. Must not spill it upon the clansmen. *Stone. She must be stone where she lived.* Almost casually she turned back and released fire at the spears that hung in the air. They burst into flames and fell in ashes. One among the front rank of clansmen burst afire too. His scream erupted slowly, a bass growl. She shuddered as the smell of burning flesh reached her and for a moment felt trapped in the very temporal distortion she had created. She had so much time here to feel the weight of her obligation. So much time to realize that she was the only one who could save the situation—and that she no more knew how to do that than she had a few minutes before.

And the clansmen kept running. Slowly, their faces torn with raw panic. Kept running because they didn't know how to save the situation either. Didn't know how to destroy the woman who burned their spears. Didn't know how to retreat. Didn't know how to do anything but continue to run, staring at the burning spears and at the gobbets of molten glass that had begun to rain around them. Because each time Keva threw fire at a spear, her fire caught the suspended sand too and melted it and liquid glass fell from the air.

She almost laughed at that. Of course! Rezni had told her, Tedni had told her, her father had told her—the panes of Pan-Vi were made from molten sand and its impurities. Now she made glass too. It rained upon the ground, and as it fell more and more heavily, the first screaming clansmen finally began to turn in flight.

Glass. Even as some clansmen fled, others took their place, bone-tipped spears drawn back to fly. *Glass.* So easily formed. The first globules were already cooling on the ground. Was there an answer in glass? If so, she must find it quickly, because Danior was bleeding. Quickly because more spears were raised.

Quickly. She caught a deep breath and let the fire-cuff blaze as she pulled sand from everywhere. Drew it into the air in thick sheets and turned her fire upon it. Turned so much fire upon so much sand that sheets of molten glass hung in the air where there had been sand. Hung fiery and bright and so hot that she felt her lips sear.

She held the sheets in place for as long as she could maintain their weight. Spears sank into them and were embedded or caught fire. A clansman who could not turn back quickly enough threw out his hands and the flesh was burned from them. Another lost his balance and toppled into the molten sheet and died in scalded silence. Others turned and ran, their robes scorched, their hair smoking.

Slowly she let the molten curtains of glass drop, folding in upon themselves until they became a thickly pleated wall. A wall to separate her from the clansmen. A wall to stop their spears, to muffle their cries. Keva exhaled and realized giddily that she had routed the clansmen. They were running, scattering back in the direction they had come. Running in total disorder.

Keva held the molten wall in place until its pleated folds began to solidify. Then she drew a deep breath and turned, uncertain what she would find.

Danior lay half-sprawled on the denuded soil, one hand pressed to his shoulder, staring at her from unbelieving eyes. His robes had fallen away in ashes. His flesh was burned dark. Even his hair seemed burned. But he stood, pushing himself to his feet, with no apparent pain.

Her flesh was burned dark too, but there was no pain and no blistering. Her hair—she raised an anxious hand to touch it, but it did not fall away in ashes. It had taken a new texture, had become coarser and duller, but it was not burned. "My hair—" she said in surprise, as if everything else—the glass wall, the vanquished clansmen—was expected, but this was not. And why did it seem that she stood taller? That her arms and legs had lengthened, that her shoulders had become broader—that even the contours of her face had altered? She raised a cautious hand and found that the lines of her face were bolder, stronger. Her eyes were more deeply set, her jaw more pronounced.

Danior watched her cautious probings and managed a half-choked laugh. "Has—has anyone ever told you the legend of Lensar and Niabi?"

"Lensar?" She did not know the name. And why did he ask her now? "No."

"The first gem master and the first barohna. I'll tell you someday," Danior promised, his voice shaky. Experimentally he drew his hand from his shoulder. "The heat—the spear burned in my arm and sealed the wound."

She stared at the puckered wound, at the blackened flesh around it. "I don't understand," she said, suddenly light-headed. Had she really done it? Really called down the sun and turned back hundreds of screaming clansmen? She could not believe so. But the wall stood before her. She felt its heat on her arms. If only she had the other thought-stone now, if only they could portion out Danior's shock and her disbelief between them . . . She touched Danior's arm, satisfying herself that he was not blistered, not burned, that he was not at all harmed. No more than she. "Why didn't you burn? Why—why didn't I?"

"Barohnas don't burn," Danior said. "But I thought I would." He examined the dark glint of his unburned flesh, laughing with relief, then gazed the length of the wall she had created. It was striated with color, its texture rough. In places it slumped shapelessly. "If you can do that again, when we return to Pan-Vi—"

Build a wall around the Greater Clan's settlement? To hold back the small-clansmen until the clans could come to some understanding? Until they could learn to live in peace? "I can do it," she said, imagining the wall she would make, tall and shining. A wall so long, a wall so tall. She gazed the length of the wall she had already built and she began to laugh too. She had made peace with her mother, she had made peace with herself. Now she wore a barohna's face and she could stay with her father as long as she wished. She could take all the time she needed to close the gap of years. She could take time to know her father and herself better. Time to learn how a barohna might live if she elected to remain in the hard-lands. Time. She turned back to Danior, wishing she could share her joy with him fully. Instead she could only say, "Can you walk?"

"Yes," he said, and gazed long at her, as if he understood her thoughts without even touching the stone that hung at his throat.

SIXTEEN
DANIOR

Sometimes, forgetting, Danior wore the pairing stone to bed and stepped into Keva's dreams, moving through the unfolding succession of images she used to teach herself what it meant to be a barohna. He saw sunlight fall in heavy waves, breaking and cresting and then being directed into carefully defined channels, all the wildness tamed and controlled. He watched reality melt under the blaze of the sunstone and saw how carefully, how painstakingly Keva recreated it, so that nothing was ultimately lost. He clutched the pairing stone in his sleep and shared the effort and the joy.

More often he remembered to remove the stone before he slept, just as he disciplined himself during the day to wear the stone but not to clasp it. Because there was no mutuality when he used the stone. He could hold it and move into Keva's thoughts. He could see what she saw, hear what she heard, learn what she learned. He could follow the entire complex tracery of her emotions. And he suspected that she guessed sometimes that he did so.

But he could not share with her. All the things he heard and saw during his days in Pan-Vi, all the things he learned stopped with him. He had only words to convey them to Keva. Clumsy words.

He wondered sometimes what had become of the other pairing stone. He had not touched Garrid's mind since the morning

Keva had called down the sun. Danior didn't know if he had remained among the Fon-Delar or if he was among the tens of men and women who had pledged themselves to the Greater Clan after Keva routed the Fon-Delar. Didn't know if he had discarded the stone or if he kept it hidden, seldom handling it.

So he was left alone with his thoughts, and it was time to return to the valley. Time to let his parents know he had survived the first seasons of adulthood. If he left now, he could reach the valley before they left for the winter palace.

If he left now . . . But he put back thought of what else he could do when he reached the valley. Because he had not yet summoned the words to ask Keva.

Tonight. He must ask her tonight, before he left. Or not ask her at all.

"Danior?"

Sighing, he sat from the cushion where he had been napping. Tedni squatted before him, his eyes bright, anxious. Unwillingly Danior steeled himself for some demand. "Is the meal set?" He had told Jhaviir he would leave immediately after eating and walk through the night, to avoid the heat of day.

"Soon. Danior—"

Danior waited, bemused by Tedni's momentary diffidence. It wasn't like Tedni to hesitate. Certainly it wasn't like him to ask instead of cavalierly demanding. "What can I give you?" Danior said, when the demand was not forthcoming.

Tedni momentarily hooded his avid eyes. When he looked up again, he had taken on some semblance of his father's easy authority. "There is a principle among the Kri-Nostri called—called the *baldoca-baldat*. The teaching of brothers," he said. "It prescribes that if there are brothers, they teach each other and show each other what they know. If one knows a place he shows the other, as I have shown you Pan-Vi and the desert. And better than anyone else could have shown you because we are Rauth-brothers. And of course because I am my father's oldest and strongest son. Then if the other prepares to travel, if he prepares to go to places the first brother has not seen, it is his turn to teach. To show. It is an obligation of brothers."

Only the watchful narrowing of Tedni's gaze told Danior that he had described a non-existent principle. Carefully Danior sat back on the cushion. Was it so surprising Tedni wanted to come with him? Wanted a brother to show him the way across strange lands—lands he might never visit otherwise? Certainly Danior had yearned for brothers to show him across other, inner lands. "Why are you asking me so courteously?" he demanded. He had learned that he could speak to Tedni as sharply as he liked and draw little more than appreciative laughter.

But Tedni didn't laugh this time. He squirmed forward on his knees, his eyes narrowing still more intently. "To show you how much I have already learned," he said promptly. "I have heard my father say that people don't speak and behave in the same way in all the lands of Brakrath. I have heard him say he had to learn to speak and behave like a desert man before he could live here.

"So I have watched you and I have watched him during his private times, and now I have decided to show you that I can master the way of other places. Of course it shouldn't surprise you that I can learn a manner when I am eldest son of the Viir-Nega and one of his best workers and strongest soldiers."

So he had already begun trying to tailor his manner for the trip. "Of course you still have a few things to learn," Danior observed, just because it needed saying.

This time Tedni did laugh, sharply. "Of course I have things to learn. And it is your obligation to teach me, since you are my Rauth-brother. I have already packed my possessions. I want you to look at them and tell me if I have forgotten anything."

"I wonder—have you perhaps forgotten to ask your father if you can go?"

"Have you perhaps forgotten that I am twelve now," Tedni demanded promptly. "So where I go is not a matter for my father to decide. Although I am sure he will want to give me his best knife and chopping blade to carry."

He was so sure, Danior reflected, that he had probably already packed them. And he wanted to see the world: the forest, the roughlands, the plain, the mountains. Wanted to learn new manners, new ways. Wanted to grow and find his own path.

It took Danior only a moment's reflection to recognize that he wanted to show him. Wanted to teach him, brother to brother. Perhaps there were even things he could learn from Tedni. "Bring me your things," he said. "I'll see if you have forgotten anything."

Tedni jumped up and returned shortly with his pouch and pack. Examining them, Danior found he had forgotten nothing. He had not even forgotten the knife and blade he was certain his father would want him to have. And by the time he repeated their conversation to Jhaviir at the table a short time later, it had become substantially altered, with Danior waking Tedni from a sound sleep and begging him to accompany him on the long journey, with Tedni packing hastily because he saw his brother did not want to travel without him. Perhaps, in his hurry, he had even forgetfully packed some things that were not his own.

Jhaviir nodded at his tale and said only, "It is as well you packed them, first-son, because of course I want you to have them." He turned to Danior. "And there is something I want you to have before you go. Resha—bring me the chest I showed you earlier." When she jumped up and disappeared, Jhaviir cast a warning eye over the younger children, who had begun to push and squirm, then turned back to Danior again. "I wonder if Tedni expected me to be surprised, when my knife and blade and best boots disappeared into his pack two days ago. If you would rather he not accompany you—"

"No, I'll be glad of his company," Danior assured him quickly.

"Good. He's eager to broaden his understanding, and you will be a good guide. Just see that he doesn't broaden himself at anyone else's expense. And now I have a request: that when you reach Valley Terlath, you give news of me to my brother."

"Of course," Danior said. News of where Jhaviir's search had finally led him. News of a people who had learned to make the desert green. News of warring small-clans who were slowly making the first uneasy steps toward peace. He glanced at Keva, at the sunstone cuff that glowed on her wrist. He would even carry back news of a barohna living in the desert—a barohna whose father was a Rauthimage. That news held hope for his sisters.

"And will you tell him that I would welcome a visit from him?" Jhaviir continued. "We didn't have much chance to become acquainted when we were younger. The Benderzic helmet took so much of his memory that he was still trying to find his way during those first years. I managed to retain my memories, but they drove me—drove me away from the valleys. Now I think we would find much to say to each other."

"I'll tell him," Danior said, wondering if his father would leave the valley, where his memories lived around him, to visit a brother who was also part of his memory. Perhaps he would, for a season.

Perhaps one day he would have to leave, for longer.

"I'll tell him," he repeated.

Then Resha came with a metal chest, scratched and battered, alien markings on its sides. The younger children fell momentarily silent, leaning forward with flaring eyes. Jhaviir raised a warning hand against the eruption of questions and demands and opened the lid. "You must select the one you want," he said.

Danior caught his breath. The chest was filled with songsilks, a rainbow of them nestled together: azure, chartreuse, crimson, emerald, lilac.

And white. Folded among the others was a white silk like the one he had seen when he clasped his pairing stone at clanhall. A white silk he knew would speak with a familiar voice.

His father's voice. Jhaviir's voice.

Birnam Rauth's voice.

He hesitated, meeting Jhaviir's gaze. All the tempting colors, all the bright songs—could he bear to wear the white silk and hear its pleading voice instead? Could he bear to carry Birnam Rauth's message with him wherever he went?

Could he bear to leave it here, unheard? For a moment, as

he hesitated, it almost seemed that Jhaviir questioned him with arched brows. Asked him silently whether he had the courage to wear the white silk—or the courage to leave it.

What if he wore it for years and never learned its secret? Never learned where Birnam Rauth was being held or by whom? Never even learned if he was still living?

But he had seen the white-stalked forest and its inhabitants. He had glimpsed the configuration of the stars through the trees. Given those details, the Arnimi might be able to consult their datafiles and tell him what world Birnam Rauth was being held on. Then, if there were a way to reach that world—

Danior considered all those things and reached his decision. He drew the white silk from the chest.

It lay smooth and cool in his hands. He licked his lips, aware of the children staring, ready to erupt into clamor. Jhaviir silenced them with a frown, watching as he unfolded the silk with trembling fingers and carefully tied it at his waist.

There was no breeze in the room, so the silk did not speak. But later, when he went on the desert, its voice would follow him. Pleading. Speaking of isolation and imprisonment in an alien tongue.

He was able to eat little, though even the youngest children urged tidbits on him from their own platters. He was too aware of the silk at his waist and of the journey before him. And too aware that he must speak to Keva soon or not at all.

He found no opportunity through the meal. He found no opportunity when he and Tedni gathered their possessions and strapped them to their backs. He found no opportunity as they walked through the lanes of Pan-Vi, with all the clanspeople carrying torches behind them. He knew then, heavily, that he should have spoken to her sooner.

They approached the great glass-wall and Jhaviir called the clanspeople to a halt. He marked the parting with a handclasp, first taking both Danior's hands in his, then taking both Tedni's. "Come back with spring, both of you," he urged. "We need good workers and strong soldiers."

Tedni, Danior saw, was suddenly overawed by the step he was taking. He turned and looked up at Danior with stricken eyes and Danior knew they must leave immediately, before he lost nerve. Danior darted an anxious glance at Keva, wishing he could speak his question here. But it was a private question and people pressed near on every side.

Apparently Keva read something from his glance. She turned to her father and said quickly, "I'm going to walk a few minutes with them. Don't wait for me."

Relieved, Danior ducked through the portal. Keva and Tedni followed. When Danior glanced back, the torches of the clan glowed through the thick, wrinkled glass of the wall, making it wink with light. Tedni turned and stared back with awe.

"Danior?" Keva urged, touching his arm.

Tensely he met her eyes. They were a barohna's eyes, far-seeing and deep. The flesh of her face and arms was burned dark from the fire she had drawn to build the glass-wall that marked the perimeter of Pan-Vi. But he had grown over the summer and stood as tall as she. And the work of the gardens had left him well-muscled. Nothing, he guessed, would ever make him feel small again.

Still he felt hesitant—as, he had learned, everyone did sometimes, even Jhaviir. Uncertain, anxious, even frightened. Perhaps he and Keva were something never seen before on Brakrath, but no new emotions had been born with them and no old ones lost. "Keva—" Unconsciously he clasped the pairing stone that hung dark at his throat. "Keva, if I ask the gem master to cut new pairing stones when I reach the valley, one for each of us—will you wear one?"

He ventured a lot with that question, he knew. He was not asking her to wear an ornament or to share an occasional thought with him. He was asking her to go where he went, to see what he saw, and to let him go always with her. He was offering to open himself to her in a way that just a short time ago had terrified him. And he was asking her to open herself in the same way.

She drew back and for a heart-stopping moment he thought she would refuse. Her hand touched her throat. She frowned. "Do you think I could use the thought-stones?"

Was that her only reluctance? Doubt? "Yes," he said. "I

know you could, now. Before you didn't know your stone was anything more than a keepsake. And you wanted no part of the power of the stones. You only wanted to find your father. But now—now you've learned to use the stones. You're not afraid of them.''

She nodded, slowly. "I'm not," she said.

She wasn't afraid at all, not since the night she had routed the Fon-Delar. She had learned that she could use the sun without burning, could use the stones without harming.

And apparently she wasn't afraid to share thoughts with him either. "I'll ask him then, when I reach Valley Terlath. I'll send a message by courier. He can have the stones ready next spring."

"Yes."

So the question he had hesitated over for days was that easily resolved. Danior felt a quick surge of elation. He was returning to the valley with a brother, with a stone mate, with word from his father's missing brother, and more—with a sure sense of himself. He had learned how little he needed legend. He had learned that tradition had no more meaning than he was willing to give it. He had learned to place his foot squarely on the path and to take one step after another. He had even learned not to fear where his feet would lead him.

Tonight they would lead him into the desert. Quickly he clasped Keva's hands. "Next spring," he said. "I'll come back next spring with the stones." And then neither of them would be alone again.

EPILOGUE
IAHN RAUTH-SEVEN

Word passed quickly, as it did in the valley. Two young men had been seen coming down the trail from the mountains, one of them the palace son. Two young men had been seen walking in the orchard, pausing to feed clumps of grass to the white-mane. Two young men had been seen climbing to the animal's back and riding it across the dike tops toward the stone avenues, toward the palace.

Two young men, one of them his son. Of course no one ran to meet them. That would embarrass the travelers. No one called out, but a few people looked up from their work and nodded a greeting. And Iahn went to the edge of the plaza to watch for their arrival.

His son—at first he thought the slighter one who rode behind the other was his son and he didn't recognize the tall, assured figure who pressed gently at the animal's neck to guide it. Then they came nearer and he did recognize his son—and saw from his face who he had become in the two seasons since he had gone.

Someone who knew his way and was not afraid to follow it. Someone who had come back to the valley but not to stay. Someone who had made the world his home.

And the way he wore his hair, knotted behind one ear, the sash at his waist—

The white sash that seemed to reach for the breeze—

Iahn caught his breath, recognizing the sash. He had seen one like it, years before, on another world. He had snatched it from the wreckage of an unmanned trader ship and hung it in a tree to hear it sing.

It had spoken instead, with a voice he later recognized as his own.

As Birnam Rauth's.

Later still, when he remembered the words the silk had spoken, he had gone to the Arnimi and they had translated them for him.

The words . . .

"Danior," he said in greeting as Danior pulled the white-mane to a halt and dismounted. He succeeded in keeping the concern from his voice. But that meant that some of the pleasure was missing too. He sounded far more distant than he intended, far less pleased than he felt. "I'm glad you've come. We're leaving for the winter palace in two hands of days."

Danior caught his hand in a quick clasp. "I thought you would be going soon. That's why I came. This—this is my Rauth-brother, Tedni. Jhaviir's son. We're going to winter in the palace so I can teach him to cipher scrolls, and in the spring we're going back to the desert."

Jhaviir's son. His attention quickened as he glanced at the boy who slid down Fiirsevrin's flank, his dark eyes glinting with barely repressed excitement. "So you have news of my brother," he said quickly.

"Yes. And his daughter. And many things."

Good news. He could tell from his tone. Danior had returned safely and he had brought good news. "Come and tell me," he said, and this time he put everything he felt into the words.

Still, as they walked toward the palace, the younger boy boasting about the exploits of the journey and about the white-mane they would mark in the forest on their return journey, he was aware of the white silk at Danior's waist. Aware of the faint sound of its voice when the breeze caught it. Aware of the words it said in its unfamiliar tongue.

I am held here, I don't know how. They keep me bound and they feed me strange substances. I can't speak, but the thoughts that leave me go somewhere. Somewhere, and I think they are recorded. If you hear them, come for me. Let me go. Set me free.

My name is Birnam Rauth and my thoughts are recorded. If you hear them, come for me.

Come for me.

Iahn frowned. Someone would have to go.

Someday someone would have to go.